Roarke pulled Sassy tight against him and massaged her shoulders. "Let's be finished with all this talk of wars and loyalties and causes," he commanded. "I'm sick to death of it."

She fought the surge of tender feelings his closeness aroused, but felt herself weakening.

"In this room there's only a wee bonny lass and the man who wants her. Outside, the wind is soft in the pines . . . and inside, the fire is warm." He pressed firm lips to his, then tightening his arms, hungrily kissed her.

Like a swift torrent, aching passion rushed through her. This was madness, she told herself. How could she surrender to this man? But when Roarke pressed her closer against him, the sheer force of her need drowned out all reason.

Other AVON ROMANCES

THE HAWK AND THE HEATHER *by Robin Leigh*
ANGEL OF FIRE *by Tanya Anne Crosby*
WARRIOR DREAMS *by Kathleen Harrington*
MY CHERISHED ENEMY *by Samantha James*
CHEROKEE SUNDOWN *by Genell Dellin*
DESERT ROGUE *by Suzanne Simmons*
DEVIL'S DELIGHT *by DeLoras Scott*

Coming Soon

LORD OF MY HEART *by Jo Beverley*
BLUE MOON BAYOU *by Katherine Compton*

And Don't Miss These
ROMANTIC TREASURES
from Avon Books

FIRE ON THE WIND *by Barbara Dawson Smith*
DANCE OF DECEPTION *by Suzannah Davis*
ONLY IN YOUR ARMS *by Lisa Kleypas*
LADY LEGEND *by Deborah Camp*
RAINBOWS AND RAPTURE *by Rebecca Paisley*
AWAKEN MY FIRE *Jennifer Horsman*

Sonya Birmingham

AVON BOOKS NEW YORK

RENEGADE LADY is an original publication of Avon Books. This work has never before appeared in book form. This work is a novel. Any similarity to actual persons or events is purely coincidental.

AVON BOOKS
A division of
The Hearst Corporation
1350 Avenue of the Americas
New York, New York 10019

Inside cover author photograph by Steven Wann
Published by arrangement with the author
Library of Congress Catalog Card Number: 91-92440
ISBN: 0-380-76765-1

First Avon Books Printing: July 1992

Printed in the U.S.A.

RA 10 9 8 7 6 5 4 3 2 1

Renegade Lady is dedicated to my husband, Milt, a determined man who taught me the importance of never giving up on a dream. One bright Sunday years ago, Milt and I met at a church picnic in California. At that time we were young, foolish, and in love. After twenty-three years of air force tours spent in the United States, Germany, Greece, and the Philippines, we are certainly not as young—and hopefully not as foolish. But we still share a Sunday kind of love.

I also want to thank my daughter Kelly Wann, an ardent admirer of Celtic culture, for helping me research this book. When Kelly was nine years old, our family made a wonderful rail tour of Scotland, and she fell instantly in love with all things Scottish. At that time she had long, golden hair, and skin so fair and creamy, her pet name was White Paws. Today she is married to a fine young man named Steven, and they have a child of their own. But in one corner of my heart she will always be the little girl with flashing green eyes who wore a jaunty tam-o'-shanter and loved the Bridge of Brigadoon and the misty Highlands. For that reason, this book is also for you, White Paws.

Chapter 1

The Virginia Frontier
March 1774

Under a giant sycamore's spreading limbs, Sassy Adair fought to preserve her virginity. Her flame-colored hair billowed out behind her as she darted over the pebble-strewn ground, holding off her attackers with vicious slashes of her knife. A blue skirt covered her dodging legs, and a white smock, belted at the waist and deeply slashed at the neck, clung to her swaying bosom. Her body was tall and willowy, her face pale and delicately molded, her eyes a flashing green.

Dressed in buckskins and coon-skin caps, two unkempt mountain men lumbered after her, grabbing at her bosom.

One of them clutched his swollen manhood, bulging beneath his tight breeches. "This here's jest fer you, darlin'!"

"And this is jest for you!" she cried, swiping the wicked blade at his belly. "Come a step closer and I'll whack off what you think you're famous for, and fry it up in hot bear grease!"

The lowlife guffawed, showing rotten teeth.

The other ruffian wiped his loose, wet lips and

snapped out a rope. "Lordy, Lordy, ain't she a feisty one!"

Sweat trickled between her breasts as she moved from beneath the sycamore nearer to the edge of the road, looking for help. Finding the highway deserted, she kept her trembling arm outthrust and flashed her knife at the men. Exhaustion had weakened her muscles, but her spirit was still strong. Her own heartbeat echoed in her ears. A backwoods girl, she knew scores of these dirty wildcat whippers, and she despised them all. Most of the frontiersmen were decent men, but some were lazy and shiftless. They misused the land, abused their wives, and spawned hordes of ragged, crying children.

The man holding the rope tied a lasso. "Why don't you jest settle down so's we don't have to rope you, gal?"

Pain tightened her side, and her breath came in short gasps. "I'll shove that goldurned rope down your throat, you mangy, yeller-bellied varmint!" Wiping at her bleary eyes, she edged backward.

All at once she stumbled over her discarded rucksack. Hooting with laughter, the men lunged forward. They were almost on her when she heard the rumble of wheels. A mail coach and team thundered around the bend, raising a cloud of dust.

The slack-jawed men froze in midmotion.

When the driver cracked his whip, Sassy's spirits sank . . . The dad-blamed rascal intended to roar past without stopping! Then, like a messenger from heaven, a handsome, dark-haired man leaned from the open window; he shouted and banged his fist against the door.

At last the driver yanked the creaking coach to a halt.

With vapid faces, the men peered through the rising dust. Their horses, tethered near the tree line, shifted restlessly and whinnied.

Clutching her knife, Sassy slumped against a thick tree trunk. Her eyes widened as a strikingly attractive man, broad at the shoulder and lean at the hip, stepped down from the coach and strode through the dust.

He assessed the scene with a sweeping glance, his hand resting lightly on a fine pistol. Lines creased his bronzed face, and between his white teeth he clenched a long cheroot. His elegantly tailored garments emphasized his muscular frame and bespoke prosperity: a fine silk shirt and a blue velvet coat with embroidered cuffs encased his torso; snug hose and high cavalry boots clung to his powerful legs. The lacy jabot at his throat set off his deep tan.

He was so dashing, he reminded Sassy of a hero the mountain storytellers spun tales about on chilly winter's nights. For months the taverns had been full of broadsheets describing the daring exploits of Captain Rakehell, the scourge of the British navy. Being mostly of Scotch-Irish descent, the mountain folk loved to hear about the colorful Scottish privateer, who stirred their Celtic pride. Yes, that's who the dark stranger reminded her of—Captain Rakehell.

Then she told herself she was being foolish. What would Captain Rakehell be doing in this part of Virginia, so far from the sea coast? This stranger was someone else. Probably the enemy.

Stunned by his magnificence, she riveted her gaze on the scar running from his earlobe to just underneath his chin. With his aristocratic nose and full mouth, the scar gave him a devil-may-care look . . . as if he didn't give a damn what he thought or did. Funny how a little thing like a scar could stamp a man's whole personality on his face, she thought.

She ran her eyes over him again, wondering why he was dressed in such finery. An aura of power and glamour drifted about him like swirling leaves. There was something else about him, too . . . something suspicious she couldn't put her finger on. Oh, he was a bold one, all right. She knew his type. Cynical. Handsome. Worldly. And every inch a Loyalist if she ever saw one.

Wasn't it just her luck to be rescued by the enemy!

As he stepped forward, sunlight gleamed over his clubbed hair; dark as the devil's heart, it hung over the back of his velvet jacket. Shoving his pistol into his waistband, he slowly traced Sassy's form. His gaze swept every inch of her skin, lingering on the soft private parts hidden beneath her clothes. Embarrassment stiffened her limbs. Why, the rogue acted like he knew how many holes she had in her drawers!

Then he flashed a wide smile that stirred something deep within her. His expression was striking—intense and strongly sensual. He projected strength, self-assurance, a reckless zest for life. Yes . . . there was an excitement about him that reminded her of the moment of anticipation before thunder crackled. With some surprise, she wondered what it would be like to be kissed by his sensual lips.

"It's apparent you need help, lass. May I be of assistance? I've had some experience dealing with hell-raisers such as these two," he said. His voice was smooth and deep, and rang with authority. Its soft burr vibrated through her like a deep chord.

He's a Scotsman to be sure, she told herself. Her tongue became tied, and she simply stared at him, feeling rather foolish.

One of the ruffians jutted out his stubbled chin. "Shoot, we wasn't hurtin' the little gal," he drawled. "We was jest funnin' with her some."

The other man picked up the rope and recoiled it. "I can tell by yer high-toned voice yer a dang furiner," he said with a cold smile. "Who the hell are ya, anyway . . . some kind of English constable?"

The stranger smiled. "I'm no Englishman. My name is Roarke MacLaren."

"Then why are ya buttin' yer nose inter our business?"

Roarke appraised the man with narrowed eyes. "Because, my friend, I choose to *make* it my business." He strode over to the man, his boots crunching over the flaky sycamore twigs that littered the ground. With fiery eyes, he tore the coiled rope from the man's hands.

"What fine specimens of manhood you are," he said, sailing the rope across the road. He grabbed a fistful of the man's homespun shirt. "I must say in one respect I'm impressed with you backwoods types. You're strong as oxen, keen-eyed, and crack shots." He hit the man on the side of the head, knocking him to the grass, and hurled his companion against a tree. "Unfortunately, you're also lazy, hard-drinking, foulmouthed, stinking, lice-infested excuses for men who'd rather taunt helpless females than engage in productive pastimes!"

The first man rose and grinned lewdly. "You jest want her fer yerself!"

Roarke snapped out his arm in an uppercut and followed it with a fist to the man's gut, sending him staggering backward. When the other ruffian lunged forward, Roarke rammed a stunning blow to the man's jaw, smashing him to the ground. Then, a muscle throbbing in his temple, he swept out his pistol. "I'll kill one of you gentlemen before you reach the trees. Which one of you shall take the bullet?"

The men scrambled for their horses, mounted, and crashed into the underbrush.

Once the horses had disappeared, Roarke turned

to Sassy with questioning eyes. "Are you all right, lass?" he asked, striding toward her.

As she met his searching gaze, excitement welled up inside her, and her heart jumped like a pea in a hot skillet. It upset her that she had such strong feelings for a man like him. With great resolution, she pressed her lips together and reminded herself that he represented wealth, position, and the English Crown—everything she hated. She shouldn't be consorting with the enemy like some doxy. Especially when she was in a hurry to rescue her father from an English gallows.

Resolution made her snatch up her rucksack and sling it over her shoulder. "Don't you come an inch closer, you low-down, egg-suckin' Loyalist," she threatened. She whipped out her knife again. "I'd jest as soon slit your gullet as look at you."

He laughed deeply. "Lord, what a welcome for your rescuer."

"I didn't ask for any help. I purt near had that trash whipped when you turned up. All you did was take the fun out of a good fight." She lifted her chin. "Come on . . . what are you waitin' for? I'll take you on, too!"

His mouth tightened as he twisted the knife from her hand with a quick flick of his wrist.

Humiliation filled her—no one had ever done *that* before.

"Where's your mount, you little saucebox?"

She glowered at him. "I ain't got no mount. My mule ran off yesterday mornin'. I'm travelin' afoot."

"Where are you headed?"

He was so close, she could smell his spicy cheroot and feel his warm breath. She looked at him closely: His roguish eyes said he took what he wanted, and asked later.

"Damn it, woman, don't stand there, silent. Answer me. Where are you headed?"

"Williamsburg," she answered, clenching her fists. "Iffen it's any of your goldurned business, I'm goin' to Williamsburg!"

He drew on the cheroot and chuckled softly. "Wait a minute, lass . . . let me get this straight. You're going to Williamsburg on foot?"

"Yeah . . . why not?"

"Why not, indeed." His eyes amused, he flicked the cheroot aside. "It's over a hundred and fifty miles to Williamsburg."

"Well, I don't care if it's ten wagon greasin's to Williamsburg—*I'm goin'*."

"Don't you realize this back country is teaming with disgruntled Shawnee?" Squinting, he boldly slid his gaze over her. "How old are you, anyway?"

"Nineteen."

"Nineteen?" he echoed with a laugh. "Why, you shouldn't be out here alone. Where's your father?"

Lord, what a predicament she was in. She wanted to tell him the truth, to confide in someone, but she just couldn't—not with him being a Loyalist. She pulled up her courage and put on a brave face. "That's between me and him, ain't it?"

He looked annoyed, but plowed ahead. "Why are you in such a froth? What's your hurry, anyway?"

She rolled her eyes and sighed heavily. "Thunderation, you ask more questions than a tax collector. Would you quit pryin' into my personal business?"

"I'm not *pryin'* into your personal business. I'm trying to help you."

"I say let every tub set on its own bottom . . . I can manage by myself jest fine."

With slow deliberation his gaze went to the spot where the men had crashed into the woods. "Aye, I can see just how well you've managed so far. You're coming with me."

"No, I ain't. I figure you're about as crooked as a bucket of greased eels. I'd rather walk over a bed of blackberry thorns than ride with you."

His eyes looked like hot slits. "Why, you ungrateful little vixen."

She tossed back her hair and started down the road. Run! Go on, get away from him, she told herself. Once he got her into the coach, she would be trapped like a wolf in a pit.

But with three great steps, he grasped her arm. "What's your name, girl?"

"Sassy Adair. Now . . . are you satisfied, your royal nibs?"

He roared with laughter. "By God, someone named you right!" She tried to tug away, but his hands were like steel bands as he steered her in the other direction. "Get into the bloody coach, Sassy Adair." His voice was cold and implacable.

Her heart beat wildly. "I've got money and my own good legs," she cried, digging her heels into the earth. "I've got everythin' I need."

"All you've got is stiff-necked pride."

"I don't want to make no long fandangle out of this. I ain't goin' with no Loyalist."

"Would you believe me if I told you I wasn't a Loyalist?"

"No, I wouldn't. Someone who looks as rich as you jest can't be trusted."

Anger tightened his face. "You hardheaded wench, I'm a Scotsman!" he thundered.

"Scots, English . . . what's the difference? You're still a Loyalist."

"Lord God above . . . no wonder your mule ran off. No doubt he couldn't stand to listen to you anymore." He clasped her waist and pushed her forward. "Do you want that riffraff who was just here to catch up with you?"

She screwed up her face and snapped, "They're

yeller. They ain't comin' back. Besides, I'm used to takin' chances."

"Well, I'm not."

With that, he scooped her into his arms and headed for the waiting coach. The driver, reins in hand, watched the proceedings with an open mouth.

Sassy glanced up at her abductor, thinking his tousled hair and glinting eyes made him look like a handsome devil. Squirming like a wildcat, she pounded on his back with her fists—she would show him he couldn't carry her off like a dad-blamed sack of cornmeal. "I'm fixin' to knock you sky west and crooked iffen you don't put me down, you big ninnyhammer!" she screamed.

His mouth remained set in a stony line, and his eyes sparkled with rage.

Legs flying, she pounded on his chest. "Why, you blackhearted rascal, I'll cut your throat the minute I get my knife!" As she struggled, she slapped his jaw with a loud *smack*.

He cocked a brow, opened the coach door, and dumped her unceremoniously on the floor. "Your knife? Why don't you just use your tongue, lass?"

Then, with a colorful oath, he climbed in after her and slammed the door shut.

Chapter 2

Inside the musty-smelling coach, Roarke sat across from Sassy, his jostling legs brushing hers as the poorly sprung vehicle bumped over the Virginia countryside. He swept his gaze over her. What a figure she had: The loosely woven smock emphasized her ripe and creamy breasts, whose nipples pressed plain and clear against the thin material, tempting him to distraction. Taking a deep breath, he cursed himself for being a rake and a rogue—she was scarcely more than a child, for God's sake!

She scrunched back into the upholstery, her green eyes glittering dangerously. "Don't be thinkin' about strikin' up any conversation. I don't converse with Loyalists. We can ride all the way to hell without talkin', for all I care." She glared at him for a moment, then for good measure added, "Chaw on that for a while."

Women, he thought. They never listened. Aye, without exception, they were a headache, and a man would do well to leave them alone. Still, there was a damn ache in his loins . . . and her perky nipples and that deep cleavage . . . and her creamy neck that needed kissing. Lord above, it was going to be a bloody long ride to the next stop, at MacKenzie's Tavern.

Sometime later, Sassy's stomach rumbled.

Roarke watched her fish into her rucksack and pull out a piece of corn pone.

She gave him a frustrated glower and met his gaze head-on. "Well, if you think I'm goin' to set here like some ninnyhammer and listen to my stomach growl . . . you're wrong!"

He laughed deeply. "Eat what you wish, lass." Blood pounded through his veins as he noticed how soft and fine her red hair was, and how beautifully it framed her milky complexion. "Why are you in such a hurry to get to Williamsburg, anyway?" he finally asked.

Like a stubborn child, she went on eating without replying.

He raised a hand to his still-stinging jaw. She was a rebellious wildcat, a dissenter: an obstinate nail jutting from a smooth board.

He leaned forward and frowned into her stony face. "*Well?* I'm waiting for an answer."

"I reckon it ain't any of your dad-blamed business. I ain't some flitter-brained jaybird that chatters my affairs all over the countryside . . . 'specially to the likes of you!" She squinted at him suspiciously. "Why don't *you* try answerin' a few questions, mister? Where are *you* headed?"

He leaned back against the uncomfortable seat. "Like you, I'm going to Williamsburg—straight through, if I can make the connection."

"You ain't stoppin' at MacKenzie's Tavern?"

"Not unless I have to."

An impish grin played over her rosy lips. "Well, I'm fixin' to spend the night there. I'm goin' to take me a hot bath and sleep the bottom out of a bed. I've been sleepin' on the ground for days now." She snapped off more corn pone and with a full mouth added, "And I'm goin' to get me somethin' larrupin' good to eat!"

He chuckled and eyed the stiff, half-burned corn pone. "What's that?"

"Pone. I don't care for fancy vittles that don't stick to my ribs."

A smile twitched on his lips as she ate noisily.

"What are *you* grinnin' at? Ain't you ever heard nobody eat pone before?" Frustration clouded her lovely eyes. "Listen," she announced, pulling herself up. "Don't think we're friends now jest 'cause I ain't fightin' and scratchin' no more. As soon as we get to that tavern, there ain't no way you can keep me in here." Her gaze traveled over his fine attire. "I reckon you'll be lucky iffen you get away with your hide in one piece. You rich types ain't too welcome in these woods."

"Aye . . . I've noticed that."

She started coughing on the dry pone.

He took her into his arms and slapped her back. "Are you all right, lass?"

A ruddy blush stained her cheeks. "Course I'm all right!" she answered, pulling away. "This pone is jest a might dry." She whipped out a corked water bottle and took a swig, swishing it around in her mouth before swallowing. "I cooked me up a whole batch of pone afore I started out—but that was a week ago."

His interest was piqued. He had seen no hamlets or homesteads nearby. Where had she come from? "You've been on the road for a week?"

She smacked the cork in place and answered, "Yeah, me and my mule, ol' Solomon, were makin' real good time, but then the lop-eared jughead up and ran off."

"Your mule is named Solomon?"

"You bet. He's the smartest ass you ever saw. I named him Solomon myself. Course, everybody in this part of the country has Bible names, even the critters."

He couldn't help chuckling. What a treasure he

had discovered under the sycamore tree! This luscious spitfire was not only soft and desirable, but also amusing. He gazed at her snowy bosom, which threatened to spill from the smock with every jolt in the road, then studied her childlike face. Who was this delectable urchin, and what was her mission? "Surely Sassy isn't your real name," he said, rubbing his chin. "What is it?"

She put away the jug of water, then tugged off an ankle-high boot made of leather and laced with rawhide string. "My real name is Rachel," she answered, rubbing her dirty foot. "Pa gave me a name from the Old Testament. He knew he couldn't go wrong with somethin' like that."

Roarke wondered where her father was and why he had let her wander the roads. "And your mother agreed?"

"She died the night I came into this hard world."

Silent, he watched her put on the crude boot. The deerskin footwear told him her family grubbed an existence from the land. Even here in the wilderness, no woman would wear homemade boots if she had real shoes. No doubt the girl had never owned an article of store bought clothing in her life.

"All my cousins have Bible names," she went on. "There's Samuel, Nehemiah, Jeremiah. And Daniel and Hosea . . . they're twins."

"Mmm . . . I would never have guessed."

She took out a strip of jerky. "The onliest kin I have that *don't* have a Bible name is my Aunt Pert in Boston."

"Boston? How did a mountain woman get to Boston?"

"She married a travelin' drummer who took her there," Sassy replied, gnawing off a bite of jerky. "Yes, sir, that man was sure 'nuf hell for travelin'! When he died she kept their nice little house on Maryborn Street." She ripped off more jerky. "Pa's own name is Ezekiel, you know."

''A man of the cloth, no doubt?''

''Iffen you mean a preacher—you're right. Folks call him Crazy Ezekiel.''

He laughed again. ''Why, for God's sake?''

She shot him an annoyed look. ''From the way he looks and his fiery preachin' style, of course. He's got shoulder-length red hair and a red beard that covers his chest. He used to have a cape, but that wore out, so now he's jest got a blanket with a hole for his head.''

Roarke could imagine the colorful sermons—short on logic and long on emotional appeal.

''When he gets wound up and starts hollerin' and moanin' and weepin', the birds nearly fall from the trees,'' she boasted with a satisfied smile. ''Iffen he ain't got a regular platform, he jest jumps up on a wagon bed to preach. Sometimes he gets folks so filled with the spirit, they faint dead away, and some of the deacons have to drag them off to the glory pen till they come to.''

''Good Lord, what's a glory pen?''

''Why, it's jest a little fenced-off place filled with hay where the spiritually overheated can cool off some.'' An exasperated sigh escaped her throat. ''Law a mercy, ain't you ever heared of one? You're duller than a widder woman's ax, ain't you?''

He laughed heartily and shook his head.

She spread her hands. ''Why, Pa's so good,'' she went on dramatically, ''sometimes horse thieves hidin' in the shadows get the shakes jest listenin' to him. They come out all blubberin' and cryin' like babies ready to repent.''

Roarke's gaze swept her hips and waist, and after lingering on her jiggling nipples, returned to her face. Smiling, he leaned back and crossed his legs, imagining how she would feel nestled close to him in bed. ''Your father sounds like quite a showman,'' he finally said.

With a thoughtful look, she considered the idea.

"Yeah, I guess he is. But he ain't a fake! He ain't lookin' for no reward this side of Jordan. He takes no heed to the weather and makes calls on the sick and sufferin' and grievin'."

"Go on, tell me more," Roarke urged, enjoying the way her eyes glistened.

"He rides all over the countryside on ol' Solomon, holdin' camp meetin's. He's got little churches shootin' up like bean sprouts all over these hills."

At that particular moment Roarke wasn't thinking about spiritual matters. With the afternoon sunlight catching on her auburn hair and her eyes as clear as a child's, she reminded him of a tousled angel—one he would like to ravish.

He took a deep breath and struggled with the feelings her heavenly face and soft drawl stirred in him. He ached to crush her lustrous hair in his hand and flutter kisses over her face and shadowy cleavage. He had never taken an unwilling woman, but she was coming dangerously close to robbing him of his self-control. Her lazy southern voice finally focused his mind on her words.

"All he takes with him is a songbook, a Bible . . ." As she bent over, a folded paper slipped from her rucksack and tumbled to the floorboard.

Roarke picked up the crudely printed political tract and scanned the inflammatory message. "Where did you get this? Surely you didn't print it yourself?"

For a moment she sat stony-faced, then she blurted out, "We've got our ways."

He pitched the tract in her lap. "It seems the word of the Lord isn't the only thing Brother Ezekiel is preaching."

"No, it ain't!" she retorted, her voice hardening. "As soon as we can get everybody together, we're goin' to drive you Loyalists out of this country and start our own country." She put away the tract and leaned forward, showing most of her magnificent bosom. "And there ain't goin' to be no kings or queens or royalty. Ever man will stand on his own two feet."

"Doesn't it sober you a little to think of all you would be casting off?" he asked, playing devil's advocate.

"I can hear you cluckin', but I can't find your nest, stranger. What in the devil are you blabberin' about?"

He sighed wearily. "You would be casting off love of empire, noble traditions, the protection of a mighty power."

"The only thing we would be castin' off is a rope around our necks!"

Roarke's lips quirked with amusement. "How long have you been a rebel, lass?"

"Long enough to know I want to be shut of ol' King George," she retorted, her eyes snapping.

"There was great violence after the Coercive Act was published last spring," he said. "Bloody, mindless violence. The protest meetings brought out thieves and lowlives. Property was destroyed—and not all of it belonged to Loyalists. Is that what you advocate?" he finished, testing her ideas.

" 'Pears you take a real dark view of things, mister. And you got an awful narrer mind, too!"

"Possibly."

She sat up straighter. "Well, life is worth gettin' worked up about . . . and so's independence! Maybe you ain't been in this country long enough to realize it, but in America we call that Coercive Act you're talkin' about the Intolerable Act. Sure, there will always be some hotheads and no-accounts, but the bulk of the colonists are good, hardworkin' folks, and all your royal *acts* and *laws* are jest drawin' us closer together. Soon we'll all be united and will send you Loyalists back across the sea."

He took a deep breath. "I'm going to tell you one last time, lass . . . *I'm not a Loyalist.*"

She scooted forward, her eyes flaring indignantly. "I know what you are," she accused, wagging a finger. "I can tell by your fancy duds you're a Tidewater planter. Only someone that rich could afford those clothes!"

He pierced her with a sharp stare and lowered his voice. "You're wrong. I own and captain a ship, you hardheaded wench. I export tobacco from Virginia to Europe." Well, it was half-true, he thought. Why should he recount all of his whole colorful past at this point?

Suspicion darkened her fine features. "You think I'm some kind of lunertic? If you're a ship's captain, what in thunderation are you doin' so far from the sea?"

"I've found that the tobacco growers and I both benefit if I buy their crops direct without the interference of an English agent," he replied. "I've just struck a deal with a large planter in the southwestern part of the colony. He'll have his tobacco at Williamsburg when I sail."

"When you sail?"

He leaned back and pulled out a cheroot, which gave off a pungent rum scent. "Aye . . . as soon as I reach Williamsburg, I'll be setting sail on the *Sea Witch* for Scotland. Most of this colony's tobacco goes through Glasgow, you know. This is what they're craving in Europe," he went on, twisting the rough cheroot between his fingers. "Tobacco for pipes, cheroots, and snuff. It all fetches a fine price."

"I suppose you're gettin' filthy rich," she challenged in a sour tone.

"That I am, since I figured out how to outfox the crippling navigation laws." At her puzzled expression, he added, "I leave America with legitimate cargoes of tobacco. But on the return trip I off-load contraband Scotch whiskey and French silks outside the harbor, then sail past the revenue cutters, avoiding customs."

A disgusted look settled over her face. "Well, it don't make no difference iffen you raise rice or ship tobacco. You're still rich and you're still a Loyalist!"

He jammed the cheroot into his pocket. "I'm not a Loyalist! My only allegiance is to Scotland. I don't care if all the bloody British drown in the sea!" His voice sizzled with frustration.

Her eyes lit up. "You're Scottish jest like Captain Rakehell. I knew you was when you first went to talkin', but I didn't know you hated the British, too. If Captain Rakehell was here, he'd help us. I reckon he's killed more redcoats than anybody. You ever heared of him?"

Roarke fell silent, then muttered, "Yes . . . I've heard of him."

When he ventured no further comment and looked away, she finally leaned back in the seat. With a weary sigh, she pulled a suede pouch from her skirt pocket and dumped the contents in her lap.

Roarke raised his brows and scanned the assortment of rocks, shells, teeth, and bits of wood. "What in the devil is all that?" he finally asked.

She shot him a withering glare. "This here is my treasure sack and these are my pretties. I've been collectin' 'em all my life. Ever onct in a while I take 'em out and look 'em over." She held up a small blue rock. "Pa found this in the creek when I was a little girl and gave it to me. Ain't it pretty?"

He smiled and nodded.

She held up a tiny baby tooth. "This here is my first tooth. It got loose when I was six and fell out jest like a kernel of corn." Placing it aside, she picked up a shell and held it in the light. "And this here is a shell a woman gave me at one of Pa's meetin's. See how pink and shiny it looks in the light?"

He examined the shell and gave it back to her.

Next she presented him with a slice of wood with a dark inlaid star shape almost at the center. "Soon as I seen this thing, I glommed on to it. That star is a little crooked, but it's plumb natchrul-lookin'. I found it on one of my rambles." After he had looked at the wood, she raked through everything again and sighed happily. "I sure got lots of good stuff in this little sack."

For a moment she sat silent, then she put away the pouch. Expectation lighting her eyes, she edged forward to begin another assault. "If you're not a Loyalist, why don't you jest join up with us? Things are fixin' to bust loose and we're trainin' men right now. I saw how you handled that trash on the road." Her gaze traveled over the light sprinkling of gray at his temples. "You must have been somethin' in your prime."

"My prime!"

"Yeah. How old are you, anyway?"

His prime, indeed! He glared at her and snorted. "Oh, I'm somewhere between thirty-three and death."

"Well, it's not too late. You're a little old, but good men are skeerce, and we need good ships, too."

He crossed his legs and stared at her.

Her eyes flamed in outrage at his silence. "You're sure set in your ways, ain't you? Haven't you ever been real stirred up about somethin'?"

"Damnation, girl, you're absolutely bursting with zeal," he finally said with a chuckle.

She lifted her dainty chin. "Mebbe I am. Life is more than big parties and fancy foods with big names that get tangled around your tongue. Life is about gettin' behind somethin' good and workin' for it. Life is good, and most people are good, too."

What an innocent she was. "Your attitude is admirable, but a bit ill considered," he said dryly.

She smacked her fist against the coach door. "By goonies, whose side are you on, anyway!"

He shrugged, then flashed her a quick grin. "My side."

Fire flickered in her eyes, matching the highlights dancing in her hair.

"It's quite simple, lass," he went on in a light tone. "Who better to be on my side than me?"

"Damn it . . . ain't there anythin' you would be willin' to die for?"

"You *do* have a way of cutting to the heart of the matter, don't you?"

Crossing her arms, she settled back into the seat and flung him a disdainful glare. "Well . . . I'm waitin' for an answer," she said, mocking his earlier comment.

"I really don't know," he stated casually, hiding his emotions. "I haven't been pressed with any life-and-death decisions lately."

"Thunderation! You're makin' fun of me again. You ain't learnt a dad-blamed thing, have you?"

The driver called to the horses, and gradually the rattling coach slowed. Roarke turned to watch the green countryside blur past the window. Soon MacKenzie's Tavern, a two-story log building surrounded by a thicket of trees, came into view. Half-fenced by a stone wall, it had a cobbled courtyard and outside tables. A brown liquor jug dangled from its brightly painted sign to notify illiterate travelers that the establishment sold whiskey.

Sassy cleared her throat loudly to claim Roarke's attention. The setting sun poured through the pane behind her, sparkling over her auburn hair; with her flashing eyes and heaving bosom, he thought she looked like a wild Gypsy wench on the verge of a tirade. "If you try to keep me in this coach, I'll holler my head off," she threatened, jabbing a finger at him.

He smiled tightly. "What a colorful imagination you have. As soon as this coach stops, I will consider our association finished," he lied. He frowned at the rustic tavern, then gazed at her again. "I have delivered you safe and sound to a remnant of civilization—poor as it may be."

Surprise filled her face as the coach clattered into the courtyard . . . then she coolly composed her features. "I'll have my knife iffen you don't mind," she demanded, grabbing her rucksack and holding out a slim hand. "It's a good London-made barlow knife paid for with maple syrup I sapped off myself."

With a smile, he handed her the knife, then picked up his tricorn from the seat.

The coach had barely creaked to a halt when she shoved down the door lever. As she clambered out, her hem caught under the half-open door, pulling her back.

Roarke chuckled while she angrily yanked at her skirt, trying to free it. With a broad smile, he raised his hat and released the garment.

Embarrassment coloring her cheeks, she whirled and headed toward the log building.

He slapped on his tricorn and cried, "Good luck, Sassy Adair. You're a bonny, stouthearted lass, if ever I saw one."

Her eyes sparked fire as she glanced over her shoulder. "Now that I'm rid of you, all my luck will be good luck!"

He watched her swaying hips as she strode toward the tavern. At the door she peeked back over her shoulder once again; then, catching his eye, she raised her chin and disappeared.

He laughed, feeling better than he had in months. What a challenging hoyden she was! And there was something in her green eyes and lush body that drove him mad with desire. His ship was waiting . . . but damn it all, it could keep on waiting. ''You're not rid of me yet, lass,'' he muttered to himself. ''Oh no . . . you're not rid of me yet!''

Chapter 3

Sassy awoke to the sound of distant thunder and soft rain. For a moment she relaxed into the bed and listened to raindrops patter against the window, then she remembered her important task. Her father was sitting in a British gaol and needed her help this very minute. Instantly she drew back the threadbare quilt, dressed in a clean skirt and smock, and splashed water on her sleepy face.

She pulled aside the muslin curtains and opened the window: The chilly morning air washed over her, carrying the sweet scents of rain and moist earth. With an upward glance, she watched moisture trickle from the tavern's shake roof; far above the roof, dark clouds tumbled through the sky, reflecting her own dark mood.

Last night she'd been too tired to eat in the noisy taproom, and had feasted on roast pork in her own chamber. And she had slept in a real bed—the first since she'd left home. She should have rested well . . . but she had dreamed of Roarke MacLaren's mocking face. Yesterday when she had realized he wasn't a proclaimed Loyalist, she had almost told him about her father, but his lackadaisical attitude toward colonial resistance had put her off. Besides, she had never met a rich man she could trust. And there was something he was holding back, too, something that just didn't set right with her. She was sure of it.

"Damn him," she mumbled, "why can't I put the good-lookin' rascal out of my mind?" Steeling her nerves, she told herself he was just another obstacle on the road to Williamsburg—like the ruffians who had accosted her.

The sound of a jingling harness pulled her attention downward; through the drizzling mist she saw a young man lead four satiny-coated Kentucky reds toward a waiting coach. Hurry up! she commanded herself, knowing the driver would be leaving soon. Reluctantly she scanned the room, eyeing the bathtub full of dirty water and the crumpled towels she had used last night. Such luxuries. Her bones still ached, but it was time to press on. She gathered her meager belongings and jammed them into her rucksack. With a backward glance at a cracked mirror, she checked her blue cotton skirt and white linsey-woolsey smock, then straightened her shoulders and left the room.

With a resolute snap in her stride, she marched down a flight of creaky stairs, admonishing herself with each step. Roarke MacLaren had vanished with the night and should be forgotten like a bad dream. There was nothing to worry about now. Hadn't the dark-eyed rascal told her he was going on? Everything had turned out just as she had wanted. She paused on the last step and pressed her lips together. Then why in the devil did she feel no joy? Why were her spirits drooping like a hound dog's tail?

Confusion scrambling her emotions, she entered the taproom, its low-beamed ceiling hung with bright copper pots. Loud, smoky, and merry, the cozy chamber smelled of fresh bread and frying bacon. A woman dressed in a mobcap and homespun gown knelt by the mammoth hearth cooking rashers of side meat. Above her sizzling skillet, a teakettle jiggled from a hook, spouting white steam. The woman's daughter worked by her side, hoisting a tray of thick-crusted loaves from a stone oven. Timidly smiling, she glanced at Sassy and tumbled the bread into a waiting basket.

Roughly dressed grandfathers, long-stemmed clay pipes jammed between their teeth, hunched around the tables conversing while they waited for breakfast. Interest warmed their lined faces as Sassy brushed past them; with an answering smile she eased onto a crude bench and caught the landlord's eye.

He was a burly man in a brown jerkin and buckled knee breeches. She ordered breakfast and asked about coaches traveling into Williamsburg. "You're in luck, miss," he replied. "We have a coach goin' out this mornin'."

As he hurried away, her spirits brightened—then she heard someone enter the room behind her back, the footsteps clear and purposeful. Her heart beat loudly, rushing blood to her cheeks. She *knew* it was Roarke, no one had to tell her, because the crowd quieted down as if a ghost had just entered. She glanced over her shoulder . . . just to be certain. Sure enough, there he stood in the taproom entrance, cocky as the Devil guarding the mouth of hell. The local farmers' eyes clouded with distaste as they scanned his fine clothes. For a strained moment, silence chilled the air, then halfhearted chatter rippled through the crowd once more.

Delicious excitement hummed through her veins while she watched him give the landlord money. Then, like a hawk homing in on a field mouse, Roarke caught her eyes. Her heart thumped uncomfortably as his gaze joined hers; a smile flashed on his bronzed face as he started toward her. Law a mercy, the rascal intended to join her for breakfast!

She bent her head and stared at the scarred tabletop, trying to think of something to say. Her stomach flip-flopped as he pulled back the bench and claimed the seat across from her. Gathering her courage, she raised her gaze and studied his amused face. "I thought you were goin' on," she whispered in outrage.

"So did I," he answered good-naturedly.

"You mean to sit there with a sly possum grin on your face and tell me you slept here last night, while . . . while I was bathin' and eatin' and sleepin' and everythin'!"

A smile lingered at the corners of his firm mouth. "Aye, I'm afraid so. After you left the coach, I got into a discussion with some farmers outside. I came in just in time to see your skirt swishing up the stairs." In a mocking tone he added, "Of course, I wouldn't have *dreamed* of interrupting your privacy."

She blew out her breath and clasped the table edge until her fingers turned white. "Well, I'll be double-dipped and fried in hot bear grease. No wonder I slept so bad last night!" She glared at him, trying to look stern. "Did you put up across the hall from me?"

He rubbed his neck. "I wish I *had* slept across the hall from you, lass," he said at last, craning his neck and stretching his arm. "Unfortunately you took the last room. I had to sleep on that blasted porch between the tavern and the storehouse, with nothing under me but a rush mat." He threw her a sideways look and massaged his neck again. "I may have had a worse night's sleep, but I can't remember when."

Her merry laughter prompted the locals to stare. "You had to sleep on the dog run? A fine Scottish sea captain like you had to sleep there?" She covered her mouth and shook with mirth, imagining Roarke laid out with the local rabble on the long, sheltered porch while she slept in a soft bed.

"Laugh if you will, lass, but I hobbled in circles for half an hour this morning trying to get my legs to work properly. I thought I might be crippled for life."

Secret excitement surged through her. "But . . . but you said you were goin' on. Why did you stay?"

He looked uncomfortable. "I couldn't make connections . . ." He was grappling for another explanation when the ruddy-faced landlord hurried to the table with two plates of bacon and thick, buttered toast. As he plunked them down, he told Sassy, "Soon as the new driver eats and the stable hand finishes hitchin' up the team, the coach to Williamsburg will be off, miss."

"*The* coach . . . You mean there's jest one coach goin' to Williamsburg today?"

"That's right . . . it's the only coach for a week."

"A week?" Whistling low, she shook her head. "Well now, don't that rang your bell?"

The man raised his bushy brows and grinned, showing broken teeth. "Course, we can put you up and feed you till another comes by."

Lord, what a turn of events this was. She had been in such a hurry to get away from Roarke, she hadn't bothered to ask about the schedule last night. Now here she was stuck with him again. She clenched the table again, pondering her alternatives.

The landlord sighed and shifted his weight. "If you want to travel, you'll have to go with this gentleman here," he said in a weary voice. "And it looks like it will be a rough trip. There's a thunderstorm brewin' in that direction, and you'll have to sleep at a one-man way station on the pass. It's hardly more than a cabin, just a place to change the team and get a little rest." He glanced at the crowded taproom, then back at her. "Well, what are you goin' to do? I've got customers to tend to."

"Jest hold your horses. I've got to think on it!"

His eyes glinting happily, Roarke ate his food and studied her face.

With trembling fingers she took a knotted handkerchief from her rucksack, untied it, and counted her money.

"If you're goin', you need to pay me four dollars, miss. I'm collectin' for the driver," the landlord prodded.

Her head shot up. "Four dollars! You might as well ask for a thousand." She tied up her money and shoved it away, thinking she should have slept outside with the rest of the poor folks.

The landlord slung the towel over his arm. "Well, are you goin' or not, miss!"

"I . . . I don't have enough," she stammered in embarrassment.

Roarke pushed back his plate, stood, and pulled out his purse.

Sassy jumped up, almost knocking over the rough bench. "No, don't take it! I ain't goin' to let this rich varmint pay it, no way. I'll work it out and go when I can." She ran her gaze over Roarke's tall body. "Why . . . why, I'd rather travel with ol' Nick himself!"

Frowning, Roarke pressed some coins into the man's hand, then moved to Sassy and took her arm. "Accept my gift and we'll be on our way."

She stamped her foot, drawing nervous looks from the breakfast crowd. "You low-down, weasel-brained porcupine. You lied to me! You said you were goin' on and you weren't. You knew this would happen. You knew I'd be trapped into travelin' with you again!"

He flashed a pleased grin. "Aye, lass, I lied. God help me, I lied. Yet another black mark has been added to Roarke MacLaren's long list of sins."

"Why, you think this is funny! You think—"

"Do you want to go to Williamsburg or not?" he broke in.

Her teeth clenched, she hastily wrapped some bacon and a piece of toast in a cloth and gathered her things; then, Roarke at her side, she exited the crowded tavern, sure that everyone there had seen her humiliation.

As she went reluctantly to the waiting coach, he pulled back on her arm, warming it with his touch. "Tell me something, lass. Why *would* you be willing to ride with the devil himself to get to Williamsburg?"

Why did he have to be so nosy? She just didn't know him well enough, didn't trust him enough, to tell him about her father. Gathering her skirt, she glanced back over her shoulder, burning to wipe the rakish smile from his face. "I'm . . . I'm jest lookin' for work, that's all," she snapped. The lie burning her lips, she snatched up her trailing skirt and entered the coach.

By dusk a full-blown storm rocked the coach. The terrible weather had slowed their progress to a crawl, and they hadn't met a soul for hours. During the morning a steady rain had peppered the hilly fields; by noon, water had swept down the gullies in rivulets; and now in late afternoon, thick mud mired the road. The driver had lit the coach lanterns, which bobbed through the heavy rain like blurry halos. Inside the jostling vehicle everything smelled of moldy upholstery and wet leather.

Roarke placed his open hand against the window, feeling the cool air that seeped around the poorly fitted door and listening to the *plink-plink-plink* of rain dripping into the coach; then, aided by the feeble coach lights, he watched Sassy wince and close her eyes while the driver cracked his whip over the backs of the stumbling horses.

She looked like an exhausted child. Her beauty

and courage had initially attracted him. Now he found himself becoming more emotionally drawn to her. Chagrined, he admitted that the little minx had already claimed a part of him.

Aye, she offered a rich sensual challenge, and he promised himself he would pick this mountain flower before he sailed for Scotland. Having never denied himself a woman he wanted, he had considered going to her last night, but he had known she wasn't ready to come to him of her own free will. And before they reached Williamsburg, come she would—that he vowed!

As they jounced over a deep rut, she stretched and caught his eye. "What time is it?" she mumbled.

He tugged out his pocket watch and held it toward the wavering light. "Four o'clock," he answered.

With a snap, he put away the timepiece and watched the misty coach lights weaving into the gathering darkness. He doubted they would make it to the way station before six o'clock. Here in the wild high country, the horses labored with increasing difficulty up the steep inclines, against the sheeting rain.

As Sassy laid her head back and nodded off, Roarke relaxed into the seat and listened to the steady rain drum against the coach roof. Then he, too, closed his eyes and let his mind drift. He remembered the first moment he had seen her. The coach had swung around a bend, and all at once she had loomed into view, fighting and slashing like a cornered tigress. With her wild auburn hair and lush body, she had taken his breath away. At that moment he knew he had to meet her. Impetuous and high-spirited, she made him laugh out loud. And she was so fresh and unspoiled, and expressed such childlike joy in life.

Roarke chuckled at the memories. And, Lord,

how she kept after him about her precious rebellion. Again this afternoon she had tried to enlist him to her cause.

"I still think you ought to join up with us," she had prodded.

Scooting his boot from a puddle of rainwater, he had sighed heavily, pulled between anger and tenderness. Indeed, she had aroused his emotions at a shocking pace—anger, frustration, amusement—and left the rest of his mind an untidy mess. How could he ever explain the tangled Jacobite cause to her? Then he decided not to try.

"It's not my war, Sassy. I'm a Scotsman. My allegiance is solely to Scotland . . . I have responsibilities there. And I would never want to live anyplace else."

"You keep sayin' that, but it sounds to me like you sail out of Williamsburg all the time."

"For the last two years I have."

Her eyes brightened. "I'll bet you have rooms there."

"Aye. I do."

"Well, there you go—you're an American!"

"No, I'm a Scotsman who lives in America on and off for business reasons. This rebellion is not my affair."

"Well, when is it goin' to be your affair? When the British lob a shot into your parlor or blockade your ship?"

Her last statement hit close to home, but he knew she would never let go if he gave her more information about his past.

Roarke laughed, and coloring it up high, said, "Look, lass, I'm a damn poor shot—I can't hit the side of a barn." He rubbed his leg. "I've got a bad leg, and limp when it's cold. Besides that, I'm a gambler, scoundrel, rogue, and general no-account. No, the American cause doesn't need Roarke MacLaren."

A disgusted look frosted her fine features. ''Well, you got one part right—the part about bein' a liar. Excuses, excuses, excuses; you've got more excuses than a spider's got eyes.''

Roarke smiled at the memory, then Sassy coughed, bringing his thoughts back to the present. He scrutinized her shadowed face. No doubt she was sick. He could imagine her sleeping on the damp earth and walking until she was exhausted to save a few pence. With amused interest he watched her pull another bottle from her rucksack, uncork it, and take a swig.

''Yet another bottle from your amazing sack. What is this one?''

Wheezing, she wiped her lips. ''It's cough elixir. I never go anywhere without it,'' she answered in a hoarse croak.

He pulled the bottle from her hand and took a sniff, then gave a lopsided grin. ''I should think not! It smells like it's a hundred and fifty proof. No doubt you make it yourself.''

She frowned as she corked the bottle and put it away. ''Pa made it. It's a little side business of his.'' Her voice was thick with sleep.

He burst out laughing. ''A preacher making liquor? No wonder Brother Ezekiel's flock is so filled with the spirit!''

She glowered and sat forward. ''Look here! I've been crossin' swords with you all day, and I'm tired of it. If Pa wants to make elixir or even make whiskey, it's his business. The British have taxed everything else, but they couldn't enforce a liquor tax in these hills with an army ten thousand strong led by ol' King George himself!''

Roarke chuckled and considered her again as she closed her eyes and rested against the seat. Despite her rustic ways and saucy tongue, he sensed her deep understanding of people and principles. But why had she lied? Clearly she was not in such a hurry to reach Williamsburg simply to seek employment.

His mind drifted to Crazy Ezekiel with his long red beard and his mule named Solomon—and his rebel propaganda. Damn the foolish old man and his childish pamphlets anyway. Where was he, and why had he let the girl go off like this?

All at once a whistling wind shook the coach, making the chained window drape smack against the pane.

Sassy sat up and looked out. Lightning flashed behind the dark, pine-studded hills, and rain fell in torrents. "I don't think we're goin' to make it, Roarke. It's rainin' too hard, and the road is jest too bad."

He caught her worried eyes and feigned a look of annoyance. At the same time, pleasure warmed him at her use of his Christian name. "What rubbish is this?" he asked, taking her cold hand. "Could this be the same lass who told me life is exciting and wonderful and worth getting worked up about?"

Before she could answer, the team floundered on a turn, sharply jostling the coach. As Roarke grabbed the leather handhold, Sassy slipped from the slick seat and tumbled to the floor. As he reached for her, the driver cracked his whip, and the horses whinnied loudly. Suddenly the coach shuddered, and with a great splintering sound, crashed to its side.

Chapter 4

Sassy cried out as the world turned upside down and the breath was knocked from her lungs; for a moment she lay stunned; then, her pulse racing, she rolled over and opened her eyes. Recognition came to her—she lay sprawled on the side of the coach, her arms and legs tangled with those of Roarke, who lay next to her. Outside, the sound of shrieking horses and scrambling boots pierced the drumming rain.

Carefully Roarke drew her into his arms and held her close. "Are you all right, lass?"

"I . . . I think so." She swung her gaze over the tilted coach. "Law a mercy," she mumbled. "We . . . we spilled over like a sack of flour!"

Cursing roughly, the driver pried open the coach door directly above them, letting in a draft of chilly air. Rain burst in, drenching them both to the skin. Lightning flashed behind the driver's head, illuminating his frightened eyes. "Are ye safe? We lost a wheel an' tipped over." He cupped his hands to yell over the wailing wind. "The damn road's jest too bad!" he warned, rain spilling from the tip of his tricorn and splattering into the coach. "Do ye want to get the young lady to the way station, sir?" he cried at Roarke. "We're almost there. The walk will soak ye both like dipped rats, but ye can dry off an' warm up there. Ye'll be safe . . . and ye can stretch out and sleep."

"Aye!" Roarke called back over the pounding rain. "We'll free the lass first. I'll lift her up, you pull her out."

Sassy felt Roarke's strong hands clasp her waist and raise her up. When she was high enough, the driver tugged her from the open door like a housewife pulling a slick kitten into the world.

Raindrops pounded her head as she slid over the coach's edge, her skirt hiking up about her thighs. At last she raked back her dripping hair and stood on shaky legs. Instantly cold water soaked through her deer-hide boots and drenched her feet, which sank into the mushy earth. She staggered away, then turned and scanned the scene. The vehicle lay on its side like an overturned turtle. One wheel revolved slowly; the other had popped off its axle and rolled away. The coach lights still flickered eerily. Behind the rearing horses, lightning streaked the night sky, highlighting the bent evergreens.

Roarke grabbed one side of the opening, and pulling himself up, scrambled out behind her. Immediately he helped the driver free the whinnying horses from the traces and place the broken shafts aside; then he turned to Sassy. Water streamed from his hatless head as he led her to the protection of a huge oak tree.

The driver followed. "The way station is jest a mile up that road," he said, pointing ahead with a gnarled finger. He peered nervously back at the wild-eyed horses, which still bucked against one another although they were tethered to a tree. "Go ahead. I can't leave them horses. They're near mad with fear now."

The old man narrowed his eyes. "I 'preciate yer help with the horses, but it's tools I be needin' now. The coach is off its thoroughbraces, an' the whip springs is twisted. Why don't ye go ahead an' take the young lady to the way station. She's freezin', an' there's rumors of Injuns about. Once ye get there, tell the attendant to bring a hammer an' pliers. Don't worry about us here at the coach," he called as he moved away. "It may take a while to get things in order."

Roarke glanced at the driver, then clasped Sassy's hand. "Come on, lass, we've a way to go, and we'll not get there standing in the rain." His jaw set, he strode ahead, tugging her along the muddy road.

Cold rain prickled her face, and thorny bushes snagged her sodden skirt as she hurried after him. As they rounded a curve, thunder boomed out and she impulsively looked back at the driver, who stood silhouetted against the angry sky as he tried to calm the frenzied animals.

"We must hurry, lass." Gently Roarke urged her forward, guiding her around a protruding boulder, silvery rivulets streaming over its edge. She stumbled ahead, her feet catching on slippery roots. Finally they topped a rise and she spied the way station a hundred yards down the road. It was nothing more than a weathered log cabin, with a crumbling stable situated up another incline, but it was a welcoming beacon, with rain-veiled light flickering from its tiny windows.

Holding her side, Sassy staggered ahead. Muck pulled at her heels, her lungs gasped for air, and her legs trembled with exhaustion. Her fingers slid from Roarke's grasp and she crumpled into the mud. With a moan, she rose, but again her legs buckled beneath her.

Roarke knelt and circled her waist with one arm. "Easy, little one," he murmured, brushing back her wet locks.

She tried to struggle up. "I jest fell. I can go on. I . . ."

He cradled her against his hard chest and stood

up with her in his arms. Even in the rain she could smell his musky scent; the strength in his arms and the sound of his beating heart warmed her spirit.

As he started up the incline, she weakly flailed her arm and murmured, "Put me down . . . I can walk."

He ignored her, snuggling her closer. "Hush, lass . . . let me carry you."

Too tired to protest, she rested her head on his shoulder, relishing the warmth of his body. Forgetting herself, she melted against him like a tired child, feeling secure for the first time in months. She felt him moving, carrying her up the incline, then they were at a rough door. Holding her in one arm, he thumped a fist on the rough panel and called above the wind.

From inside came the scraping of latches. Then the door banged open and a tall man carrying a lantern loomed in front of them.

Dawn light flooded into the loft window, caressing Sassy's face. In her dazed state everything felt warm and cozy and smelled of hay and wood. Yawning, she wiggled into the mattress. Somewhere in the back of her mind she realized the storm had passed. Well, the weather may have improved, but her disposition hadn't, she thought, pulling the deer-hide cover over her chilly shoulders. Her body still ached, and outside the cabin, a nest of blue jays chattered and shrieked, sabotaging her efforts to fall asleep again.

With a groan, she looked at her muddy clothes spread over a rickety chair, then down at the buckskin shirt she now wore, given to her by the way station man.

Finally she sat up and peered over the railing at Roarke, who slept on the ground floor in a rude bed—a platform padded with a cornhusk mattress and covered with deer hides. His ruined finery lay heaped on the floor at his side. Naked to the waist, he slept peacefully on his back, one tan arm thrown over his head. Warmth flowed through Sassy as she remembered the feel of those strong arms around her body last night. It was a good thing the coach could be repaired and they could continue on today, she thought, wondering how long she could resist Roark's potent allure.

Brushing back her tangled hair, she remembered the driver and way station man. Thunderation, it was dawn! Why weren't they back yet? Perhaps they needed help.

With a weary sigh, she got up and looked over the railing at the rest of the cluttered room. Hickory stools and a huge table and puncheon benches—split and peeled logs with legs—furnished the cabin. Shelves full of crockery and tall knotty pine cabinets offered the only storage. On one side of the cabin battered pots and pans littered a blackened hearth over which hung a set of deer antlers. There was little else except barrels of staples, gun racks, and pegs for clothes.

Everything was so still. Then, as Sassy listened to the squawking blue jays, another sound caught her ear. Muffled hoofbeats thudded outside the cabin, sending a chill down her back. She peeked through the window—and the scene below made her gasp.

Bathed in dawn's pink glow, a band of painted Indians were sliding from their ponies. Clad in buckskin leggings and beaded moccasins, they stared at the way station for a moment before fanning out to explore. Feathers dangled from their long hair, and quivers of arrows bounced against their tanned backs as they gathered in front of the stable. As silent as shadows, one brave opened the stable door and another crept toward the front of the way station.

Her heart pumping, Sassy eyed the thick batten

door. It was hung on wooden hinges and had strong latches and an extra bar for use in time of Indian attack. Thankfully, Roarke had secured all the latches before they had fallen exhausted into their hard beds.

Hearing soft whinnies, Sassy pressed her face back to the window. Another Indian was trotting his mount over the wet soil; on a long tether he led four matched Kentucky reds—the horses from their wrecked coach! The other Indians proudly brought out a string of four dapple grays from the stable.

Her legs trembling, Sassy moved to the railing and scrambled down the loft ladder. She hurried to Roarke and shook his brawny arm. "There's Injuns outside," she whispered hoarsely. "They're stealin' the horses!"

With a soft curse, he rose from the bed, a pair of borrowed buckskins clinging to his slim hips and long legs. He jerked on his muddied boots and strode to a downstairs window. Sassy stood on tiptoes to peek over his broad shoulder as the Indians drove off the horses and disappeared into the dewy forest.

In one swift movement, Roarke grabbed a flintlock and a powder horn, then slammed back all the latches and threw open the door.

Sassy clenched her hands and ran after him. "Where are you goin'?"

"To see about the others." His face taut, he left the cabin and started down the muddy incline. "*You* stay there!" he ordered over his bare shoulder.

For a moment she watched him jog down the road. Then, her heart pounding, she tore out after him. The soft earth gave way beneath her bare feet as she scampered down the slope, the rain-washed forest flying past her. By the time she reached the curved road, Roarke was far ahead of her. "Wait.

Wait for me!'' she called, her long buckskin shirt slapping against her thighs.

Without looking back, he streaked ahead, the flintlock swinging at his side. Her bare feet made sucking sounds in the cool mud as she followed his swift form, and fear for the men's safety consumed her thoughts.

When she finally caught up with Roarke, he glared down at her. ''It's a fearful hardheaded woman you are, Sassy Adair!'' he said, but he slowed his pace a bit so that they could run on together.

Pain coursed through her legs by the time they sighted the overturned coach. Roarke rushed ahead, then returned and loosely caught her arm. ''You needn't go any farther,'' he warned.

With all her strength, she broke free and shot ahead. Her heart somersaulted as she spotted the two men lying on the ground, arrows protruding from their bodies. His tricorn floating in a nearby puddle, the driver lay sprawled near the coach. His arm jutted out awkwardly, and his stiff hand looked as if he had clenched a pistol. The tall way station man was crumpled over a tangle of harness.

Feeling a warm hand on her shoulder, Sassy turned and fell against Roarke's broad chest. ''Lord, how terrible,'' she breathed. ''Jest to think they were killed while we slept.''

He pulled her closer and caressed her back. ''Aye, from the looks of it, they were dead before they could fire a shot.''

She skimmed her gaze over the bodies, then buried her face against him once again. ''It could have been us.''

''Luck was with us, lass. Last night we were protected by the rain and darkness. And this morning we were locked in the way station, asleep.''

''They killed them . . . jest for the horses,'' she said hoarsely.

"Aye, I'm sure that's what they wanted . . . that and weapons. The driver should have given them the damn horses."

Shivers tingled over her as she scanned the wooded hills, their tops gilded in the fiery dawn. "Pa says Shawnee ain't interested in anythin' but horses and guns. Mebbe they won't come back."

He tightened his arms around her. "I think you're right. They have what they want. And they have no idea there are weapons in the way station." Gently he turned her away from the coach and, sighing heavily, circled her waist with one arm. "You should be safe," he said, leading her back down the road. "But you have *two* problems to worry about now."

Her gaze locked with his. "Two?"

"Aye, lass," he quipped with a grin. "Unless someone else comes along this isolated road, you'll be detained in getting to Williamsburg . . . Like it or not, you're stuck with me for another week!"

Chapter 5

Inside the way station the scent of cooked meat and whale-oil lamps permeated the air. A rust-colored skirt wrapped about her chilly legs, Sassy sat near the glowing hearth reading a well-worn almanac; Roarke leaned against the mantel, studying a map. Earlier in the day they had retrieved her precious rucksack and his luggage from the wrecked coach, and with heavy hearts, had buried the hapless men. The painful task had brought them together and cast them both in quiet, reflective moods. Left to her own devices during the afternoon, Sassy had washed clothes and cleaned the cabin while Roarke searched for game.

They had just finished a simple supper of rabbit stew, and now relaxed around the crackling fireplace. As Sassy flipped another page in the ragged almanac, she started coughing. Roarke placed the map on the mantel and retrieved her cough elixir and a spoon. She skipped her gaze over him while he poured the medicine. How breathtakingly handsome he looked in a white shirt with a lacy jabot and cuffs, and a pair of buckskins that molded his lean hips. She marveled at the way the two very different garments complemented each other. Buckskin and silk matched up by a whim of fate—just like her and Roarke, she thought.

Firelight caressed his harsh face as he felt her forehead, taking her temperature. His warm hand sent shivery feelings down her spine. When she licked the spoon, she met his sharp eyes. "I'll be all right," she murmured, picking up the book again. "I've jest got a little cough."

"I'm surprised you don't have pneumonia after what you've been through," he remarked, putting away the elixir.

His deep, warm voice made her feel as if she were wrapped in a soft quilt. She remembered how wonderfully secure she had felt when he had carried her from the coach, and how she had wanted to stay in his arms forever. And there had been a flame of passion—she had felt it crackle between them. With that same spark of desire flaring within her now, she watched him light a cheroot in the flames, pick up a musket and rag, and seat himself near the sputtering logs. The fire gilded his hair and warmed his craggy features. She imagined she could hear the sound of her own heart over the snapping flames as she gazed at his bent head.

The Kentucky rifle, five feet long, rested across his legs while he polished the brass patch box on its stock. When he glanced up and smiled, the message in his eyes was clear. Law a mercy, she felt her insides melt every time the rogue looked at her. How much longer could she resist him? she wondered. And Lord, when would someone come up that washed-out road and rescue them! Suddenly things seemed altogether too quiet. Standing, she snatched a raw turnip from the table and walked toward him.

"You're real partial to that gun, ain't you?" she asked with a chuckle.

He tossed the polishing cloth aside and rose. "Aye, that I am," he replied. He studied the gun in the amber firelight. The maple stock was polished until it looked like tortoiseshell. "It's a fine weapon," he remarked, replacing it in the gun rack.

"Why is it so special?"

He ran a hand through his thick hair and reclaimed the bench by the fire. "You'd have to be Scots to appreciate it, I suppose."

"Why's that?"

"Most of the Scottish weapons are smooth-bore muskets, and wildly inaccurate."

"Sounds like you've had lots of experience with 'em."

His countenance darkened. "Aye . . . unfortunately I have."

She took a place at his feet and spread out her skirt. Tell me about Scotland," she coaxed. "Lord knows we ain't got nothin' else to do." Settling down for a good story, she bit off a chunk of turnip and studied his tense face.

He studied her with guarded eyes. "What do you want to know?"

"Where's your home . . . what's it like?"

He cast a warm gaze over her and smiled. "I'm from the western Highlands—it's a wild region full of red deer and grouse and swift mountain streams. Dangerous, foggy channels separate the mainland from the offshore islands. I grew up with the sound of crashing waves in my ears. All along the coast, the sea reaches into the river valleys to form deep, narrow bays."

She stared at his sparkling eyes, mesmerized by his soft Scottish burr. "Did you grow up near a big town or a city?" she asked softly.

"No, I didn't. People along the coast are fishermen and live in small villages . . . Those in the inland valleys are crofters. Towns are few and most often lie in sheltered bays where there is safe anchorage for ships. Weapons, furnishings, velvets, all luxuries, have to be brought in from the South."

"You talk so fine. I suppose you went to a lot of

big schools?'' she stated, biting off another mouthful of turnip.

''No, my brothers and I were educated at home by special tutors.''

''How many brothers do you have?''

''I had an older brother who died. His name was Robert. My younger brother, Kevin, still lives at home.''

Sassy sighed wistfully. ''Your pa must have been dreadful rich.''

Roarke chuckled and tousled her hair. ''Aye, he was a laird.''

''A laird?''

''A chieftain, the owner of a landed estate, the head of his clan,'' he said.

She had never met anyone so handsome, so rich, so alluring. She thought of the first moment she had seen him step from the coach dressed in gold-braided finery; he had walked into her life like a fairy-tale prince or the famous Captain Rakehell she admired so much. And now they were sitting peacefully before the fire while the night wind whispered in the eves. ''I'll bet your house is real grand, too,'' she finally said.

His lips quirked upward. ''It isn't a house, it's a castle, lass.''

The words momentarily took her breath away. She had seen a picture of a castle in an almanac once, but never thought she would talk to anyone who lived in one. Blinking her eyes, she swallowed and muttered weakly, ''A . . . a castle?''

He laughed. ''Don't be too impressed, love. Donkinny is rather small as castles go.''

''You said your father *was* a laird. He's . . . he's dead now?''

Pain hardened his face. ''Aye, he was killed . . . A few years later, my mother died of grief.''

Sympathy flooded her heart. ''So you took your

father's place?" she guessed. "You're one of them lairds, too, now?"

A proud, somber look shadowed his eyes. "That I am, and a very serious responsibility it is, lass. My clan, my people, look to me for leadership and protection."

A secret sadness washed through her as she considered the differences in their backgrounds. Like her, he had grown up in a wild, isolated land, but how different the rest of his life had been. He had been well educated, while she had spent three years on a rough bench in a one-room schoolhouse. Her father was a dirt-poor preacher, while Roarke's had been some kind of Scottish royalty—and Roarke was his heir.

Unanswered questions skipped about in her mind. Why had Roarke deserted his people and his castle? And why had his face clouded up like a thunderstorm when she had asked if he had experience with Scottish weapons? "Why did you leave it all?" she asked.

A muscle twitched in his jaw as he stared into the fire. She knew she was losing him, that he was closing a door between them. What was wrong? What was he hiding? Suppositions about his past plagued her. Something just wasn't right!

She tossed the turnip aside, then stood and walked to the loft ladder, struggling with her feelings. "I think you're keepin' somethin' back from me. Of course someone as rich as you could have no sympathy for a bunch of poor colonists. Why, you're practically royalty yourself," she cried over her shoulder.

The fact that she was keeping something from *him* seemed totally irrelevant.

He strode across the room and pulled her into his arms. "I'm a MacLaren, and that's all I am." She could feel his warm body and smell his manly scent; quivering with anger and passion, she pulled back.

"Why are you afraid of me?" he asked.

"I . . . I jest don't trust men, 'specially those that don't tell the truth!"

"I have a feeling you don't trust anyone, lass." His fingers trailed a fiery path down her arms. *"Trust me,"* he ordered, his dark eyes holding hers. Passion roughened his deep voice. "There's a whole world of pleasure waiting for you," he added, clasping her trembling hand. Confusion engulfed her as he turned her palm upward and pressed his hot mouth against it, shooting a tingle up her arm.

She sucked in her breath, suddenly shy and embarrassed. She felt as if she were sinking into deep water—as if she were drowning. Her knees shook and her pulse thudded as she met his bold eyes. She started to turn her head, but he caught her chin in his hand. His fingers were light and gentle, yet a powerful force seemed to hypnotize her. Before her emotions could betray her, she jerked away and scrambled up the ladder.

Well rested the next morning, but still thinking of Roarke, Sassy felt only a few doubts nibble at her mind when she tried to untangle the puzzle of his past. She still couldn't bring herself to completely trust him, but a deep yearning urged her to recapture the closeness they had shared when they had talked of Scotland. With a minimum of pleading, she convinced him to accompany her on a morning walk. They hurried through breakfast. The air was heavy with the sweet scent of periwinkles when they left the way station.

The beautiful day set Sassy's blood and spirits aglow. Her heart beat faster as she scanned the landscape that stood out against a perfect sky. In the distance, creeks snaked over the woody slopes like silver ribbons. Closer, stately, vine-covered oaks towered above the road, sheltering it with overhanging limbs. Wild honeysuckle flooded the air with fragrance, and birds trilled sweetly as the pair strolled into a tree-shaded meadow. Sassy bent to pick some flowers and frightened a covey of quail that burst into the air with a great whir of wings.

Roarke, wearing another lace-fronted shirt and his newly acquired buckskin breeches, regarded her sternly. "Did you take your cough elixir?" he asked. "You don't want to get sick."

The hem of her blue skirt swished through the dewy grass as they walked side by side. "Don't have a cryin' blind fit about it. If I get a fever, we can jest mix up some rattlesnake venom with sweet sage tea . . . That'll take care of it."

He threw her a sidelong glance. "Fine. I'll fetch a basket of rattlesnakes to take back with us."

She frowned, then stooped to pick some fresh-faced daisies, dislodging a purple butterfly. "Don't make fun of the mountain cures," she said over her shoulder. "They've been passed down from generation to generation."

"Forgive me. I didn't mean to blaspheme."

With a grin, she turned and looked at him. Sunlight filtered through the tall trees behind him and danced over his black hair. Impulsively she brushed a bit of leaf from his glossy locks, then trailed her fingers over his shoulders and down his arms.

Lord, why had she done that? Her heart ran away with itself as she met his dark eyes, heavy with unspoken need. Struck with his powerful presence, she traced his roguish face, knowing she would remember each line for the rest of her life. She desperately needed to create some kind of distraction to break the mounting desire between them.

"If—if you ever go bald," she stuttered, feeling

her joints weaken with desire, "jest rub your scalp with onions till it's good and red, then rub it with honey." She watched laugh lines crease his tanned face. With a scowl she added, "Don't laugh. It helps!"

"I'm sure it sells a lot of new hats, too."

She walked on, stopping every now and then to add a flower to her bouquet. "If you get warts, you can rub them with blood from a black-feathered chicken. Course, if they're *real* bad, you'll have to use the hand of a corpse."

She sauntered ahead, her steps crushing the tender grass. "Drinking vinegar with rusty nails will cure a nosebleed. And a bullfrog baked in butter will bring down a cyst," she added with a backward glance. When he roared with laughter, she stamped her foot. "Well, it works, you know!"

He caught up and clasped her shoulders, making them tingle. "It doesn't do much for the bullfrog, does it, lass?" he commented with a chuckle. His hot gaze roved over her face, and she quivered inside; her heart hammered, making her lightheaded. From his taut expression she sensed he was holding himself in check. As they studied each other, a now familiar spark of desire darted between them.

His rakish features hardened; a sweet throbbing pulsed between her legs, both disturbing and delighting her. Her mind raced wildly—she opened her mouth to speak, but found she couldn't. A flush stung her cheeks as she stared at a wild pear tree ablaze with white blossoms.

She gasped as he traced his thumbs over the sides of her breasts, searing them with warmth. Trembling, she edged away, but he clasped her waist and drew her back. "Sassy, what do you really want?" he asked.

She looked back at him, feeling her blush

deepen. "Why, to get to Williamsburg so I can . . ." She bit her lip.

His eyes were hard. "So you can what?"

It was difficult to concentrate with him standing so close. "So . . . so I can get a job."

He led her to the pear tree, then sat down on a log and gently pulled her to his side. Snatches of bird song enlivened the quiet atmosphere, and bees flitted among the flowering shrubs. He caressed her trembling hand. "I don't believe you, lass. I don't know what you're afaid to reveal, but perhaps in your own good time you will tell me. Not what you want just for today or tomorrow . . . but for years from now."

How easily he had seen through her lie about Williamsburg. But perhaps she could give him a truthful answer to his last question. She studied his roguish features, now dappled with wavering shadows. Maybe her first assessment of him had been wrong. Under his obvious cynicism, she sensed something else . . . sensitivity and loyalty. Maybe, just maybe, she could trust him. "I'd . . . I'd like to see this country stand on its own feet . . . become independent."

He shot her a look of disbelief. "Surely you must want something personal, something for yourself."

She slid her gaze away. "Oh, jest a happy family, I suppose," she said with a nervous laugh, glad she had put some space between them. "You know, jest sittin' with the ones you love around the fire at night, spinnin' or workin' on somethin'. The firelight playin' off the babies' faces, and everyone safe and warm and knowin' they was real loved."

"No mansion on a hill or a fine carriage or regal frocks?"

She laughed softly. "I wouldn't be refusin' those things, mind you," she answered, taking a daisy from her bouquet and twisting it thoughtfully in her fingers, "but it seems like after a while they might get in the way of real livin', even become a burden." She tossed back her hair. "Me belongin' to the man I love, and him belongin' to me, and us followin' our dreams. Seems to me that's what is real important in life."

His brown eyes deepened. Gently cradling her chin, he raised her face and lowered his lips, searing her mouth with a kiss full of wild desire. He tightened his arms around her quivering body and drew her closer. A deep warmth radiated over her back where his arm encircled her. She inwardly fought the demanding kiss, but felt herself relaxing . . . dissolving. "You're so unspoiled, so idealistic," he murmured against her lips. His husky voice washed over her like the mountain sunshine, fluttering sweet tremors through her body.

Resolutely he pulled her against him, holding her firmly; with one hand he supported the back of her head as he brushed his lips against hers again. At first she inched back, but he strengthened the embrace and lightly flicked his tongue over her lips. "Open your mouth, little one," he coaxed. His tongue played over her lips, then finally slipped between them.

Sighing, she closed her eyes and melted into his arms, unable to fight her aching desire any longer. She could smell his male scent and feel his rough stubble pressed against her face. Her flowers spilled to the ground as she lifted her arms around his neck. Like a flooding tide, excitement welled up and engulfed her.

At first their kiss was gentle, then it became more insistent. He plunged into her mouth and found her breast with his fingers. She moaned as his tongue plundered deeper and he teased her nipple through the thin material of her smock. All at once she found herself kissing him back, as if she couldn't get enough of him.

Slipping his hand into the deeply slashed garment, he cupped her breast and rolled the aching nipple in his fingers, making her whimper with pleasure. Her nipple rose and tingled; it ached with wild pleasure. Aflame with desire, she felt the sharp pulse between her thighs throb even faster.

With great skill he worked a hand under her skirt and caressed the inside of her trembling thigh. Inch by inch he seared a path toward her hidden sweetness, melting her joints and making her head reel. When he slipped his fingers beneath her underclothes, she gasped and tried to pull away, but he pressed her closer.

Possessively he twined his long fingers into the curls that guarded her womanhood and teased them while he darted his tongue in and out of her mouth. Passion spiked through her, tingling her nipples and between her legs with unspeakable pleasure. Her mind fogged; her blood roared in her ears. She felt his thick manhood strain against the buckskin breeches and throb long and rock-hard against her. He held her palm to his swollen shaft, then stroked her moist femininity until her body shuddered.

Gradually from deep within her a voice echoed through her mind. *This is wrong!* Had she lost her mind? How could Roarke, who had doubtless loved scores of sophisticated women, love a callow backwoods girl? What was he feeling . . . scorn, amusement? Pure lust? As her blood cooled, fear and humiliation stabbed through her. He was trying to take her virginity—and what was worse, she was enjoying it!

With a jerk, her eyes flew open and she twisted away; tears rolled down her cheeks as she threw down her skirt. Her vision blurry with tears, she stared at his dark, unreadable face. "What kind of woman do you think I am?'' she cried, scrambling to her feet.

He stood and clasped her arm. ''Sassy, wait!'' But she pulled away.

''I thought you were a gentleman, *Laird MacLaren.* But you're no better than them ruffians on the road!''

Pain choking her throat, she ran back toward the way station.

Chapter 6

Three days had passed since the incident in the forest. Every time Sassy thought of what had almost happened, her face burned with humiliation. How could she have been so weak . . . so foolish? Since then, she and Roarke had scarcely spoken. They hadn't argued, but their cool politeness created an unbearable tension. As Sassy performed mundane housekeeping tasks, she kept thinking about the feel of Roarke's darting tongue in her mouth, his fingers on her nipple, his rigid manhood pressed against her stomach. Worse yet, she had dreamed about him . . . dreamed they had made love. And she had awakened moist and throbbing with desire.

Roarke's daily hunting trips had provided the only relief from the nerve-shredding tension. Then, a few hours ago, Roarke had wandered to a small mirror on a shelf and examined his ears. Piqued with curiosity, Sassy had walked to his side and asked what he was doing.

"I'm seeing if my ears have grown long and fuzzy," he said. "We've eaten so much rabbit stew, I expect them to flop over any second."

Sassy chuckled at the remark, and when he turned about and wiggled his nose like a rabbit, she laughed until tears moistened her eyes. The light moment eased the strain between them.

Now while they relaxed on a puncheon bench near the glowing hearth, a fragile sociability blossomed. The aroma of savory roast quail lingered in the air as Sassy picked up the old almanac and thumbed through it.

Roarke grinned and in a friendly tone commented, "You seem to read very well." To her embarrassment, her heart started beating like crazy again as she basked in his attention.

His face seemed to have softened a bit, and the light in his eyes told her he wanted to lift her spirits. For once, she felt like cooperating. "Yeah, I can read little words real good. It takes me longer with the big 'uns."

"You learned to read from the almanac, did you?"

"That and the Bible and *Pilgrims' Progress* and Dilworth's speller."

He studied her face. "Sassy, you look a little tired . . . troubled somehow. Is something bothering you? Something besides what happened in the meadow?"

She blushed at his mention of the incident, then considered his question. Lord, she just couldn't tell him about her troubles—at least not yet. "I . . . I jest ain't sleepin' good," she said lamely.

He smiled. "When I was a boy in Scotland, I used to count the waves as they crashed against the rocks when I couldn't sleep."

"Yeah, I know what you mean. When I was a little girl in Potter's Lick, I'd look out the cabin window and try to count all the stars in the sky." She laughed softly. "Course, I'd always lose count and have to start all over again. Sometimes I'd put a sweet potato under my pillow."

"Why?"

"Old Widder Smith was half a witch, and she told me it would make me have sweet dreams."

"Did it work?"

"Nearly always."

He laughed. "I suppose children are the same the world over. Simple and trusting and able to believe in magic."

How she wanted to confide in him, but pride and fear held her back. "Yeah. Then they grow up and . . . and they change," she said, feeling he was getting too close.

For a moment he sat quietly, then he shrugged and smiled again. "Well, if you won't tell me about your troubles, tell me about your village. Tell me about Potter's Lick." His voice was light and cheerful, and she began to feel less threatened.

A warm feeling came over her as she put down the almanac. "Well, Potter's Lick ain't much," she said, "but we're right proud of it. We have a meetin' house, a buryin' ground, a store, and two taverns."

With dancing eyes, he watched her stand and pace around the table. "Who lives there?" he asked.

She threw him a look of mock outrage. "Why, all kinds of folks!" Spreading her fingers, she counted them off. "We have a blacksmith, a gunsmith, a carpenter, a tanner, a cobbler, and a cooper who makes barrels and tubs."

His brows slanted upward in surprise. "So many . . . Why, you're describing a metropolis, lass!"

Her low spirits bubbled up like spring sap. "Saturday everybody comes into town to swap or sell or jest have fun," she continued. "The men have their boots all blacked with soot and bacon grease and are swingin' homemade walkin' canes. The women are dressed in calico and wearin' black silk bonnets with little linen caps underneath. Most of the younguns are barefooted."

"Did I hear you mention fun?" he asked with a glint in his eye.

"Yeah. The women gossip, and the men visit and smoke, and the boys plague the gals . . . or race horses, or have cockfights." She laughed and, placing her hands on the table, leaned forward. "It ain't hard to have a good time—the tavern sells whiskey for twenty-five cents a quart! Sometimes somethin' comes up during the week, too."

"Oh, really?" Amusement laced his deep voice.

"Sure. We make parties of huskin' bees and bring a lot of good home-cooked desserts. Some of the mountain women can make cakes and pies and cobblers that's so good, you want to rub 'em in your hair. We have a lot of fun at sugarin' time, too. In the spring when we're boilin' maple sap, we sit in the firelight and drink spicewood tea and laugh and talk."

His eyes merry, he arched his brows, waiting for more.

As she strolled toward him, her full shirt brushed against some of his folded clothing, stacked on a chair. With a tinkle, a small gold object fell to the floor. As it winked in the firelight, she picked it up. "Why, this is real pretty," she said, examining it. "What is it?"

"It's a religious metal of Saint Jude—the patron saint of lost causes." He studied her face, then added, "I received it years ago."

She turned it over, then sat down next to him and placed it in his hand. "I think I understand. It's kind of like the pretties I carry in my sack, ain't it?"

His eyes deepened and he chuckled. "Yes, quite a lot, I suppose. It brings back lots of memories, and just having it makes me feel better . . ."

She frowned and cocked a brow. "But you're rich. You don't need to depend on anythin' to make you feel safer, like . . . like I do."

He smiled and shook his head. "Riches can buy you luxuries, but they can't protect you from life's hurts, little one. And no one can shoulder all of life's troubles by himself. In the end, we must all depend on people to share our burdens." He laid the metal aside and took her hand. "In a time of need, medals and charms are fine comforts, but real people can help most of all." He caressed her hand with his thumb. "Won't you tell me what's bothering you?"

Her spirits lowered as she thought of her father's commitment to the cause, and the trouble it had brought. When she stood and wiped away a tear with the back of her hand, Roarke's face softened.

With a heavy sigh, he rose and took her into his arms. "Sassy, I want you to tell me why you're crying . . . and tell me the truth," he demanded. "I have a feeling it has something to do with this rebellion of yours . . . and your father."

Her throat tightened with emotion. Lord, if she could only trust him! He could be so warm and tender. And she had been with him long enough to realize that he was like no other man she had ever known. Still, a tiny part of her held back.

Then, as his arms pressed her closer, a wonderful sense of security flowed through her, melting away the last of her doubts. She had been alone and afraid for so long, and had wanted to confide in someone so desperately. A burden was lifted from her, for in his voice she heard sincere concern. Before she knew it, the whole story gushed from her trembling lips like water bursting through a dam.

"The soldiers took him over two weeks ago," she said, biting back tears. "I was in the woods pickin' herbs, and when I came back, the cabin was empty. I rode ol' Solomon into the village, and everyone told me what had happened. The soldiers that took him were British redcoats. They told the townsfolk Pa was bein' taken to Williamsburg to stand trial for treason. That he had passed out tracts stirrin' up folks to disobey British rule."

"Which was true, of course," Roarke murmured.

Her throat aching, she slipped from his strong arms. "Yeah. It's true . . . every word of it," she admitted in a shaky voice. "But he don't deserve to be hung, to be killed for fightin' for what he believes is right!"

Roarke narrowed his eyes. "Surely you knew this would happen. You—"

"Reckon we didn't think," she cut in. "We jest knew we had to do what was right!" She noted his hard face, then nervously paced around the room. "They said they was goin' to make an example of him . . . put the fear of the law into all us ignernt backwoods bumpkins." She clenched her hands until her nails bit into her palms. "Not a man tried to stop 'em. When I got to town, the soldiers had carried him clean away."

Roarke's eyes were deep and warm as he caressed her shoulders, shimmering warmth over her arms. "So you set out to save him, did you?"

"Yes, but ol' Solomon ran off! Then that low-down trash jumped me! Then you came! Then that storm wrecked the coach! Then—"

He brushed a kiss on her bent head and flicked away her tears with his thumbs. "There, there, my brave lass."

"If I had jest come back from the woods a little earlier. If I had jest started sooner. If—"

"If . . . if . . . if, how many times I've used the word myself. Don't go on so. Once we get to Williamsburg, I'll go with you to see your father."

"You . . . you will?"

He pulled her tight against him and massaged her shoulders. Warmth radiated down her back. "Of course I will. Let's be finished with all this talk of wars and sides and loyalties and causes," he commanded. "I'm sick to death of it."

She fought the surge of tender feeling his closeness aroused, but felt herself weakening . . . softening.

"In this room there's only a wee bonny lass and the man who wants her," he stated quietly. "Outside, the wind is soft in the pines . . . and inside, the fire is warm." He pressed firm lips to hers, then tightening his arms, hungrily kissed her. Sighing heavily, she closed her eyes and relaxed against him, relishing his tender passion.

With a will of their own, her arms encircled his broad shoulders. A few days ago in the meadow she had pulled away from him because she thought she felt only physical desire—but this was more than desire! His touch made her feel so safe and secure and warm. And just the sight of him or the sound of his voice made her heart race. Never in her nineteen years had she felt like this . . . like laughing and crying and singing all at the same time. Yes, she was sure this was more than desire. It had to be something very special.

Amazement filled her heart as his lips captured hers in a slow kiss; his tongue traced her mouth and opened it to explore. Like a swift torrent, aching passion rushed through her, matching his own desire.

At the same time an angry part of her brain cried out against the emotion. This was madness! A host of disturbing questions plagued her mind. With her strict upbringing, how could she, innocent in the ways of love, surrender to a man she scarcely knew? Indeed, wasn't this the man she had fought against like a wildcat only days ago? And how could she consider enjoying such shameless pleasure when her father was in danger?

But when Roarke pressed her closer against him, the sheer force of her need drowned out all reason.

She had resisted him once—she couldn't manage it again. As his manhood brushed hard and rigid against her abdomen, her heart fluttered crazily. Already throbbing with pleasure, she felt herself become moist and ready.

His eyes hazed with passion, he raised his head. "I'm going to love you, lass. I'm going to show you what love can be," he promised, effortlessly scooping her into his strong arms.

Roarke settled her on the bed in the loft. The sweet odor of pine and hay floated around them, and under her she felt the smooth deer hide. Her pulse pounded erratically as she considered what was happening . . . what *she* was letting happen. In the dim light she scanned his rugged features: the dark hair flopping rakishly over his forehead; the square, stubbled jaw; the firm mouth; the dark eyes, stormy with hunger.

She watched him sit to discard his boots, stand to unbutton his silky shirt and peel off his buckskin trousers. At last, the soft light to his back, he towered before her in naked splendor.

She shot her gaze over his well-defined body, devouring it. Smooth, tanned skin covered his broad shoulders, his muscular chest, his sleek belly. A mat of thick hair tapered from his chest toward his large, aroused maleness, which looked hard and satiny, jutting from his shadowed groin.

As he lay down and pulled her against him, she felt his warm breath against her cheek, felt that hard maleness through her skirt, already fitting snugly between her thighs. Blood roared in her ears as she stared at him, listening to his ragged breathing, tremulously waiting. Passion made his eyes warmly languorous . . . Perspiration sheened his tense face.

Then, with sure confidence, he took her into his arms and covered her mouth with a kiss, sending passion racing through her body like fire over dry kindling. Her pulse quickened when his tongue invaded her mouth and his arms tightened about her. She caressed the bunched muscles of his back, then traced his lean hips.

His eyes warm and dreamy, he took her fingers and placed them around his shaft; her eyelids fluttered down as her hand closed about him . . . and she felt him grow harder yet beneath her trembling fingers. A thrill ran through her when he groaned and throbbed deep and warm inside her closed palm. A stubborn bit of conscience still clawed into her, trying to pull her back, but she knew it was too late.

Slowly he broke the drugging kiss. "Let me undress you, little one," he murmured against her mouth. "Don't be afraid. I'm going to teach you what it is to be a woman." She looked up through half-closed lids. Her heart almost burst with tenderness, for she now realized she had wanted this union since the moment they met.

He moved an arm under her, then with his free hand, pulled the smock over her head and tossed it aside. Pale and creamy in the dim light, her breasts pressed against his hair-covered chest. He gathered one pearly mound in his dark hand and drew on the nipple. She gasped as he moved to the other breast and gently tugged at the nipple with his teeth, making pleasure explode between her legs.

Almost reverently he settled her back into the mattress, then popped open the waistband of her skirt. Lifting her hips, he tugged the clothing down her legs and past her feet, then slipped off her tattered undergarment.

The tie had loosened and slipped from his clubbed hair, which now fell freely about his face, giving him a wild, rakish look. His gaze melting into hers, he lay at her side and leisurely rolled her nipples with his fingers. She shuddered and clenched her thighs together, already bursting with pleasure. Confused feelings still stormed against her heart. Who was this man, this gorgeous stranger who had stolen the spirit right out of her? And Lord, oh Lord, why did she feel as weak and helpless as a kitten when he touched her?

"Relax, love," he commanded, cupping and stroking her breasts. "Relax and let me show you how wonderful it can be."

His hands smoothed down her arms, then her legs, leaving them warm and glowing. He bent his dark head to kiss her quivering inner thighs, leaving a fiery trail. When he moved to suckle her breast again, she felt the moist head of his shaft move over her thigh. His tongue flicked at her nipple again and again until it was rock-hard, then he nibbled at it and roughly nuzzled her breast. She could feel his prickly beard and his teeth against her tender flesh; a hot flush stung her face and rolled over her breasts.

His warm, musky scent claimed her senses as he brushed her lips with his and traced her mouth with his tongue. As she closed her eyes, a delicious indolence crept through her: She could feel herself becoming heavy . . . relaxing into the bed. Then, becoming more demanding, he took her mouth in a deep kiss. His tongue flicked between her lips, traced her teeth, then plunged deep into her mouth; a sweet fire surged through her body.

She gasped as his fingers teased the tangle of curls around her femininity, then entered to stroke the fount of her desire. Relentlessly he flicked the aching bud until tears rolled from her eyes and a warm ache filled her. What had happened to her? Reality had skittered out of control. This perfect ecstasy had dissolved all her thoughts, all her memories . . . all her troubles. Every inch of her skin tingled with delight. She felt free and wild, like a mountain stream darting over bright pebbles . . . sparkling and flashing in the light.

Roarke's shaft became so hard, he thought he would burst with desire, but he wanted to look at Sassy once more before she was his. He raised himself to scan her lovely face. Could this lush flower be the savage hellion he had fought for days? She was so soft, so tempting, so delicious. He had always taken women as the lightest diversion, but now strange feelings battled deep within his heart, feelings he didn't understand. Had the little witch hypnotized him? He knew a female like Sassy could only mean trouble. But he mentally shrugged the considerations aside—he wanted her as he had wanted no other, and he intended to have her!

Her glorious hair fanned out about her on the deer hide in a tangle of silken curls. He brushed a shiny lock away from her forehead and caressed her flushed face; as she opened her eyes, her long lashes cast shadows on her cheeks. Her flaming hair set off her green eyes, shiny and dilated and sparkling with passion. As smooth as a rose petal, her pink lips were slightly parted, showing a flash of pearly teeth. A pulse throbbed in her white neck, tempting him to taste it. He kissed her face, her quivering eyelids, her delicate ear, her sweet-smelling hair. Again he was at her neck, roughly nibbling at the pulse, making her moan. He savored her beauty. He wanted to *devour* her, to completely lose himself in her soft femininity.

Lord, how he wanted to plunge into her, to bury himself in her velvety softness. He found her lips and kissed her gently, then roughened the kiss by forcing her mouth wide open for his plunging tongue. He could taste her and feel her smooth teeth and the silk of her tongue. He cupped the weight of her heavy breast in one hand and rolled her nipple in his fingers again, then slid his hand between her legs to part her moist tangle and flick his thumbnail over her slippery bud of desire, driving her to a fever pitch.

Her head sank back into the bed as he spread her trembling legs and lowered himself over her. He settled the head of his hard shaft inside her wet womanhood, firmly rubbing it against her. She cried out in delight.

Sassy was light-headed with pleasure. Gasping for breath, she watched him position himself over her. His face was intense, all lean planes, and his maleness was thick and hard. Its velvety tip glistened with milky seed.

"Put your legs around me, little one," he urged.

Obedient, she slipped her legs over him. She whimpered and caressed his silky hair, then traced down his neck and corded back and clenched his buttocks. She could feel his body warmth, hear his raspy breath, and smell his wet seed. She moaned as if she could bear no more and pressed her hands against his tight buttocks, begging for entry.

"Oh, lass, you feel so wonderful," he moaned, settling into her. He fluttered kisses over her face and eyelids, and with a masterful stroke, slid into her at last, huge, strong, and powerful. At first she stiffened and gasped at the burning sensation. Then, as he began to move slowly and confidently, she surrendered her trust, wanting him to stroke her deeper.

What a concentration of fire and beauty ran through her body at that moment. Groaning, she dug her fingernails into his back and arched her hips toward him. Pulling back a bit to protect her from his weight, he started a tantalizing rhythm, plunging deeper and stronger as she rocked up to meet him.

Each masterful stroke fired her excitement, and she gasped and drew him closer yet. Now her hips twisted beneath him as she struggled to meet his faster pace; exaltation rolled through her, and she felt warm and glowing, as if she might burst with pleasure at any moment. As he relentlessly continued, flames darted from her womanhood to her belly, taking her to another plane of existence.

At last they could contain their ecstasy no longer. As Sassy cried out in joy, they exploded in a starburst of sensual delight which lasted for long moments. Afterward, they clung to each other until their racing hearts slowed, then Roarke moved to his side and held her against him. Love's tender afterglow shimmered through Sassy's body. As Roarke fluttered kisses over her face and hair, a feeling of deep security flowed over her. With a sigh, she relaxed into the mattress, and it seemed she was floating, gliding like a swan over sun-dappled water.

Wonderfully content, she drifted into light, peaceful dreams and dozed, Roarke's arms protectively about her. Then she heard a sound, a bothersome noise . . . a muffled banging. Roarke stirred at her side, then rose up on one elbow. Groggy, she ignored the noise until it became louder and more insistent; then, sitting up herself, she glanced out the window and saw lanterns and heard voices. The window blazed with light.

"What's happenin'? What's wrong?" she muttered.

"*Everything,*" Roarke muttered dully, pulling her close to his side. "A coach has arrived."

Chapter 7

Three days had passed. The morning after the travelers had arrived, everyone had boarded the coach, and the driver had headed for Williamsburg. Now, still journeying eastward, the vehicle rattled over the Virginia countryside, trailing dust behind it. Inside the jostling coach, an old lady in widow's weeds clasped a hand strap, then scooted forward on the frayed velvet seat and eyed Sassy. She had bright eyes, as sharp and piercing as pebbles.

"Oh, my dear, you'll just love our city. I know you will," she drawled in an aristocratic southern voice. "It being the seat of government, the British lieutenant governor lives here." The old lady's face was overpowdered, and she looked lonely—a tiny old woman, her mourning garments faded and patched, her face spiderwebbed with wrinkles.

The leafy mountains had melted into rich plantation land as the coach rolled across Virginia. It had traveled through lush countryside feathered in the light green of spring, through tiny villages snuggled among the pine trees, beside babbling brooks and glistening lakes, and over log roads and wooden bridges . . . always bearing east toward Williamsburg.

Sassy, listening to the woman, scanned the

musty-smelling coach, studying her travel companions. Dressed in his last silk shirt and a rust velvet coat and breeches, Roarke sat next to her, his tense jaw bearing evidence of his frustration with the old woman, who had chattered on for hours. Across from Roarke, his mouth agape in sleep, a young dandy in burgundy slouched next to the pinched-faced widow.

Sassy heard the woman's words, but she found it difficult to concentrate. Her emotions reeled as she considered the lovemaking she and Roarke had shared in the way station. Lord, what did he think of her now? she wondered. She cast a quick look at his hooded eyes and closed countenance.

From their sly glances, she was sure the coach driver and the young dandy knew she and Roarke had been making love . . . and she guessed the old woman also knew. Nervously she smoothed down her plain blue skirt and adjusted her white smock, wishing there were some way she could erase the memory from their minds.

How tangled her emotions were. Part of her rejoiced at having made love, but another part—a strict part that prized her virginity—felt shaken. Did Roarke MacLaren love her, or had she let the sound of the wind in the eaves and his soft voice hypnotize her? She forced down her feelings. Surely he did love her and they would be married. Hadn't he offered to accompany her when she visited her father in the Williamsburg gaol, and hadn't he suggested they share a room after the visit?

She needed to decide how she really felt about him. But how could she when he was sitting so close, making her blood sing with excitement, her face flush with warmth?

The old woman called sharply to rouse Sassy from her thoughts. "You're not listening, my dear!"

Wearily Sassy raised her brows. "I can hear you jest fine, ma'am."

With a doubtful look, the old woman rattled on. "You're in luck. You're visiting our city during the convening of the courts and assemblies. Everyone who is anyone will be here, and there will be a fair in market square."

Sassy's attention drifted away again. How could she sort out her feelings about Roarke when her father's life was in jeopardy? Her thoughts were consumed with the problem of saving him. To whom should she speak? Had she tarried too long? Perhaps they had sent him to another gaol. Would she have time to save him before . . . before they hanged him?

The bell in the steeple of the Burton Parish church rang out loud and clear, startling her.

"Well, for pity's sake," the old woman exclaimed, jerking back the window drape and peering out. "We've already passed the College of William and Mary, and we're entering town." She grabbed Sassy's arm and tugged her toward the dirty pane. "Here, look for yourself!"

Set on a low ridge in rolling countryside, Williamsburg lay before her; despite the pastoral setting, the town pulsed with life. As their coach creaked down Duke of Gloucester Street, she saw ladies in bright farthingaled gowns walking together, chatting in the morning sunlight; dressed in velvet and buckskin, dandies and frontiersmen bustled past the white clapboard homes and mellow brick buildings.

Roarke leaned close to Sassy and pointed out the sights. She could feel the hardness of his thigh and smell his masculine scent as he casually draped an arm about her shoulders. "Look to your left," he suggested, caressing her arm. "There's the Governor's Palace." His voice was magic, deep and smooth and strong.

Ignoring her quickening heartbeat, she gazed beyond the velvety Palace Green to the Governor's Palace, with a British flag snapping smartly from its dome.

Soon market square sprang into view. The square swarmed with farmers and craftsmen selling vegetables and tinware. From the crowd she heard the resounding clang-clang-clang of a hammer and a raucous burst of laughter.

Now in the pleasant tree-lined heart of town, Sassy saw neat shops and stately homes set back from the street on half-acre lots, and a row of taverns with memorable names: the Golden Staff, the Road To Ruin, the Quiet Smile.

Ahead of them, a steady stream of traffic moved down the wide, sandy street toward the redbrick capitol. The cream of Tidewater aristocracy poured into the shady capitol grounds in sporty carriages—the ladies in bright silks, the men in snowy stockings, velvet suits, and tricornered hats.

Presently they entered a poorer section of town; Sassy's heart fluttered with apprehension when Roarke told her the gaol was located down a side street they were approaching. As the coach turned a corner, she noticed a freight wagon rumbling across the street ahead of them. Its load covered with canvas, the wagon moved in front of the coach's team. Alerted by the driver's yell, the teamster hauled back on his brake lever; at the same time, the coach driver yanked back his wild-eyed horses. Despite their efforts, the front wheel of the coach cracked into the wagon, jamming it sideways.

Roarke was jolted against Sassy, then instinctively tightened his arm about her while the other passengers clung to their hand straps. His eyes blazing, the driver spilled from his seat and strode over to the wagon. In the ensuing argument he ripped the canvas from the wagon, revealing three pine coffins. Sick fear overwhelmed Sassy as her trembling fingers touched the door lever.

Roarke frowned down at her. "Lass . . . what's wrong?" he demanded.

Unable to speak, she scrambled from the coach on trembling legs. She heard Roarke leave the vehicle behind her.

The two drivers were still arguing: "Dammit, man, are ye bloomin' blind, runnin' in front of me like that!"

The wagon driver wore a face as sour as hard grapes. "I . . . I jest didn't see." His jaw hung ajar in surprise. "I couldn't help it!"

"What gives ye priority? What are ye carryin' here . . . dead royalty?"

"No. They're jest criminals. They was hung yesterday . . . I saw it all. One of 'em was a crazy ol' preacher with a long red beard. I'm takin' em off for burial."

Sassy's heart slammed in her breast and tears stung her eyes; the words sliced through her mind like shards of glass. Her lips quivering, she felt Roarke standing behind her clasping her arms. It was a mistake, she whispered to herself. The driver made a mistake!

She eyed the cheap pine coffins, faintly hearing the drivers' words through a thick mist of emotion. The coffins were rough and knotty, and sap oozed from them; the carpentry work was so shoddy that bits of bark still clung to the wood. She spotted the name Nate Hooks crudely scratched on the side of one of the long boxes. Then, her heart in her mouth, she found her father's name scratched on the coffin above it.

The name jumped out at her with the force of a blow.

Defeat and regret knifed through her . . . She had fought and she had lost. Her throat ached and her stomach felt leaden. A twisting pain swelled up into her breast as death's brutal reality chilled her spirit. Her father was dead. *Dead.* He who had been so vital, so alive, so filled with life.

Now he was gone, to be carted off to a Potter's Field in a cheap pine box like a criminal. She ran her trembling fingers over the splintery wood, tracing his carved-out name. Lord, why hadn't they bothered to print his name in ink? Why hadn't they allowed him that simple decency instead of carelessly scratching his name with the tip of a knife?

She pulled from Roarke's hands and threw herself against the rough coffin. Somehow she was aware that the drivers had stopped talking, and once again she felt Roarke's comforting hands on her shoulders . . . but everything seemed distant and far away.

She knew she should think of her father being in heaven and rejoice, but she didn't want to let him go! He might have been just a half-illiterate circuit-riding preacher, but how he had lived, fighting for what he believed and drinking deeply from life's cup.

"I'm so sorry, love," Roarke said deeply. Warmth and compassion threaded his voice as he turned her around in his embrace. She cried against his broad chest like a helpless child. At last she lifted her head and gazed tearfully over his shoulder to see a British flag waving from the capitol building. Yesterday as the British had feasted and enjoyed their parties, her father had been executed. Maybe some of them had even watched the hanging as an entertainment. Now she had a single goal in life: She wanted to tear to shreds every British flag in the colonies. Whatever it took . . . whatever she had to endure . . . whatever the cost . . . she vowed to see that hated flag brought down.

The next morning dawned cold and dreary. Roarke had left his room early to attend to some business in Williamsburg while Sassy sat by herself. It had rained during the night, and on the other side of the mullioned windows the wind whined past the second story of the inn, sweeping over the garden, shaking the freshly budded lilacs. Sassy snuggled into the window seat and wrapped her rust-colored skirt about her legs, then leaned against the cold pane, watching a plot of yellow jonquils bend to the ground. Unbidden tears flooded her eyes, and taking out a damp handkerchief, she wiped them away. She felt empty and drained. Tired. Defeated.

Trying to raise up her spirits, she lovingly caressed her father's old Bible, her only inheritance. The young British officer had been so correct, so impersonal, as he handed it to her at the gaol and told her that all her father's other effects had been burned.

All his other effects.

Tears came to her eyes again as she thought of his clothes, the worn blanket with a hole cut for his head, and his broken boots that had walked the Virginia frontier. Those with power, those with authority, had burned them . . . but they had been afraid to burn the Bible. There it had lain on the officer's desk. Worn and tattered, just waiting for someone to claim it. Just waiting for her.

She drew a long, ragged breath and scanned the room. The innkeeper had laid a fire to chase away the chill. Crumbling logs sent out sparks that danced against the blackened hearth; firelight played over the whitewashed walls and sagging beams, coloring the room with rosy light. There was a wardrobe, a canopy bed hung with rose velvet curtains, and three wingback chairs in a like fabric arranged around a heavy table. There were end tables and quilt boxes, dark oil paintings and shiny warming pans, small carpets and bits of decorative china. It was a fine room. A fine room paid for with Roarke MacLaren's money.

She had been forced to accept his generosity just as she had been forced to accept his help in paying for her father's funeral. The rector had been sympathetic. "We can forget that the deceased was executed as a criminal," he said. "Was he not another laborer in the vineyard of the Lord?" So her father had had Christian words said over him, and he had found a quiet resting place in a decent little cemetery . . . and there was to be a tombstone. Roarke had already paid for it and given the rector instructions.

Sassy swallowed back her tears and put away the handkerchief. Roarke had been so kind. She looked at the bed again, the bed where she had slept the night in his arms. There had been no lovemaking, only comforting words and tender caresses as he soothed her grief. Early this morning as she half dozed she had heard him quietly moving about the room getting ready to go out and attend to business. It gave her a sense of security to think that now that her father was gone, she had Roarke; through her sadness she felt a bit of excitement and admitted to herself that she was falling hopelessly in love with him. Still she harbored some misgivings about their conduct in the way station, for she had given away her virginity without benefit of marriage.

She thought of her father again. He had died alone—without hope.

Lord, if she could only talk to him now, if she could only make him know she had tried to reach him! At last she opened the Bible to the Twenty-third Psalm, a passage that he had used to teach her to read. Her eyes widened when she saw an inked message in the yellowed margin next to the text. She sank down in a wingback chair and started to read.

"Sassy, by the time you find this, I'll be gone," the message said. Her heart raced. In the crudely inked words she heard her father's rough country voice as clearly as if he were standing by her side. "I want you to go to your Aunt Pert in Boston. John Williamson, the owner of the Golden Staff Tavern, will lend you money for the coach fare. Take care of Pert. She is old and needs you. You two can abide together. Remember that I love you. I knew you would come, darlin'. Cling to our cause and never give up hope. Love, Pa."

Sassy blinked back fresh tears. How clever he had been, knowing she would read the psalm if she found the Bible! A letter might have been lost or burned, but he knew even the British wouldn't burn a Bible . . . Neither would they bother to inspect it. Joy rose up in her heart. *I knew you would come, darlin'*, he had scrawled in a trembling hand. Thank the Lord, a flame of hope had warmed his last days.

She had seen the Golden Staff from the coach yesterday. She had always known that a tavern owner in Williamsburg supplied her father with the rebel pamphlets, but he had stubbornly held back the name of the man and his establishment, trying to protect her. Now, to provide for her welfare, he had cleverly revealed that information. At the same time, he had protected his source. And everyone had laughed and called him Crazy Ezekiel!

Then Sassy realized her father's advice complicated her relationship with Roarke. Which direction would their lives take now that they were in Williamsburg? Yesterday she had been too distraught even to consider such things. But deep in her heart she knew they must make plans for the future. After their lovemaking, she couldn't think of being separated from him.

Hearing footsteps in the hall, she placed the closed Bible on the table and smoothed out her skirt. Seconds later, Roarke entered; in the low-ceiling room, he loomed larger than ever. As usual, she was struck with his handsomeness, his virility. He wore a dark blue velvet jacket and knee breeches, dazzling white stockings and silver-buckled shoes. Quietly elegant, his clothes were obviously well made and expensive. They set off his broad shoulders and hard, muscular body, which was plainly evident even under the soft velvet.

A serious look darkened his face as he removed his tricorn with a bronzed hand and sat down. "Are you feeling better?" he asked, running his gaze over her.

She sank into the chair opposite him. "A little. Have you finished your affairs in Williamsburg?"

"Aye, I have." His words rang with finality. He watched her chafe her chilly arms, then rose and strode to the hearth. Kneeling, he stirred the flames. She watched his muscled arms move under the velvet while he attended the fire, and she remembered how safe and warm she had felt in his embrace. Lord, how she wanted to be in those arms right now.

When fresh flames crackled about the logs, he stood and walked back to the table. "Did you sleep well?" he asked as he reseated himself.

"No, I kept thinkin' about Pa."

They sat in silence. Outside, the wind whined about the inn; inside, the fire popped and whispered about the logs. "I know your pain is very sharp, lass," he finally offered.

She rose and paced about the room with crossed arms. "It hurts me that his death meant nothin' to those who ordered his execution."

"Perhaps you should think of those whose lives he touched."

"That's jest it," she replied, still pacing. "He

always struggled and fought and tried to help so many—and no one was there when he died."

"I'm sure a chaplain was there."

She whirled about angrily. "Someone should have been there that counted! I don't want someone to say an empty prayer, then forget him. I want his memory preserved. I want folks to never forget him or what he did." It suddenly struck her that the best way to preserve her father's memory was to dedicate her life to his work. Surely she could align herself with the rebels in Boston; the owner of the Golden Staff would tell her who they were.

Roarke's heels rang on the bare planks. "Sassy, your father lived a good, full life and accepted the consequences of his deeds. I'm sure he wouldn't want you grieving for him, or planning memorials. He would want you to live as he lived. To follow your heart." His face softening a bit, he clasped her arms. "I need to talk with you."

She looked up at him, hoping he might make a commitment to their love. Perhaps this would be a good time to tell him about her father's request. "Yes, we need to talk. We need to talk about Boston."

"Boston?"

She eased away from him, then walked to the table and opened the Bible. With a soft voice she read the scrawled message.

A thoughtful look passed over Roarke's face.

"I want to go to Boston," she said, hurrying back to his side. "We can sail there on your ship. Why, we could live there. You could sail from Boston jest like you sail from Williamsburg!"

Frustration leaped into his eyes. "You would ask me to move to Boston? To cast off my obligations like a worn jacket? To forsake my country, my clan, my crew?"

She felt a stab of pain, and her throat tightened with emotion. "But I thought—"

"I have a shipload of fine Virginia tobacco in the channel," he interrupted in a firm tone. "A crew waiting. Responsibilities in Scotland."

"Scotland?" she murmured weakly, shaken by his betrayal.

"Aye. I never said I was going anyplace else, did I?"

Her face flushed with humiliation, and a suffocating hopelessness overpowered her. "No, but . . . but after what happened in the way station, I thought . . ."

"I'm sorry if I hurt you, but I never pretended to be noble. The tide is right and I must sail today. I have a carriage waiting."

She ran to the wardrobe and opened the doors. His clothes were gone. He had packed and taken out his things while she had slept this morning in ignorant bliss. Searching for words, she stared at his handsome face, feeling sick and light-headed. Lord, how could she have dreamed that he would stay with her?

He sighed heavily. "You assumed everything, lass. I admitted I was a scoundrel and I made no proposal. I know this is a terrible time for you, but it seems fate played the cards against us. Our lives are going in very different directions. Surely you can see that. Accept what we've shared and leave it at that." His voice sounded businesslike, and she felt shocked and paralyzed.

"But we made love," she said on a strangled sob. Her heart raced as she listened to him tread over the planked floor.

He placed some paper money on the table. "You may need this before you get to Boston."

He was paying her. Treating her like a whore when she had given him her heart. Fresh pain made her body tremble. How keenly aware she was of the difference in their social stations. "I don't want your money! What about us?'' she cried, spreading her hands.

''I have people waiting for me . . . depending on me in Scotland.'' He gave her a look of regret, then placed his hand on the doorknob.

''Roarke!''

''I have to go now.''

She moved to the table, tears choking her throat. ''I should have known. You took advantage of me; now you're usin' your responsibilities to run off. You jest wanted someone to warm your bed!''

She felt weak, and her vision blurred. The man who had been so tender, who had held her in his arms last night, was leaving. She hurled the money at him.

He stood silently for a moment as it fluttered to the floor, then left and closed the door behind him.

From the hall, she heard the sound of his swift footsteps fading away. Tears streamed down her cheeks, and she clenched her hands until her nails bit into her palms. Angrily brushing away her tears, she ran to the window. She watched him stride to a waiting carriage; her heart beat crazily.

It had started to rain again, and the wind whipped at his coat. He looked devastatingly handsome as he ducked into the carriage and slammed the door shut. Her heart twisted with pain. How she longed to race after him. To fall against him and feel his arms about her, taste his lips, feel safe and warm and glowing with happiness once more.

She stood at the window and watched the carriage roll into the mist. She watched it until it turned and she could no longer see it. Finally she stood alone with only the sound of the ticking clock and the light rain against the window to keep her company.

Gathering her strength, she picked up the Bible and pressed it to her thudding bosom. She had wantonly chosen her fate and cast aside her virginity for a fleeting pleasure. And what a price she had paid! Gradually she controlled her flowing tears. She was at a great crossroads in her life; she knew she must fight through her terrible pain and go on living.

At that dark moment she turned her sights toward the Boston patriots and Aunt Pert's comforting arms.

Chapter 8

Three months later, Dr. Joseph Warren gazed at his fellow rebels seated about a table in Boston's Green Dragon Inn. The inn was dim and smelled of yeast, but copper pots gleamed from its rafters, and planters of light pink begonias brightened the lace-draped windows. "We know the British are building up their troops, but we have no idea how many they are transporting over from England or when they will arrive," the doctor said in a deep, firm voice.

Sassy found it difficult to concentrate on the doctor's words. Life had dealt her several mighty blows since she had left Roarke, and even Aunt Pert's loving concern hadn't been able to ease her pain. Poor Aunt Pert, Sassy thought, glancing down at her new pink cotton dress with its lace-edged sleeves. Her kindly aunt had welcomed Sassy into her home, bought her pretty frocks, and provided dancing lessons as a diversion—but the old lady had failed to raise her spirits.

Sassy's heart still ached when she thought of her father's death, but it was nothing compared to the anger she felt at Roarke. How could he have seduced and abandoned her, as if she were nothing more than a tavern wench? She also hurt with a deep, secret pain she had shared with no one. With a sigh, she tried to focus on the positive aspects of her life. At least she had the rebel cause to buoy her spirits.

The laughter of noon patrons that filtered from the noisy public room brought Sassy's wandering thoughts back to her surroundings. By the light pouring through the Green Dragon's leaded-glass window, she studied the famous doctor. Tall, dark, and well built, he radiated a confident air and, like John Hancock, sported stylish clothes. According to Sean O'Reilly, the Green Dragon's burly proprietor, Dr. Warren was the most skilled physician in Boston and often treated British officers. He was also the colonists' most valuable spy.

The innkeeper hunched his thick shoulders and slapped a beefy hand on the table, interrupting the doctor. "One moment, sir. How do ye *know* the British are plannin' on bearin' down on us?"

Dr. Warren looked thoughtful. "They're bound to be up to something. They've been drilling the Royal Marines and exercising their horses more frequently." He laughed dryly. "They're also practicing their marksmanship."

Mary O'Reilly, the innkeeper's wife, leaned forward, her ample belly shaking with laughter. A kindly middle-aged woman in her fifties, she wore a drab cotton dress; a tattered mobcap covered most of her silvery hair. "They *need* to be practicin', I say. There's not one of the loobies that can hit the side of a barn!"

Sassy felt a little of her old spirit return; she liked her outspoken hostess, who reminded her of a sensible mountain woman. A few days after Sassy had arrived at Aunt Pert's home, she had visited the Green Dragon on the advice of the owner of the Golden Staff in Williamsburg. Both Mary and Sean had welcomed her to their establishment with open arms. After listening to her story, they had suggested she return to meet the rebels who congregated at their inn.

Soon Sassy had found herself passing out propaganda pamphlets in Boston, just as her father had done in Virginia. The O'Reillys' son Jack, who now approached the table with a tray of hot spiced rum, often lifted her drooping spirits. A tall, lanky boy of thirteen, he had a shock of unruly red hair and freckles like his mother.

Pulling a comical face, he offered Dr. Warren a tankard of hot buttered rum with a warm, spicy fragrance. "Here ye go, sir. A little somethin' to wet your whistle," the boy quipped. "I already took your horse around to the back and made sure it was well hidden. 'Twould not do for a column of lobsterbacks to recognize that white blaze."

Dr. Warren slapped Jack on the back. "Boy, you have a fine, shifty mind, and your talent is wasted here. I think I'll put you to work spying on the British."

When the O'Reillys' laughter had died down, Sassy said, "Sir, you spoke of spyin'. Do the rebels have a large intelligence ring?"

The big man leaned back and flashed a wide smile. "Yes, indeed, we follow British movements very closely. In Massachusetts we have a Committee of Safety to make quick decisions and monitor the British. One of my colleagues, Dr. Benjamin Church, is very involved with that committee." He rubbed his chin. "Our spies live cheek to jowl with the British soliders, and are able to gather much information."

The comment saddened Sassy, for these days everyone lived cheek to jowl with the British. Since the authorities had begun enforcing the hated Quartering Act, Boston's citizens had had to feed and lodge British soldiers in their own homes, whether they liked it or not. And there was nothing she or anyone else could do about it.

Mary caressed her arm. "Why so glum, dear heart? What's wrong?"

"I . . . I was thinkin' about the British. Like the doctor says, they're all over the city, walking the streets like lords. I jest wish there was some way I could help the rebels besides passin' out pamphlets."

Dr. Warren drummed his fingers on the table. "Perhaps there is another way you can help. Samuel Adams is keen to know when the British will be transporting more troops to Massachusetts."

Adams's face loomed in Sassy's mind. She had seen him at a meeting at Faneuil Hall only a few days ago. He had looked unkempt and watery-eyed, and he had been shaking with the palsy. But he had been filled with such fire and spirit, she had been instantly drawn to his message.

"The British officers are holding a masked ball at the Wainwrights' Beacon Hill mansion on Friday," Dr. Warren continued. "The affair will provide a wonderful opportunity for someone to gather information about British troop movements. Would you care to attend?"

Excitement rose in Sassy's breast, and for the first time she appreciated her dull dancing lessons. "Yes, of course, I'd love to go. But I don't have an escort. I don't—"

Mary touched her arm once more. "Don't worry, dear heart. Leave the details to me and Sean. We'll find someone to escort you."

Jack set down his tray and pulled a battered watch from his pants pocket. "It's one o'clock already," he said, throwing Sassy a meaningful look. "Time for us to be makin' our rounds. I'll get our baskets and meet you at the door."

After saying good-bye to the others, Sassy joined Jack at the door. As they left the rosy brick inn with its copper sign hanging in front, and walked down the busy Boston street, she saw sparkling windows and well-swept doorsteps and shiny brass knockers.

Anticipation welling inside her, Sassy glanced at her basket, which was filled with juicy red strawberries wrapped in paper cones; the basket was partially covered with a cloth. Under the packages of fat strawberries were piles of political pamphlets, crudely printed by the Sons of Liberty on a press located in a storeroom at Old North Church. Sassy was among only a few people who knew of the press's whereabouts. It was a measure of the trust the O'Reillys placed in her that they had confided such secret—and potentially dangerous—information in her.

"Come on, slowpoke," Jack called with a grin as he strode up the street. "We've got folks waitin' on rebel news."

Sassy lifted the hem of her gown and followed Jack, who seemed to know the home of every rebel sympathizer in the city. After receiving a list of house numbers from Jack, she worked one side of the street while he worked the other. Although her basket was heavy, she enjoyed selling the strawberries as a cover for her real purpose, knowing the rebel supporters eagerly awaited news about the gains the patriots had made.

As Sassy paused to take money from a lady, she spotted Boston Common between two tall brick homes, where English soldiers in red uniforms marched over the field, accompanied by crisp orders and the faint *ra-ta-tap-tap* of snare drums. A British flag fluttered in the breeze. Instantly the image of her father's scarred coffin flashed through her mind.

With renewed vigor she went on her way delivering the pamphlets—all she could do to help the rebels that day. But next week, she thought with a thrill of excitement, she would do much more than pass out pamphlets.

Next week she would gather needed information for Samuel Adams himself.

The skirt of Sassy's green taffeta gown rustled crisply as she entered her aunt's home on Maryborn Street a few days later. "Where's Aunt Pert?" she asked the maid who had opened the door.

"She's in the back, pruning roses, miss," the girl replied, adjusting her mobcap.

Sassy sighed. Home from another dancing lesson, she was eager to tell her aunt of her progress. She decided to change her delicate satin dancing shoes, then go outside and find her aunt in the garden.

As she crossed the foyer and ascended the stairs, she considered her situation. She had a cozy home and a kind companion. She should have been happy—but she wasn't. She entered her bedroom and closed the door behind her. Hung in blue silk, a big canopied bed dominated the room, which included an assortment of chairs, screens, and benches.

It was within this room that Sassy could let down her guard and truly be herself. Every night after her aunt shuffled off to bed, Sassy would sprawl on her bed, stare at the silky canopy, and think of Roarke. Sometimes she cried, although she told herself she was crazy to do so. How foolish to cry over a man who had used her . . . and left her. Left her for his fancy obligations and his own country. How could she cry for a man like that? Yet deep in her heart she knew their lovemaking had touched her soul.

As Sassy opened the wardrobe to change her slippers, her gaze went to a neatly folded nightgown placed on a shelf behind a row of shoes. With a trembling hand she shook out the garment and held it to her bosom. The lacy nightwear was the first gift Aunt Pert had given her after she had arrived on her doorstep from Williamsburg. For Sassy, the garment was a reminder of Aunt Pert's love, as well as her own secret pain.

Emotion tightened Sassy's throat as she contemplated the much-washed gown. This was the gown she had been wearing when she had suffered a miscarriage in May. How frightened she had been when she had realized she was pregnant! The odor of cooking meat had nauseated her, and she had been so tired and listless. At first she had blamed her illness and exhaustion on the long journey to Boston, but when she had missed her monthly flow, she had realized with a stab of fear that she was with child.

In one respect she welcomed the pregnancy, for she loved and wanted children. If she were married, this would have been a joyous occasion. But she had seen enough women in Potter's Lick who had given birth to bastard children to know what awaited her and her offspring. Roarke had ruined her life. His betrayal cut into her heart daily. *How angry she was at him!*

Late one night she had bitten her lips to stifle the pain of sudden, severe cramps. No one knew she had suffered a miscarriage that night. Not her aunt, or her friends at the Green Dragon. No one. She had faced the event with mixed feelings. Part of her was desperately sad, numb, and confused; another part felt relief. For a few days she had pretended to have pain from her normal monthly flow, then had returned to her daily life, trying to forget. But in her heart she knew she never would.

She put away the gown, realizing she mustn't dwell on the dark memory. She had to go on with life and never look back. Turning from the painful past to the present, she changed her shoes and went to find Aunt Pert.

As she left the house, her heels made crunching noises on the gravel path. In the walled backyard a faint breeze stirred the air, and butterflies flitted from one blossom to the next. Cherry trees and flowering shrubs sweetly scented the air. Between the trees, the sky was a bright scrap of color, a piece of gay blue silk. Seeing the top of a frilly sunbonnet bobbing against the garden wall, Sassy walked down a path of paving stones, passing a small greenhouse.

Aunt Pert was dressed in a sprigged muslin gown and a gardening apron full of spades, her silvery hair arranged in fat sausage curls. She held a pair of scissors, and a basket of roses swung from her ample arm. As she heard Sassy's footsteps, her face flooded with pleasure. "Darlin', how lovely you look!" She caught Sassy's hand and twirled her about. "Well, how did you do today?"

Sassy thought of the dancing lesson . . . the steps she had missed . . . and her spirits drooped. "I suppose I did toler'ble well . . . but these Boston dances seem kind of stiff, don't they?"

Concern shadowed Aunt Pert's eyes. "Now what's wrong, child? You look so sad."

Sorting out her thoughts, Sassy looked at the roses that blossomed in neat beds and ran rampant over the garden wall, perfuming the air with their extravagant fragrance. "It's . . . it's jest that I still feel so rough sometimes, like a wild brush colt right out of the woods," she said at length. "I feel like folks will know I ain't what I pretend to be . . . that I ain't had no learnin'." She clenched her hands. "I mean, like I *haven't* had no learnin' . . . I mean *any* learnin'." She bit her lip. "Oh, you know what I mean, Auntie."

A silvery laugh came from the old lady's lips. "Hush, dear! Don't you know I felt that way ever so long after I came here? And my speech wasn't any better than yours. Never give it a thought. Your country ways will fade away, and soon you'll feel quite at home here. You're changin', darlin'."

She ran her eyes over the lovely gown and Sassy's upswept hair. "Lord, how you're changin'!"

Sassy's eyes moistened as she listened to a hummingbird hovering over a trellis of heady jasmine.

"My dear . . . what's wrong now?" Aunt Pert crooned.

"That's jest it. I don't know if I want my country ways to fade away. Sometimes I get a yearnin' to ramble through the woods or wake up and run through the wet grass and never give a thought to books or what's proper and what's not. There are so many rules here. Here everythin' is jest like that ol' minuet . . . all stiff and formal. And it seems the further I get away from mountain livin', the further I get away from Pa, and I don't ever want to do that!"

Tears welled in Aunt Pert's troubled eyes. "Yes, you're quite right to feel that way, darlin'. But you know you'll never lose him, don't you?" She set the rose basket down and caressed Sassy's arm. "He'll always be there, guidin' and helpin' you, and the best of him will stay with you forever."

Sassy searched the old woman's soft face. "Oh, Auntie, do you really believe that?"

"Yes, darlin', I do." She kissed her cheek, then picked up the basket again. "Let's you and me go around to the front of the house now. I have some propagatin' to do. Someday I'm goin' to grow the perfect rose, you know."

As they strolled to the front of the tidy home, where June roses bloomed in neat rows beside the front walk, Sassy thought of her aunt's passion to produce a perfect rose—a rose of a new color. As the older woman knelt next to a fragrant blossom, Sassy secretly doubted the project would ever succeed. The deep red and fragile pink roses were just too different. Like her and Roarke, some things were never meant to be combined.

Nevertheless, she patiently watched Aunt Pert

trim the petals from a rose in preparation for cross-pollination, then apply pollen from another rose with a small brush. Finally she tied a little cloth sack over the seed pod to protect it from other pollen. Smiling, she gazed up at Sassy with satisfaction. "Now, when that seed pod is mature, I'll collect it and ripen the seed; then I will start some new seedlin's."

Stiffly she stood and looked at a potted rose near her front door. "Will you bring me that seedlin', dear? I think it's strong enough to survive outside now."

Sassy fetched the tender seedling and knelt as her aunt planted it; at last Aunt Pert rose and dusted her soiled hands. "There! We'll see how this seedlin' does. I already have some wonderful crossed roses in my greenhouse that should be ready to bloom next year." As Sassy stood as well, her aunt glanced up at the sky. "I declare, the sun is very warm today."

With a gentle smile, she took her niece's arm and guided her back into the house. "Enough talk of roses. Let's go inside and have some lemonade, dear. There's a rash of fancy balls comin' up soon. And there are loads of young gentlemen here in Boston. With your fiery hair and angel face, you'll be settin' their hearts racin', if I know anythin' about men. Before the year is out, I'll be plannin' a weddin'."

Sassy wanted to tell Aunt Pert she had no intention of putting herself on the marriage market. How could she think of another man after Roarke? And there was her work with the rebels to consider, though her aunt knew little about it and disapproved altogether.

"If we could just get you invited to *one* military ball, your fortune would be made," Aunt Pert went on. "Why, the young officers would be swarmin' to my door like bees to a honey hive. You know, with all this unpleasantness, General Gage has ordered over more troops . . . and more officers. They're all young and lonely and mighty susceptible to a pretty face."

Sassy knew her aunt thought a girl should marry and bear children. The kind old lady had been cosseted by a husband who had sheltered her from the world. She knew little of politics and preferred to remain ignorant. To her, the coming revolution was just so much unpleasantness she would like to avoid. How could Sassy tell her sweet aunt that the O'Reillys were providing her with an escort to a ball so she could spy on the British?

Sassy smiled. "Why, Auntie, didn't I tell you I'll be goin' to a costume ball at the Wainwright mansion the end of this week?"

The old lady stared back at her in puzzlement. "No, you didn't. I . . . I didn't know you knew any of the officers, dear."

"Well, I do. I met an officer in my dancin' class." Sassy bit her lips, regretting the white lie, but she knew it would be best to protect her aunt's innocence.

As they climbed the front steps, the old lady paused and patted a handkerchief over her damp forehead. "This is a wonderful surprise, darlin'," she said, slightly out of breath. "Thank the Lord you have an escort to the ball!"

Yes, thought Sassy. Thank the Lord and the rebel owners of the Green Dragon Inn.

Chapter 9

Late that same night, Roarke sailed the *Sea Witch* into Boston harbor under cover of darkness, easily passing the British revenue cutter anchored in the mouth of the bay. Lights gleamed aboard the cutter, and the night wind snatched sounds of merrymaking from its open portholes. Farther into the bay, a stone lighthouse cast a soft glow over the water and over the church steeples ringing the harbor. As Roarke eased the packet into port, the damp, earthy scent of land was strong in his nostrils. Long Wharf, now stilled in the wee hours, slid past the ship like a dark arrow pointing to the city.

Having often performed this stealthy procedure, Roarke's crew adjusted the sails for a quiet berthing. Roarke guided the *Sea Witch* past brigs and schooners, sloops and merchantmen, finally locating a quiet, half-hidden berth. At last the packet's anchor splashed into the inky water. Pride swelled Roarke's breast as he studied the ship's clean lines picked out in the moonlight. She was sleek and elegant, built for speed and beautiful to behold.

With a warm glow, he remembered her performance earlier that day . . .

A stiff wind had blown from the southwest, and the packet had sliced through the green sea like a knife, throwing spray from her bow. Standing on the quarterdeck, Roarke admired the full sails standing out bold and white against the blue sky. "Another reef out of that foretopsail, and give it to her!" he boomed over the sound of the waves.

Two hands scrambled aloft; the reef points were cast adrift, the halyards manned, and the sail snapped out her increased canvas to the wind. The *Sea Witch* clipped along at a breathtaking rate, flinging salty foam as far aft as her gangway. Her spars and masts creaking, she sped through the sea.

Hands on his hips, Roarke paced the deck, glancing aloft at the strutted sails, then to windward; his chanteyman, Duncan MacPhee, stood in the gangway with a dark scowl. A life on the Atlantic had lined and toughened the old seaman's face. A warm familiarity existed between the two men. Many years ago Roarke's father had entrusted his son to Duncan, commanding simply, "Teach the lad to sail." When Roarke had first stepped on a ship, Duncan's hard, callused hand had pulled him aboard. He had guided the boy through the rigging and ropes and taught him the names of the sails and how to tack a course. He had been a mentor, a friend, and often a father to the lonely boy whose own father was either occupied fighting the British or negotiating peace with the battling lairds.

Now Duncan pulled down his tam-o'-shanter and approached the boy he had once taught, now a man . . . now his master. " 'Pon my word. She's flyin'. Ye're runnin' the heart out o' her."

"She's going handsomely. She'll hold."

The old man shook his grizzled head. "I canna' understand it. Are ye daft, lad? A week after we unloaded a cargo of fine Virginia tobacco in Scotland, ye were ready to return to America. Why are ye so set on makin' port at Boston?"

Roarke gazed at the shining sea and held his tongue.

"Ye dallied about Donkinny Castle lookin' like ye were ready to spit fire, then ye announced we were takin' on a cargo and sailin' fer America again. Ye never bothered to tell me or even Master Kevin why," the old man ranted on. " 'Twas all business, ye said, but I knew ye was lyin'. Now yer runnin' the *Witch* like the very devil is followin' our wake." He wagged his head again. "I've known yer moody ways since ye were a lad. But somethin' is heavy on yer heart. For God's sake, what is it, lad?"

Roarke sighed heavily, knowing the old sea dog would keep pressing until he gave him an excuse.

"As I said, it's a matter of business," he replied dryly. "I'll sell the Scotch whiskey in the hold and take on another cargo in Boston."

"Business, is it? What business have ye in Boston when the lairds have their blood up ready to fight? There's MacDougal, and MacNeal, Gordon, and Robertson, and dozens of other clans that have pledged, ready and waitin' fer ye to lead 'em into battle."

Roarke knew he was right. The British Crown had tried to stamp out the clans, but the people clung to them, vowing allegiance to their chieftains and looking to them for guidance. Many of these chieftains had in turn pledged their allegiance to Roarke. A small but determined army stood behind him.

Duncan softened his voice dramatically. "Ye have the funds now, and the British are weak. The French have taken the heart out of 'em, and they have their hands full with these rebellious colonists." He spread his gnarled hands. "Why, ye've got Bonnie Prince Charlie himself thinkin' o' comin' back to the Highlands! The time is ripe, lad. It wouldna' take more than one good push now."

"Do you think I don't know that!" Roarke snapped. He studied the old man's stricken face, instantly regretting his harsh words. The possibility of driving the English from Scotland had always glittered before him like a golden dream. Pockets of rebellion had flared since the Battle of Culloden, yet the British had managed to keep a whip hand. But the time *was* ripe now. Riper than it had ever been.

"We'll return to Scotland as soon as I've finished my business in Boston," he stated in a firm voice. Resolutely he left the old man.

"Roarke MacLaren!" Duncan called after him in a sharp tone.

He glanced over his shoulder at the old seaman whose jacket ruffled out in the wind.

"Is yer business in Boston worth yer dream? Is it worth yer rebellion?"

The question rolled into Roarke's brain with mind-numbing force. He stood there, watching Duncan walk away with a rolling gate, then clenched the rail and stared out at the swiftly moving sea, asking himself the same question.

Aye, the chance of victory was slim, but it was the best chance they would ever have. Even a partial victory would bear sweet fruit: Old border lands would be returned to Scotland, old wrongs would be righted, his father's death would be avenged. And there was a chance, a wild, tempting chance, they might place a Stuart on the throne in Holyrood Palace . . . It shook the heart to think of it . . .

Now, as moonlight shimmered over a forest of masts and rigging in Boston harbor, Duncan's question echoed in Roarke's mind yet again. Mixed emotions swept through him like a stiff gale. At first he had thought Sassy was like other women he had known, yet somehow she had fastened herself in his heart. Once he had returned home, he had realized his feelings for her went deeper than physical attraction; her warmth, wit, and passion for life fascinated him. Although they were completely unsuited to each other, something about her had drawn him back to her. He had to have her in his bed and in his life.

No doubt she had already recklessly involved herself in some dangerous political work that might cost her life. He looked at the outline of the city silhouetted against a night sky sprinkled with stars. Somewhere in this city of sixteen thousand people, an old lady named Aunt Pert lived on Maryborn Street, and Sassy was with her, feverishly plotting to overthrow the English Crown.

He had to find the hardheaded hellion and protect her from her own foolishness. He had to see she didn't end up with her head in a noose like her stubborn father. And he had to convince her to return with him to Donkinny Castle. Knowing Sassy, he realized this would be no easy task. At the same time, his passionate commitments called him back to Scotland.

Without a doubt, Roarke MacLaren was a man divided.

"You *must* be still and let me dress you, darlin'. Your escort for the ball will be here any minute now!" Clenching a petticoat with wide panniers, Aunt Pert moved toward Sassy, who stood near her canopied bed, already wearing a low-cut corset that revealed most of her bosom. After Sassy stepped into the quilted petticoat and the back strings were tied, the old lady slipped taffeta underskirts and a heavy ball gown over her head. Once the back lacings were secured, she said, "Now, go look at yourself, dear."

Sassy stepped up to a tall cheval glass. She had never seen such a fabulous gown. Aunt Pert had paid a seamstress to copy the coronation gown of Queen Maria Teresa of Hungary from a sketch in a Boston newspaper. When the drawing appeared, it had been the talk of the town, and Sassy knew the ladies at the Wainwright mansion would recognize the historical figure she portrayed.

Sassy turned sideways and studied her reflection. The panniers were twice as wide as normal, the skirt had yards of fabric, and the décolletage was daringly low. The blue gown's tight sleeves hugged her arms to the elbows, then spilled into riots of artfully gathered silver lace. Although the panniers gave the skirt great width, she remained very slim in profile. The huge skirt was split to reveal the taffeta underskirts that swished as she moved. Why, she looked beautiful. It was a gown fit for a queen. What woman could resist it?

Breathless, Aunt Pert clasped her niece's shoulders and plunked her down in front of the dressing table, then brushed her long hair, twisted the locks atop her head, and pinned them close to her scalp. She hummed happily as she worked, hairpins slipping from her mouth to the floor. At last she went to the wardrobe and took out a large box, then placed the box on the dressing table; with great care, she retrieved a silvery wig.

Sassy eyed the fanciful creation, thinking it looked like a big haystack. "I still don't see why I have to wear that funny thing."

"Why, dear, if you're goin' to be dressed as Queen Maria Teresa, you must look like her in every way," Aunt Pert said, easing the outlandish coiffure over Sassy's own hair. "The wigmaker spent all yesterday afternoon dressin' it." Aunt Pert tucked every one of Sassy's auburn tresses out of sight, and securely pinned the wig into place. The transformation was startling, for the wig gave Sassy a sophistication she did not usually possess. At last the old woman tied silver ruching around Sassy's neck and slipped a rose into her low décolletage.

"Law a mercy, are we done now?"

"No, dear, we must fix the feathers and set the patches. It would not be correct to attend a ball without feathers. The queen herself set the vogue."

"All right, all right," Sassy said with a groan, "but jest give me a little one. I don't want to look like an ol' turkey gobbler!"

Aunt Pert laughed softly. "Very well, dear." She selected a blue plume and firmly attached it to the wig. "Now, what shall it be . . . a moon, a heart, or a star?" she asked, pouring black patches into her hand. "And where shall we put it?" she added, weighing the question with great importance.

Suddenly from downstairs there was a firm *rat-a-tap-tap* on the front door.

The old woman jumped and spilled the patches onto the floor. "Oh, there he is!" she exclaimed, pressing a ringed hand over her heart.

Sassy raised her brows. "Lawzee me, why are you so nervous, Auntie? Your maid can answer the door."

The old lady's eyelids quivered like butterfly wings as she pressed a lace handkerchief to her brow. "Yes, but I must greet him. Do you remember everythin' I've told you about manners, dear?"

Sassy patted her aunt's plump arm. "Yes, of course. We've been havin' manner lessons for days now. Remember?"

Four more sharp raps resounded from below.

Her eyes wide, Aunt Pert rushed from the bedroom and slammed the door, rattling the pictures on the wall. Sassy heard her trotting down the stairs and greeting her escort for the ball. A man's deep voice floated up from below, but his words were too muffled to understand.

Sassy shook her head and chuckled. Poor Aunt Pert and her nerves, she thought. She slipped her feet into jeweled mules and slipped a black velvet mask into her reticule. She glanced at her reflection one last time. The snug bodice and flowing lines of the skirt magically transformed her figure: Suddenly it was enjoyable to be a lady. Self-confidence rose in her breast—surely no British officer would be able to resist her!

In fine spirits, she walked down the stairs and entered the foyer, her taffeta underskirts rustling softly. She met Aunt Pert, who was on her way back to the stairs. "Oh, he's handsome, darlin', very handsome indeed," the old lady said excitedly. "I know you'll have a lovely time."

As Sassy listened to her aunt slowly ascend the stairs, she idly wondered whom the O'Reillys had chosen for her escort. Whoever this mystery man was, handsome or not, she was sure she could handle him. No doubt he was some weak-livered fop she could bend to her will.

Anxious to see the man who had set her aunt's heart racing, she opened the sitting room doors. Instantly her gaze went to a tall man standing at the fireplace with his back to her: The silk shirt, snug breeches, and tall suede boots of a pirate clothed the man's powerful body. Anticipation swelled in her breast as the mysterious figure slowly turned.

Her heart leaped to her throat as her eyes locked on Roarke MacLaren's sun-bronzed countenance.

Chapter 10

To Sassy it seemed that all the breath had been knocked from her lungs—just like the time she tumbled from the roof while helping her father shingle their log cabin. The accident had almost rendered her senseless, and she felt the same way now: shocked, stunned, dazed. At the same time the sight of Roarke's face filled her with wild joy. The conflicting emotions made her legs weak and her pulse beat erratically.

Roarke was garbed as she imagined Captain Rakehell would be dressed. But Captain Rakehell was a hero she could admire, not a scoundrel like the man standing at the other end of the room. Her first impulse was to burst out in a tirade against him—but she bit her tongue and reined in her emotions. *No,* she decided. Why should she tell him how badly he had hurt her, and lose the rest of her pride? Hadn't she already made a fool of herself over him? It was best to remain cool and let him believe she had never given him a second thought after he left her. Fighting for breath, she rested a trembling hand on the doorknob and stammered, "How—how did you get here?"

An amused smile played over Roarke's mouth. "On the *Sea Witch*, of course."

There was that hypnotic voice, that soft Scottish

burr, that deep resonance, stirring her blood and firing her heart once more. As his gaze enveloped her, she read warm approval in his eyes . . . then suddenly she caught a hint of mockery on his lips. Why, he thought this was all amusing sport! He thought he could play with her emotions at will . . . leave her brokenhearted in Williamsburg, then show up in Boston and expect her to act as if nothing had happened.

In the space of a heartbeat anger crowded out any joy she felt at seeing him. Damn him anyway! Did he think he could just saunter into her life and rearrange it whenever he wished? Did he think the world revolved around him and him alone? "I can't believe you're here," she finally exclaimed.

"Well, you better believe it, because I am here . . . here to take you to the ball."

She trembled with anger. After telling her he *must* leave for Scotland, he had returned to America and was now lightly suggesting he take her to a ball . . . as if they had seen each other just yesterday. It didn't make sense! And how in the devil had he found out about the ball?

Anger sharpened her voice as she narrowed her eyes. "Iffen you think I'm goin' anyplace with you, Roarke MacLaren, you're fishin' with a rotten line."

"We'll see about that."

"How did you know where to find me?"

"I've docked in Boston many times. On one visit, I heard a rumor that the Green Dragon Inn was a meeting place for American rebels. My instincts told me someone there could direct me to you."

"But the ball—"

"I told the O'Reillys I knew you in Virginia," he cut in. "At first they seemed suspicious of me, but I said we were old friends. I gave them so many details about you and your father that I finally won their trust. When I discovered they were looking for an escort to take you to the Wainwright mansion tonight, I volunteered."

She pressed her lips together, angry at the O'Reillys; then she realized they had been deceived by his silvery tongue and smooth manner just as she had been. "I still don't know why you came here in the first place," she snapped.

He straightened, looking even taller. "To take you to the ball, of course," he replied lightly.

"*No,* why did you come here—to Boston?"

A veil of secrecy fell over his rugged features. "I have business in the city."

Certain he was lying, she met his challenging glare with courage, but when he moved forward, her heart started hammering. His stride was casual and self-confident, and he carried himself with dignity.

"You must think I'm crazy . . . Mebbe you jest think I'm dumb as a box of rocks," she ranted on.

He moved closer.

Stepping back, she pointed a finger at him. "You know somethin', Roarke MacLaren? You're the vainest man I ever saw in my whole life."

"Why?" He laughed, nearing her.

"Because you think you can jest walk off in Williamsburg, then take up with me like I was some rag doll whenever you please. You think I'll be dyin' to fall right back into your arms. Well, believe me, *you're wrong*. And I got a wagonload of other stuff to say to you, too!"

He caressed her bare arms, moved his hard hands up and down them, warming them with his touch. At first she struggled and beat against his chest with her fists, but he strengthened his grip; then his arms were around her, setting her body ablaze.

As his lips neared hers, she looked into his smoky eyes. "Why should we talk when we can do this?'' he muttered thickly. Then he was kissing her, snatching the very spirit from her body.

Slowly she quit struggling, then she instinctively slid her fingertips over the silken shirt, feeling his powerful shoulders and muscled arms under the privateer costume. As he pulled her to his broad chest, his legs and abdomen pressed against her. By now she was lost in the warmth and nearness of him, lost in the scent of his spicy cologne and the feel of his heart beating against her bosom. Tender feeling rolled over her, taking away her anger, leaving her limp and yielding. It was so wonderful to be in his arms again. So wonderful!

Slowly he traced her lips and entered her mouth with his tongue, making her throb with pleasure, making her go hot and shaky all over. The kiss rushed warm, savage feelings through her body, leaving her weak with their intensity. She delighted in the powerful sensations she had craved since they had parted in Williamsburg.

At last his lips broke away to nuzzle her throat and sear her deep cleavage. When he slipped his warm fingers into her bodice, her aching nipples strained over the top of the low-cut corset and hardened with need; she sucked in her breath as he flicked them with his thumb.

''Sassy,'' he whispered. ''*Sassy.*''

Fire shot through her, burning away her resistance, her will to fight. Bravely she tried to dam up her feelings, deny him a response, but her passion broke through like a mighty river.

Her lips were searching his when she remembered how he had seduced her and left her as if she were a trollop. Now, unbelievably, he expected her to yield to him again. Did he think she hadn't a scrap of pride? Furthermore, she knew he was lying about his business in Boston. No doubt he had come to persuade her to warm his bed again. After her bitter humiliation, she would never consent to such an arrangement. She would show him Sassy Adair made her own decisions!

And there were other considerations beside her pride. She had important work to do here in the colonies. Lord, why couldn't he see that her cause was just as important as his precious responsibilities, which he was always so vague about anyway.

She could taste bitter defeat on her tongue . . . If she gave in now, all would be lost. Resolve stiffening her spine, she pushed down her passion and pulled away from his arms.

"I know what you want," she said hotly. "You want to seduce me again." She raised her chin. "I've got more pride than that . . . and more sense, too! Why don't you jest leave this second? I have important business to attend to."

"Aye, I'm sure you do," he said knowingly.

She met his sharp gaze head-on. "Why did you tell the O'Reillys you'd take me to the ball anyway?"

His lip curled with frustration. "Because I knew once you were there, you'd manage to get yourself into trouble."

"I don't need your protection," she stormed. "And I ain't goin' to the ball with you!"

"Aye, you are. You are because you'd give your soul to go so you can spy on the British."

She stiffened and widened her eyes.

"Don't play the innocent with me, missy," he warned, anger blazing in the depths of his eyes. "I know you have a specific mission. The O'Reillys told me you're trying to find out when more British soldiers will be arriving in Boston."

He strode to the double doors and opened them, then extended his hand with an air of authority. "You'll go to the ball with me or you won't go at all!"

Hands on hips, she smiled tightly, hoping she

looked smug. "And may I inquire how we're goin' to get in? I ain't seen an invitation yet."

Flashing a broad smile, he pulled a card from his pocket and held it before her. "The O'Reillys are a talented family. When I arrived at the Green Dragon they had already forged an invitation for you and your escort. For tonight," he added, scanning the fancy calligraphy, "we're Lieutenant and Mrs. Colin McCrann."

She knew he was forcing her to be with him, using the same tactics he had used to force her to travel with him from MacKenzie's Tavern . . . and it made her blood boil. Damn it to hell, somehow he had trapped her again.

Lifting her cumbersome skirt, she swept past him with a raised chin. *Lord,* the things she endured for the rebels!

She marched through the foyer and out the front door, his jaunty laughter ringing in her ears.

As Roarke led Sassy through a slow minuet, she glanced about the Wainwrights' elegant ballroom. The walls were of white paneled wood decorated with gold molding, and the floor was polished parquet. Chandeliers full of blazing candles hung from the high ceiling, and French doors opened onto a long verandah. In a corner, a group of musicians dressed in velvet and wearing white wigs played a harpsichord and stringed instruments. Dancers in colorful costumes moved gracefully about the huge chamber, which smelled heavily of perfume and powder and burning candles.

The room's ornate surroundings and stately music made Sassy feel out of place, but Roarke's commanding air gave her a measure of reassurance. Like the ballroom's swirling colors, her mind blurred at the thought of being back in his embrace. His exciting nearness made her more lightheaded than the tangy champagne she had sipped minutes earlier. Her body tingled from his close presence, and she looked deeply into his eyes, glittering through the openings of a black velvet mask. Again that warm, tender feeling rushed over her, stirring her emotions as violently as the day they had first met. Thank goodness the trip to Beacon Hill had been short, but now that he had found her, what would happen later?

A burst of laughter brought her attention back to the ball. It seemed that the cream of Boston society was at the Wainwright mansion. Most of the ladies were costumed as royalty from the pages of history; softly waving plumes, flashing gems, and gauzy confections adorned their powdered wigs. Several of the gentlemen were dressed as Roman emperors or famous highwaymen—a few wits sported comical costumes or harlequin suits. Black masks concealed everyone's identity.

Except for one man.

Sassy's gaze kept straying to a tall officer standing near the arched windows who was holding a drink in one hand. Dressed in a resplendent parade uniform, he had a bearing and manner that spoke of discipline and authority. A striking black patch covered one eye. His other eye roamed over the dancers as if he were searching for someone.

"Look at that strange officer by the windows," she whispered to Roarke.

As he guided her in a slow circle, he glanced at the man but didn't speak.

"Do you know him?" she prompted. "Who is he?"

He was silent for a moment, then replied flatly, "That's Colonel John Blackhurst. I'm surprised you haven't heard of him." His brow creased above the black mask. "He's notorious in this city. He's on General Gage's personal staff. He's famous for that eye patch . . . and his cruelty."

Sassy stared at the officer again. He stood out

from everyone in the crowd, and he looked so silent, so alone. ''He's in uniform, and everyone else is in costume,'' she said. ''He must think it's beneath his dignity to put on a costume—he must be a very special man.''

A deep laugh rumbled from Roarke's throat. His eyes twinkled through the mask.

''What are you laughin' at?'' Sassy demanded.

They were about to make a turn, but he skillfully maneuvered her away from the other dancers. ''No doubt he *is* brilliant—he's an intelligence officer,'' he said as he walked her to the other side of the ballroom. ''But I'd call him more of a pit bull dog than a very special man. Whenever General Gage needs to plan an especially distasteful operation, he calls on Blackhurst.''

''Why, he must know almost everythin' about everyone then!'' Sassy exclaimed.

''Aye, he does. I've heard he has information about British officers as well as suspected rebels. I'm sure he has a large, dog-eared notebook on your friend Samuel Adams.''

Sassy twisted about and gazed openly at Blackhurst.

''Stop staring at the man!'' Roarke commanded, turning her around.

''I want to meet him!''

He pulled her closer, leading her past a candlelit buffet table piled with cold meats and dainty pastries.

She looked up at him, pouring all her frustration into a hot glower. *''I said I want to meet him.''*

''By my faith, you're the most stubborn woman I ever met.'' Clasping her hand, he led her toward the verandah. ''He's exactly the kind of man you shouldn't meet, you little hellion.''

Sassy's heart jumped as she noticed Blackhurst moving through the crowd, working his way closer to them.

Roarke swore under his breath. "Now you've done it," he muttered darkly.

Before they could reach the open verandah doors, Blackhurst touched Roarke's arm. "I'd like to claim a dance, if I might," he announced in a clipped British accent.

"I'm sorry, all of the lady's dances are taken," Roarke replied.

Sassy's pulse was racing with excitement. Tall and slender, Blackhurst appeared to be about fifty years of age. Everything about him was neat and precise. His uniform and person were immaculate; his brass and leather gleamed; his gray hair was clubbed back in a tight military manner.

"Oh, I'm sure the lady has one dance left for a poor soldier," he stated in chilling tones. He bent to kiss Sassy's hand; his lips were cold and hard, and they sent a chill up her spine. "My name is Colonel John Blackhurst. And who might you be, lovely lady?"

Roarke's eyes glittered in warning through his mask, but the colonel's cold blue eye mesmerized her. Before she knew it, she found her lips saying, "My name . . . is Sassy Adair."

"And what a lovely name it is." The colonel took her arm with a proprietary air. "Shall we dance?"

Roarke clasped his dark hand on Blackhurst's shoulder. "I said the lady's dances are taken."

The older man scanned him coolly. "I seem to recognize your voice. Yes, there is something quite familiar about you. Have we met?"

"No . . . I'm Lieutenant Colin McCrann, just arrived in Boston."

For a time Blackhurst gazed at Roarke's thick hair and large hands, studying him. "Oh, I see," he stated at length. "Your voice tells me you are Scottish . . . Your manner tells me you're unimpressed with rank. All the king's lieutenants should be so forceful." He glanced back at Sassy. "And what do you say to my request, dear lady?"

She gazed at Roarke's clenched fist. She could tell he was holding himself in check, and truth be told, Blackhurst's coldness frightened her, yet she felt compelled to draw some information from the man. "I . . . I think I have time for one dance."

The colonel smiled icily, then glanced back at Roarke. "With your permission, sir."

Roarke bowed his head and stepped back.

Sassy looked at him as Blackhurst took her hand; she knew from his hard lips and stiff body that he was boiling mad.

The colonel led her away to join a group engaged in another minuet. From the ceiling, chandeliers dazzled light over the dancers, picking out glinting embroidery and flashing colors. As they danced, there was the swish of silk, the crisp rustle of taffeta petticoats, and the click of high heels on the polished floor.

While they paraded to the minuet's precise strains, Blackhurst smiled down at her, chilling her spirit like a north wind. His gaze glittered with cold intelligence; when he stared at her, she felt he knew what she was thinking. At that moment she realized it would be very difficult to extract any information from this man. Still she had to try. "Colonel Blackhurst, I've seen so many new British regiments comin' into Boston lately. Has General Gage asked for more to be sent from England?"

"Although I work closely with the general, I'm not privy to all his plans."

Sassy held her tongue, knowing this wasn't the time to ask more questions. Over his shoulder she could see Roarke glowering in the corner.

"I detect a country accent, Miss Adair," the colonel said. "Are you from the frontier . . . one of the southern colonies perhaps?" he drawled as they made a turn.

"Yes, Virginia's my home," she replied.

"A lovely spot. Lovely indeed."

While they danced, Blackhurst made small talk and answered her questions with one-word replies. Gathering her courage, she told herself she was here on important business; she couldn't fail the rebels. She had to try to question the officer again.

"Colonel, when do you expect new troops to arrive?"

"I didn't say any new troops *were* arriving. Why are you so interested in the plans of the British army?"

She had an awful feeling *he* was interrogating *her*, and longed to pull away from him; she longed to wash her skin where he had touched her, to wrap herself in a quilt and warm her blood again—but he clasped her hand firmly. "I . . . I was jest wondering, that's all."

"Strange. Most young ladies your age are interested in gowns and balls, not troop movements." He looked at her intently, as if he were trying to remember something, then he asked, "How is your father employed?"

"He was . . . I mean he's a circuit-ridin' preacher." As soon as the words left her mouth, she knew she had made a mistake. Undoubtedly a man in his position reviewed the names of men hung for treason in *all* the American colonies. He had probably read the report written by the officer in Williamsburg, and from her last name knew that she was the daughter of a notorious rebel. Lord, why hadn't she been clever enough to use a false name?

Alarm quickened her mind when Blackhurst guided her away from the other dancers. "I must go now," she said. "I—"

"No, no," he interrupted, clenching her wrist until it hurt. "Let's talk a bit." She looked back for

Roarke, but he had vanished into the press of dancers. The scent of cloying perfume made her stomach churn as the colonel pulled her toward the open verandah doors.

"Shall we get a breath of fresh air?" he suggested, his fingers biting into her flesh as he urged her forward. Her heels clicked over stone paving, then the cool night air, heavy with the scent of greenery and roses, washed over her. Chinese lanterns glowed like orange moons the length of the long porch, and over the railing Boston shimmered at the foot of Beacon Hill.

When the colonel snatched off her mask and tossed it aside, she felt weak and woozy, and clammy perspiration popped out on her brow; her hands were ice-cold. Before she could fight him off, he pulled her toward him and had his arms tight about her. The swift action made her heart lurch, and his rude abruptness shocked and offended her. Tears blurred her vision, and she was crushed to think he had so little regard for her. With a racing heart, she stared at his shadowy face and tried to wrench away. "Leave me alone, you ol' devil. How dare you try to manhandle me!"

Blackhurst lowered his head and murmured, "Don't be so unfriendly, you little jade. Don't you know who I am?"

"Yeah, I know who you are. You're a low-down stinkin' skunk who's trying to take advantage of me!"

He laughed and pressed his mouth against hers; the taste of his thin lips was rank and disgusting. Groaning, she squirmed and beat against his chest.

In the back of her frantic mind, Sassy heard purposeful steps, then a large hand clamped on Blackhurst's shoulder and shoved him away. His eyes going wide with fright, the colonel stumbled against the railing. Before he could fully stand, Roarke slammed an uppercut to his jaw; as the blow connected, Blackhurst crumpled to the stone floor. With a strangled sob, Sassy hurried to Roarke's side; through the shadows she watched Blackhurst pull himself up, his gaze fiery with hatred.

"You'll live to regret this, my fine Scottish friend," he vowed, wiping blood from the corner of his mouth.

"The regrets will be yours, Colonel."

Roarke clasped Sassy's trembling hand and guided her into the bright ballroom. As he pulled her across the polished floor, several dancers stared openly at them. Sassy could tell from their startled faces that they sensed something was wrong. "Let's go, lass," Roarke ordered, leading her toward the mansion's large entryway.

Thinking her legs might buckle under her, she hurried to keep up. "Where . . . where are we goin'?" she asked, shaken by his anger.

"To the *Sea Witch!*" he answered sternly.

She could only follow him, anxiously wondering what awaited her there.

Chapter 11

Even after they arrived at Boston Harbor, Sassy and Roarke's heated conversation continued as it had all the way to the waterfront. Slamming the carriage door, Roarke glared at her, the silvery moonlight emphasizing his angry face. "Let's go to my cabin . . . I want to show you something," he ordered.

She lifted her skirts from the dirty street and frowned. "Only if the coach driver waits!"

A cynical chuckle floated into the darkness. "Perhaps you'd like to search me for weapons, too," Roarke suggested.

"I know all about your weapons. That gilded tongue of yours is sharper than a snake's tooth, and I won't be left here on foot!"

"As you please, then," he replied in a weary voice. "I've never held a woman against her will." He spoke to the carriage driver, and the man raised his tricorn and nodded in understanding. "Now, let's go," Roarke commanded, pulling Sassy toward the shadowy gangplank.

When she stepped aboard the gently swaying *Sea Witch,* the tangy scent of the harbor filled her nostrils, and all about her was the lap of the sea against the hull. "Here, this way," he added. Curious, she followed him, scanning the dim waterfront maze of Fiddler's Green. Taverns, pawnshops, and clothing stores lined the shabby street; from the shop fronts, signs with anchors and crossed harpoons creaked in the night breeze. Like pointed lances, the ships' bowsprits extended over the narrow street and almost touched the run-down buildings facing the harbor.

Roarke led Sassy past the mainmast, where a British flag fluttered in the moonlight. She sensed that the crew must be ashore, for the ship itself was silent. As her heels tapped over the planks, the sound of a distant buoy bell echoed; hazy in the late night mist, a forest of masts and rigging jutted from neighboring vessels. They descended to his cabin by a handsome flight of stairs with mahogany handrails . . . A dull light glowed through a louvered door at the bottom of the steps.

"Wait here," Roarke commanded as he went ahead. She could hear him moving around the cabin, lighting more lamps. Soon long fingers of brightness streaked across the stairwell.

The first thing she saw when she stood on the threshold was a sideboard made of polished teakwood and brass; leather-bound volumes of Shakespeare, Voltaire, and the Greek classics covered the surface.

"Don't stand there . . . Come in, lass."

Surprised at the cabin's opulence, she stepped onto a plush carpet and eyed the rest of the sumptuous room, which smelled of a delicate Oriental spice. Curtained with gold brocade, a bed with immaculate white sheets and a soft cashmere blanket occupied the corner. There was a long desk with charts and a buffet stocked with brandy and sweets; an open box of cheroots rested on a silver tray.

Arms crossed, Roarke stood in the middle of the room, looking like an angry pirate. "Now, for God's sake, lass, will you tell me why you insisted on attracting Blackhurst's attention when I told you not to look at him?" He sat down at the desk and crossed his booted legs. "I know you want to gather information about the British, but you could have questioned another officer. Blackhurst is a viper."

Anger raised her temperature several degrees. Who was he to question her? Did he think he could just sashay into her life and change it all around after she had set her course? "I can take care of myself," she stormed. "Why are you talkin' to me like I was a child?"

Avoiding his hot eyes, she looked at the aft of the ship, where, over the rudder, a sweep of bowed windows draped in red velvet looked out to the sea. Upholstered in the same material, a window seat ran under the windows that glowed with soft moonlight. "I thought you were goin' to show me something, not plague me with questions!" she ranted on, glancing back at him over her shoulder.

"Aye, I *do* have something to show you." Roarke walked to the sideboard, selected a Virginia twist, and lit it in the flame of a nearby whale-oil lamp. Then, the cheroot clenched between his white teeth, he lifted a pamphlet from his desk. "You know, lass, for a bright girl, you can be infernally hardheaded at times," he snapped, turning her about and shaking the folded paper at her.

Her heart skipped a beat when she saw what he was holding. Surely the O'Reillys hadn't informed him of her involvement in passing out rebel pamphlets. She knew they kept that secret very close. Her mind raced as she braced herself for his next statement.

He drew his brows together in a scowl. "While the O'Reillys were attending to other customers, I decided to check on my mount. I took a shortcut through the inn's storeroom on my way to the stable and found a bundle of these pamphlets on the floor. Evidently someone had bumped into a covered box and dislodged them." He narrowed his eyes. "You're passing out rebel propaganda just like your father was in Virginia, aren't you?"

Knowing she had been caught, she tossed her head. "What if I am? You already knew I was gatherin' information for the rebels."

"Asking British officers questions is one thing. This is another. You can play a curious little girl if the British become suspicious of your questions. If they catch you passing out these pamphlets, you'll hang." He pitched the pamphlet on his desk and moved toward her. "I'm sure the Sons of Liberty are behind this, and I want you to avoid them."

"Why! Why should I avoid them?"

"Why, indeed! They're the most radical political group in America. They destroyed large quantities of stamps in Philadelphia."

"That's wonderful! Tell me more."

"All right, I will," he retorted. "In New York they threw bricks at soldiers and set the lieutenant governor's coach ablaze. And right here in Boston they destroyed the office of the chief tax collector and burned the records in the Admiralty Court."

"Don't you think I know that? They're doin' what they think is right, jest like Pa."

He jabbed a long finger at her. "They're doing what will get them hung!"

"I thought you hated the British!"

"I do. That doesn't have a damn thing to do with what I'm talking about. I visited the editor of the largest newspaper in Boston yesterday. He said there's a rumor of a secret printing press in the city run by the Sons of Liberty." He slanted his eyes at the pamphlet, then back to her. "Both of us know that rumor is correct." He scowled at her again. "Blackhurst has openly sworn to find the press and hang everyone associated with it."

Sassy remembered her conversation with Blackhurst at the ball, and feared he already knew she was a rebel.

"Don't think your pretty face will save you, lass," Roarke went on. "After he has tired of you, he'll string you up right beside the others." He rose and threw her a challenging stare.

Standing taller, she raised her chin. "Don't stare at *me*. Save some time to worry about *yourself*."

"What are you talking about?"

"You know what I'm talkin' about." With a wise nod, she went to the bowed windows and ran her fingertips over the velvet draperies. Then she turned and let her gaze rove over the cabin, noticing bits of Oriental china, oil paintings, and other pieces of fine art. The window seat was littered with a sexton, compass, and one of Roarke's elegant jackets. She picked up the expensive piece of clothing and held it at arm's length. "How did you get so rich, anyway? How can you afford all these paintin's and fancy dishes and fine clothes?" She flung down the jacket. "Why, this place looks like a floatin' palace."

From the desk she picked up an ornate bronze clock. "Everywhere I look I see somethin' that cost money," she added, slamming down the clock.

He sat on the edge of the desk, squinting through a haze of cigar smoke. "We went over this when we first met," he recited tiredly. "I export tobacco and import Scotch whiskey and French silk."

"No . . . no, there's somethin' more," she blurted out, her gaze on the scar on his jaw. "Somethin' you're holdin' back. I've always known that. I can jest tell it by the look in your eyes."

With a husky laugh, he drew on the cheroot. "You have a vivid imagination, lass."

"Why did you bring me here anyway? I have a feelin' you want to talk about more than my politics."

Standing, he stubbed out the cigar in a small brass tray, then came to her and wrapped his arms about her. "Aye, I do. I want you to return with me to Scotland."

She widened her eyes in surprise. "After you abandoned me in Williamsburg? I can hardly believe you have the gall to speak those words."

"If my words won't persuade you, perhaps this will."

He pulled her against him, his gaze hungrily devouring her heaving bosom, then slowly—very slowly—he raised his eyes to hers. Excitement flooded the pit of her stomach as he lowered his head and brushed her lips with his. How often she had dreamed of this. How often she had ached for this moment . . . but spurred by her pride, she twisted away.

"Oh, no you don't!" Quickly he snapped her face about and brought her against him, imprisoning her in a steely embrace, then he took her mouth again. No longer gentle, his lips plundered her mouth, setting her blood afire. She could hear his ragged breathing, feel his thudding heart, as he deepened the hot, leisurely kiss, potent with feeling. A drugging heaviness spread through her limbs.

When his hand cupped her breast, he raised his head and softly said, "The British will be closing the harbor soon. I must return to Scotland. I need to attend to clan responsibilities and speak with my brother, Kevin. Come with me."

Doubt and indecision assailed her. How could she say no when her whole body was aflame for him?

He kissed her eyelids. "Listen to your heart, lass. What does it say?"

Her heart cried out to go with him—but all of her instincts were telling her to be wary. Yes, her better judgment was telling her the rogue was trying to sway her with sweet seduction; her better judgment was telling her if she stayed a minute longer, her resistance would crumble. Stop him, stop his straying hand that was inches away from taking her to paradise!

Like a sudden sea breeze, a chill came over her, cooling her blood, and fear crept in to melt away her pleasure. Using every ounce of her strength and discipline, she caught his hand. "I ain't listenin' to my heart. I'm listenin' to my head."

He laughed gently and kissed her forehead. "What do you mean, bairn?"

She pushed away from him and gazed at his puzzled face. "*I mean I'm listenin' to my head.* I want to be part of somethin' that will last. I want to have a part in changin' this country. I want to have a part of this comin' rebellion. And I can't do it from Scotland."

Frustration clouded his face. "Each day you stay in Boston increases your chances of being captured. If you come with me, you'll be safe from Blackhurst."

"Do you think I'd leave my friends when they need me—jest to keep myself safe?" She shook her head. "You can't forgive me for doin' what I have to do, can you?" she asked as she walked away from him.

With a heavy sigh, he raked back his hair. "Lass, are you sure this is the kind of life you want? You might change your mind later."

She blinked back hot tears. "Yeah. This is the kind of life I want. And I ain't changin' my mind—now or later!"

Before he could say another word, she ran from the cabin.

Sassy sat hunched over a desk in Aunt Pert's sitting room studying the scattered contents of her treasure sack. How unhappy she was! Instead of obtaining valuable information for Samuel Adams, she had failed in her assignment and possibly revealed her identity as a rebel. Outside, rain dripped from the roof, and inside, the upholstery and drapes smelled musty; with a shiver, she paused to pull a light shawl tighter about her. It had been chilly and rainy for days now, almost like fall instead of June.

Returning to her dreary musings, she picked up her father's blue rock, then a small brooch from Aunt Pert. The trinkets soothed her nerves and made her feel closer to those she loved. The last few days she had slept little, obsessed with thoughts of Roarke even more than her failure as a spy. Her heart in turmoil, she had constantly rehashed their discussion aboard the *Sea Witch*. She knew she had done the right thing, but she was angry at herself for missing the good-looking rogue.

When the clock struck five, she put everything back into the treasure sack and tucked it into her chemise. Her aunt's neighbors the Trimbells would be here soon for tea, and it wouldn't do for them to see her mooning over her private mementos. A few moments later a carriage splashed over the puddled cobbles and jangled to a stop in front of the house.

Knowing her aunt was still napping, Sassy sighed heavily, rose, and walked to the foyer. Near the front door, she glanced at herself in the mirror and smoothed down her wrinkled pink dress. Fluffing up her loose hair, she studied her reflection. Her complexion seemed duller, and dark smudges lay under her eyes, which had lost their usual sparkle.

A carriage door slammed, then brisk footsteps told her that this was not Master Trimbell and his wife, but someone else. The visitor gave the door knocker several smart raps.

Carefully she opened the door to peek out. By the time she realized who was standing there, John Blackhurst had pushed the door all the way open.

She staggered backward as he shoved his way into the foyer. Her pulse hammering, she gasped and ran her eyes over him: Dressed in a smart red uniform dotted with raindrops, he glittered with polished brass and colorful medals. His silvery hair was tied in place with a black ribbon, and his beaded boots were glassy with polish. Her gaze riveted on his stark eye patch, then moved to his good eye, which gleamed brightly.

Outrage rose in her soul at this violation of her privacy. "What are you doin' here?" she burst out. "Get out. Get out this minute!" She rushed for the door, trying to slip past him. "I'll call a constable. I'll have you thrown out!"

Blackhurst snatched her arm, catching the shawl in his hand. "You'll do no such thing," he said, flinging the garment aside. His fingers bit into her skin and he pushed her back. Through the open doors he eyed the empty sitting room, then smiled broadly. "Alone. How very convenient." With a cold grimace, he pulled her into the room, and shoving her ahead of him, deposited her on the sofa.

"How . . . how did you know where I live?" she asked in a strained voice.

"A mere formality. I had you followed after the ball, of course."

She stared at him as he paced about the room with a military air, looking as if he had just commandeered the parlor for a staff meeting. Her pulse raced wildly, but at the same time, anger overrode her fear. Impulsively she moved forward to call Aunt Pert—then she realized the gentle lady would be frightened to death. What could she do anyway? No, let her sleep, let her be protected from this monster.

Blackhurst stood with his booted feet planted apart. When he lifted her chin in his fingers, she pulled her head away—but he jerked it back, holding it rigid. From the edge of her vision, she could see he wore a huge gemstone ring mounted in a high setting. "Don't play the haughty vixen with me, Miss Sassy Adair. I've come here to talk, and you'll listen to every word I have to say!"

She composed her face and steeled her heart, vowing to give him no sign of fear.

"Ah, that's much better, my dear," he said. "Perhaps we can speak like civilized adults now."

Her eyes followed him as he swaggered about, finally pulling a small leather notebook from his spotless uniform. He sat down beside her and presented the notebook as if it were a holy relic. "Do you know what I have here?"

Alarm nipped at her heart. Had he discovered her connection with the rebels? All she could do was remain silent.

Blackhurst stood and slapped the notebook against his open hand. "No, I'm sure you have no idea, do you? I'm sure he gulled you also."

"Who are you talkin' about?"

A cold smile flickered over his thin mouth. "Roarke MacLaren, my dear. Who else?"

Her lips trembled and with a will of their own, sputtered, *"Roarke?"*

Using his thumb, the colonel ruffled through the stiff pages. "Yes, indeed. I have recorded his whole history here in this journal . . . It makes highly colorful reading. One might think it was fiction, but every word is true." He glared at her and in a patronizing tone, added, "You didn't believe that story about him being a Scottish sea captain, did you? Yes? Well, you are naive, aren't you?"

He took her hand; iciness shot up her arm and she tried to pull away, but he held her fast. In a raspy voice he hissed, "My dear, Roarke MacLaren

is none other than the infamous Captai
scourge of the British Crown. He is a
pirate!"

Her heart lurched at the words that w
ered with brutal malice. She was shock disbe-
lieving. That scoundrel Roarke MacLaren couldn't possibly be the man she had admired from afar, a man about whom romantic legends were told.

Blackhurst went on in oily tones. "For the last ten years he has pillaged English merchantmen. The man has amassed a fabulous fortune."

He released her hand, but towered over her, demanding her attention. "He is very clever, you know. He usually waits for the merchantmen to stray from their convoys in a fog before he attacks. The warships rarely give pursuit, for he is also a master of quick sailing and sharpshooting. There have been many bloody confrontations. He was once attacked by a man-of-war carrying a host of men and fourteen guns. After the battle, it was the English deck that was red with blood. Eighty of our men were killed before he sailed away. Think of it. Eighty good English sailors dead because of him."

"How do you know this is true?"

He arched his brows and smiled. "Because I was there, in transit to America. I shall always remember it. The roar of the cannon, the smell of the bitter smoke and fresh blood, the men's screams, the sound of Captain Rakehell's voice as he called orders, urging his men to kill and pillage." He widened his blue eye. "Oh yes, I was that close." He thumped his eye patch, making a hollow sound against the shiny material. "Close enough for him to take my eye."

"Roarke took your eye?"

"Yes," he said, pacing about the room, "and I swore to find him. I knew I would never forget his voice." He turned and smiled. "It's very deep, very distinctive, isn't it? For an observant man like

,self, it's unforgettable." He snapped the notebook shut and put it away. "I've carried this notebook for years, adding to it as his exploits increased. Several years ago he left the seas and disappeared. Many said he had gone to the Caribbean to retire, but I always suspected he would turn up in the colonies. The man is a celebrity in England, you know. His notoriety ranks with the most famous highwaymen, and there is a fabulous price on his head. The British Admiralty would give a king's ransom to see him swing from a gibbet."

"If you knew who he was, why didn't you take him at the ball? And why are you tellin' me all this?"

He moved close, so close she could smell his damp wool uniform and feel the cold brass buttons brushing her arm. "How thoughtful of you to bring up my next point," he said, gazing at her lewdly. "I was hoping you'd know, but since you're so unsophisticated, I suppose I'll have to tell you. In return for certain . . . favors, I would be willing to hold my tongue about Captain Rakehell. Just think of it, my dear. Within your hands you have the power to protect your lover." He stared at her. "He is your lover, is he not?"

Blackhurst's proposition sank into her with full force. He wanted her to become his mistress or he would turn Roarke in to the Crown! Outrage twisted inside her, and she stood and drew back to slap his face.

With an upward swipe, he caught her hand, deeply scratching her forearm with the sharp mounting of his ring. "You should feel flattered," he said, tightening his grip. "There is a sumptuous purse waiting for the man who brings in Captain Rakehell. And I'm prepared to forgo that reward—at least for a while."

She winced in pain and held her stinging arm, wanting to spit in his face, but an inner strength stilled the action. She studied Blackhurst's nervous manner, telling herself he was deranged and dangerous—better to play it safe and cool, better to lie through her teeth than incite him further. And what did a vow mean to a madman? It was no vow at all. Then she thought of Aunt Pert, who would be coming down the stairs at any moment. She must remove this monster from her home and send him away before he could frighten her gentle aunt.

A brittle hardness laced her voice. "Very well. I guess I ain't got no choice. What terms do you have in mind?" She listened to her own words, unable to believe she had spoken them.

Instantly he released her arm. His face lit with surprise and delight. "I must say, you're responding quite well now that you understand the matter. Perhaps you have more sense than I thought."

Outside, there was the sound of horses, and another carriage splashed through the puddles. Thank God, Master Trimbell and his wife had finally arrived. "You better get out of here! My aunt has company comin' and they jest rolled up. They'll be at the door any minute."

With an angry scowl, he clenched her arm and strode to the foyer, his manner becoming cold and businesslike once again. "Meet me at my home at eleven tonight." He tossed his card on a table, then turned to go; opening the front door, he paused in afterthought. "Don't think about warning our beloved captain. The navy has closed the port, and my men are everywhere. I have the notorious Captain Rakehell in a jug with a tight stopper." Suddenly he clenched her jaw, digging his fingertips into her cheeks. "And don't try to run away from me. Wherever you might go, I would hunt you down and seek my revenge." The sharp words hung in the air as he turned to leave, staring rudely at the Trimbells on his way.

Sassy greeted the older couple as if nothing had

happened. After she escorted them into the sitting room, she left to awake her aunt, ascending the stairs on quaking legs. She felt rage at Blackhurst and rage at Roarke. No wonder Roarke had cleverly kept his past hidden, she thought, her jaw hardening. He could scarcely tell her he had a price on his head! Then a new thought nettled her pride. While she had begged him to join the rebel cause, he had put her off with excuses about inexperience. To listen to him, he was no more than a peaceful sea captain concerned about his clan in Scotland. All that when he had engaged the British in active conflict for more than a decade!

Yes, she thought, reaching the upstairs landing. While she had told him her deepest secrets, he had manipulated her like a simple child, denying her access to his past. At that moment she could have choked him, yet deep in her heart she knew that she couldn't let Blackhurst have him, and neither could she give herself to the monster. Somehow she had to find the courage to save them both. But how?

As she tapped on Aunt Pert's door, the stinging scratch on her arm, now bright red, caught her eye. The sight of her own blood spurred her resolve. Somehow she *would* warn Roarke and help him escape. And after Roarke was safe, Blackhurst would have nothing to hold over her . . . Then she could tell him to go to hell, where he belonged!

By ten o'clock that night it had stopped raining, but a heavy fog shrouded Boston. Lamplight glowed in the mist along the waterfront. As Sassy crept up the gangplank of the *Sea Witch,* the pungent scent of the harbor enveloping her, she clutched her long cloak and shivered in the chilly air. Far below the tarred boards, the sounds of lapping water and muffled buoy bells mingled with her creaking footsteps. With each step she thought of Aunt Pert asleep in her bed; how she had hated to slip from the back of her house like a common sneak. But how could she involve her aunt in such degradation and danger?

Near the ship she lifted her sweeping cloak so it wouldn't snag and peered over her shoulder. In the swirling fog she could see no one. Had Blackhurst followed her? Was he even now lurking in the shadows watching her?

Suddenly a rough hand seized her arm and pulled her aboard the packet. Her heart jumped wildly. Stumbling on a coiled rope, she clapped a hand to her mouth, stifling a scream. Her stomach knotted with fear as she stared into a lined face, shadowed under a tam-o'-shanter.

"I'm Duncan. Who be ye?" a gravelly voice demanded.

Her heart settled down a bit when she realized the old seaman was one of Roarke's crew. "M-my name is Sassy," she stuttered between dry lips. "I've come to see your captain."

The old man raked her with a disapproving gaze. "Guess ye're a bit o' fluff he's ordered up for his pleasure. Well, ye'll have to wait," he explained sourly. "He's gone ashore. I canna' tell ye where he's gone or when he'll return." His eyes snapped with contempt. "The cabin's below, the door's open." Tossing her another hard look, he walked away.

Sassy realized he thought she was a loose woman and disapproved of her for it, but she didn't bother to correct him. She fumbled to the aft of the *Sea Witch,* remembering the path Roarke had taken. Once she was down the stairs and safe in his softly lit cabin, she felt better.

As she slipped off her damp cloak, she noticed several of his belongings scattered about. She caressed his velvet jacket, scented with tobacco and a subtle sandalwood aroma from his Chinese sea chest. With a pang of anxiety, she pressed the jacket against her bosom and inhaled its exotic fragrance. Wherever he was, he was in danger. Surely Blackhurst's men were stalking him. She ran her fingers over the angry red scratch on her arm and thought of the man who had promised to hunt her down.

Icy fear flooded the pit of her stomach. Lord, the colonel's men had probably tracked her here. If they didn't already know where the *Sea Witch* was located, they did now! How could she have been so careless? She should have sent word to the packet and asked Roarke to meet her in a tavern. Her panic had put them both in jeopardy. With a worried sigh, she tossed the jacket aside and looked out the aft windows, seeing nothing but the faint impression of a forest of masts. In the cottony fog even the noise of the waves and the buoy bells seemed muted.

For a while she walked about the gently moving cabin to relieve her nervousness—then she looked at the hands of the ticking clock. *Ten-thirty.* Soon Blackhurst would be expecting her at his home. If she didn't come, he would make a beeline for the *Sea Witch.* She knew he would.

Lamplight caught on a cut-glass brandy decanter, drawing her attention. Without thinking, she clasped the sparkling container and poured herself a drink. When the fiery liquid burned her tongue, she made a face and swallowed it anyway. Soon the brandy put a numbing mist between her and her troubles.

Five minutes later she poured another drink. Then yet another.

Clasping the decanter against her bosom, she examined the bed, so inviting with its snowy white sheets. Somewhat dizzy, she decided to sit down—just for a bit. Well, why shouldn't she if Roarke was going to be so blasted slow in coming? she thought, yanking back the ringed bed curtains. After a few more drinks, she set the decanter on a bedside table and stretched out on the mattress. The liquor, gently swaying cabin, and soft harbor noises all worked their magic. Soon she was fast asleep. She dreamed of her father, Roarke, and Blackhurst's bright blue eye. Lost in darkness, she tossed and turned, burrowing into the soft bed.

Then there was a strong hand on her shoulder, shaking her, and a deep voice was calling her name.

Numb and groggy, she flicked open her eyes and saw Roarke's face. Half-asleep, she blinked, thinking she was still dreaming.

"Wake up, lass. It's time for breakfast," he said.

Under her she felt the rocking of the ship. Not the gentle movement of the harbor, but the rhythmic buck of sea waves. Quickly she turned her head and glanced aft to see sparkling sunlight streaming through the bowed windows . . . and clear blue sky!

With a gasp, she shot to a sitting position, instantly regretting her mistake. Her head spun wickedly, and her stomach threatened to toss up its contents. "What time is it?" she muttered. "Why is the ship movin' so?" She clasped her throat. "And law a mercy, why am I so sick?"

Roarke sat beside her and settled his warm hand over hers. "Easy, lass. It's nine in the morning."

"Nine!"

"Aye, you're sick because you're unaccustomed to spirits and you drank half a bottle of brandy last night. To answer your other question, the ship is pitching because we're in choppy water far from Boston Harbor . . . on our way to Scotland."

Chapter 12

"Scotland!" Sassy held her spinning head and stared into his amused eyes. You . . . you kidnapped me!"

Roarke grinned broadly. "That I did, lass. I came back and saw you laid out cold as a dockside drunk, and shamelessly seized the opportunity."

She lurched to her feet, wanting to kill him. "I can't believe it. I jest can't believe it!" Holding her pitching stomach, she staggered to the windows and peered out. Golden sunlight dazzled through the panes, warming her face and hurting her eyes. Waves peeled back from the stern, and water foamed over the ship's wake; the clear horizon tilted to the side; a few crying birds wheeled over the white-capped water. There was not a sign of Boston or any other land to be seen. *She was at sea.* She had been snatched from port by a ruthless villain. She was cut off from everyone she knew in the world except Roarke MacLaren. And if she had anything to do with it, she wouldn't know him much longer, because he would be dead—by her hand!

Ire erupting inside her like steamy lava, she whirled about and aimed a glower at him. He was lounging in a leather chair, idly rolling a cheroot between his fingertips. Dressed in a full-sleeved shirt, snug breeches, and high jackboots, he looked exactly like the pirate she now knew him to be.

"You couldn't have left port. The British closed it!"

"Wrong," he replied, cool as chipped ice. "The British are *trying* to close it. They don't have enough men-of-war in the harbor yet. There were plenty of holes to slip through—with the fog, it was easy. My crew is accustomed to moving swiftly and silently." He jammed the cheroot in his mouth and leaned back at his ease.

"How in the name of God could you have done it!"

He flashed white teeth and lit the spicy-smelling cheroot in a low flame, making her queasy stomach draw up in a knot. "It was easy. You were so inebriated, you were sleeping like a baby." He took a long draw and knitted his brow. "Oh, by the way, did you know you snore when you're drunk?"

She staggered across the cabin, intending to slap him, but her stomach rebelled. Woozy, she pressed a hand over her mouth and looked above his head, watching a lantern swing crazily. "Why is the ship rollin' so?"

Deviltry danced across his face. "Perhaps it's *rollin'* because you're still drunk."

She glanced at the sparkling brandy decanter on the sideboard and decided to swear off liquor for the rest of her life. Nothing was worth this agony.

Roarke nodded at the rumpled covers. "The chamber pot is under the bed," he added flatly.

She rushed forward, retrieved the clean chamber pot, and tossed up the remains of her last meal in Boston. With a groan, she shoved away the receptacle and crawled onto the bed. A bitter taste coated her tongue, and tears oozed from her eyes; her stomach pitched violently. "Take me back," she ordered in a strangled voice. "Turn this rollin', buckin' prison around and take me back to Boston this second!"

He stood, his eyes frosty. "I can't do that, lass. I've lost too much time already. I have important business to attend to in Scotland."

She clenched her fists and struggled up, but another wave of nausea flattened her on the pillow.

Observing her with cool detachment, Roarke puffed away on his cheroot. "God Almighty, I'm glad I'm not you today. The sky is clear, but the wind is up. Even some of the seasoned hands are sick. With your brandy head and the rough water, you're in for a hard time."

In truth, she felt like dying, but she hoisted up enough strength to say, "No, it's you who'll be in for a hard time, Roarke MacLaren, 'cause soon as I'm well enough, I'm goin' to kill you, you vile pirate!"

He chuckled deeply and tapped the ashes from his cheroot. "Vile pirate, is it? You know, I rather like that phrase. It's very colorful."

"It's the truth. That's what you are, ain't it—*Captain Rakehell?*"

A surprised look crossed his face and he slowly approached the bed.

She gazed at the muscle throbbing in his jaw. "Why didn't you tell me you were the terror of the seven seas?" she demanded.

"Who told you I am Captain Rakehell?" he muttered, taking a seat on the bed.

"Who else? Colonel Johnathan Blackhurst."

"When?"

"Yesterday afternoon. He came to Aunt Pert's house with his little notebook. He said it's jest chock-full of stuff about you. He says he was on one of them men-of-war you tangled with, and you caused him to lose his eye. He recognized your distinctive voice, as he calls it, at the ball." She watched his face take on a serious expression as he absorbed the information. "He told me you had a fabulous price on your head."

"And you came here last night to warn me?" he asked, trailing a lean finger along her cheek.

"Yes, God help me, I did," she replied, brushing away his hand. "And it's the biggest mistake I ever made!" Raising her head, she looked toward the windows and peered at the frothy sea. "This is how you repay me, by kidnappin' me!"

Roarke stood and laughed heartily. "What a great joke. When Blackhurst didn't search me out after the costume ball, I thought he had believed that I *was* Lieutenant Colin McCrann. I knew he wouldn't report our little scuffle, for he wouldn't want anyone to know he had been bested. When I left port last night, I had no idea he was ready to close in."

"I wish I'd brought him with me! If I could, I'd turn you in myself," she snapped. "You lied to me three times. In the mountains. In Williamsburg. And in Boston."

He paced to the bright windows and turned about, fixing her with a hard look. "I didn't lie. I just didn't reveal everything about myself."

"Oh no! You said, 'The American cause doesn't need Roarke MacLaren, lass. I'm a damn poor shot, I've got a bad leg, and I limp when it rains.' "

He chuckled. "I had to put you off someway. You were after me every minute about your cause. If I'd listened to you, I'd be singing 'Yankee Doodle' and shelling Boston Harbor, wouldn't I?"

With a tremendous effort, she raised herself up on one elbow. Light poured in the window and burnished his manly face. "Oh, you were clever as a tree full of owls, weren't you?" she stated acidly. "While I was spillin' my guts to you like some looby, you kept back a whole chunk of your life."

"Just a chunk."

"But what a big ol' colorful chunk it was, Captain Rakehell!'' At that moment she ached to cram the cheroot down his throat. ''What about poor Aunt Pert, left all by herself now?''

''I'm sure she has many friends to take care of her needs.''

''But she'll be lonesome!''

''You can write her every day if you want.'' A smile brushed his lips as he strolled back to the bed and leaned over her. ''You know, lass, we have a strange plant in Scotland I've been meaning to tell you about.''

She rolled her eyes. ''What in thunderation does that have to do with what we're talkin' about?''

''Quite a bit. It's a weedy thing called the *woman's tongue.* It has wee pods full of dry seeds which rattle continuously in the wind.''

Her hand shot up, but his long fingers clasped her wrist.

''If I live to be nine hundred years old,'' she ground out between clenched teeth, ''I'll never forgive you for takin' me away from my cause jest when the Sons of Liberty needed me the most!''

''I saved your neck, you hardheaded hellion,'' he snapped, releasing her wrist and walking away. ''One more week in Boston and Blackhurst would have connected you with the rebels and slapped you in prison. Shortly afterwards you would have been hung!''

She slid from the bed and staggered over to him, clutching the back of a chair to brace herself against the ship's roll. Nausea twisted through her, but it was nothing compared to the rage she felt at that moment. ''I would have been hung happy then. My rebellion means more than anythin' in the world to me!''

He pierced her with a keen stare. ''Damn your rebellion, lass! This is a Scottish ship. I am a Scottish privateer, and we'll soon be on Scottish soil.

From now on, the only rebellions we'll be discussing are Scottish rebellions!"

"Scottish rebellions? What in the world are you talkin' about?"

A dark look veiled his face. "It was just an expression. A figure of speech." Angrily he banged a series of folding shutters over the windows, dimming the room.

Then, with a stony face, he stalked from the cabin.

The rest of that day and night, Sassy thought she would die. She was as sick and weak as a newborn kitten. The ship rolled and pitched in the choppy waves while she dozed in fitful snatches, dreaming of Blackhurst and his promise to find and punish her. Once, when she awoke to the sea's roar against the hull, she considered finding Roarke and again demanding he return her to port. But when she lifted her head, another wave of nausea crumpled her against the pillows.

Late in the night someone held a cup to her lips and commanded, "Drink," but the darkness blotted out the face. There were mumbled words, the scent of cigar smoke, and gentle hands on her body. Afterward she slept deeply and dreamlessly.

On the morning of the second day the sun's warmth awakened her; when she blinked, light sparkled into her eyes—someone had opened the shutters. She noticed the waves had stilled and the ship rocked peacefully like a hammock in a gentle breeze. New hope buoyed her spirits until she discovered, with some shock, that someone had taken off her gown and dressed her in a long shirt. Enraged, she sat up. Merciful heavens, all she had on was pantalets and the loosely woven shirt! What had happened to her corset and underskirts and gown?

Smelling sandalwood, she noticed that Roarke's

Chinese sea chest stood open. The distinctive aroma of cigar smoke lingered on her tumbled bedding. Yes, someone had violated her privacy while she slept—undoubtedly the infamous Captain Rakehell himself. She rubbed her temples, waiting for her numb brain to thaw out; obviously he had drugged her and removed her gown while she lay helpless. Fresh anger stirred inside her. How dare he take such liberties when she was too sick to utter a word of protest. She'd just get up, find him, and give him a piece of her mind!

Feeling shaky, she slid from the warm bed—just then, there was a knock on the door. In a flash, she climbed back onto the mattress, shot under the bedding, and jerked the sheet up to her chin. "Roarke MacLaren, you stay out of here until I get my clothes on!"

The door creaked open and Sassy reached for an expensive Chinese vase at her bedside. She was about to throw it across the cabin when an old man entered, accompanied by a small Scottish terrier. Dressed in a tam-o'-shanter, a striped jersey, and white duck pants, the man carried a tray of food whose pungent aroma made her somewhat nauseous. She squinted at him, realizing it was Duncan, the wiry seaman who had grabbed her arm when she had first slipped aboard the packet. "Oh, it's . . . you," she stammered, replacing the vase.

A smile split his leathery face and he clicked the door shut. "Aye, it's me." His embarrassed gaze moved over her. "I owe ye an apology, lassie. I dinna' know ye were Master Roarke's lady when ye boarded the *Sea Witch.*"

"I ain't!" She raised up a bit. "Did he tell you that? Why, I ought to—"

"Hold on, lassie," he ordered. He walked across the room, the dog obediently trailing his heels. "Ye'll make yerself sicker. I have food for ye."

She glanced at the tray. "I . . . I don't think I can eat yet."

"Aye, ye can and ye will." He placed the tray on the bedside table and pulled up a chair. When he snapped his fingers, the little terrier curled up at his fet. "Are ye feelin' better?" Duncan asked, running a concerned gaze over her.

"A . . . little." She traced her fingers over the satiny counterpane, then nervously tugged it higher.

"Easy, lass. Ye canna' be worryin' what I'm thinkin' now," he advised, taking a seat. "It was me who undressed you . . . an' gave ye the potion, too."

"You?"

"Aye. Ye have no reason for embarrassment. I do the doctorin' on this packet. I've set bones and sewed up wounds, and God help me, I even took off a poor devil's leg once."

She stared at him, reassessing him.

"I know what ye're thinkin'. Ye're thinkin' I look like a broken-down seaman, and that's what I am. But I can still sing a chantey and doctor the crew. That's what Master Roarke keeps me for."

"My gown . . ." she began.

He patted her arm with his rough hand. "Whisht! Now, jest dinna' be worryin' about that, lassie. Master Roarke bade me doctor ye . . . Ye was sufferin' terrible last night." He pointed at the desk where blackened Virginia twists littered a tray. "He sat right there and watched ye half the night himself. Then he came and woke me from a sound sleep to mix up some potion fer ye. It's a rest medicine, it is."

Sassy liked the old seaman immediately. His homespun ways reminded her of her own father. And she liked his dog. Leaning over the side of the bed, she patted the terrier's black head.

"The gown and the corset was bindin' ye, lassie,'' Duncan went on. ''I thought ye'd rest better if ye could move around a bit. Everythin' is there,'' he added, pointing to a brass-trimmed mahogany wardrobe.

Her gaze shot to the polished wardrobe, then back to his face. ''Was . . . was Roarke here when you . . . ?'' She trailed off, blushing.

''When I undressed ye? Aye, he was. Ye were fightin' us both in yer sleep till the potion took hold, then ye was limber as a rag.''

She had been drugged and stripped bare above the waistline while she was helpless; just thinking about it heated her face with humiliation. Yet another offense she'd add to Captain Rakehell's long list of sins.

Duncan laughed and rubbed his nose. ''Master Roarke said ye was rough as any Highlander he'd ever fought.'' Still chuckling, he uncovered a bowl of something that looked like cornmeal mush. Beside it lay cold sliced pork.

Duncan spooned up some of the mush. ''Nay, dinna' be lookin' hard at what I brought ye. 'Tis the best thing fer a sick stomach. That and the cold, salty meat. It'll put strength in yer blood.'' He swung the spoon to her lips and raised his bushy brows.

Gradually she sat up and let him feed her. The creamy mush tasted salty and good against her tongue. After she had swallowed the first bite, she smiled and said, ''Why, that ain't too bad. It kind of reminds me of corn pone afore it's cooked.''

Duncan chuckled, and kept patiently feeding her a few bites at a time.

Between mouthfuls she asked, ''You always call Roarke *master* instead of *captain*. Can you tell me why?''

''Aye, I can. I called him that when he was a boy. His father bein' such a famous laird, it seemed fittin' that I use *master* afore his name.''

"You knew him as a boy?"

He scraped up the last of the mush. "Knew him? I near raised him. The great Laird MacLaren died when the boy was only six. O' course, he spent most of his days learning his books, but whenever he could, he came runnin' to me with his face glowin' like the mornin' sun . . . and we would sail." He shook his head and laughed. "What a braw lad he was. He had sailin' in his blood, he did. That's where his heart is, the sea and Scotland."

Sassy mulled over the information. "Do folks really call him Captain Rakehell?"

Duncan nodded. "Aye, they do. And the name is well earned. He's twisted the tail o' the English lion more than once."

"The British say he's a pirate."

"Nay, Master Roarke is no freebooter. He's a privateer who uses letters of marque."

"What's a letter of marque?"

The old man set the bowl down and sighed. For a moment he rubbed his temple as if he was choosing his words carefully, then he leaned forward again. "When countries is fightin' each other, they all offer letters of marque . . . The English do it, too," he explained. "A letter gives a captain the right to seize enemy ships. The captain turns over the captured ship and a percentage o' the cargo to the country that issued the letter—but he keeps the rest of the cargo."

Sassy ate some of the tangy pork and tossed a bit to the dog. "It sounds like piracy to me," she said with a full mouth.

"Nay, pirates honor no man, but privateers abide by articles o' war."

She ate more of the meat and considered his words.

"Privateerin' is a powerful quick way to make money," Duncan added at length.

"I suppose so. This is the fanciest place I've ever slept in." She felt somewhat better now that she knew Roarke's exploits had been legal, but she still couldn't understand why he wanted to amass so much money.

Duncan caressed the dog's head. "I thought I'd leave Tam with ye while ye're gettin' better. She's a gentle-natured dog and fine company. And I can tell she already likes ye."

"I never thought of anybody carryin' a dog on a ship."

"Aye, Tam's a ratter, and a fine one, too. Nary a mouse gets by her sharp nose."

Sassy ruffled Tam's ears, and the terrier thumped her tail playfully. "I like the idea of havin' some company, and I've been missin' dogs and cats and all kind of critters since I left the mountains."

They both sat quietly while she petted the dog, then she righted herself, and catching Duncan's eyes, said, "Tell me somethin'. Why does Roarke hate England so? And he mentioned something about a Scottish rebellion. When I asked him about it, he turned my question aside. Can you tell me about that?"

A wretched look glazed the old seaman's face. "It's a long story, lassie. Perhaps he'll tell ye himself one day." He stood and walked to Roarke's books, then chose one and brought it to the bed. "While ye're gettin' better, ye might take a look at this. It'll help ye understand him better."

Sassy glanced at a red-and-gold-bound history of Scotland, then laughed. "Why should I want to know about Scotland? I'm from Virginia, from the colonies." She tossed the heavy book at the foot of the bed. "And that's where I'm goin' back to as soon as I get loose from Captain Rakehell."

Duncan signaled his dog to stay, then went to the door and opened it. As he left, he glanced back over his shoulder and sighed. " 'Tis a pity ye have no hunger to read about yer new home."

"New home?"

Duncan paused for a moment. "Aye, Master Roarke is a fearfully determined man, ye know." He left, closing the door behind him.

Chapter 13

Feeling better as the day progressed, Sassy got up that afternoon and played with Tam, then she picked up the history of Scotland and peeked between its covers. After listening for footsteps in the stairwell and positioning the book where she could easily hide it, she turned the cover and began to read. As minutes passed, she became absorbed in the words. From what she could tell, the Scots were a warlike, clannish people who often fought among themselves—just like the families in the Blue Ridge Mountains. She still wondered about this mysterious rebellion Roarke had mentioned, but from the look on his face, she knew he would never answer her questions.

Lost in the book, she jumped when someone creaked open the cabin door.

Thinking it was Roarke, she shoved the book aside, but before she could hide the volume, an old man ambled in with a tray of food. The years hung on his stooped shoulders like a heavy weight, and he wore ragged clothes; a cowlick sprouted from his head. Somewhat embarrassed, he set down the tray and touched his silvery forelock. "I be Old Angus, missy. Duncan was busy, so I brung yer food." His faded eyes strayed to the book. "What . . . what are ye readin'?"

"Jest a book about Scotland. Do you like to read?"

He chuckled and shuffled his cracked boots against the floor. "I wish I could," he uttered in a roughened voice. "I always wanted to, but dinna' have a soul to teach me."

Sassy's heart went out to him. "Well, you have someone to teach you now."

His ruddy face glowed with joy. "Ye will? Ye'll teach me?"

"Is a tomater red? Sure I'll teach you." With a smile, she stood and snapped the heavy history book shut. "Come back when you can spare a minute. Before we get to Scotland, I'll have you makin' out words real good."

He tugged his forelock again and backed away. "Oh, thankee, miss. Thankee kindly," he babbled, closing the door behind him.

Later, when Duncan came to walk Tam, she asked him about Old Angus.

He shrugged and sighed. "He came to Master Roarke while we was docked in Boston, beggin' to sign on fer the journey to Scotland. He said he wanted to go home and die among his kin. O' course, the old man's sailin' days are over, but Master Roarke, havin' such a kind heart, he hired him aboard out o' pity."

After Duncan left, she pondered what he had told her, wondering if Roarke MacLaren actually had a heart after all. She flopped down on the bed. No, she thought, Roarke might have a sentimental streak for his fellow Scots, but when it came to women, he had a right smart way to go!

That evening Duncan presented her with a sailor's jersey, belt, and trousers, saying her dress was unsuitable for going about the deck. By now Sassy burned to ask him questions about Roarke. Where was he? What was he doing? Why hadn't he returned to his own cabin? But pride stilled her tongue. Duncan removed several items—charts, shirts and breeches, cheroots—every time he left the cabin. Obviously the articles were for his beloved Master Roarke.

The next day at breakfast she stood with Tam by the bowed windows, watching the churning wake. Pleased to hear footsteps, she whirled as Duncan entered the cabin, whistling a tune.

" 'Pon my word, ye're the bonniest sailor I've ever seen, lass!" He plunked down the tray and ran his eyes over her loose hair and body, now encased in the jersey and wide-legged trousers.

She smiled at her new friend, then took a seat at the desk to eat. As she sat down, she felt her treasure sack in her pocket; just knowing it was there made her glow with contentment.

"Ye'd feel better if ye stirred about, lass. It's a glorious day atop. The sea has smoothed out, and the air is fine as wine."

With a disinterested shrug, she lifted a metal cover from her plate and sighed.

Duncan braced his hands on the desk and caught her eye. "Look here, lass, ye canna' avoid him forever. Eat, then go atop. Master Rourke is busy now anyway."

"Thanks. I'll think about it."

"That's my bonnie lassie, see that ye do," he advised, leaving the cabin with Tam at his heels.

Sassy considered the old sailor's words while she ate her breakfast. He was right. She couldn't avoid Roarke for the whole voyage. And why should she *want* to avoid him? By cracky, didn't she have a few words to say to him now that she wasn't as sick as a dog? Darn right she did! With a clang, she slammed the metal cover in place, then rose and dusted off her hands. Pirate or privateer or whatever the devil he was, Roarke MacLaren would find he couldn't whisk her from one country to the next without her consent and expect her to meekly accept it.

As she left the cabin and climbed the narrow stairs, a gust of fresh air brought the scent of the sea and the odor of fresh paint. When she emerged on deck, sunlight dazzled her eyes and great rattling sounds pounded against her ears. Squinting, she saw that the rigging was swarming with sailors, each dressed much like herself in striped jerseys and duck pants. Some of the men shinnied up taunt ropes, while others hung over the yardarms, clutching lacings. Bone white against the deep blue sky, sails ripped from their fingers and exploded into the wind.

She gazed above the mizzenmast and spotted a blue flag with a white cross fluttering in the salty breeze. She knew it was the cross of Saint Andrew and represented Scotland and Scottish pride. Evidently now that Roarke was away from Boston, he had decided to haul down the Union Jack and fly his true colors.

As soon as the sailors spotted her, they whistled and shouted and ogled her openly.

Suddenly strong fingers pressed into her shoulder. With a gasp, she whirled to face Roarke. The rascal looked wonderful in snug breeches and a flowing buccaneer shirt, a scarlet kerchief at his throat. The silky shirt billowed over his broad chest, and his tied-back hair glistened in the clear morning light.

''Stay out of the way,'' he ordered, pulling her to his side. ''We're changing tack.''

As the ship rolled, she stumbled and clutched his hardened arm. ''The sailors are on the riggin'. I ain't in the way,'' she said.

Ignoring her, he cupped his hands and boomed out, ''Reef out the royals, and put your backs to it!'' Instantly the men scurried to the very top of the mizzenmast, and soon the sail popped out to the wind, cracking like a gun. When the operation was completed, Roarke glared down at her like a malevolent giant, and clenching her arm, steered her toward the wheel.

She rushed along, hopping over coils of rope, trying to match his long strides. "Lemme be! Turn my arm loose, you big looby. I ain't some idjit you can march around like I ain't got good sense!"

"Come on, shake a leg."

"You better take me back to Boston this second, you . . . you Bluebeard!"

He shot her a crooked smile. "You're wasting your breath, lass."

She pulled away and shook her finger at him. "Did you know, I'm goin' to have you arrested for kidnappin' me the minute this ship docks? I think the British would be *real* interested in knowin' about Captain Rakehell's latest crime."

He yanked her forward. "I don't care what you think. Neither does anyone else."

She sucked in her breath and ground her teeth, but by that time, they were already at the wheel.

Roarke nodded at the sandy-haired first mate. "I'll take over now, Mr. Cameron."

The mate touched a finger to his cap and respectfully backed away, but not before moving his gaze over Sassy. Roarke glowered at the man, then took the wheel in his large hand and parked Sassy by his side. "Where in the devil did you get that outrageous outfit?" he demanded, staring at her bosom. "The jersey fits like a second skin."

"Duncan gave me these clothes," she shot back, raising her chin.

"I should have known. I suppose you have him dancing to your tune now?"

"Don't say anythin' against Duncan! He's the only person who's been nice to me since you stole me away onto this floatin' torture rack!"

He scanned her snug attire again, looking as sour

as a green peach. "Don't you know not to come on deck while we're changing tack? One look at you and some mother's son will fall from the top gallant yardarm."

What was wrong with the man now? Did he think she had graduated from a naval academy? She stamped her foot. "I'd 'preshate it iffin you'd tell me what you're talkin' about!"

Roarke sighed heavily and turned the big wheel. "Changing tack is an intricate operation, and the men have to have their wits about them. You might have distracted them and caused an accident."

Well, wasn't he full of himself, she thought sarcastically. Somehow he always managed to make everything that went wrong seem like it was her fault; anger blazed down to her toes. Fine. Jest let him mess with her—she'd fight him like a mad shrew with a toothache. "What are you goin' to do if I make another mistake, Captain Rakehell? Tie me spread-eagle to the riggin' till sundown or put me on half rations for ten days?"

His face remained rock-hard.

She narrowed her eyes at him. "Consarn it! What in the hell is wrong with you, anyway? You look like you've been eatin' rocks for supper and bugs for dessert."

He threw her another sour glance. "Nothing is wrong with me that a little sleep wouldn't cure. Since you decided to become sick in my quarters, I've been sleeping in Duncan's cabin—in a hammock." He raked her with a dark glower. "Lord, the man snores like a bear with a stopped-up nose."

Amusement brimmed up inside her. So that's where he'd been while she occupied his soft bed. "He snores worse than me?" she asked with false sympathy. "Why, you must really be sufferin'." Then she shot a hot gaze over his brawny physique, filling it with as much contempt as she could muster. "I'd thought an old buccaneer like you could sleep on a rock pile."

"I can. But I choose to sleep in my own bed, and that's where I'm sleeping tonight!"

"By goonies, not with me, you ain't!"

"Oh yes, I am, lass! You can sleep with me or in the fo'c'sle with all those lusty hands who were whistling from the yardarms."

"Duncan will—"

"No, he won't!" he cut her off. "I personally ripped that hammock down, and I'm having a long talk with Duncan this afternoon. He's babied you long enough." He traced a finger along her chin and smiled wickedly. "Now that you're feeling better, I'm claiming my bed—and you."

She shrugged from his hand and backed up, stumbling in her haste to get away.

He turned and shouted at her as she hurried across the deck. "We're having dinner in my cabin at eight sharp, and later we're going to bed. Do you understand!"

She spun around, clenching her hands. "You don't have to beller at me like some addled bull," she snapped back. "I understand you. I understand you're a stuck-up, muleheaded, stiff-necked Scottish bastard that don't know 'Come here' from 'Sic 'em'!"

She thundered down the stairwell, an idea forming in her mind. Her hand flew to her throat when she nearly collided with Duncan, who was coming up the steps. "Oh, lawzee me, there you are! Thank God I found you. I need your help," she said.

He looked puzzled. "Och . . . what is it, lassie?"

She grinned, feeling a warm, satisfied glow wash away her anxiety. "Where can we find some wood . . . and a hammer, and some big nails?"

At exactly eight that evening the steward placed several covered dishes and a bottle of wine on the table, then, with questioning eyes, looked at his captain. Roarke nodded. "You may leave now, lad. We will serve ourselves."

The laird of Donkinny Castle was freshly bathed and shaved, and a damp forelock flopped above his glittering eyes. Like an Oriental emperor, he sat at table in a loose Chinese robe of red silk which revealed a wedge of his hair-covered chest and his muscled forearms. A whale-oil lamp swung above the table while he uncovered the dishes, inspecting each one.

He smiled at the pungent aromas of braised chicken, savory potatoes, and buttery vegetables. "The cook has outdone himself. We'll have a fine meal," he added as he uncorked the wine.

Like a prisoner coming to her execution, Sassy had elaborately arranged her hair and dressed in her pink silk gown with ruching and ruffles. Still she felt drab in comparison to Roarke.

As the steward picked up the tray, she stared at her plate and listened to the waves slap against the hull; when she heard the steward close the cabin door, she snapped out her napkin and waited for more instructions. She knew there had to be more . . . because for the last twenty minutes Roarke had lectured her about her behavior aboard the *Sea Witch*. "You will stay in this cabin until nine every morning," he had said. "You will wear loose, modest clothing on deck. You will immediately go below when the hands are changing tack."

She had listened to *you will do this* and *you will do that* until she thought she would burst. With a sly smile she glanced at his bed, now hidden by the closed brocade drapes. Only one thing kept her from losing her temper—the surprise Captain High and Mighty Rakehell would find when he finally saw the bed!

Roarke heeped her plate, then started eating.

As Sassy tasted the well-cooked food, she looked over her elegant place setting. ''I suppose you bought this fine china with your privateerin' money, *Captain Rakehell?''*

He regarded her coolly. ''No. As a matter of fact, I liberated it from one of King George's flagships.'' He handed her a filled wineglass and smiled broadly. ''With the king's compliments, my lady.''

''Seems to me all this privateerin' and piratin' and buccaneerin' kind of run together. Why'd you get into privateerin' anyway?''

A dark look crossed his face. ''Money, naturally.''

She nodded, but suspected he still hadn't told her everything about his motives. ''Yes, I'll bet there are lots of women ready to jump into bed with a rich scalawag like you.''

''Of course, I keep four mistresses in every port,'' he replied in a sarcastic tone. He sighed and swirled the wine in his glass. ''But for some reason, I seem to be attracted to you. I can't understand it, because you're obviously all wrong for me.''

She slapped down her fork. ''Well, you're sure 'nuf wrong for me!''

''You'd turn down the advances of Captain Rakehell, your hero?''

''Captain Rakehell *was* my hero—until I found out he's you. You think you're the greatest thing since sour mash whiskey, don't you? Well, if you were the last man in the world, I wouldn't come near you. I can't *wait* to get off this ship.''

Roarke was silent for a moment, then he shook his finger at her. ''Do you know you're your own worst enemy?''

She raised a brow and dragged her gaze over him. ''You want to bet on that?''

He tossed his napkin on the table and leaned forward. ''You need a lot of taking in hand, lass.''

His voice was as sharp as slivered glass. "And I'd like to give you a few words of advice."

She burst out laughing and widened her eyes. "Oh, this is goin' to be as good as possom gravy. The King of the Pirates is goin' to give *me* advice on good behavior. That's just what I need. I ain't had any advice in the last thirty seconds."

Roarke's eyes flashed with anger. "*You*, young miss, ought to be the privateer. Your tongue's as sharp as any saber I ever lifted." His fiery eyes told her their conversation was over.

They ate the rest of the sumptuous meal in silence, the noise of their scraping forks and the crashing sea the only sounds. Sassy's nerves twitched and trembled, and the rich food congealed in her stomach. Sipping water, she gazed at Roarke's stern face. Lord, if their conversation had made him this mad, what would he do when he saw the bed?

Using the tip of a knife, Roarke removed the cork from a bottle of wine; with a dry smile, he poured the liquid into Sassy's crystal glass, then filled his own. "Don't be so sour. Have some wine. I think you understand your sailing orders now."

"Yeah, I understand 'em, all right. What are you goin' to do if I disobey? Keelhaul me or tie me over a cannon and give me twenty lashes?" Earlier in the day, she had planned to be cool and emotionless throughout dinner—but he made it impossible.

He glowered at her over the rim of his wineglass. "Burn me, you're an impertinent wench." He swept his gaze over the cabin, which he'd furnished that afternoon with a makeshift dressing table, complete with a small mirror, combs, and brushes. "What more do you want? I've set up your own corner of the cabin, and the ship's cook does his best to please you." He glanced at his books, then drilled her with another look of disapproval. "You will have nothing to do all day but eat, groom yourself, and read. You're being pampered shamelessly by both Duncan and myself. Is there anything else your ladyship requires?" he ended in a mocking tone.

She shot to her feet. "Yeah. Her ladyship requires her freedom! I ain't some pet bird you can cage up and pacify with caraway seeds. I want to be in Boston, where I can help the Sons of Liberty. I want to carry on Pa's work. I want to hear Samuel Adams and John Hancock." She smacked her fist on the table, rattling the dishes. "I want to be in America, not sailin' to the other side of the world, jailed up in some cabin with orders not to stick my head out the door."

His eyes flinty, Roarke stood. "Why don't we just dispense with the rest of the meal and go straight to bed?" He smiled wickedly. "So I can keep my promise about claiming you."

Lord, here it comes, she thought. This is just what she had been waiting for. She would go along with his orders, because she knew what would happen when they tried to get into the bed. "All right, fine. Let's do jest that."

Thoughtfully, he cocked a brow. "What did you say?"

She kicked off her slippers and pulled pins from her hair. "I said, fine. Let's do jest that. Are you hard of hearin'? Maybe you're jest gettin' teched in your old age?" Whirling about, she presented him with her back. "Here, quit lollygaggin' around and untie these lacin's so I can skin off this dress. We don't want to waste no time!" His warm fingers sent shivers over her body, but she stubbornly ignored them. A few wiggles freed her from the gown, which she kicked aside; then, tugging up her low-cut corset, she stared at his confused face. "Well, don't stand there like a preacher in a whorehouse lookin' like you don't know what to do," she prodded, pulling up her black silk stockings. "Strip off that robe. Do you want to go to bed or jest sit up and talk all night?"

Puzzled, he reached for the belt of his robe . . . just as Duncan burst into the cabin holding some charts. Roarke pushed Sassy behind him and glared at the old man, who instantly lowered his eyes.

"Ye told me to bring these charts."

"Not now, man!"

"I'll be out o' here at once," he stammered, chucking the charts aside and backing from the cabin.

As soon as the door snapped shut, Roarke shed his robe and tossed it over a chair. Sassy's eyes widened at the sight of him. In the way station the light had been dim. Viewing Roarke in a good light . . . in all his naked magnificence . . . was a little more than she had bargained for. Hot blood pounded through her as her gaze drank in his tousled hair, tanned skin, broad shoulders, lean belly . . . A warm, drugging sensation sweeping over her, she quickly averted her eyes . . . but it was too late. Blood stung her cheeks as her gaze crept back for a further inventory; yes, she thought, nature had been *real generous* with him in all departments.

Her heart fluttered as he pulled her into his arms and seized her lips. Just as she expected, her fingers itched to caress his hair-covered chest and muscled shoulders, and her hands ached to smooth over his slim hips—but she reined in her feelings. She sternly resisted the emotions that threatened to overpower her, and coolly wrapped her arms around him. Damn it anyway! She would show him he couldn't soften her resolve with his skilled touch.

When Roarke scooped her into his arms, she closed her eyes and, trying to look demure, prayed for strength. For a moment she thought she might faint; but using all her discipline, she flicked open one eye and watched his face.

Gently he broke the kiss, then he reached out to rip back the bed curtains. She bit the inside of her cheeks to keep from laughing, for at that moment the look on his stricken face was worth twenty lashes. Following his hot gaze, she stared at the mattress, where, with Duncan's help, she had nailed a high board down the middle of the bed. At both ends the plank was nailed to horizontal boards, which in turn were secured to the head-board and footboard.

As Roarke relaxed his grip, she slid from his arms, bounced off the edge of the mattress, and landed on the floor. Overcome with a fit of giggles, she sprawled on her back, watching him glower at the divided mattress as if it were a five-headed flame-breathing dragon. His eyes sparking fire, he whirled, snatched up the Chinese robe, and shrugged it on. "You couldn't have managed this by yourself. And I know who helped you." Clenching one hand, he strode to the door, wrenched it open, and bellowed up the stairwell, "Duncan MacPhee, I swear by all that's holy, I'm going to keelhaul you!"

Chapter 14

Roarke turned and pointed a finger at Sassy. "I'll be back to deal with you later," he said, and slammed the door behind him.

Still chuckling, Sassy got up and put on her seaman's clothes; she had just sat down in a leather chair when Roarke returned with an ax and a hammer.

He strode across the cabin and began to chop the partition from the bed. Sassy watched with pleasure. As the bosun piped the early night watch, she sat cleaning her fingernails with a knife and listening to the *whack* of the chopping ax and the *ping* of the flying wood chips as they shot across the room. The longer he worked, the angrier Roarke became.

Cursing under his breath, he tossed away the ax and picked up a hammer. Thirty minutes later, he pulled out the last of the long nails with a screech and removed the device fixed to the headboard. He glowered at Sassy and traced his fingers over the nail holes. "I suppose you realize you and Duncan ruined a fine piece of furniture."

Secretly she regretted the damage to the bed, but she had no intention of admitting it. Without looking up, she replied, "Buy another one, Captain

Rakehell. We both know you've got enough money to burn a wet mule."

Roarke turned to face her. "You little hellion! Don't you know a few planks of wood won't stop me if I want to take you?"

"I've dealt with your kind before," Sassy said, rising from the chair. "You'll have to hog-tie me first, you scoundrel, 'cause I plan on puttin' up a mighty battle."

Roarke tossed the hammer aside. "You keep that tongue of yours going at a murderous rate, don't you?"

"Of course I do. It's my only weapon against you." She pointed the little knife at him to emphasize her words. "Is lovemaking all you ever think about? Ain't there a ship somewhere that needs pillagin'?"

He flashed her a grin. "What's wrong, lass?" he asked. "Are you still afraid of me, bloody rogue that I am?"

She cocked her brow. "Why should I be afraid of you? You've already kidnapped me and ruined my life. What else can you do to me?"

A bitter smile stole over his lips. "Quite a lot, actually. A captain has complete authority aboard his ship. If you're interfering with the smooth operation of this vessel—and I'd say you've definitely been an interference—the articles of war say I can tie you, bind you, flog you, even keelhaul you."

"Are you sure this ship ain't goin' to hell instead of Scotland?" she said, pointing the knife at him again.

He strode toward her. With a quick move, he twisted the knife from her hand and threw it on the table. "It's only fair that you get a taste of what you've given me. Compared to dealing with you, pillaging ships is child's play. Why do you persist in plaguing me with your stubbornness?"

"Why do younguns like to wiggle their toes in the mud? Jest because it's so much fun."

He pulled on his shirt, trousers, and boots, then turned to her. "I'm going on deck. The air is getting too oppressive in here." With that, he stormed from the cabin.

Sassy fell into the chair. How would she ever manage to live with him after this? she wondered. She glanced at the mangled bed, picturing him on deck harassing some hapless seaman unlucky enough to be awake.

And what would the sleeping arrangements be now? She considered sleeping in Duncan's cabin, then remembered how he snored. Realizing she had to share a cabin with Roarke or sleep on the open deck, she decided in favor of having a roof over her head. Well, she might have to share his cabin, but she certainly didn't have to get close to him!

An idea forming, Sassy left the cabin. A short time later, she returned dragging an old mattress Duncan had taken from the fo'c'sle. Throwing down the mattress far away from Roarke's bed, she claimed a piece of the floor. She knew the sight of the mattress would enrage Roarke, and that he would probably chastise Duncan again, but she had no choice.

They would have to work out an agreement about who occupied the cabin at certain times. She could always pretend to be asleep when he came in after making his last rounds on deck.

With a weary sigh, she lay down on the coarse mattress and tried to rest.

Three hours later, Sassy heard the bosun pipe the late night watch; after restlessly tossing and turning, she had found sleep wouldn't come. As she lay on the hard mattress, she thought of the hot words she and Roarke had exchanged. She knew that putting the partition in the bed had been a childish prank, but it had given her a measure of satisfaction and control over her fate.

She wondered if she would ever tell Roarke about the miscarriage. The memory seemed too private and painful to pass from her lips. Her mind spinning, she sat up and told herself she needed some fresh air. How could she sleep with her thoughts in such turmoil?

Wiping a sleeve across her damp brow, she leaned out the open windows where a moist warmth rode the stirring breeze. Idly she rose and went to the velvet window seat, and watched moonlight glimmer across the ship's wake. Over the sound of the churning water, a sea chantey and concertina music came to her from the deck.

Eventually curiosity got the better of her.

She left the cabin and jogged up the stairwell. On deck, the mingled scents of salt air, hemp, and tar came to her. Moonlight silvered the calm sea, and glittering stars studded the sky. Purplish clouds rode low on the distant horizon.

The sound of a rustling sail prompted her to look upward. A gentle breeze now blew from the west, shaking the slack canvas overhead, and toward the bow, shadowy sails were moving in the freshening wind. The cool air felt good against her face as she strolled along the deck, following the music.

The aroma of tobacco made her heart race. She glanced at the rail where a tall figure stood smoking a cheroot. She turned to go back, but a deep voice stopped her. "What are you doing on the deck at this hour?"

She stood for a moment, then turned, staring at Roarke. For some strange reason, she was fascinated with the way his white shirt shone in the darkness; the way the moonlight played on his tied-back hair. Her breath caught in her throat as soft moonbeams whispered over his craggy face;

then, despite her misgivings, a powerful need pulled her toward him. "I . . . I couldn't sleep," she murmured at last.

He took a long draw from his cheroot. "Neither could I," he admitted, raking her with a knowing glance. "It seems arguments do little to promote sleep."

After the argument they'd had, she was surprised they could converse so freely. Evidently the sea air had cooled his anger, as it had hers.

At last he nodded at the sea. "Have you ever seen dolphins?"

She felt hypnotized by the quiet strength stamped on his features and found it hard to speak. "No . . . no, I ain't," she muttered.

He smiled. "I've been watching them for thirty minutes. A school is following the ship."

She approached the rail and looked down; large, silvery forms streaked beside the *Sea Witch*, playfully leaping from the water. Without speaking, she and Roarke stood by the rail and watched the racing dolphins. Music and laughter wafted on the breeze, and in the darkness below, waves slapped the hull. The scent of Roarke's cheroot warmed her senses and relaxed her tense muscles; despite her lingering anger, just being near him made her glow with sensuality.

Although he was watching the dolphins, she sensed his mind was thousands of miles away . . . At last she stole a look at him. "What are you thinkin' about?" she asked softly.

"I was thinking of Scotland. We'll be there before you know it."

She sighed heavily. "That's what I'm afraid of."

He chuckled. "Cheer up . . . Scotland's a beautiful country. At harvesttime the lowland grain fields gleam golden in the sun, and near the coast, the purple heather meets the sea and dazzles the eye."

She noted how his eyes took on a faraway look as he spoke. Had a man ever been so in love with his country?

"In the Highlands," he went on, "there are crofters' farms and fishing villages almost hidden beneath the cliffs." He regarded her keenly. "But the thing that stands out in my mind are the hills and the locks. There are hills upon hills in the Highlands—and rushing rivers. The mountain burns crash down and foam through gorges full of leaping salmon. And in the straths, they meander wide and deep over grassy land dotted with white sheep."

Spellbound, she listened intently to everything he was saying. The moonlight spilled over his hardened face, highlighting the lines about his eyes and mouth—yet his words were soft and gentle. Could this man with the dreamy look be the notorious Captain Rakehell?

He tossed his cheroot into the sea and smiled at her. "And the old people talk about the kelpies."

"The kelpies?"

"Aye . . . water spirits. They come out at twilight to help or hinder mankind as they see fit."

"You sound like a poet when you talk about Scotland. Are all Scots so in love with their land?"

"Aye, I suppose they are." He studied her face for a moment, then gently took her into his arms. Her heart fluttered wildly like a bird caught in a trap, but she relaxed against him. As she nestled in his arms, the feel of his hard body stirred her desire, and she curled her arms around his neck. *This is madness,* she thought, struggling with her emotions. She had fought his advances, first by avoiding him, then by taunting him, and finally by building the partition in the bed. Yet, as deep passion swept through her, she knew how badly she wanted to be in his arms.

Before she could bat her eyes, his lips found hers, skittering fire over her mouth. Pulling her closer, he lovingly cupped her hips and trailed his fingers over her thighs. With a soft groan, he parted her mouth and traced the tender inner surface of her lips, then his hand was at her breast, teasing her nipple through her clothes. As he smoothed his hand over her swelling curves, every inch of her skin tingled with desire. He was a master, she thought, at whipping her senses to a fever pitch. When he fully entered her mouth, his kiss became more insistent and she ached to quench the flames racing over her body. His wandering fingers ignited a fire in her abdomen, making her shudder with longing. She was floating . . . spinning . . . drifting.

Slowly he raised his lips and murmured against her ear, "Why are you resisting me, lass? It's the first time a woman ever has."

His words settled on her as gently as a snowflake. At the same time they chilled her heart. Drawing back a bit, she studied his dark features. Even as desire glowed through her like warm wine, she said, "How can you ask that when you thought so little of me that you seduced me in the way station and then abandoned me in Williamsburg?"

As she voiced his actions, new anger swirled within her. Besides abandoning her, he had violated her freedom, he had no respect for her cause, and he had treated her like a convict aboard his ship. She eased back even further; his eyes flickered with an erotic warmth that spoke volumes. "I shouldn't have walked over here," she blurted out. "This is jest what I thought you'd do."

He gave a roguish grin. "I'm a vile pirate, remember? I have no morals where women are concerned." Resolutely he pulled her against him and again covered her mouth with his.

Lord, it was happening just as it had a moment ago. Her joints felt weak and her legs were trembling and her heart was hammering out of control. With a stab of fear, she realized she would submit to him in a matter of minutes, then would hate herself for it later. No, she told herself. She would *not* submit to him again. Weak with emotion, she pulled free from Roarke's arms.

He smiled at her tenderly. "You move away from my arms, but your reaction to my kisses proves you're still attracted to me."

Standing near the rail, she watched the waves roll toward the horizon. "I'm attracted to you, all right, but I could never trust you. I don't think you'll ever give your heart to any woman—especially one like me." Her words lacked the sharp tone of three hours earlier, but their quietness carried great conviction.

Roarke was silent for a moment before he answered, "As I said, a few boards wouldn't have stopped me if I'd meant to take you, but they did make me realize how unwilling you are to share my bed."

"I'll be puttin' my mattress on the deck tonight," she murmured. "Tomorrow I'll clean out that little storeroom next to Duncan's cabin. It's small, but big enough to sleep in. There's no need for me to disturb your privacy."

"You don't need to do that. We can share the same cabin for sleep, and I won't try to seduce you. I've never ravished a woman against her will."

"No. I've made up my mind." Using all her courage, she glanced at Roarke's shadowed face, then walked away.

The quickening wind cooled her flushed face, but her heart still raced and her legs felt weak. Thank the Lord, she had had the strength to save herself this time. But every time he kissed her, she weakened a little more.

How long could she hold out against him, and what would happen when they reached his castle in Scotland?

Chapter 15

Three weeks later, Sassy and Duncan relaxed at the rail of the *Sea Witch,* bathed in a golden sunset; talking excitedly, they watched the first sight of rocky shoreline as the packet passed the sacred isle of Iona, the burial place of Scottish kings. Then, thirty minutes later, the ship met a fleet of fishing boats leaving on the evening tide, their sails like amber flames in the dying sun. Soon after that, just as Tam joined them at the railing, Sassy spotted what she believed was Scotland.

Duncan pointed at the dim coast. "Aye, there she be, lassie," he announced warmly, confirming her thoughts. "There she be. Scotland!"

At first she could see only a blurry smudge on the horizon. Then, as the *Sea Witch* sailed closer, the smudge became fiords and channels. Gradually huge cliffs took shape, sheltering gleaming sand beneath their sharp outcroppings. Already she realized Scotland was a land of mountains and moors, of glens and rough cliffs, of stark peninsulas and green coves. Neat houses, their windows twinkling in the twilight, ringed the base of the fiord; fishing boats bobbed in the bay; piers loaded with milling people jutted into the harbor.

And above the village of Killieburn—above everything—Donkinny Castle sat on a high hill, brooding over the landscape.

The sight of the castle reminded her of Roarke and the time that had passed since they had stood at the rail together watching the dolphins. She had avoided him as much as possible and refused all his dinner invitations, choosing to eat with Duncan. For the benefit of the crew, she and Roarke had worked out a strained peace, but she could only wonder what would happen at Donkinny Castle. At this very moment her meager belongings rested in a bundle at her feet ready to be taken there, for like it or not, she was penniless and must accept Roarke's hospitality. Just for a while, she fervently hoped.

Now the *Sea Witch* entered the hidden harbor, sheltered on either side by high cliffs. Duncan clasped her arm and grinned. "I can hear the pipes. They're playin' 'Highland Laddie,' to welcome Master Roarke. They saw our sails and the flag of Saint Andrew from the cliffs and knew we were comin' home."

Gently the *Sea Witch* glided into berth like a leaf floating on a smooth pond. With a great splash, her anchor was dropped and men sailed lines ashore. A crowd had gathered on the quay. Old seamen dressed in blue jerseys, stout breeches, and sea boots smiled broadly and shouted jests. Wearing kerchiefs and full skirts, fishwives dabbed at their eyes and waved greetings to sons aboard the ship. Their kilts swinging proudly, a band of Highlanders clenched bagpipes and strutted beside the now-docked packet.

"Everyone acts like they're havin' a celebration," Sassy remarked, studying the cheering crowd. "But I thought it said in the Scottish history book that the kilts and tartan were outlawed by the British."

Duncan chuckled and tugged on his ear. "Aye,

they were. But on an occasion such as this, Highland pride outshines any British law. Besides, Master Roarke often breaks that law just to defy British authority.'' Duncan's eyes sparkled. ''Look how happy they all are. Everyone in Killieburn has a son or nephew or cousin who's aboard this ship. But mostly they're happy because their chieftain is home. Master Roarke will be busy fer a long time judgin' disputes and settlin' arguments. Killieburn depends on its laird, and he's been away for many a moon. Doubtless there will be feastin' and Highland games to celebrate.''

Sassy thought of Roarke's younger brother Kevin and wondered why he hadn't taken care of clan business while the MacLaren chieftain was absent. ''What about Kevin? Doesn't he live at the castle, too?''

''Aye, he does, but he's not cut from the same cloth as his brother. The lad wastes his time moonin' fer the days o' knights and ladies. Nay, Master Kevin canna' take care o' his own affairs, much less the clan's.''

''But shouldn't he be here to meet his brother?''

''Aye. He *should,* but he ain't. He's probably off in the hills, dreamin'.''

As Duncan finished speaking, a carriage rattled over the cobbled quay, and on the deck behind her, Sassy heard commanding footsteps. Roarke put his hand on her shoulder, and she turned, feeling a disturbing warmth in the pit of her stomach. His breeches and buccaneer shirt had been replaced with a fine black velvet suit and snowy stockings; lace hung from his neck and wrists, and ornate buckles glittered on his polished shoes. Dressed in the elegant clothes, he looked every inch the laird of Donkinny. As she met his even gaze, a tingly excitement radiated through her.

''Now that we're anchored, I'm taking you to the castle,'' he said in a voice that brooked no dissent. "I'm leaving Mr. Cameron in charge of beginning the unloading operations."

Stalling, she looked down at her pink silk dress, which had begun to show signs of wear. Anxiety swelled in her heart, and she sought an excuse to delay. "But I . . . I was talkin' to Duncan," she spluttered.

Rourke clasped her arm. "Duncan has work to do. He must pay the seamen who live in the village."

Her throat tightening with emotion, she scanned the old seaman. "When will I see you again?"

"I canna' say, miss. Tam and I will be stayin' on the ship to watch over things while it's in port."

Sighing deeply, Sassy picked up her bundle, then waved good-bye to Old Angus, who was standing near the quarterdeck, coiling a rope.

With slow steps, she walked beside Roarke, leaving the *Sea Witch* with both dread and anticipation.

Ten minutes later the carriage bumped over the steep road, carrying them both toward Donkinny Castle. On one hand, she could scarcely believe it. She, Sassy Adair, the daughter of a backwoods preacher, was going to spend the night at a real castle. On the other hand, she had begun to think of the castle as an ogre's lair. Her mouth dry, she studied Roarke's hard face, then nervously glanced away. They rode in silence until the coach jostled in a rut and Roarke's knee brushed hers.

Her gaze locked with his. His jaw twitched and his eyes flashed. Was he upset about something that had happened aboard ship, or was he just mad at her as usual? What was he thinking . . . What was he planning?

Finally Sassy's natural curiosity and exuberance overcame her fear. Scooting to the edge of the seat, she peeked from the open window. Wildflowers and yellow butterflies dotted the edge of the winding road, and in the meadows, summer's warmth released the scent of heather and wild thyme. In the strong sunset, pines and birch, bent by a prevailing wind, cast long shadows on the rolling hills. She looked back over her shoulder to see green waves pounding the white shore.

Then, without warning, the coach made a sharp turn and the castle loomed into sight. Sassy widened her eyes in awe. Built on a crag above the crashing waves, the castle's square-toothed parapets and soaring spires stood out in stark relief against the red sky. Surrounded with tall evergreens, the castle seemed like a world unto itself . . . a world lost in time.

"How do you like your new home?" Roarke asked.

"My home's in America. We've been over this a hundred times," she stated wearily, "and there ain't no use goin' over it again. Don't you remember our agreement? I'm goin' to be forced to stay until I can get my bearin's—then I'm goin' home."

Looking dark and inscrutable, Roarke raised his brows. "We'll see, lass . . . we'll see."

Sassy felt all hot and nervous again. Trying to remove herself from his gaze, she sat forward and peered at the castle, eyeing the tall, flashing windows, glittering like gold in the sun's last rays. The breathtaking sight pricked her childlike wonder. "Law a mercy, Donkinny Castle sure has a lot of windows," she blurted out. "Aunt Pert has a lady that comes in once a month to wash her windows. Do you have a housekeeper to do yours?"

Roarke laughed. "My *housekeeper* is a man. His name is Mr. MacDonald—actually, he's my steward. He sees to all my affairs while I'm away. I'm sure he's arranged for several people from the village to wash the windows."

"Shouldn't your brother—"

"No," Roarke said. "Mr. MacDonald takes care of my affairs."

Sassy thought it was strange that Roarke didn't want to talk about his brother. While they rode the last bit of the way to the castle, a host of other questions plagued her mind. Duncan had already told her she would be a Sassenach, an outsider; as a stranger in a strange land, how would she find the help she needed to escape Roarke's grasp? And how could she ever get back to America when she had no funds or connections?

Now, just as day folded into the purplish dusk, the jangling carriage rocked to a halt before Donkinny Castle. Soon there were brisk footsteps, and a kilted servant opened the carriage door and helped her out. Roarke followed, and putting his hand behind her, escorted her up the wide entry steps, his fingers warming her back. She stared at the tall doors and the torches flaring beside them; they reminded her of two outposts of hell. She wondered what waited on the other side of those doors—a foe or a possible friend who might help her get back to America.

When the kilt-clad servant opened the doors, light spilled over the smooth stone steps. Sassy blinked and stared at another servant as he extended his hand and respectfully stood aside. She gasped at the entry hall with its marble floor and mahogany-paneled walls. All about her, suits of armor towered in every corner, and bright flags and ancient claymores decorated the high walls. Momentarily a dapper older man in a green and blue kilt and a handsome dark jacket rounded the corner. Despite his age, he pulled himself up like a soldier reporting for duty, bowing his silver head to Roarke.

"Mr. MacDonald," Roarke announced with some warmth, "I've brought a guest with me from the colonies—Miss Sassy Adair. She will be staying in my mother's room and using her things," he added, his voice echoing in the huge marbled entry.

The steward touched his frothy jabot but asked no questions and didn't seem curious about her relationship with Roarke. Maybe the infamous Captain Rakehell brought strange women home with him all the time, Sassy thought wearily. Again she scanned the impressive entryway, feeling small and insignificant with her bundle of pitiful belongings. When she noticed Roarke had walked away and Mr. MacDonald was following, she hurried after them.

Roarke led the way into a chamber with a parquet floor and rosewood paneling. Dark pictures of fierce-looking Scots in Highland garb dotted the walls, which also displayed medieval weapons and fine stag heads. A huge table and carved chairs filled the middle of the room, and a long sideboard with silver plates rested against one wall; a magnificent chair dominated the end of the room like a king's throne. Roarke frowned at Mr. MacDonald. "Where is my brother? Why isn't he waiting for me here in the chieftain's room?"

Mr. MacDonald flushed and nervously adjusted his silver cuff links. "He isn't to be found, sir. Of course, we received word from the village that the *Sea Witch* had been sighted . . . but afterwards he disappeared."

Regret showed in Roarke's dark eyes. "Take care of Miss Adair," he ordered. "Give her anything she wants." Then a veil dropped over his emotions and he fixed Sassy with a brittle stare. "I must return to the *Sea Witch*. No doubt Mr. Cameron and I will be up late going over the ledgers. I'll see you at breakfast."

He turned on his heel and strode from the room. His abruptness surprised her; they had been here ten minutes and already he had devised a new way to embarrass her. And she was puzzled about his relationship with Kevin.

She gazed about the huge chamber until Mr. MacDonald coughed discreetly.

"This way, miss," he said, extending his hand. "I'll show you to your room. Since you'll be eating alone, I'll have your dinner sent there." Still clutching her ragged bundle, Sassy followed the older man, her head full of questions. Already she was beginning to hatch a plan.

Before they entered the room that was to be hers, Sassy ventured, "Mr. MacDonald, do you think you could get me a sailin' schedule? I'm curious about when the next ship leaves Glasgow for America."

The steward gave her a respectful nod and replied, "Yes, of course, miss. I'll bring it later with your meal." Then he ushered her into the lovely room.

Sassy could scarcely believe her eyes. There was a pastel carpet and French furniture covered with needlepoint upholstery, and a great marble-manteled fireplace, and a wonderful bed right out of a fairy tale. Everything was so fine! she thought, mentally comparing the outside of the foreboding castle to the richness inside.

Mr. MacDonald opened an armoire and laid a beautiful blue dress over a chair. "You may use these clothes if you like," he offered. Delighted with everything, Sassy paced about the room, fingering the gorgeous furnishings. Looking a little bewildered at her enthusiasm, Mr. MacDonald cleared his throat and announced, "I'll be leaving now, miss."

A while later, a tasty meal was delivered to the room. Sassy ate it, then, full and contented, removed her old dress and, with a weary sigh climbed into the high bed, wearing her tattered shift. She slipped between the cool silk sheets and considered all that was on her mind. How were Aunt Pert and the O'Reillys? Had the British found the secret printing press yet? How would she be received in Scotland? And how long would it be before she could return to America? As she mulled over the questions, exhaustion weighted her limbs. Finally it seemed a dark velvet curtain was drawn over her mind, and she fell into a deep sleep.

Early the next morning, cool air wafted over Sassy's bare shoulders, awakening her. She tugged up the silky sheet, yawned, and burrowed into the bed . . . until she remembered she had just spent her first night in a real castle. With a start, she sat up and gazed about her, trying to convince herself she hadn't dreamed the whole thing.

Yes, all the fine furniture and brocade drapes and gilt-framed paintings were still here.

She looked at the gauzy canopy over her head, then moved her gaze down the richly carved four-poster bed to the puffy counterpane where she had discarded her frayed pink gown. How she had come up in the world!

In high spirits, she ran to the billowing curtains, her bare feet sinking into the thick carpet. Outside, shade trees and clipped hedges surrounded a lovely garden of scarlet rose beds, marble benches, and green grass. Below the gardens she spied the roofs of the village, and beyond that, the rolling sea.

Hurriedly she dressed in the gown Mr. MacDonald had offered her last night. The elegant creation had belonged to Roarke's mother and was a little old-fashioned, but to Sassy, it was lovely. Made of blue taffeta, it swept low over her breasts and nipped in at her waist.

Like a child on Christmas morning, she raced to a tall wardrobe and threw open its doors. Bright as flowers, dozens of gowns crowded the cedar-scented wardrobe, tempting her to trace her fingers over their silky skirts. Still exploring, she opened the dresser drawers, finding them packed with dainty undergarments. She seated herself before the mirror and brushed her hair.

Pleased with her efforts, she thoughtfully picked up the sailing schedule Mr. MacDonald had brought last night. With great interest, she ran her finger down a column of dates and studied the fine print beside each entry. When she tucked the folded paper into her shift and glanced back at the mirror, her eyes snapped with anticipation. Maybe, just maybe, she could carry off her plan.

Then from the other side of the windows the call of a lark beckoned her to stroll in the garden before breakfast; she left the bedroom, walked down an arched corridor and a wide staircase, and was soon outside.

The rising sun warmed her face. A few clouds floated by, as if they had all the time in the world, and on the horizon, the blue of the sky melted into the green of the sea like a painter's dream. Meandering through the fresh garden, she drew in a long breath, recognizing the scents of roses, lilacs, and heady hyacinths. Gravel crunched under her feet as she paused to touch a blossom still cool with morning dew.

Rounding a flowering hedge, she saw a stranger sitting by himself reading. He was perched cross-legged on a marble bench, poring over a huge volume bound in leather. He wore a frayed velvet jacket and projected a soft, dreamy look. Although she guessed he was near thirty, his bearing gave him a younger appearance. He looked so much like Roarke, she knew it had to be his brother—but Kevin was like a pale watercolor compared to the vibrant oil painting that was Roarke.

Kevin gazed up as she came forward, and looking puzzled, he closed his book.

"I know who you are. You're Kevin, ain't you?" she said.

"I am, but how did you know?"

"You couldn't be anyone else. You look jest like your brother."

He tried to smile, but sadness gathered in his eyes.

"Who . . . who are you? And where did you come from?" he asked.

She smiled broadly. "My name is Sassy, and I'm from Virginny—a place called Potter's Lick. Lately I've been livin' in Boston with my Aunt Pert, tryin' to figure ways to fight the British, but Roarke kidnapped me and brought me to Scotland." She stamped her foot. "Lord, jest thinkin' of it makes me feel like eatin' fire and spittin' smoke!"

His face paled. "He . . . he kidnapped you?"

She flopped down on the bench beside him and nodded her head. "Yeah. Don't it beat all? Does he bring women here all the time?"

"No, you're the first one." He ran his gaze over her gown. "And you're the first person he's ever permitted to touch Mother's clothes."

"The nub-headed son of a buck stole me away from Boston while I was passed out drunk," she ranted on, scarcely hearing his words. She laughed at his shocked expression. "What's the matter? You surprised I had a tad too much likker?"

"No. I . . . it's just that I've never heard anyone call Roarke anything like that."

"I can believe that! Around here everyone scrapes to him, don't they? I've seen people bowin' and touchin' their heads like he was a king or somethin'."

A solemn look settled over Kevin's face. "Aye, he commands great respect here. Do you know his full title?"

Sassy shook her head.

Kevin took a deep breath. "Well, Roarke is actually Roarke MacLaren of Donkinny, Chief of Clan MacLaren, Laird of Donkinny, Laird of Oban, Laird of Mallaig, Laird of Lochalsh, Baronet of Scotland, Representer in the Male Line of the Celtic Earls of Donkinny Since 1275."

Sassy's brows flew up. "*That's* who he is? I thought he was just Roarke MacLaren, Common Thief and Privateerin' Cutthroat."

"No. He's a great noble—most of the clansmen call him *the* MacLaren," Kevin said seriously.

"*The MacLaren*? Well, believe me, *the* MacLaren is jest like everybody else," Sassy said with conviction.

Apparently surprised into speechlessness, Kevin stared down at the closed book.

"What are you readin'?" she asked, hoisting up the heavy volume.

He looked up with bright eyes. "It's a book of medieval history, all about knights and ladies and tournaments."

She laughed and ruffled through the illustrated pages. "Why, this looks real interestin'. Do you think you could tell me about it sometime?"

"Of course I could! And I can show you around Donkinny Castle. I know every rock in it." He put aside the book. "And I can teach you archery. I practice with the longbow every day. Would you like that?"

She had never seen anyone so eager for a kind word or a friend. "Yeah, I would. Some of the boys back home had bows and arrows like the Injuns. Course, they never let me have a try at it."

"We can have a wonderful time."

She cleared her throat awkwardly. "Yeah, but I won't be here long. As soon as I can earn my passage, I'm goin' home." With a weary sigh, she clenched her hands. "I'd take a ship tomorrow if I had the money. It may take a while, but I know I can earn my passage back somehow." Noticing his sadness, she added warmth to her voice. "Don't worry. We'll still have lots of time to do things together. I want you to show me everythin' about this castle . . . and tell me about it, too."

He stood and walked around the bench. "All right, I will," he said, motioning at the castle turrets. "I know all about castles and sieges," he went on, his voice coming alive. "There are hundreds of good stories."

"Who told them to you? Roarke?"

His expression fell. *"No,"* he answered. "He was always gone privateering against the British. Mr. MacDonald raised me after our mother died. Roarke has always been disappointed in me. I . . . I just can't seem to be like him."

"Why should you be like him? Everyone's not alike. Even the critters ain't alike. A coon don't try to be like a rabbit, and a possum don't try to be like a fox. They're smart enough to know better."

A smile broke over his face, then he laughed, looking happier than before.

Sassy glanced at the castle and saw a servant approaching. Reaching them, he announced, "The laird is up an' aboot. Ye best come fer yer breakfast now." With a stolid face, he turned and strode away, his kilt swinging smartly.

Sassy clasped Kevin's arm. *"Come on.* Leave this readin' and let's go meet the rascal!"

"I don't know what to say. I can't bear to face him."

"I know, I know . . . but you *can* face him, 'cause I have!" She chuckled and tugged him along the garden path, telling him about all the times she had tangled with his brother. "Jest growl back at him," she advised. "He may snap at you a little, but you're too big for him to eat."

By the time they had reached the dining room, she had convinced him to smile. She blinked when Mr. MacDonald whisked open the tall doors to reveal Roarke standing with his back to a fireplace large enough to roast a stag.

It was the first time she had seen him in Highland dress, and her heart jumped at the sight. He wore a black jacket with silver buttons that perfectly fit his broad shoulders, and a kilt of the dark green and blue MacLaren tartan. A frilly jabot set off his tanned face; a rich furred sporran hung from his waist; and a silvery *skean dhu* dagger flashed from the top of his hose.

She noticed an annoyed look crossed Roarke's face as he spied his brother. "Kevin, I missed seeing you last night. How have you been?"

"I've . . . I've been fine," Kevin stammered.

Roarke extended his hand at the table while he waited for them to take their places.

Despite his magnificence, Sassy felt her old anger stirring up, and turning to Kevin, she quipped, "From his dress, the MacLaren must be expecting the king to join us for breakfast."

"That will be enough, Sassy." Roarke's voice rang out in the large room. His stern gaze raked over her. "If you must know, I plan to visit Laird Dunsworth this morning. He holds dearly to the old customs and would be offended if I appeared otherwise."

He waved his bronzed hand at the massive table set with fine china and silver. Kevin obediently took his seat, and Sassy followed, thinking Roarke needed only a crown to complete his lordly appearance. No wonder everyone was afraid of him.

When his chair had scraped into place, two servants entered with heavily laden trays and placed breakfast before them. There was oatmeal drenched in butter, herring fried to a golden turn, rashers of bacon, fresh eggs, floury baps and rolls, scones and oatcakes, marmalade and honey.

At first they ate in silence, then Roarke shot a dark look at Kevin. "As soon as the Highland games are over in a couple of days and the villagers have had their fill of merrymaking, I want to confer with all the other lairds. Have you spoken to them since I left?''

Kevin put down his fork, looking guilty. ''No, I haven't spoken with the lairds. I haven't had time.''

''What have you been doing?''

''Studying, writing—''

''I thought we agreed you were going to speak with the other lairds while I was away,'' Roarke cut in.

''There just wasn't time. I . . . I couldn't arrange it all.''

Roarke thumped down his knife. ''There is always time to practice archery or moon over some book, though, isn't there?''

Sassy stood and tossed down her lace-trimmed napkin. ''Roarke MacLaren, you've got enough tongue for six rows of teeth, ain't you!''

Roarke glared back at her. ''I suggest you stay out of matters you know nothing about.''

Hands on hips, she strode to the head of the table. ''And I suggest you start actin' like a human being instead of a snappin' sow.''

His jaw hardened. ''I would appreciate it if you would keep a civil tongue in your head while you're living under my roof.''

She smiled crookedly and tapped a finger on his chest. ''Well, I won't have to be civil very long, because Mr. MacDonald brought me this sailing schedule last night.'' She drew the folded paper from her bosom and waved it in his face. ''It says there's a ship sailin' from Glasgow to Boston soon—and I'll be on it!''

''Where, may I ask, are you going to get the fare?'' he questioned coolly.

''I don't know, but I'll get it somewhere. I'll earn

it. I'll borrow it. Mebbe I'll jest knock somebody in the head and steal it!"

Kevin stood up, nearly upsetting his chair; he swallowed and raised his chin. "She's right. You shouldn't try to keep her here against her wishes."

A stormy light flickered in Roarke's eyes. "It seems you two have already teamed up against me." His face set in cold resolve, he put down his napkin. "Very well," he said to Sassy, "I'll take on the both of you." He turned to Kevin. "I suggest you direct your courage to greater things than defying me," he said, and then he left the room.

Sassy looked at Kevin's disappointed eyes and rubbed his shoulder. "From the way he's acting this mornin', it seems *the* MacLaren got up on the wrong side of the bed."

She hated the tension between the two brothers. Families should be happy and close together, like her and her father and Aunt Pert. What had happened to antagonize Roarke and Kevin?

She didn't understand everything yet, but she swore that before she left Scotland, she would bring them together.

Chapter 16

A few days later a twilight breeze wafted over the castle gardens, carrying the lush scent of roses. Dressed in a summery blue silk dress trimmed in lace, Sassy walked toward Old Angus, who was cultivating the soil about the rose bushes. Sassy carried several letters in her hand. With plenty of leisure time, she had written carefully worded notes to the O'Reillys and her friends in the Sons of Liberty. More important, she had poured out her heart to Aunt Pert, telling her about her stormy relationship with Roarke. When she reached the old man's side, she smiled and asked, "Will you do me a favor, Angus?"

"Aye, I'll be glad to." He wiped his soiled hands on his old shirt, then stabbed his shovel into the ground. After the *Sea Witch* had docked, Roarke had hired the homeless sailor as a castle gardener, extending his charity a little further.

Sassy placed the letters to America into his soiled palm. "Will you take these to the post coach for me?"

The cool breeze ruffled the old man's hair as he took the mail. "I'll be glad to see to all yer letters. There's no use for ye to go into Killieburn when I make the trip every day." He looked at the glowing sunset and tucked the envelopes into his vest.

With a broad grin, he touched his forelock. "Well, good evenin', miss. Guess I'll be goin' back to the village now, it bein' nearly dark."

Sassy watched the old man disappear into the shadows, then she looked at the castle where lamplight glittered from the tall windows. With a sigh, she headed for the library, intending to read before dinner.

The huge chamber was empty and smelled of leather and old books. Oil lamps glowed on several long tables and pooled the room with soft light. There were comfortable chairs and writing desks scattered about; one corner was screened with an ornate Chinese panel covered with delicately painted peonies and fat goldfish. Yet another piece of booty Roarke had seized from an unsuspecting ship, she thought with a snort of derision.

Sassy felt herself relax. When she strolled the castle corridors, she invariably met Roarke. And outside he seemed to loom from the very earth itself. She would take a walk in the garden only to find him standing there with a wicked grin on his face, or bump into him at sunset on a graveled path. Here among the gold-stamped volumes, she could escape his eyes and find a moment of privacy. Here she could be herself.

She stood on tiptoes and pulled two leather-bound volumes from the high shelves, then carried them to a table and settled down for a good read. One book was a volume of Shakespeare's plays, the other a romance, which she opened to the first page.

"The romance is a poor choice. The plot is weak and the characters insipid."

Sassy's heart pitched as she glanced over her shoulder. Roarke was standing beside the Chinese screen, holding a whiskey bottle in one hand and a glass in the other. Dressed in a loose-fitting shirt with lace-trimmed cuffs and snug trews, he looked as if he had just tumbled from bed. His lids drooped seductively, and a lock of hair flopped over his amused eyes.

She slammed her book shut and stood. "Why didn't you tell me you were there?"

He moved toward her. Humor lurked in his eyes, and she had the uncomfortable feeling he was making fun of her. "Pardon me, I wasn't aware that I needed to inform you I was using my own library. How thoughtless of me."

How she longed to wipe that sly smile from his face. Putting her hands on her hips, she glanced at the screen. "What were you doin' behind that screen anyway? Spyin' on me?"

He laughed deeply and held up the whiskey bottle. "I was drinking, of course. There's a sofa behind the screen. A cozy nook indeed. I set it up myself to escape life's constant demands."

She raked her gaze over him. "Yeah, I suppose bein' the world's greatest pirate is kind of demandin', ain't it?" She turned to go.

"Stay awhile," he said, clasping her wrist.

"I have to go now," she replied sourly.

He glared back at her with a patronizing air and released her arm. "I suppose you do." He poured himself another drink, then sat down at the library table and placed the bottle and glass before him. His eyes dark and bold, he ran his gaze over her. "You look tired. Are you sleeping well?"

"No . . . I've been dreamin' about Blackhurst. How he threatened to track me down iffen I didn't come to his house. You said that once I left Boston, I'd be free of him, but you were wrong. He still haunts my dreams." She hadn't meant to reveal the information, but the words dropped from her lips before she could hold them back.

"Forget him," he shot back. "We're well away from his clutches. He can do nothing to you now."

She watched him lift the sparkling glass to his

lips and empty it in one gulp. "Don't you think you've had enough?" she blurted. "God hates a man who can't hold his likker."

He slammed down the glass and laughed deeply. "Where in the hell did you hear that?"

She wondered what demons had prompted him to indulge so recklessly this evening. What was he trying to forget? "I didn't hear it. I've always known it. And I know a drunk man when I see one. What in the hell's wrong with you tonight?"

He frowned and stared at a shadowy corner of the library. "I don't think you'd want to know, lass."

He had never offered to tell her anything about his past before . . . but he was weakening now. She could tell. If she was clever enough to ask him the right questions, maybe she would discover the private demon that drove him so mercilessly. Curbing her anger, she took a seat on the other side of the library table and in a calm voice said, "Yes, I would. Tell me about it . . . please."

His eyes were dark with pain, and she felt as if he were reliving another life.

"I was thinking about my father . . . This is his birthday," he finally answered.

"You said he was dead."

"Aye. He is dead. He was a Jacobite."

Although Sassy had read about Jacobites in the volume of Scottish history, she was confused about their goals. "Tell me about 'em," she urged in a quiet tone.

He eyed her closely. "A Jacobite is a supporter of the Stuart claims to the throne of England. Roman Catholics and Tory Anglicans often feel more support for the Stuarts than for their successors." He refilled his glass and set down the bottle. "There have been Jacobite battles since 1688, and there was an uprising when I was growing up."

"And?"

"My father was killed after the battle of Culloden. The English shot him, just like they hanged yours."

Compassion tugged at her heart. "You said he had died. You didn't tell me he had been executed."

"He was taken prisoner at the battle and later placed before a firing squad. My mother had just given birth to Kevin. Once my father was killed, she never recovered; she withered and died of grief for him."

Sassy studied his anguished face. She sat absolutely still, not wanting to break the spell that had prompted him to open his heart to her.

His eyes hard, he went on in a bitter voice. "The English placed an agent over our land. He lived in the castle and acted as an administrator. My older brother, Robert, was legally the new laird, but the agent overrode his authority. I worshiped Robert and hated the agent." He chuckled bitterly. "As a boy, I put thistles under the agent's saddle to make his mount pitch, and played other childish pranks on him."

He stood up, clenching the whiskey glass in his hand.

"By day, Robert and I were proper boys, tutored at home. At night, we recruited young men from the village and raided the British troops who were building roads in the area. Of course, in the end we lost everything."

"Your castle. You said—"

"Aye. We managed to keep that," he interrupted. "We managed to keep our small holding on the roughest coast in Scotland. But we lost our land. It was divided and given to English lords."

Her throat aching with emotion, she ran her gaze over his scarred jaw. "Your scar . . . ?"

"A memento from a skirmish with English authorities," he stated. "One night Robert and I were out on another raid. During the skirmish, one officer shot him while another slashed my face with his sword. I led Robert's mount to a secluded glen and lifted him to the ground. He died in my arms that cold night. In the wee hours I buried him in the castle garden."

He sighed heavily; his face was all hard planes. "All over Scotland the rebels were outmanned and outsupplied. We had nothing but our dreams. The coffers were empty . . . No one had the means to wage a real resistance. We needed funds desperately. The lads who had ridden with us against the English disbanded."

He paused and stared at the glowing lamp; anger seared his voice. "I was hardly more than a stripling then, but there was nothing left for me in Scotland but bitterness, so I left Kevin with Mr. MacDonald. To satisfy the curiosity of the English, he told everyone that Robert and I had gone to sea."

Sassy was surprised to learn that the mild-mannered steward had participated in such a deception.

"At the age of eighteen I signed on with a merchant ship sailing from Glasgow. Duncan came with me. For seven years I learned my trade and saved my money. By then I had enough to buy my own ship—the *Sea Witch.*" He took a gulp of the whiskey. "Then I had a *new* dream—a dream to seek vengeance against the English at sea."

She rose and went to him. "And Captain Rakehell was born?"

Rage exploded in his eyes. "Aye. For a decade I raided British merchantmen for the French and the Dutch."

"Blackhurst said you took his eye . . . that he was a noncombatant."

"Aye. There was a terrible raid. We found more men aboard the English ship than we reckoned.

The decks were slick with blood. I rounded the quarterdeck and met Blackhurst with a pistol raised at my head. My pistol was empty, useless—but I clenched a sword. My arm shot out impulsively, and the blade met his face."

She struggled to understand his previous secrecy, which to her mind bordered on deceit. "Why didn't you tell me about Blackhurst and your privateerin' in Boston?"

A thoughtful look passed over his features. "An old habit, I suppose. I never told anyone. I couldn't afford to trust anyone when there was a price on my head."

She glanced about the sumptuously furnished library. "Your privateerin' has made you rich—richer than anyone I've ever known."

"Aye. I've amassed a fortune, but it's not for my personal use, lass. It's a fortune intended to arm and mount an army." His voice deepened. "And dozens of the lairds have sworn allegiance to me."

So this was why he had been so desperate to get back to Scotland. And this was why he had gone privateering—to support some secret rebellion! "You always sidestepped my questions about a Scottish rebellion. Why didn't you tell me about it on the *Sea Witch?*"

"I thought . . . I supposed you wouldn't understand my passion. That you *couldn't* understand."

She respected his motives, but wondered how much of his passion was motivated by Scottish patriotism and how much was tinged with a need for revenge. Besides that, his mission seemed impossible. "Lord, you dream big, don't you? Do you really think you can run the English out of Scotland?"

"There's a chance, a wee chance," he said with a bitter smile. "And a man's dream is always worth fighting for, isn't it?"

"Do you really think you and a few dozen clans can do it?"

He placed his glass on the table and clasped her shoulders. "Think about what you're saying. You and a handful of zealots are going to throw the English out of the colonies, aren't you?"

"But that's different. That's—"

"No." He cut her off. "It's not so different. You're trying to stir up a new rebellion, I'm trying to stir up an old one. And there's a chance that Bonnie Prince Charlie will come back to the Highlands." His face glowed with emotion. "He's living in France now, but I've already spoken with his brother in England. If the prince does return, all of Scotland will rally to him."

Stunned by the news, she smiled. "For a pair with a common enemy, we sure do fight each other a lot, don't we?"

"Aye, we do, lass." He pulled her into his arms and regarded her tenderly. "Why don't we make love instead? Under the circumstances, it seems our patriotic duty." His eyes glinted with sensual promise. Slowly . . . gently, he covered her mouth in a kiss. She could taste the whiskey flavor of his tongue and feel it snaking into her mouth; it was weeks since they had kissed, and her lips ached for his.

His fingers eagerly feathered over her cheekbones and neck, then strayed inside her bodice to find her breasts. His touch sent pleasure through the core of her being, and the library itself seemed to glow with warmth. And she felt a deep hunger for him. Felt it far down in her bones. When a moan escaped her throat, he pressed her against him and she felt the ridge of his manhood under his breeches.

He raised his head. "See how I want you?" he murmured, taking her hand and brushing it against him.

Instinctively she clutched his hardness with her trembling fingers . . . and he kissed her again. By now her head felt light. Driven by a white-hot need, she clasped both arms around his neck and met his driving tongue with hers. Every nerve in her body tingled with pleasure and she felt her control dissolving. Their bodies melted together and burned with passion for long moments before he lifted his mouth again.

"Let me carry you upstairs to my bed," he suggested hoarsely.

No, a voice cried out in her brain. Think what you're doing. Think what he's doing. He took your virginity, abandoned you, left you to struggle through a miscarriage by yourself, then selfishly kidnapped you. And he's never proposed marriage or made *any* commitment to you. He only wants to satisfy his lust. You're playing a dangerous game. A dangerous game you can't win.

Her emotions cooling, she pulled back from him. "Does it ever bother you jest a little bit that you're an overbearin', egotistical bastard?" she asked, emphasizing each word.

He chuckled deeply. "Not particularly," he drawled. "I can live with the guilt." His eyes dark and dangerous, he lowered his mouth to hers again, but she pulled away.

"You're drunk!" she cried indignantly.

"Aye, drunk enough to do this." He yanked her to him and kissed her again, this time savagely, without mercy. Her emotions whirled within her as she wrestled away from him yet again. Anger knotted in her bosom, and her breath came hard and fast. How she wanted to slap his handsome face!

"I won't be eatin' dinner with you tonight," she said in a tight voice. "I'm cuttin' back on my vittles—until about 1800."

Gathering up all her dignity, she picked up her

books, strode from the room, and slammed the tall library doors behind her.

For the next seven days Sassy avoided Roarke. Then Mr. MacDonald told her that her presence would be required at the Highland games. Not knowing what to expect, she gathered her courage and met Roarke at the castle drawbridge on a fine August afternoon. Outfitted for the summer games, he wore full Highland dress honoring his position as chieftain of the MacLarens. Black cock feathers gleamed in his bonnet, and a plaid was draped over his shoulder, held in place by a cairngorm brooch blazoned with his coat of arms. Sassy eyed his costume, then caressed her own silk blouse and velvety basque. Roarke had provided her with an ensemble appropriate to the occasion, with everything of the finest materials. "Come, lass," he said, offering his outstretched hand. "It's time for the games to begin."

Sassy clasped his hand and gazed longingly beyond the drawbridge, which lay open in the afternoon sun. Since the incident in the library, she had searched for employment in Killieburn, but to no avail. How she needed a bit of diversion! Daily her mind wrestled with one problem: How could she get enough money to go home? Her footsteps ringing hollowly over the wooden planks, she stole a glance at Roarke's handsome face. She had been forced to accept his hospitality—and by all rights, he owed her passage home—but she would die before she asked him for anything. With a sigh, she decided to put away her gloom and enjoy life . . . just for one day.

As they left the drawbridge, her heart beat with excitement at the beauty of the Highlands. The heather in all its glory slashed wildly across the landscape, and the scent of roses and sun-warmed grass floated on the light air. Bluebells and larkspur nodded over the grassy slopes. All about the castle grounds tiered fountains spilled water, and hawthorn hedges trembled with creamy blossoms.

A proud look glinted in Roarke's eyes as they strolled across the sweeping lawn. Seeing them come from the castle, the villagers who had assembled for the summer games cheered wildly. Sassy smiled at them, then up at Roarke. The balmy day held such promise, she found it hard to be mad at anyone—even him.

While they moved about the lush grounds, she scanned the crowd. This was not a great gathering of many clans, but rather a small and intimate affair honoring Roarke. A raised platform for dancers jutted from the center of the green, where teams of performers competed in the Highland fling and the Reel of Tulloch.

A great oak loomed on a rise near the platform, and as they neared its shade, a man fluttered his plaid over the grass. "My laird," he said, catching Roarke's eye, "will ye and yer lady not rest for a while?"

Roarke nodded his thanks, and the smiling man walked off to join the games. Then the laird of Donkinny Castle knelt and extended his arm, offering Sassy a place by his side. Her heart racing, she took his warm hand and settled herself on the plaid. Spreading out her full skirt, she scanned his rakish features, thinking how handsome he looked. He rode every day now, and the sun had deepened his tan, making his flashing smile even brighter.

She leaned back on one arm and sighed. Lord, if he were only ugly, or dull, or mean-spirited, it would be so much easier to resist him, she thought. Even now he projected an appeal that coiled about her senses like an alluring aroma. Trying to distract herself, she glanced into the distance. Midsummer's breath was on the land, and on the moors heather covered the earth . . . Far beyond the distant trees, faint traces of snow glittered on the craggy mountaintops.

"It looks like you're enjoying yourself for a change," he remarked with a smile. His voice was deep and rich, and sent a shiver up her arms.

"I am. With any luck, I'll be on my way home soon," she bravely predicted. "I feel like I've been in a prison since I arrived in Scotland."

His dark eyes twinkled as he caressed her hand, making her pulse flutter. "Aye. The vile pirate's prison."

There he was, using that silvery tongue, forcing her lips to curve upward. She bit back a smile, for when she laughed, her resistance was at its lowest. "Correct," she came back evenly, pulling her hand from his. She gazed about the crowd, trying to look cool and disinterested. Since she had heard the story of his youth, she felt she understood him a little better, but his hardships didn't give him an excuse for the shameless way he had treated her. She would show him he couldn't insult her in the library with his advances and then one week later jest with her as if nothing had happened. "Yes," she went on in a businesslike tone, "soon I'll be home fightin' for my cause."

All was silent except for the sound of a bee droning in a flower cup. Roarke sighed heavily and fondled her hand, shooting sparks up her arm. "Lass, let's make a vow," he suggested. "Let's vow to avoid politics for one whole day. I won't talk about Bonnie Prince Charlie if you won't talk about the Sons of Liberty."

Sassy was feeling particularly generous. "All right, 'nuf said. I get your meanin'," she replied cautiously. "But jest for today. Then I've got a whole lot of talkin' to do."

Roarke laughed and ran his gaze over her appreciatively. His eyes were looking into her heart a little too deeply . . . so she turned to where brawny lads in kilts were tossing cabers. A circle of women cheered them on as they hurled the huge logs over the grass. On another slope villagers struggled in a tug-of-war.

A mood of relaxed good humor ran through the crowd. The Highland dress was worn with pride, and everyone was having a wonderful time. Families picnicked on the flowery grounds and visited comfortably with one another while their children waded in the cool brook. In the background, the pipes skirled in a spirited tune; later an ox would be roasted for feasting. It was a wonderful day. A perfect day. The most perfect day since Sassy had arrived in Scotland.

Cautiously she returned her gaze to where Roarke rested back on his elbows, studying the crowd. As a chieftain, he had a personal relationship with his people and seemed to take pride in their accomplishments; she knew he had a great feeling of worth for the individual man. His countenance looked more relaxed today than it had since he had arrived home—then, as Kevin walked by, his expression sobered. She knew he was remembering their constant arguments.

"What's the matter? Are you thinkin' about Kevin?" she ventured.

"Aye," he replied.

In the short time she had known Kevin, he had impressed her with his intelligence—but compared to Roarke's strength, his demeanor lacked confidence. When the young man was out of sight, she casually remarked, "You know . . . Kevin is right good-lookin' in his own way . . . and he's pert near the smartest person I ever knowed, too."

Roarke plucked a nearby thistle and hurled it aside. "He's brilliant—he's already written a scholarly book on medieval castles, and he speaks Latin and Ancient Greek—but he moons about like a dreamy old woman. I wish he were more manly."

Watching golden sunlight dapple his troubled face, Sassy thoughtfully said, "You know, onct I knew an ol' woman in Potter's Lick who caught a baby wolf when its eyes was still squinched shut. She fed it on a rag tit sopped in milk and petted it like a baby." She laughed a little. "That ol' wolf grew up gentler than any dog you ever saw. At night when the wolves got to howlin', it would jest cuddle up by that old woman's legs. It didn't have a lick of spirit."

"What are you trying to tell me?"

She swung her gaze toward Mr. MacDonald, who stood near the dancers. "I like Mr. MacDonald real good, but sometimes he's fussier than any ol' woman I ever knew. And I bet he'd jest die if he got a speck of dirt under his fingernails."

Roarke threw back his head and laughed. "That he would!"

She leaned closer as if she were revealing a great secret. "Well, jest think about it," she said. "Who raised Kevin? Your father was dead and you were off to the high seas. There's a lot of difference 'tween feedin' and educatin' a youngun, and raisin' one to think he'll be somebody. You don't know you're a wolf unless you run with the wolves."

Roarke uttered not a sound, but his eyes said her words had touched his heart.

"Kevin's raisin' can't be undone," she went on, "but he can be given a chance to shine. That's all he needs—a chance to shine. I bet he'll have the grit to meet a real test when it comes." She gazed at him earnestly, but had the wisdom not to press the subject.

With a grin, Roarke leaned over to pick another thistle and twirl it between his fingers. "Only the Scots would have a thistle as a national flower. But in a way I suppose it does represent our thorny spirit."

She smiled to herself, liking his choice of words.

"I prefer the softer flowers myself," he added, then tossed the thistle aside and snapped a bluebell from the grass. His eyes never leaving hers, he placed the flower behind her ear. "This is for you, wise lassie." His fingers brushed her face as he lowered his hand. The touch resonated through her, setting her blood aglow and warming her spirit. She felt a strong, almost tactile intimacy between them, pulling at her heart and vitals. And with a stab of fear, she also felt herself beginning to yield . . . her resolve melting.

Her knees trembling, she rose awkwardly. "I . . . I want to see the games."

Afraid to look at his face, she gathered her skirt in her cold hands and walked into the crowd, her strides swift and deliberate.

Sassy visited with the MacLaren clansmen for a while. As she strolled the castle grounds, she saw Kevin sitting under a birch tree reading a book. Like his brother, he was garbed in Highland finery, but he lacked the authority to carry the flamboyant dress. It touched her heart that even during this great outdoor gathering, he had chosen to read. When she neared him and cleared her throat, he tucked the book into his vest and stood up, looking surprised. "Oh, there you are," he said. "I missed you this morning. Are you well? You look upset."

"I've—I've got a headache," she stammered, realizing he was clever enough to know she was lying.

"I'm sorry. Is there anything else? Is there any way I can help?"

She drew in a long breath and replied, "No, I was jest thinkin' . . . wonderin' how I would get back home. It's jest like Duncan said, all the jobs are taken . . . and no one wants to hire me." Blood warmed her cheeks. "They think I'm Roarke's lady—that I belong in the castle."

Kevin lowered his eyes, then lifted them to meet her gaze. "I'll give you the money," he offered bluntly. "My mother left me a special fund. I'll ask Mr. MacDonald . . . He'll have it in a few days."

Her hands flew to her mouth. "No, no! I didn't mean that. I wasn't askin'—"

"I know you weren't," he interrupted, "but I have no use for it anyway. Since it can't buy me passage to the Middle Ages, it might as well buy you passage to America." He hung his head again. "I know what it's like to be a prisoner here."

Tears pricked her eyes and she clasped his hand. 'I'll pay you back when I get home. My aunt's lawyer can send you a letter of credit."

"Fine . . . if that's what you wish."

She searched his eyes, a little surprised by his spirit. "Roarke will be mad as a wet hen, you know."

"He always is," he said with a chuckle. "Are you happy now?"

She swallowed back her tears and smiled. "Oh, yes. Real happy. I'll be goin' home!"

Chapter 17

Sassy spent the rest of the afternoon wandering the castle green and meeting people. At last she returned to her room to rest. Now she lay on her bed, listening to the laughing villagers leave the grounds.

The chamber had dimmed to a rosy glow. Knowing the sun was just setting, she rose and pushed back the velvet drapes. To the west, a great ball of fire slid into the sea, drenching the sky with red light. Below, on the shadowy lawn, dancers strolled arm in arm toward Killieburn. For some strange reason she could not fathom, the sight of the loving couples made her eyes blur with tears.

Her thoughts in turmoil, she walked to a mirrored dresser and glanced at her appearance: Her eyes were tense, her hair mussed, her countenance tight. How disgusted she was with her lack of courage. "You're jest a big coward," she cried, jabbing a finger at her reflection. But what could she have done—spend the afternoon under Roarke's hot gaze?

Groaning in disgust, she sank down on the bed's silky counterpane. With a trembling hand, she took the sailing schedule from a night table and ran her finger down the column of dates. A ship left in one month. In one month she would be free of Roarke's grasp. She would see Aunt Pert. Help the rebels. Be free to do or think what she pleased.

It seemed she had only one worry—avoiding Roarke until she left. Finding no solution to the problem, she rose and paced about once more; then she heard footsteps in the hall. Almost before she could shove the sailing schedule under her pillow, Roarke knocked and opened her bedroom door. Her heart turned over at the sight of him. His Highland regalia a blaze of color, he filled the open doorway, a bouquet of freshly cut roses in his arms. She raced her gaze over his bronzed face and broad shoulders. He projected a powerful allure that tugged at her heart each time she saw him.

"I brought flowers for your room, lass . . . from the castle gardens," he announced with a flashing smile. "Did you enjoy the games?"

"Yes . . . they were wonderful," she said.

He placed the sweet-smelling roses in a vase on her dresser, then lit a lamp, warming the room with golden light. "I passed Kevin on the grounds this afternoon," he remarked casually. "He seemed shaken. Is there a problem?"

She swallowed the lump in her throat. "No. Th-there's no problem."

He gazed at her doubtfully. "It's a shame you had to leave my side," he added, moving toward her. "We were talking so well, not arguing for a change."

She watched him draw closer, thinking she had never seen a better-looking man. His eyes still danced with mischief, and he radiated a warmth that she found almost irresistible. When he touched her face, she felt a vibration deep inside her.

"Why did you really leave?" he asked huskily, now so close, his velvet jacket brushed her arm and she could see the golden flecks in his pupils. His voice was deep and strong; it made her tremble.

When their eyes met, a strange shyness overcame her and she found it hard to speak. "You know why I left." She felt a tug in her womanhood and a flutter in the pit of her stomach.

With an impulsive gesture, he lifted her hand and kissed it, then gently pulled her into his arms; a heady joy rose inside her as his hands trailed fire down her back. For a moment there was a tenderness in his gaze that tore at her heart, and she felt an unreasonable guilt over her plans to leave. Why did it have to be like this? Why did she have to make this terrible choice? Why did the decision hurt so much?

"Were you afraid I would do this?" Slowly he lowered his head. He kissed her first on the eyelids and cheeks; then, warm and moist, his tongue flicked over her trembling lips. At first as he pressed his mouth to hers, there was a dreamlike quality about his lips that made her think of satin and silk and rose petals. Then he deepened the kiss; shivers raced over her arms and she trembled inside. Tantalizing . . . persuasive . . . commanding, his lips continued their sweet exploration.

Now he was gently nipping and biting, devouring her softness as he pulled her tighter, pressing his hard maleness against her; when he plunged into her mouth with his tongue, excitement exploded deep within her. For a moment time seemed to dissolve like the morning mists on the moors. The soulful kiss reminded her of fire and velvet and the rising sun and everything beautiful and exciting. Like water to a parched soul, it was a kiss to drink down in great drafts.

Gradually she struggled away from him, fighting back her tears. "Don't do this! I'm leavin'," she cried, gazing at his passion-heavy eyes. "I'm leavin' on the next packet."

He looked at her blankly. "You haven't the money."

"Yes, I do," she carelessly revealed. "Kevin is lendin' it to me!"

A surprised look flashed over his face, making her hurt deep inside. Then he dropped his hands and moved away. Raising a brow, he nodded cynically. "Well, it seems our young wolf is showing his teeth at last."

"Yes, and I'm happy for him," she shot back.

He paced about the room, then returned to her side and clasped her shoulders. "What would you say if I refused to let you leave?" His voice rang with authority.

She clenched her hands and swallowed her rising emotions. "I'd say you were bein' true to your colors—selfish as always. Do you think I would ever stay with you after what you've done to me?"

His eyes hard and brittle, he studied her face. "I insist you tell me why you won't sleep with me. There's something more, isn't there? Tell me the truth!"

All the hurt and anger Sassy had ever felt toward Roarke rose in her breast, demanding release. Before she could stop them, hot words rushed from her lips and disclosed her painful secret. "Yes, there is! After you seduced and abandoned me in Williamsburg, I learned I was pregnant. I had a miscarriage in Boston!" she blurted out.

He stared at her, surprise and disbelief stamped on his face.

"Late one night I felt the pains, but I didn't call for Aunt Pert. I was so ashamed, how could I involve her in such a thing? How could I hurt her? I took care of myself, then a few days later began my life again, trying to forget I'd ever met you!"

For a moment his eyes glittered with emotion. His pained expression momentarily softened her anger, then she reminded herself he had no morals where women were concerned. Hadn't he already demonstrated that?

"Why didn't you tell me?" he finally asked in a soft voice.

"Why should I have told you? I wanted your love, not your pity." Painful emotion tightened her breast. "I'm sorry I just told you. At least I had my pride . . . Now that you know, I don't even have that."

Roarke dropped his hands from her shoulders and hardened his jaw.

She watched him turn and stride from the bedroom. As his footsteps rang down the castle corridor, she collapsed on the bed and wiped her moist eyes.

She bit her lips and held back her tears. She refused to break down. She had made her decision. She had set her course.

Soon she would be on her way home.

A few days later, Roarke met with the Highland lairds to discuss the political situation and the chances of staging a successful Jacobite uprising. With a frown, he surveyed the combative scene taking place in his own chieftain's room and noted the meeting was far from a success. Fat Laird Ferguson was crouched in front of Ramsay, shaking a finger in his face; Lairds Leckie and Campbell were shouting at each other in one corner of the room, while Lairds Black and MacAdam were bellowing conflicting opinions at the top of their lungs. Lairds Fletcher and MacNish sat at the long council table drinking spirits and ignoring Kevin, who was scribbling on a paper. It had all been going on since noon.

Roarke had fed them enough food for a Roman legion, but that hadn't placated their hot tempers. Disgusted with their childishness, he strode to the diamond-paned windows and gazed over the castle grounds toward the moors. The rumble of discordant voices continued to drone behind him, but he pushed the irritation from his thoughts. A far more important problem weighed on his mind.

He studied the distant mountains: The mists shrouding the peaks crept downward like ghostly fingers, wrapping themselves about the rocky crags. With a heavy sigh, he remembered the afternoon Sassy had told him about the miscarriage. Since then he had thought of little else. Now the drifting mists reminded him that time was passing.

Soon it would be time for her to go.

Lord, if he had only known she was with child when he had left Williamsburg. What she had endured by herself! What she must think of him! With a long sigh, he realized he couldn't change the past, but he *could* devote every free moment to proving to her that he really cared. He must court her and charm her and indulge her with special treats. He must show her he wasn't an unfeeling brute. But time was swiftly running out. He clenched his fist in frustration, knowing he would give everything he had for another chance to win her trust. One thought constantly hammered at his brain: Could he change her mind about him and keep her from leaving the Highlands?

Damn the little heller anyway, and damn Kevin for helping her! Who would have guessed that he would have chosen this time to show a little spirit? At first Roarke had thought of trying to reason with Sassy about their past—but the words had lodged in his throat. For talking to Sassy Adair like a reasonable person was damn near impossible. But, Lord above, how he wanted her . . . What he would give for another chance to win her love!

The angry voices broke into his dark reverie, prompting him to turn back to them. The lairds' eyes bulged; their faces were flushed; their jugular veins throbbed—the more they argued, the more they liked it. No run-of-the-mill bully, Laird Dunsworth had pushed the other bullies aside and demanded everyone listen to him. To take the edge off his boredom, Laird Murray had challenged Dunsworth's principles. Principles? thought Roarke. The old man's only principle involved not getting more than twenty feet from a whiskey bottle.

MacGruder was bellowing again, and Roarke knew the other lairds would soon join in if he didn't intervene. He looked at the bright trews, kilts, and silver-topped sporrans. The room was filled with the aristocracy of Highland dissenters—who were all dissenting with one another. Could two Scots agree with each other on anything? They had produced little all day but confusion—in that matter, they were making wonderful progress. Yes, they were all bigoted, hot-tempered, died-in-the-wool liars. And they all had a nostalgic yen for good old hand-to-hand, eye-to-eye, snot-slinging, blood-spurting, bone-crunching warfare—just like their fathers before them.

And lucky him . . . they were all on his side.

Roarke's disgust melted into sympathy as he noticed Kevin staring at a paper filled with fine handwriting. He was dressed in the fine trews of the MacLaran tartan, but looked like a lost orphan. His head bent, he dipped a quill into an ink pot and doodled on the margin of the paper. Roarke regretted every moment they fought with each other; he didn't mean for arguments to arise—but they always did. The lad couldn't help that he was quiet and moody. As Sassy said, he just needed a chance to shine, more opportunities to display his keen mind.

As Kevin looked up, Roarke caught his eyes, passing him a silent message they had earlier agreed upon.

"My brother has a few ideas he would like to put forth," Roarke announced over the lairds' contentious voices. "He has given our cause a great deal of thought."

The old men looked at Roarke with surprise. Slowly they quieted, seemingly more out of curiosity than respect for Kevin. At last they all sat down around the huge table and stared at him.

After a stiff silence, Kevin began haltingly. "First, I believe we should postpone all action for the moment and invite some of the Lowland lairds to share our discussion. After all, most of the skirmishes would take place on border lands. They more than anyone would want a successful rebellion—they would be the first to feel retaliation if we fail."

Dunsworth shot to his feet, his jowls quivering. "Lowland lairds, you say? A fine passel of soft old women they are, is what I say! We'll be carrying them in wagons with warming stones before we've met the English."

MacGruder smacked a fist on the table. "He's right! I came to fight and I say we fight, not invite the whole of Scotland to tea parties to talk about fighting!" He scanned the other lairds. "I say Highlanders should have the main say in this rebellion. After all, didn't we suffer the most at Culloden? The wounded were bayoneted where they lay, and it was the Highlanders, not the Lowlanders, who were executed and transported to the West Indies.

Roarke understood MacGruder's rage. It was true the English had vented their anger on the Highlanders rather than on the Lowland Scots. In an attempt to break the Highlanders' spirit, they had dipped the tartan in mud and forbidden all weapons—even the pipes. And after the battle, seven hundred men, women, and children had died from starvation and fever on the hellish Tilbury prison ships.

Still, this matter concerned all Scots.

Roarke looked MacGruder straight in the eye. "Perhaps it would be best if we postponed talking for the moment. Let Kevin proceed to his next point."

As MacGruder reseated himself, Kevin rattled his paper. "In the matter of arms, I propose we buy weapons from the French, who have always been friends of the Highlanders."

"The French?" MacNish shouted. "What part has a Highlander to play with them limp-wristed Frenchies?"

"France gave a home to Charles Edward Stuart!" Kevin shot out.

An ancient laird with snowy whiskers stood up and banged his crooked walking stick on the floor. "The French are fine for whores or cheese, but I'd rather do business with real men." The other old men present hooted with laughter. "Try the Dutch, I say. They're honest and blunt like us . . . and they won't cheat us!"

Another laird, who had apparently been asleep, roused himself with a great smacking of lips and spluttered, "No, no, no, you're all wrong! We could get the guns cheaper from the Spaniards!"

Yet another laird told Kevin, "Be quiet, lad, and leave the planning to experienced men."

With those words, all the lairds stood and began arguing with one another. So loud was their din, Roarke could hardly hear himself think. He watched them clasp each other by the lapels; he watched them bellow and rage; he watched them curse and jab each other in the chest.

From the corner of his eye he saw Kevin leave the table. His heart sank as his brother moved between the battling lairds and quietly slipped from the room.

A knot in his throat, Roarke sat down to collect himself. His carefully engineered plan to display Kevin's fine mind had failed. The hardheaded old men had shouted him down before he had had a chance to convey two points. Roarke stared at them now as they argued. Shut up and listen for a change! he wanted to shout . . . but he knew he needed their support.

Angry, he stood and snatched up Kevin's discarded paper; then at the top of his voice he bellowed, "Sirs, take your chairs!" The whiskery old men threw him surprised glares that asked, "Why are you so upset?" but gradually they calmed down and gathered at the table.

Forty minutes later, Roarke finished forcefully presenting all of his brother's arguments. Some of the diehards still grumbled under their breath, but they voted to invite the Lowland lairds into their union and convene later at Laird Dunsworth's castle to finish discussing where they would buy arms.

As they filed from the chieftain's room, Roarke went to the grog tray and poured himself a whiskey. Wondering how they had made any progress at all, he walked to the window and pulled back the drapes. He blinked when he saw Sassy riding down the winding castle road. She was dressed like a laddie in a kilt, jacket, and hose. A jaunty Highland bonnet, complete with a perky feather and green ribbon, flashed against her red hair.

Yes, the costume was unconventional for a woman, but she looked undeniably gorgeous. He also noticed her kilt rode up above her knee and showed off her shapely legs; he wondered where she had gotten the outfit. Probably from Mr. MacDonald, or Kevin, or even Duncan, who came to the castle to visit her. Even Old Angus could have brought it to her. Hadn't Roarke seen him leaving Donkinny with her letters for the Glasgow mail coach? They all spoiled her. Spoiled her outrageously!

When Kevin joined her on a fine stallion, anger surged inside Roarke like a swelling tide. *Wait a minute.* What was Kevin carrying? Damn it to hell . . . fishing poles! The blackguard was going fishing with *his* woman after he had left him in a chieftain's room full of grouchy, foul-breathed, rotten-tempered old lairds who couldn't agree on the time of day!

As the pair rode away, Roarke scanned Sassy's mount, a high-spirited mare given to unpredictable behavior. His jaw hardening, he slammed down the whiskey glass, knowing he must go after her.

Sassy glanced over her shoulder at Kevin as they left the castle. No horseman, he loosely bounced along on his mount, clutching their fishing poles under one arm. Feeling her gaze upon him, he smiled and hurried to catch up. She thought he looked much better than he had only minutes before when she had found him brooding in the garden.

"I've failed again," he had announced with a sigh. "I've failed Roarke. I was to present our plan and had everything worked out, but the old lairds shouted me down." He looked up from his place on the garden bench and tossed a pebble to the ground. "Some of those old mossbacks haven't had a new idea in years. All they want to do is raid and pillage with no objective, as the clans have done for years. No wonder the English think we're backward." He had stood and raked a hand through his windblown hair, then gazed at her earnestly. "I have some ideas for the rebellion myself, but I can't hold my own with them. The old death's-heads cut me off every time!"

Now as he galloped toward her on a black stallion, she felt sadness tug at her heart; in his Highland garb he looked almost as handsome as his brother, but she knew he was aching inside. As he neared, she put on a bright smile. She was glad she had suggested the fishing trip to cheer him up. It would be good for her, too.

He reined his stallion close to her dappled mare. "Let's ride to Loch Tay," he suggested. "I've fished there before. With any luck we should get a fine string of trout before sunset."

She glanced back at the castle as they rounded a curve. Was someone standing at the window, looking at them? Probably just Mr. MacDonald. It couldn't be Roarke. Since she had told him about the miscarriage, there had been only awkward silence between them. Sometimes it seemed he wanted to speak to her, but she always made some excuse to leave the room. Could anything good come of their conversations? She doubted it. Thank goodness she would have to endure him for only a few more days, then she would be on her way home. Despite her hopeful future, a strange weight pressed against her heart. She ignored it, determined to cheer up Kevin.

Letting him take the lead, she galloped along behind, listening to the *thud-thud-thud* of her horse's hooves. The scents of earth, horse, and leather were soothing to her senses, and it was good to be in the deliciously light misty air. A moist wind cooled her face, and now and then she felt a touch of rain on her face. The nights had been chilly for this time of year, and the first touches of autumn foliage glowed in the distance. It had been a day of sunshine and showers, and clouds skimmed over the mountains, making the rocky slopes brighten and darken with drifting light and shadow.

When they neared a crofter's farm she raced toward Kevin, enjoying the feel of the fine mare thundering over the open land. Reigning in her horse, she touched his arm. "What are they doin'?" she asked, watching a man and woman digging in the earth. A wagon and team waited nearby.

"They're cutting peat blocks." He pointed to a spot near their cottage where hides covered a pile of blocks. "Those blocks are drying. By the time winter is over, the crofter and his wife will have burned every block. Peat burns evenly and has a wonderful scent." He rode off and motioned for her to follow.

Passing the peat cutters, she studied the cottage. The roof was of thatch, and posts supported the walls, but vines drooped over the welcoming doorway; and in the trees birds chirped merrily, giving the place a homey feel. A huge oak drooped over the roof, its bright red leaves contrasting handsomely with the dark thatch and the misty blue mountains. Behind the cottage, long-horned sheep with black faces dotted the craggy ridges.

Half an hour passed, and then Sassy and Kevin rode through a glen forested with birch and oaks. Red berries brightened the fragrant woods, and occasionally a cliff crowned with purple heather was visible over the trees. Warbling birds darted across the wide woodcutters' path as the horses trotted ahead . . . Then, with sudden drama, glistening Loch Tay loomed into view.

The loch lay peacefully beneath the gathering clouds. Its waters nipped into the land in long inlets and flashed back the reflection of a tall mountain. Along the pebbly shoreline, sunlight glinted on the waves, and the wind rustled through the surrounding birch trees like the songs of angels. "Oh, it's lovely!" Sassy cried. Over the center of the loch a golden eagle spread his wings and circled effortlessly.

Kevin pointed at an ancient oak near the shoreline, its foliage orange and gold. "Let's race to that tree. Bet I can beat you!"

"You've got a bet!"she said, slapping the mare

on her glossy rump. With gales of laughter, they left the shady forest and raced toward the shore like carefree children. At first Sassy was far ahead of Kevin, but then she heard him pounding ahead, gaining ground. Looking back to see where he was, she frowned and swatted her mare once more.

To her surprise, Kevin's mouth formed the word *No!* and he waved his hand . . . but it was too late. While her head was turned, the mare whinnied and pitched forward. Sassy's heart leaped as she shot from the side of the horse and crashed to the rocky ground. Stunned, she looked at the dirt clinging to her scraped and bloody arms . . . then searing pain ripped through her leg and darkness tumbled over her.

After the last of the grouchy, arthritic lairds had been loaded into carriages and wheeled away, Roarke changed into trews, then mounted his own steed and raced toward Loch Tay. Kevin must be taking Sassy there to fish; he had often said it was his favorite place. As Roarke left the castle grounds, a storm rumbled over the misty crags, and wind swept down the slopes, making the leafy oaks and slender evergreens tremble. When he reached the moors, rain clouds were floating down the foothills and trailing through the high meadows like drifting cannon smoke.

The first drops caught Roarke near the crofter's cottage. Their work interrupted, the man and his wife abandoned the peat cutting and clambered into the wagon, then headed back to their cottage. Anxiety tugged at Roarke's mind as he gave them a cursory glance and galloped on. Why had Kevin let Sassy ride the high-strung mare? Why hadn't he used better judgment? Fifteen minutes later, when he entered the dripping forest, his anxiety grew to sharp concern. Drawing in a long breath, he thundered down the woodcutters' road, his mount's hoofs spraying wet earth behind him.

Steady rain was splattering his shoulders by the time he reached Loch Tay. As he entered the clearing, his heart jumped in his chest. There, a hundred yards in front of him, Sassy lay sprawled on her back, one arm thrown above her head. Kevin knelt by her side, holding her hand. With dangling reins, their mounts cropped stubble nearby.

Sassy looked so still, she appeared to be dead. Roarke's mind raced wildly. He kneed his mount and rode toward her.

As Roarke slid from the saddle, Kevin looked up with brimming eyes. "A rabbit ran in front of her," he said. "The mare was galloping along at a fine pace, but when she saw the rabbit, she went crazy. Sassy shot off her back. She . . . she landed on her side, but her head jerked back," he added, his voice breaking. He lowered his head to get control of his emotions, then gazed at his brother again. Rain streamed from his slick hair and soaked into his fine jacket. "Her . . . her leg was bent under her, too."

Roarke squelched over the wet grass, knelt, and placed his hand over her heart. His own heart hammered a crazy tattoo, for he feared she had broken her neck. Searching for a heartbeat, he started to speak to Kevin, but felt his chest tighten with anger and decided to wait. At last, he felt the stroking of her heart under his spread fingers. Unspeakable relief washed over him, misting his eyes with tears. He trailed his fingers over her face, and was rewarded with a low moan. Her eyes fluttered as she returned to consciousness.

Rain pounded against them as Roarke ran his hands over her arms and legs. He caressed her face again. "Sassy . . . listen to me," he commanded, taking her cold hand from Kevin and clasping it in his own. "What do you feel in your arms and legs?"

She opened her eyes, and giving him a dazed look, groaned. "My leg . . . my right leg is hurtin' so much!"

"Can you move your other leg?"

"Yeah," she said weakly. "I think so."

"Well, try, damn it. Try!"

Slowly she moved her left leg.

Roarke looked at Kevin's frightened eyes. "She was knocked unconscious and broke her leg—badly. Thank God it wasn't her neck as well."

"We . . . we were racing," Kevin explained. "She was looking back at me and didn't see the rabbit dart in front of her. I tried to warn her, but it was too late."

Roarke clenched his jaw, trying to control his anger. "Why did you let her ride this mare? You know the horse is high-strung."

"She was already mounted. We were in a hurry. I . . . I just didn't think."

The words *you never do* almost shot from Roarke's lips, but he saw Kevin's hand tremble and managed to stifle the comment. The lad was already suffering enough. "Ride back to that crofter's cottage," he commanded. "Have them fill the wagon with hay and bring it back here. We'll take her back to the castle."

"But . . . but there isn't a real doctor in Killieburn anymore. He died while you were away."

"Duncan can set her leg. And he has laudanum in his medical supplies. Now, get going!" Roarke watched Kevin scramble atop his horse and gallop away, then he looked back at Sassy. The driving rain had plastered her hair to her head and wilted her frothy jabot to a sodden rag. Lying in the grass with mud splattered on her white face, she reminded him of a stricken child.

"I'll be outta your way soon . . . This leg ain't

goin' to slow me down none. You'll see,'' she offered lamely.

He placed a finger over her lips. ''Hush, love.''

Still she continued to speak, her words interrupted with moans of pain. ''I'll . . . I'll be gone afore you know it.''

Roarke smiled as the cold rain soaked through his jacket. ''No, I'm afraid you won't, lass. You won't be able to put any weight on that leg for a long while, much less walk. And the ship you were so set on taking was the last one scheduled out of Glasgow till spring. Winter comes with a swift force in the Highlands. By the time your leg is mended, the sea will be too rough to travel. Nothing passes over the Firth of Lorne in winter.'' He sighed and pressed his lips to her trembling hand. ''Despite Kevin's generosity, you'll be forced to winter with me . . . at the vile pirate's castle.''

Chapter 18

When Sassy woke up the next day, she realized something was wrong, for she couldn't move her leg. With a swift rush of depression, she remembered her fall at Loch Tay and the painful ride in the crofter's wagon back to Donkinny Castle. How cold and wet and miserable she had been, and how her leg had hurt. Roarke had been there at her side, cuddling her body against him and rearranging a tattered blanket over her legs when the gusty wind blew it aside.

Feeling dizzy and stunned, she raised her head and glanced at the bedroom windows where light sifted between the closed drapes; a grandfather clock in the corner of the bedroom told her it was eleven o'clock. She could scarcely believe she had slept so late. It must have been the laudanum, she thought, recalling Duncan had given her the medicine for the pain. After she had swallowed the bitter dose, she remembered Roarke's concerned face, the warmth of his hand clasping hers, and Kevin's frightened eyes as he stood at the foot of her bed. Soon drowsiness had swept over her, and she had felt Duncan's hands on her shin, sure and gentle—then there was deep slumber and forgetfulness. He had set her leg and applied the tightly bound splint while she slept.

Sassy tossed the sheet aside and looked at her leg sandwiched between the long splints. She wiggled her toes, and was glad she could move them. Her leg still ached, but the sharp pains had subsided. Still, the sight reminded her she would have to winter in Scotland with Roarke. How much precious time would be lost. And now that she was immobile, she couldn't sidestep his advances as she had so easily done before.

As Sassy considered her confinement, a rosy-cheeked maid entered the bedroom and pulled back the drapes. The girl helped her with her personal needs and gave her a warm sponge bath, then changed her into a lacy nightgown. Afterward, the maid brought an early lunch and promised to return often to see if she needed anything.

By two o'clock a gray gloom had settled over the castle grounds and soft rain pattered against the bedroom windows. When Sassy heard the door open, she expected to see the maid again. Instead Roarke towered over her. He wore a lacy shirt and trews and soft suede boots. In one hand he carried bright yellow chrysanthemums wrapped in gay paper. Nestled in the crook of his arm was a little wooden chest. Concern shadowed his eyes, but a soft smile hovered on his firm mouth. "The maid said you were awake, that you had eaten. How do you feel?"

An uncomfortable feeling rose in her bosom, for she felt he was being too charming, and this time she couldn't escape that charm. Then she told herself he was only being courteous. She would be polite to him, but that was all. She wouldn't smile or laugh or in any way make him think she enjoyed his company or was softening her resolve to return to America. "I feel well 'nuf, I suppose," she said at length.

He closed the door behind him and came closer to her bed. "You look depressed," he added with a wry smile. "Aside from being thrown from your horse, breaking your leg, and being jolted over the countryside in the rain, what's wrong with you? Do you want to talk about it?"

"Yes . . . I mean, no. I . . . I—"

"I was worried about you, lass," he said, interrupting her. He sat down next to her and laid the blooms on the nightstand. "You could have broken your neck." He put his warm hand over hers, and tingles shot up her arm, making her feel even more uncomfortable.

"I know," she replied weakly.

"Now, why are you so unhappy?" he asked, caressing her hand with his thumb. "I know you're disappointed because your trip has been postponed, but think of it as a mere delay. Thank God you weren't hurt worse. Duncan says the fracture was clean and should mend nicely."

She glanced out the rain-spattered window and sighed. "I know I should be thankful I'm all in one piece, but I'd like to be free to run in the sunshine or have a picnic or somethin'. It's just so . . . so—"

"Gloomy?" Roarke cut it. He playfully cocked a brow. "Aye, we Scots invented gloom. Why do you think we drink so much whiskey and fight among ourselves?" He regarded her tenderly. "But we've learned to live with it. In fact, every Scot carries a piece of sunshine in his soul to warm himself on such days."

She felt rather foolish for complaining, especially when he was being so amiable. Wondering what she would say next, she glanced at the yellow chrysanthemums. " The flowers are pretty. It makes me feel better jest to look at them."

He grinned broadly. "There were a few left in the garden. I had Old Angus out early this morning cutting them. The maid will find a vase when she returns." He took the small chest and held it in front of her as if he were presenting a great treasure. "I've been after the cooks, too." He nodded at the chest. "Go ahead, open it."

Carefully Sassy lifted the lid to reveal all types of attractively arranged homemade candies: fudges and toffees, divinities and chocolate-covered fruits, and a row of Scottish shortbread, each cookie stamped with a thistle design. Her eyes widened.

"I've never seen so many good-lookin' things to eat," she cried out in delight. "The cooks must have been workin' since dawn."

"Aye, they have. Everyone in the castle hates me today." His mouth twitched as he drew another flat box from his vest pocket. "Here, open this one, too."

Sassy pulled the loosely tied string and opened the package to find a flat yellow cake. Perplexed, she tapped it with her finger.

"It's supposed to be corn pone," Roarke offered in apology. "I remembered you were eating it the first day we met. I tried to describe it to the cooks. I suppose it's more like a flat cake with a little corn in it, but you can pretend it's corn pone."

Emotion choked her throat. It was going to be hard, very hard, to resist his charm if he kept this up. Perhaps she could favor him with just a tiny smile—but that was all. Roarke's eyes lit up as she smiled and softly said, "Thank you."

He walked to the windows and gazed out at the rain. Half turning, he commented, "You know, lass, this looks like a fine day for a picnic to me."

"What do you mean? It's damp and rainy and chilly. No one could have a picnic out there but three frogs, and two of them would have to be doctors."

Roarke laughed and made his way to the door. "I think you're right, but I'm the laird of Donkinny Castle, and I say there will be a picnic." He glanced at the chest of candy. "Don't eat too many sweets, now. I don't want you to take the edge off your appetite. We'll have our picnic at six this evening." He left the room before she could ask any more questions.

Later the maid came, then Duncan and Kevin arrived for short visits. Still feeling sore and tired, Sassy took a short nap and awoke about dinnertime, remembering Roarke's promise of a picnic.

True to his word, he appeared just as the clock was striking six, carrying several lighted candelabras; a maid followed him with a picnic hamper. Sassy raised up in bed and watched him set the candelabras about the room, then spread a blanket before the fire. He opened the basket and, with the maid's help, arranged a sumptuous meal of roast pheasant and all the trimmings before the crackling flames. He then set fine china and crystal and silver on the hearth and had the maid gather and arrange chair pillows on the blanket before he dismissed her. At last he extinguished the lamps so the bedroom was lit with only soft candlelight and the fire's glow.

Flashing a bright smile, he came to the bed and tore back the covers.

"Wait! What are you doin'?" sputtered Sassy as he slipped his arms beneath her.

"I'm carrying you to our picnic," he said, lifting her from the bed. "I know you're a fearful hardheaded woman, but I'll not have you fighting me about it. I've already talked to Duncan. He said if I move you very carefully, it will be all right. Don't struggle so, or I'll have *him* mad at me, too."

Gently he carried her to the hearth and laid her on the pillows, then snatched a cashmere throw from a chair and covered her up. "Just relax," he commanded, uncorking the champagne and pouring her a glassful of bubbly liquid. His eyes twinkled as he handed her the wine, then he went to the tall windows and opened one a bit, filling the room with the scent of rain.

On the blanket, he filled Sassy's plate with the perfectly cooked pheasant and hand-fed her some of the more succulent bites. While she drank champagne, she noticed that he was treating her like a fine piece of china. She knew it wasn't just because of her broken leg. He seemed to be exerting considerable effort to be charming and not to offend her or do anything that would upset her. Perhaps in his way he was asking her to forgive him—though at this point she couldn't find it in her heart to do so. It was one thing to laugh and drink champagne with him before the firelight. It was quite another to give him her heart.

As soon as she had sipped half her wine, he refilled the glass. "Roarke!" she chided. "Are you tryin' to get me drunk?"

"Don't be silly," he replied. "It's good for your leg. It'll help the pain."

In the middle of the meal, there was a knock at the bedroom door and a man dressed like a Gypsy entered with a violin. Sassy stared at him in disbelief as he stood playing classical music. Replete and happy, she finished the wonderful meal and drank glass after glass of champagne. Outside, lightning flashed, and inside the snug room, the candles glittered and the flames crackled. Only Roarke would have thought of a wonderful treat like this.

After the violinist finished serenading them and left, Roarke looked at Sassy and raised his brows. "He's not a real Gypsy, of course, but he was rather good, don't you think? Mr. MacDonald has been searching Killieburn for a violinist all day. After working for my family all his life, the man threatened to quit my employment this afternoon. I can't understand why he's so touchy lately."

"I wonder why?" Sassy said with a laugh.

Now Roarke pulled a book of romantic poetry from the wicker basket and read her love poems as she relaxed by the fire—"The Passionate Shepherd," by Christopher Marlowe, and several of Shakespeare's sonnets. She thought about a line of the bard's poetry which stated that true love did not try to alter the object of its love. Had Roarke chosen the sonnet to make a point?

Later he carried her back to the bed and covered her up, tenderly tucking the bedding around her. When he bent to brush his lips against hers in a good-night kiss, she turned her head, feeling her heart thudding within her breast. Disappointment filled his face as he caressed her arm, then left the bedroom.

The romantic picnic by the fire had touched her heart, and despite her resolve to remain unmoved, she couldn't help feeling closer to him. She was proud she had resisted his kiss, but as she contentedly drifted into sleep, the last thing she thought of was his dark eyes and smiling face.

Kevin leaned forward in his chair, gazing earnestly into Sassy's eyes. "The chessboard is our battlefield, and the pieces are our soldiers."

Nestled on a sofa in the library, she watched him set up a chessboard on a table between them. She felt warm and comfortable, and a glass of brandy stood on the table at her fingertips. Roarke sat near the sofa reading a volume of Shakespeare's comedies. His picnic by the fire had kept him on her mind for the last few days, and her building desire for him made her decide to resist his tender advances all the harder.

After sharing dinner that evening, he had carried her downstairs for a change of scenery. Kevin had soon joined them near the crackling fire. Pouring himself a brandy, he decided to teach Sassy how to play chess. After a long lecture about the pieces,

they were finally ready to play. Outs
wind blew from the moors and whippe
castle, making their place by the fire see
and cozy.

Sassy moved a pawn forward. "Is that right
she ventured.

"Right," Kevin said. "Just think of pawns as foot soldiers who never retreat."

After a few more moves, she stared at his keen eyes, looking for approval.

"Not bad, but this would be even better." He returned her pawn and made another move for her.

Roarke glanced up from his reading. He was wearing a dark vest with silver buttons and a contrasting white shirt. Lamplight gilded his clubbed hair. "Don't try to best Kevin in this game," he warned. "It's damn near impossible."

Kevin grinned at his brother. "And who taught me? Every clever move, I learned from you."

Sassy eyed Roarke. "I thought you were gone privateerin' when Kevin was growin' up."

He closed the book and laid it aside. "I was gone most of the time, but made frequent trips back to the Highlands. Kevin learns quickly."

Sassy studied his dark eyes, and couldn't resist the opening he had left her. "Yes, I agree, he learns quickly—unlike some people I know." Her voice held just enough humor to let him know the comment wasn't malicious.

He smiled and nodded knowingly. "I feel it might be unwise to respond to that statement."

Ignoring the chess game, she glanced at his book. "What are you readin'?"

"The Taming of the Shrew," he replied with twinkling eyes. "Perhaps it would be better if I dipped into *The Comedy of Errors* or *Love's Labors Lost.*"

"Why don't you try *Much Ado About Nothin'*?"

Kevin cleared his throat. "I think I'll go to my room now. I have some reading to do, and Roarke s a better teacher anyway." He lifted his brandy glass and took a sip, then set it down. "Good night, Sassy. I'll visit you tomorrow."

She smiled as he left the large room.

Roarke moved to Kevin's chair. "Well, now that we've managed to embarrass Kevin into leaving, we have the whole room to ourselves."

"I suppose we do," she replied, picking up another chess piece.

Roarke moved his knight.

Sassy laughed softly. "The gallant knight brings fear to his enemies, for you can never be sure where he will strike next."

Roarke chuckled and lifted his brows in surprise. "What is *that* supposed to mean?"

"I don't know . . . It's jest sometin' Kevin told me a while ago."

"Did he tell you anything about attacking and capturing?"

She regarded him evenly, understanding they were talking about more than chess. "No, but he told me about blockin' and defendin' myself. He said it was the most important part of winnin' the war."

Roarke's eyes shone with passion. He studied her face for a long minute; then, with a heavy sigh, he focused on the board. They played chess for almost an hour, but finally he looked at her and shrugged his shoulders. "It seems we are in a stalemate," he remarked. With a tender smile, he slid his gaze over her. "Sometimes there is no choice but to stay where you are and resume the conflict on another day."

"Yes. I believe you're right."

Slowly he leaned across the chessboard and brushed her lips with his; then he claimed her mouth in a fiery kiss that spread warmth through her limbs. Even as desire coursed through her body, her stirring conscience warned caution. Resolutely she pulled away. Emotion choked her voice. "I'm not ready to turn my heart loose again," she whispered. "I jest can't trust anymore."

His eyes were soft as he said, "Love beareth all things, believeth all things, hopeth all things, endureth all things."

It touched her to hear him quote the Bible verse from Corinthians, but she held a tight rein on her heart. "Are you down to quotin' Scripture to try to win me over? I don't think the writer was talkin' about man-and-woman love there. Do you?"

He chuckled and sighed. "No, I don't. But at this point I'd be happy for a little brotherly love." Sadness darkened his eyes as he scooped her up into his arms. "Let me carry you back to your bedroom. It's getting late."

As they left the library and he carried her to her room, she considered his words. Was she being too hard on him? Could she find it in her to trust him again?

He laid her on her bed and pulled the covers up to her chin. At the door, he turned and glanced over his shoulder. "Did Kevin explain to you how to end a chess game?"

"Yes. He said you must checkmate."

"There's another way, too. So that the game may not continue unnecessarily, a player may lay his king down on its side and simply say—I resign."

The significance of his words was not lost on her. "I ain't much for quittin'. It kinda goes against my grain."

He smiled and thoughtfully nodded his head. "That's what I thought you'd say."

After he left, she pondered their discussion. She knew he was courting her, and she was loving it, every minute of it. It would be so easy to give in, so very easy, and so pleasurable. But what price would she pay for her pleasure?

No, she thought. She wouldn't resign the game.

She knew she was softening and would have to guard her heart well. She tossed and turned for a long while, but finally fell asleep, vowing not to respond to his courting.

A week had passed since Roarke and Sassy's chess game in the library, and he had daily showered her with attention. He had served her breakfast, brought her little gifts, and entertained her with humorous stories of Highland characters he had known in his youth. Roarke bitterly regretted her accident, but at the same time he was grateful for another chance to show her that he cared for her.

Now as they sat by the hearth in her bedroom talking about the battle of Prestonpans, he studied her delicate face and watched the firelight play over her auburn hair. He thought how hard it had been to restrain his passion for her. He wanted her so much, but he knew one false move would scare her away. Hadn't he found that out during their chess game when he had tried to kiss her? Restrain yourself, he thought now as he offered her a glass of sherry. Be tender and gentle with your advances and don't frighten the girl.

She took the glass in her hand and sampled the liquor. "So Johnny Cope was a British general?" she asked with wide eyes. Dressed in a simple winter wrapper, she sat in a wingback chair, her splinted leg propped on a stool. With the fire's glow warming her face, she looked to Roarke like an angelic child eager to hear one more bedtime story.

"Yes. General Sir John Cope was the commander of the royal forces against Bonnie Prince Charlie in forty-five. After he lost the battle and fled, the Scots captured his coach and gave it to Old Laird Robertson." He chuckled and sipped some sherry. "A scarred veteran of many rebellions, the old chieftain rode back to his castle in the fine coach and kept it until he died. It was his greatest triumph."

She smiled. "I suppose you've had your share of triumphs as a privateer."

"Aye. Each English ship I've plundered was a triumph for me. But more than that, it was a triumph for Scotland."

A dark look crossed her face. "Are you sure?" she asked.

"Of course! Everything I've done, I've done for Scotland."

She looked as if she wanted to say more.

He leaned forward and clasped her cool hand in his. "I've had many triumphs, lass, but they pale in significance compared to the brightness of your smile."

She blushed and pulled her hand away. "You know it's useless talkin' that way. Why do you keep on?"

He chuckled and relaxed into the soft chair. "You're a hard woman, Sassy Adair. A hard, hard woman."

She grinned and shrugged. "Yes, I am hard. But *life* is hard. Hard and full of blisters."

He could only laugh at her words, but in the back of his mind he wondered what it would take to melt her icy resolve. He had given her sweets and flowers, poems and trinkets. He had given her everything, but it still wasn't enough. Then, with a flash of insight, he understood what she wanted. She wanted a part of him. She wanted his heart.

Sassy lay in bed, playing with Tam; she giggled as he licked her face, demanding more affection. What a little rogue he was. Happily she ruffled his ears, then snuggled him beside her, ordering, "Calm down, now. Your heart is racin' fit to bust!"

His moist eyes pleading, he begged for more

play. Finally he placed his nose between his paws. Sassy caressed Tam's furry head, tossed back the sheet, and stared at her toes peeking from the long splint. Over a month had passed since the accident at Loch Tay, and she was still confined to bed.

Despite Tam's cheering presence, melancholy began settling into her bones like a spell of bad weather. Drawing in a long breath, she turned up her bedside lamp, then looked out the rain-streaked window. What a dismal, joyless day it was! Just like the day before it: no sun, no chirping birds, just clouds and wet moorland, which accentuated her loneliness. Even worse, it was her birthday. Her spirits drooping, she listlessly picked up a dog-eared book and began to thumb through it—yet again.

There was a soft rap at the bedroom door and Roarke entered, prompting her to pull the sheet up to her chin. He was dressed in his buccaneer clothes but had added a fur vest for warmth; he had also tied a large kerchief about his head, and he squinted through one eye.

"What are you doin'?" she asked with a laugh, despite her resolve to not respond to his antics. "You look like a pirate!" Tam rose and pricked up his ears with interest.

Playing the fool, Roarke stalked toward her and sat on the creaking bed. "Aye, lassie, it's a pirate I am an' a pirate I'll stay!" he growled in the broadest Scotch burr she had ever heard. His deep voice stirred her senses and sent her heart racing. She knew he had been out and about the estate, for he smelled of the damp earth and evergreen trees.

"I've jest arrived from plunderin' the Caribbean o' its riches," he went on in a cracked voice. "I'm in port fer a few days o' drinkin' and wenchin', then I'm off to cut more throats."

He covered her fingers with his warm hand, and

her pulse fluttered wildly. She tried to bite back her smile, but his twisted-up face was so funny, she burst out laughing.

Gently caressing her fingers, he glowered at her. "Laugh at me, will ye? Well, I'll have ye know I'm the vilest pirate that ever lived. When the lassies laugh at me, I tax 'em with a fee."

"I'll bet you do," she returned, still laughing. "You already have more money than ol' King George himself." His nearness made her blood sing, and happiness rose up inside her.

He leaned back with an offended air. "Money? Nay, I don't tax 'em fer money. I tax em fer a kiss!" Before she could stop him, he had pressed her to him and wrapped his arms about her. She beat on his chest and tried to push him away. "Nay. I'll have my fee!" he growled. As their eyes met, he dropped his acting, and passion blazed out of him, shaking her with its power and smothering her protest. Moving adroitly, he seared her neck with shivery kisses and fluttered them over her face.

A tremulous weakness welled up inside her while his mouth roamed over hers, and her nipples tingled under the thin nightgown. Without thinking, she circled his neck and leaned against him, feeling his beating chest; the tender kiss was slow and dreamy, and rushed warmth all the way to her heart.

Lightly his hand found her breast, and a shudder ran through her, making her hardened nipples ache with pleasure. As his lips raced over hers, demanding a response, a warm tide of elation rose up inside her. Now his fingers caressed her nipple with tantalizing pleasure, and he slipped his tongue between her lips, sending her heart thumping. And for one glittering moment all she felt, all she saw, all she heard, was love—bright, chiming love, as wild and sweet as a nightingale's song.

How she wanted to tell him she loved him; but

was she ready to stay in Scotland forever with no hope of ever seeing America? The question shot into her brain and left her with one answer. Gradually the glorious magic dimmed and flickered, and reality settled over her like a fine mist, leaving her empty and desolated.

Her heart aching, she broke the kiss and pulled away. "No . . . this is wrong—wrong 'cause it can't lead to anythin' good. Don't you understand I'm leavin' soon as it's warm?"

Roarke rose from the bed and tugged off the pirate kerchief. For one unguarded moment a dull, resigned look darkened his features, then he regained his composure. Slowly he reached into his vest, pulled out a velvet packet, and tossed it on the bed.

Tam tumbled across Sassy's legs and sniffed at the packet, but she took it from him and raised her brows.

"It's your birthday," he said quietly. "I thought you might want this."

A great lump lodged in her throat. "How did you know it was my birthday?"

"Duncan told me when he came to visit yesterday." He regarded her silently for a moment, then said, "Open it."

When she opened the packet, she saw something that looked like a small leaf made of gold. "It's a little leaf," she said with a smile.

"It's a laurel leaf, the MacLaren plant badge."

"Plant badge?"

"Aye, every clan has a tiny piece of Scottish vegetation that belongs to them and them alone. The laurel belongs to the MacLarens. There is a picture of it on our emblem and on the crest we wear on our bonnets. This talisman was created by one of my ancestors centuries ago after the Battle of Bannockburn as a lucky charm. The MacLarens have passed it from hand to hand since 1314. It brings great luck for the holder—but you can't keep it forever. You must pass it on or the luck will vanish."

"Who gave it to you?"

"My grandfather pressed it into my hand before he died. I was but a wee lad then, yet I knew the significance of such a gesture," he said, looking into her eyes. "I think I've had it long enough now. I wouldn't want the luck to fade."

"I must give it away someday?"

"Aye." He moved his gaze over her. "To someone you love. That's the rule. You must pass it on to someone you love."

Emotion welled in Sassy's bosom as she put the leaf back in the velvet packet. With this romantic gesture he had told her he loved her.

As he started to walk away, he glanced over his shoulder, taking on the pirate character again. "Sorry I can't stay, lass, but I need to keelhaul a few men before dinner," he added with a grin that almost hid his pain.

She watched him cross the room and close the door behind him, all the while fighting an urge to call him back. With a trembling hand, she pulled her treasure sack from beneath her pillow and added the velvet packet. The laurel leaf touched her heart, but at the same time it saddened her, for she knew their love could never be. Just like the roses Aunt Pert tried to cross—they were just too different. They were both involved with their own revolutions, their own countries. How could any love be strong enough to bridge the differences between them?

Chapter 19

Frigid cold gusted from the north early that year. In Killieburn shopkeepers closed their shutters and wrapped themselves in furs, trying to keep warm. In the countryside, the crofters stuffed rags under their doors and huddled about peat fires, drinking hot tea. On such a raw day Sassy sat at a library table in Donkinny Castle, gowned in a fur-trimmed dress of blue wool. The room smelled of old books and ink, and all was silent except for the sounds of a crackling fire and a ticking clock. A servant had just left tea and scones on a table beside the hearth.

Sassy thanked the girl, then, ignoring the food, opened a thick volume and studied an illustration of two jousting knights. Kevin had recommended the book. He had recommended many in the last twelve weeks while she recovered from her broken leg. Twelve weeks! she thought as she stared at the woodblock illustration. Twelve precious weeks had been wasted in Scotland while exciting things were happening in Boston. And now winter whistled about the castle, further dampening her spirits.

A sudden gust of wind rattled the library windows, making her tighten a shawl about her shoulders. It was cold and damp and miserable, but a little flame of hope flickered in her heart—for today the mail coach was due to arrive from London via Glasgow. True to Roarke's prediction, the bitter weather prevented sea traffic on the Firth of Lorne, but a few British packets still arrived in London with mail from the colonies.

Old Angus had faithfully mailed her letters to Boston when she had first arrived here. Surely he wouldn't fail her today. If the mail coach managed to get through the snow between England and Scotland, he would meet that coach and deliver her correspondence. Perhaps she would have a letter from Aunt Pert or someone in the Sons of Liberty; those precious letters would have to last her all winter.

She snapped the book shut, then rose and poured herself some tea. Carrying the cup and saucer, she strolled to the window. Her leg still ached a bit, but Duncan had removed the splint last week, and at least now she could walk.

Drinking the tea, she gazed over the glistening evergreens to the mountains. Snow silvered the high peaks and moorlands, glinting in the rosy twilight; it swirled over the meadows; and near the castle, it drifted against the stone walls, catching in the crevices. Like the snow, her thoughts drifted over the weeks since her accident.

Roarke had supplied the winter's few bright spots. How he had courted her while she was convalescing. He was always there with an interesting bedtime story or small gift to divert her attention. And he made her laugh. Dammit! Why did he manage to do that when she wanted to stay mad at him? Every time she thought of the golden laurel leaf he had given her, emotion stirred within her. But then, she always remembered if he hadn't kidnapped her, she wouldn't be in this awful country, away from the excitement in the colonies.

A cough brought her thoughts back to the present. She turned to see Old Angus standing at the open library doors. Dressed in trousers, a fur vest, and a long jacket, he looked half-frozen—but he clutched a ream of letters in his grimy hand.

Meeting her gaze, he snatched off his damp tam-o'-shanter and grinned. A broad smile split his face as he stepped forward in dirty boots; Sassy started to scold him, but she remembered he had been working in the castle gardens, making a compost pile.

"I brung ye these letters, missy, jest like I said I would. The mail coach came jest an hour ago. I waited while the driver dug 'em out o' his pack. I knew how bad ye were wantin' 'em!"

In high spirits, she led him to a cluster of wing-back chairs placed before the roaring hearth. "Here, you jest sit down and rest a spell," she offered. "The tea is still hot. Have some and warm up."

He hung his head. "Och, it ain't fer the likes o' me to be drinkin' tea in the laird's castle. I jest come to bring ye these letters."

She took his arm and urged him into a chair. "Why, you're nearly frozen. Have some tea, and some cakes, too! Roarke MacLaren has enough money to buy all the tea in China!"

With a nervous chuckle, Old Angus seated himself and waited for her to pour the tea. When she handed him the dainty cup, he passed her the letters. Her heart raced as she sank into a chair across from him and riffled through the mail. Most of it was from Aunt Pert, but a few letters bore addresses of friends in the Sons of Liberty. Joy flooding her heart, she opened the letters and scanned them while Old Angus drank his tea. Then, realizing she was being rude, she said, "Oh, thank you, Angus! You'll never know what these letters mean to me."

He placed his tea aside and chuckled. "Aye, lassie, I will, 'cause I've been homesick meself. I know what it is fer the heart to yearn fer home." He coughed again and peered at the letters. "It seems that most of them are from yer aunt, but there's some others, too. Who are they from?"

"They're from folks in the Sons of Liberty," she admitted openly.

"The Sons of LIberty? That sounds like one o' them political groups."

"It is. We're American patriots and we're fixin' to throw the British out of the colonies. Jest you wait and see!"

At last the old man asked, "How many do ye have in the group?"

Sassy's head rose and she caught a gleam in his eyes.

"Oh, I don't know for sure. I was one of the few women, and I was jest gettin' to know everyone when Roarke kidnapped me from Boston." With a happy sigh, she picked up a letter and ran her gaze over the florid script.

"Do . . . do them Sons of Liberty print up pamphlets and all that?"

She glanced up at his curious eyes. He had been in the room long enough to warm up, but his face looked flushed, and a wild excitement fired his eyes. Placing the letter aside, she gave him her full attention. "Yeah, they do. But . . . but why are you so interested in our group? To listen to you, a body would think you wanted to join up!"

He stood so quickly, he almost spilled his tea. "Nay. I . . . I was jest askin' a few questions," he stammered, plunking the cup on the table. "It was jest the foolishness of an old man." He turned and started for the door. "I've got to be goin' now."

Sassy walked across the room with him, patting his arm. "You keep up on your readin', now. We'll be havin' a lesson real soon. I want to see how well you're doin'."

"I'll be rememberin' that, miss," he replied.

Then, with a nervous smile, he tugged on his tam-o'-shanter and disappeared down the hall.

When he was gone, Sassy returned to her chair and read her mail. Homesickness swept over her as she devoured every line of Aunt Pert's letters—then, on the last page of the last letter, she saw a grimy thumbprint. At first she laughed to herself. Aunt Pert had been working among her roses again before she wrote the letter. But it was so unlike her not to wash her hands after gardening. Frowning, she held the letter close to an oil lamp; the print was deep and dark, and far too large to belong to Aunt Pert.

A sick feeling flooded the pit of her stomach. She checked every page of her other correspondence. The letters from her friends in the Sons of Liberty also had thumbprints on them. *No,* she thought, surely Old Angus couldn't have read her mail. Why would he do such a thing? Why would the activities of an old lady or a foreign political group be of any interest to him?

She tossed the pages aside and examined the envelopes, which she had hastily ripped open at the ends. Some of the flaps looked ragged, as if the letters had been steamed open and sealed again . . . but she couldn't be sure.

As she pondered the puzzle, a maid entered the room to remove the tea tray. A girl from the village, her face beamed with ruddy good health. "Oh, I see ye got yer mail, miss," she said politely.

"Yeah," Sassy replied, distracted. "Old Angus brought it a while ago."

"A while ago!" the girl echoed. "The mail coach came this *mornin'*. I know, 'cause my cousin got a letter from her mother in Glasgow." Shaking her head, the girl picked up the tray and turned about.

Sassy watched the maid leave, feeling hurt and empty inside. Old Angus, whom she had trusted, whom she had taught to read, had opened her letters. But why? Why would he invade her privacy when she had taught him the skill in the first place?

And Roarke had been good to him, too. Out of pity he had hired a useless old man aboard the *Sea Witch* just so he could return home, then he had provided him with another job.

She went to the fire and gazed down at the crackling flames. Should she speak to Roarke about the letters? He was planning a trip to England in a few days, and since getting a message from the South, he had immersed himself in political business. Maybe this wasn't the time to tell him the old man he had befriended was a snoop; still, Sassy felt she must inform him.

Quickly she left the library and found Roarke on the second floor of the castle in Mr. MacDonald's office, going over household accounts. Thankfully the steward had stepped out for a minute to see the head cook, so she could speak in private.

Nervously she handed the letters to Roarke and explained the situation. "I'm sure those fingerprints don't belong to Aunt Pert," she said. "See how large they are?"

Roarke studied the letters, then thoughtfully rubbed the back of his neck. "I can understand how you feel, but no harm has been done. Out of boredom and curiosity, an old man has peeked into your privacy."

"But they were my letters. I—"

Roarke stood and clasped her arms, interrupting her complaint. "I hardly see Old Angus as any kind of spy. He is nothing more than a harmless old man with only a few years left to live." He glanced at the letters again, then gave them back to her. "He's certainly guilty of snooping, but I think that's all."

"Don't you think we should watch him?"

He raised his brows and nodded. "Yes, we'll

certainly keep our eyes open, but I think you are being a little too suspicious."

Her mind full of questions, Sassy left Mr. MacDonald's office and went back to the library to reread her letters. How important was it that Old Angus had opened her mail? she wondered. Was he just a harmless old man who had made a mistake, or something more?

Bundled in leather and furs against the cold, Roarke relaxed in the saddle, letting his mount have his head. Moonlight cast a silver glow over the road, and the gorse and weeds glittered with hoarfrost. Twinkling brightly in the cloud-swirled sky, the distant stars guided his way over the snowy moors; occasionally cottages dotted the bright expanse and sent up plumes of fragrant peat smoke that drifted into the darkness. Nothing was audible but the wail of the wind and the lulling thud of his horse's hooves.

The two-week trip to York had been long and hard—but rewarding—and now he was almost home. Breathing a sigh of contentment, he turned up his collar against the moaning wind as a sudden turn brought him to where he spotted a blotch on the horizon. Soon the blotch grew larger, and at last Donkinny Castle appeared against the sky, golden light glowing from its tall windows.

As he thundered homeward, the letter in his fur vest rested warm against his chest, lightening his spirits. From Cardinal Henry of York, it fired the Jacobite cause with the possibility of success. Ten days ago he had met the cardinal in icy York Cathedral. The cleric had eased down beside him on the pew and whispered, "Here it is, just as I said in my message." With trembling fingers he had handed Roarke a letter stamped with a red Stuart seal. Roarke's pulse had raced. The letter. Lord

God above, how long he had waited for such a letter.

Satisfaction swelled within him every time he remembered the meeting. He finally had the letter, and Sassy would be waiting at Donkinny for him. Even now his heart stirred at the thought of her creamy skin and fiery hair. They would share tender moments and cozy evenings near the fire, and they would talk and laugh and be closer than ever. Aye, she would be there . . . waiting at Donkinny.

Her vision strong upon him, he touched spurs to his mount, passing crofters' cottages and ancient stone fences built by generations of determined Scots. Soon the castle loomed around a bend, surrounded by glistening fir trees; light spilled from its towers and streaked over the snowy battlements. The sound of a barking dog greeted him as he clattered over the drawbridge . . . Once inside the cobbled courtyard, he slid from the saddle and tossed his reins to a waiting servant.

With a few long strides he was inside the castle, enveloped in warmth and light; quickly he skinned off his gloves and tucked them away. He headed down the long hallway toward the dining room, knowing Sassy would be there eating dinner on a small table beside the fire, as was her custom. As he neared the chamber, the smell of braised beef stirred his appetite; he pushed open the dining room doors and saw her—even lovelier than he had envisioned.

She looked up with a start. Dressed in a blue skirt and a black velvet jacket trimmed with fur, she had draped a MacLaren tartan about her shoulders. A MacLaren tartan. The sight pulled at his heart, making him devour every curve of her soft body. The flames turned her flowing hair to fire, and a silver brooch glinted at her throat. In the firelight's glow she stood out like a figure in a dark Italian oil painting.

She put down her fork with a clink and stared up at him. "I didn't think you would be back so soon."

Roarke pulled off his damp hood and sat by the hearth, enjoying the warmth. "Neither did I," he replied, tossing the headgear aside. "I finished my business in England early. There was no need to stay." He wanted to say, *There was no need to stay when you were here* . . . but he bit off the words.

There was fresh tea and she offered it to him. As he accepted the cup, his hand brushed hers, and desire sparked between them. Sassy's eyes darkened and her hand trembled. Had she missed him as he had missed her? he wondered. A deep need welled up within him, making his groin tighten. Lord, how he wanted to take her into his arms and make love to her right on the dining room floor—but that was something a vile pirate would do.

"Have you eaten?"

He gulped down some tea and placed the cup on the hearth. "No, lass. I'll eat later." He tugged the muffler from his neck and raked a hand through his damp hair.

For a moment they sat in silence listening to the fire crackle and the wind wail. While she was confined with her broken leg, he had revealed to her things about himself he had never told anyone. She was no longer the amusing girl he had desired and taken in Williamsburg, or the fiery woman he had wanted and kidnapped in Boston. She was much more. They had shared themselves and their dreams, and to him she had become a complete human being—the woman he loved.

A deep intimacy welled up between them, binding them together. Before he could touch her, she nervously glanced up and asked, "Was your trip successful?'' Her words sounded tiny in the big room.

Pride warmed his heart as he replied, ''Aye. Very successful.'' Working a hand under his vest, he slipped out the letter and handed it to her.

She scanned the finely written page and raised her brows.

''Look at the signature on the bottom,'' he urged.

''Charles Edward Stuart,'' she muttered, giving each name great emphasis. Her face paled.

''Aye, Bonnie Prince Charles himself. He's an old man now, not the fair-haired lad who sported with Flora MacDonald and danced at Holyrood Palace, but he's ready . . . ready to come back to Scotland. He'll be our rallying point. There will once again be a Stuart in Scotland.'' He took the letter, refolded it, and placed it back against his heart.

''You . . . you saw him?''

Roarke stood and paced before the fire. ''No. He's in France. I saw his brother, Cardinal Henry of York. He acted as our intercessor.'' Excitement flowed like wine through his veins as he spoke. All his years of defying the British agent, all his years fighting in the Highlands, all his years of privateering, all his years as Captain Rakehell, had come to this—one folded page of finely written lines lying against his heart. He looked at Sassy again, wanting to share his joy with her. ''This is what I've been waiting for. With this letter, all the lairds in Scotland will be ready to fight.''

''From what I've seen, all the lairds in Scotland are ready to fight each other!'' she said with a laugh. ''Who has the patience to lead 'em?''

''*I* will lead them,'' he replied with conviction. ''In his letter the prince names me as his representative.''

Her eyes widened. ''When are you goin' to show the letter to Dunsworth and the other lairds?''

"I'll show it to *all* the lairds at the same time. No one will feel slighted and say they were the last to see the letter . . . and it will have the most impact presented to the group as a whole." He looked thoughtful. "I think I'll take advantage of a festive occasion and invite all the lairds, even the Lowland lairds, to a New Year's *ceilidh*.

"Well, you've finally done it, ain't you?" she murmured with trembling lips. "At last you have the power to make your dream come true."

He knelt by her chair and took her hand in his, grazing his thumb over the palm. "Perhaps. It will still be very hard. But perhaps now I will succeed."

He looked into her eyes and caught a glint of passion that pulled at his heart.

"That's wonderful. I'm real happy for you," she offered.

Slowly he cupped her face, then his lips brushed hers in a kiss full of tenderness and fire, a kiss calculated to set her soul aflame. As he pressed her closer, the sweet smell of her hair flooded over him, spurring his passion. As he caressed her breast, soft flames fanned out in his belly, radiating pleasure through his limbs. Aye, God help him, this was the woman he loved, this stubborn little renegade, this single-minded hellion who had captured his heart with her fierce spirit.

A smile curled his lips as he eased away his mouth. He felt her heart somersaulting against his and saw the passion in her smoky eyes. "Tell me you feel nothing now, lass. Tell me my kiss has left you cold."

Her eyes glistened and she eased away, standing. "Yes, I feel somethin', but I can still think, too. What about America?" she asked stiffly.

The anger in her tone made his temper rise. "What about it?" he asked, coming to his feet. "I'm sure Samuel Adams and all the other American zealots are working feverishly, whipping up the rebel cause. I'd say open warfare is imminent."

She turned and stared at him. "But I won't be there, will I?"

With a huge sigh, he took her into his arms and caressed her silky hair. "Is it more important to you than us?" he asked, studying her sad face.

"Could you stay in Boston while the Scots were fighting the British?"

The question lanced into his heart like an arrow, and he couldn't find words to answer her. Speechless, he stared at her, knowing no force on earth could keep him away from the Highlands.

"No, I thought you couldn't," she said at length, pulling away from his arms. Her voice was sharp and cut into his pride. Without another word, she walked from the room.

As her quick footsteps receded, then vanished, he placed a hand on the mantel and stared down at the dancing flames. In these last weeks as he had courted her, it seemed they had made some progress in their relationship. But now he saw that this problem of priorities still stood between them. Who would step aside so the other could find happiness? It seemed neither. It seemed they were at a great impasse.

Lord Almighty, how he wanted this woman: He wanted to spend all his life with her; to take her to bed this minute; to kiss her eyelids and keep her warm; to make love to her; to plant his seed deep within her and never let anyone or anything hurt her. But loving Sassy Adair was a thorny problem, involving many sacrifices. She would have him go to America with her. She would have him abandon his clan and his cause. She would have him accept her politics as his own.

He slammed his fist against the mantel. No, he thought with deep conviction, he wouldn't sacrifice the cause he had worked for all these years.

No, he wouldn't escort her about the bloody world, like a besotted lover, unsure of his own mind. No, a thousand times no, he would never leave Scotland!

Chapter 20

In December Roarke made a trip south to invite the Lowland lairds to his *ceilidh;* his heart high and his carriage chock-full of holiday treasures, he returned on a wintry Christmas Eve. A short time earlier, Kevin had donned a fine kilt and jacket, and seated Sassy before a dinner of roast goose. Since Roarke couldn't predict the time of his return, the pair would enjoy an elaborate but quiet meal. Faced with an overwhelming abundance of food, Sassy and Kevin had just begun to eat when footsteps rang out in the corridor. Quickly Sassy smoothed out the skirt of her blue wool dress; with a racing heart, she glanced at the open dining room door.

As Roarke entered, he thumped snow from his Highland bonnet and sailed the hat aside. He was heavily dressed against the bitter weather in trews, a fur vest, and a long coat. Dark stubble shadowed his face, and moisture glistened in his black hair; his eyes twinkled merrily.

"Good evening!" he called out in his deep-timbred voice, warmed with humor. "It seems I've arrived just in time to share the Christmas Eve goose."

Their arms filled with presents, two servants trailed him into the vast chamber, which had been decorated for the holidays with scarlet ribbons and pungent pine boughs.

Good health and well-being radiated from Roarke's tanned face. He was a stunning man, a devastatingly handsome man, and Sassy was secretly thrilled he had returned; but her heart warned her against a display of affection. So putting an amused note in her voice, she stood and tossed down her lace-trimmed napkin. "Well now, I suppose I should be honored—the MacLaren is home."

"Perhaps I should build up the fire," Roarke remarked, flashing a wide smile. "I'll vow, it's colder in here than outside."

Sassy rolled her eyes and sat down, then watched the servants hover about Roarke like honeybees around a hive. She knew how much Charles Edward Stuart's endorsement meant to him, for his face had beamed with happiness as they had shared their nightly dinners. Weeks had passed since his return from England, and every morning he rode out to encourage some Highland laird to join in the rebellion; every evening he stormed into the castle full of political news. She could not forget the glow on his face, the light in his eyes, the joy in his voice, as he had told her the stubborn old men were softening their resistance against buying guns from the French.

Roarke peeled off the last of his outer garments, and an attendant snatched up the pile of damp wool and whisked it away; other servants arranged the Christmas presents around the sweet-smelling bayberry candles on the sideboard; yet another hurried an extra place setting to the table and splashed whiskey into his master's glass.

Roarke sat down at the dinner table and placed his whiskey aside.

"How are things in the South?" Kevin ventured.

Roarke chuckled. "Good and getting better. To

my surprise as I made my rounds from castle to manor house, I discovered even a few of the placid Lowland lairds are leaning our way. And most of them accepted my invitation to the *ceilidh*. The castle will be full for the New Year's holiday." He refilled Kevin's and Sassy's wineglasses, then raised his tot of whiskey. "A toast on Christmas Eve," he proposed, gazing at Sassy with dancing eyes. "A toast to the Sword of Wallace."

She raised her glass and cocked her head. "You're drinkin' a toast to a sword? I've heard Kevin mention Sir William Wallace, but never his sword. What are you talkin' about now?" she asked.

"Sometimes I forget you're not Scottish," Roarke said with a laugh. "I suppose Christmas Eve is as good a time as any to tell you the story. Lord knows it's being told to children all over the Highlands this bitter night."

Kevin set his glass on the table and nodded in agreement.

Roarke's countenance took on the dreamy look she knew so well. "Wallace is the national hero of Scotland," he began. "He organized resistance to King Edward I, and in 1297 his army defeated the English at Stirling Bridge. Then another English army was sent, and in the summer of the next year he was defeated at Falkirk."

"Did the English execute him?"

Roarke's eyes darkened. "No. Not then. For the next four years he took refuge in the Highlands. Some say he then went to France and Italy, but in 1305 the English arrested him in Glasgow."

Kevin leaned forward and in an icy tone added, "At that time they took his sword, a symbolic act of humiliation. In London he was charged with treason. He denied it, for he had never sworn allegiance to Edward, but he was condemned and executed the same day."

"And the sword?" Sassy asked.

Roarke curled his hand into a fist. "His sword was taken to Warwick Castle, where it still lies in an armory. Every Scot dreams of bringing the Sword of Wallace back to Scotland. To do so would strike a great blow to the very heart of the English. Often we toast the sword at Christmas, hoping the coming year will find some Scot brave enough or clever enough to bring it back."

The romantic story stirred Sassy's fancy. "Have any tried?"

He drained the whiskey in one gulp, then smacked the glass on the table. "Aye, a few have tried, but they have died for their efforts. For four hundred seventy-six years the sword has languished in enemy hands." A thoughtful look flickered over his face. "Nothing would fortify Scotland more than the return of the sword—but at this point that is impossible." He rubbed his stubbled jaw. "I hope the letter from Bonnie Prince Charlie has the same effect; I need something powerful to unify the lairds," he added, frustration coloring his deep voice. "We Scots are the most independently minded people in the world . . . Unfortunately our strength is also our undoing. It's hard to get us to agree on anything—especially something as complicated as plans for a rebellion."

Running a hand through his damp hair, he strode to the hearth, where a Yule log burned. "I'm looking forward to the *ceilidh*," he commented, skimming his gaze over Sassy. "Perhaps the holidays and a barrel of whiskey will soften up the old bandits." He chuckled, his tone brighter.

Before she could reply, approaching steps resounded outside the dining room. In a moment Duncan entered. Snow caked the old sailor's heavy clothes, and weariness lined his face.

"I need to speak with ye, Master Roarke," came his strained request.

Roarke pulled his brows together and nodded a greeting. "Aye. Of course." He left the room with Duncan.

Kevin stood and tossed his napkin on the table. "I'm going to my room now," he said with a smile. "I have a book on medieval sieges I want to study." His eyes were warm as he regarded Sassy. "Merry Christmas, and sleep well."

She smiled at him as he quickly left the room. What a dreamer he was—but what a kind, gentle dreamer. She knew he hadn't joined Roarke and Duncan, for she heard him continuing down the corridor.

Left alone, Sassy picked up her heavy silver fork and toyed with her food. What were Roarke and Duncan discussing? What news had lured the old seaman away from his snug quarters aboard the *Sea Witch?* Murmured words floated into the room, but their meaning escaped her; still she detected a note of concern in the men's tones. And this was no quick message concerning the ship, for she had almost finished her meal when Roarke returned to the dining room.

Instead of sitting down, he paced before the sweet-smelling fire, his face tense and drawn.

"What was that about?" Sassy piped up, turning about in her chair. "Your face is as dark as the inside of a coffin."

He strode to the heavily laden table and sat down; wordlessly he shoved back his plate and stared straight ahead; his eyes sparkled with angry fire.

Hadn't his good mood dried up fast! she thought sourly. A sensible woman, a prudent woman, would have remained silent, but frustration sprang up inside her, and she leaned forward, her brows raised. "I said—"

"My conversation with Duncan was private," he said, cutting her off.

Stung, she blinked at his blazing eyes. After all his weeks of tender courting, what had prompted him to snap at her? What had she done to provoke the great MacLaren?

His gaze as stormy as a sea gale, he clasped her arm. "I don't want you to leave Donkinny without me or Mr. MacDonald," he ordered. "And no more riding out by yourself. Whenever I'm gone, you'll stay strictly inside the castle."

Sassy stared at him in silent wonder. "More rules?" she cried. "You'd think I was a child the way you're tryin' to take care of me. I'd like a little more freedom than that."

Roarke looked at her sternly. "I'm concerned for your safety. I don't want you slipping on the snow and falling. You need to be careful with your leg in case it isn't completely mended."

She pulled free of his grip. "I feel like I'm on that floatin' prison of yours again. Why don't you jest lock me up?"

He stood, his jaw hard. "I'm sorry. That's my final word on the matter."

Christmas day dawned cold and cloudy. When breakfast was over, everyone gathered in the chieftain's room and Roarke handed out presents; there was something for everyone, including Mr. MacDonald and Duncan. Afterward, they enjoyed a huge meal, and Sassy felt in need of exercise; about two o'clock she decided to take a ride. What a surprise she had when she arrived at the stable and found the servant wouldn't saddle her horse! She marched back to the castle. True to his word, Roarke was already thwarting her plans. Evidently orders had been given to the lowliest servant in Donkinny that her freedom was to be restricted.

Determined to get some exercise, she bundled up for a walk and stormed outside again. Soon she recognized Duncan striding across the snow toward her. Clad in heavy winter clothes and a muffler, he scarcely resembled the old sailor she knew so well.

"Where are ye goin', miss?" he called, waving his hand for her to wait for him.

She looked over her shoulder, a little nettled with the man she usually liked so much; nevertheless, she slowed her steps. When he reached her side, he matched his pace with hers. Pine needles crunched under their feet and the frosty air nipped at their cheeks as they strolled down the road leading to Killieburn. "You were watchin' me, weren't you?" she said in a strained voice.

He shoved his hands in his pockets and hung his head. "Well, miss, I . . ." Frosty breath puffed from his mouth.

Sassy studied his uneasy expression. "I know you were. And I saw Roarke lookin' at me from a castle window when I was walkin' to the stable a while ago. "Did you know the boy wouldn't saddle my horse?"

"It's Christmas day, miss. I suppose he thinks he deserves a day o' rest."

"No, it's not just that," Sassy retorted with a frown. "Kevin is the only one who seems normal today. You and Roarke and Mr. MacDonald have been watchin' me like hawks since last night when you came to the castle. I hadn't gone thirty feet down this road when you came after me. What did you tell him to make him so protective of me? I want to know."

Duncan shook his head. "I canna' be repeatin' the words I said to Master Roarke. It ain't fittin'. I canna' break a vow."

She widened her eyes. "A vow? You mean he made you take a vow of silence?"

Duncan touched her arm, forcing her to stand still. "Now, miss, I canna' be tellin' you what I said, but I know we should be returnin' to the castle." He glanced at the smooth, gray sky. "It's goin' to snow again and ye should be inside, where it's warm. And all this walkin' isn't good for yer leg." He took her arm. "I'll escort ye back to Donkinny, then I must return to the *Sea Witch.*"

Sassy considered insisting that she continue the outing, but they had actually gone quite a way and the weather did seem threatening. So she let Duncan gently turn her about and they returned to the castle together.

Sassy considered the strange situation. Since she had broken her leg, Roarke had been gentle and tender and had courted her as if she were a great lady. Just this morning he had presented her with several elegant gowns, bottles of scent, jewelry, books—everything a woman's heart could desire. Yet now he had put new restrictions on her movements. Law a mercy, she thought, it just didn't make sense. The man who had given her the golden laurel leaf had become her jailer. What in the name of God had Duncan told him on Christmas Eve?

The rest of the week flew past and the New Year's Eve *ceilidh* was soon upon them. A jewel-clasped plaid at his shoulder, Roarke stood near the great windows of the chieftain's room watching the last of his guests enter Donkinny Castle. The road leading downward to the village shone like a silvery ribbon, and as the chieftains' ladies swept through the snow, their long capes trailed behind them, glinting in the moonlight. The chieftains themselves were dressed in fine kilts, trews, and Highland jackets. Aye, the castle would be full, Roarke thought warmly. Even the Lowland lairds had come. Mr. MacDonald had already ordered extra provisions from the village, for most of his guests would be spending the night.

The skirl of the pipes and the rattle of drums

pulled Roarke's attention away from the frosty pane; sharp and sweet, the lively music stirred his blood and reminded him of his proud Scottish heritage. Their faces bright, the assembled guests laughed and applauded while a line of musicians in Highland dress entered the great chamber, which was decorated with greenery and glowing candles. A troupe of sword dancers and singers, also colorfully dressed, trailed the musicians over the shining parquet floor.

As the procession passed, Roarke scanned the noisy crowd, searching for Sassy. For a moment a sea of faces and colors danced before his eyes. Finally, among the dark, fur-trimmed costumes he spied a flash of red hair.

Sassy stood by the great hearth, where several giant logs burned brightly. A low-cut green taffeta gown Roarke had brought from the Lowlands molded her slender figure; wide-eyed and fragile-looking, she projected a graceful, innocent air and made the other women seem dowdy and overdressed. His mother's emeralds glinted at her white throat and ears, and burnished by the flames, a riot of glossy curls crowned her head. The wide, farthingaled gown emphasized her full bosom and dainty waist, and she drew admiring glances from every man in the room.

Exhaling a long breath, Roarke studied her face. As usual since Christmas Eve, a pout was on her lips and defiance gleamed in her eyes. He knew she was sulking because he had forbidden her to ride or go to the village. Undoubtedly he had been too stern with her, but Duncan's news had chilled his heart, and since that night, he had been afraid to leave her by herself for even a minute.

His vigilance had exacted a high price. What he would give for a smile tonight, he thought wearily.

Resolutely he strode across the room and caught her eye. At first she turned away and tried to lose herself in the crowd, but he pushed fat Laird Ferguson aside and caught her slim arm.

She lifted her chin and glared at him.

"I see Mr. MacDonald brought you the gown and my mother's emeralds," he said. "I thought you might like to share my rule tonight," he offered, glancing at two thronelike chairs at the end of the room. "The laird and his lady always preside over the New Year revels just like a king and queen."

She glared at him, her posture stiffening with defiance.

With a deep chuckle, he met her stormy gaze. Flashing a smile, he placed his hand at the small of her back and steered her ahead with unhurried purpose.

As they moved forward, he skipped his gaze about the gorgeously decorated room, making a mental note to compliment Mr. MacDonald: scarlet-ribboned greenery and holly hung above the dark paintings and on the mantel, and the heavily laden buffet table groaned with suckling pig, mince tarts, and mulled wine, their mingled aromas permeating the air. Everything, from the brass-armed chandeliers to the tall windows, was immaculate—even the claymores and colorful flags seemed brighter tonight.

When Roarke and Sassy reached the end of the chamber and took their seats, the other lairds and their ladies, who sat in chairs circling the room, applauded loudly. Then the wild, sweet notes of the pipes melted away and sword dancers trouped forward with a flurry of yells.

Dressed in kilts, billowy shirts, and leather jerkins, they strode proudly to the rattle of the drums. In the firelight's glow, they placed their swords on the floor, then with quick, elaborate steps, danced over the blades. After a series of complicated figures, the glinting swords were brought together to form a star.

Roarke stole a glance at Sassy, who was watching the dancers with a stoic face. His eyes roamed over every inch of her luscious body, caressing her curves. The green frock set off her lovely face and snowy breasts, making them appear unbelievably white. With her blazing hair, she looked like a petulant angel, angry because she had been barred from heaven for some earthly infraction.

At last she lowered her eyes before his admiring gaze.

"Smile, love!" he urged with a grin. "Laird Fletcher is watching you with a wary eye. Soon all the lairds will be saying I'm keeping you here by force."

She shot him a withering glower. "Well, ain't you?" she said in a rough whisper. "Ain't that jest what you're doin'?"

"Of course not, lass," he replied with a note of sarcasm. "You're free to go anytime."

She glanced at the thick snow swirling outside the windows and shook her head. "Of course. I'm free to leave anytime I want—in a foreign country in four feet of snow."

He chuckled heartily. "We must all brave the Scottish winters, lass."

"And what's goin' to happen when spring comes?" she asked with a toss of her head. "Don't you think I know what's goin' on? Every time I stick my head from the castle, either you or Mr. MacDonald are watchin' me. Why don't you jest put a leash on my neck?"

He raised his brows and watched the dancers file away. "Perhaps I should."

Her fingers turned bone white as she clenched the chair arms. "When the first ship leaves next spring, I'll be on it," she vowed with trembling lips. "Kevin promised to give me the money."

Roarke glanced at Kevin, who was standing in

the corner being argued down by Laird MacNish. "My brother's generosity humbles me."

Sassy started to say more, but a group from the village began playing a ballad appropriate for dancing. Some of the ladies peered at Roarke, mentally prodding him to dance so they could also take the floor. With a weary sigh, he rose, slanted a look at Sassy, and extended his hand. "I would not ask for myself, lass, but we must dance so the others may enjoy themselves."

For a moment she looked at him woodenly, but at last she stood and gave him her hand. Roarke could almost hear a sigh of relief from the ladies as he set the example and moved across the floor with Sassy. As he held her soft body in his arms, he remembered the sparkle in her eyes when she was happy, her laugh when she was amused, the tenderness of her lips against his as she sighed. He remembered the look in her heavy-lidded eyes as he caressed her breasts, and the way her nipples hardened under his fingers. He remembered the silkiness of her inner thighs, the touch of her fingers on his back, the warmth of her breath against his cheek, the smoothness of her tongue against his lips.

As they danced, he pressed closer, feeling his maleness thicken with desire. She stiffened, but he put a hand to her chin and held it where he could see her glinting eyes . . . so defiant, so bold. He could feel her thudding heart beating against his chest and hear her quickened breathing. Slowly he moved his hand to her back to caress her tight muscles. As he did, he tried to memorize everything about her. The sweep of her bosom. The glow of her creamy skin. The luster of her fiery hair. The way she stirred his heart like no other.

Finally the last strains of the dance faded away and everyone applauded as Roarke and Sassy resumed their seats. Sassy seemed warm and flustered. A pulse throbbed in her neck and a blush colored her cheeks. Had she enjoyed the dance as much as he had?

Remembering his duties as host, he reluctantly directed his gaze to the great hearth. A girl from Killieburn stood before the flames, just beginning a song. She was healthy and robust, and her voice carried a soft, plaintive quality. She sang "The White Cockade," "Charlie Is Me Darlin'," and "Come O'er the Stream."

Roarke watched tears glisten in the grizzled lairds' eyes while they listened to the Jacobite songs. Aye, the whiskey and warmth of the season had worked their magic. As soon as the ladies had gone to bed, he would gather the men around the hearth and present them with the letter from the prince. They would drink more whiskey and laugh, one in the spirit. Then in the spring . . . It made his heart race to think of what would happen in the spring.

Singers, dancers, pipers, storytellers . . . They filled the evening, and the hours passed by quickly; before they knew it, the grandfather clock in the corner was chiming midnight. Now it was time for the lads from the village to burn out the old year and ward off evil spirits. Knowing what to expect, the laughing lairds and ladies strolled to the windows, sipping from cups of hot mulled wine.

Without permission, Roarke took Sassy's hand again; the feel of her silky skin warmed his heart and made him want her all the more. "Come to the window with me," he urged, rising and gently pulling her to her feet. "I want you to watch an old Scottish custom."

The chattering group respectfully parted as they approached. Outside the castle a group of young men from the village packed fuel-soaked rags into netted globes of wire attached with chains to long poles. After the rags were lighted, the men swung the fireballs far above their heads, and the fiery arcs blazed through the darkness while the men paraded before the castle.

Some of the ladies broke into applause. "Now we'll all have a happy new year!" one of them cried.

Roarke wondered about the prediction. He eyed Sassy, who leaned against the window casing, listlessly watching the fiery spectacle. While the other ladies laughed and cheered, her face showed not a trace of emotion. Aye, he thought painfully, his rebellion was going well now—but what of his courtship? He knew she resented the restrictions he had placed on her, but dammit, they were for her own safety. He had considered repeating Duncan's words to her, but had decided against it. Duncan's news would unnecessarily terrify her. She might as well be happy while she's here, he thought. As he studied her sad face, he remembered the evening one week ago when Duncan had told him . . .

"I have news for ye, Master Roarke," Duncan had announced in the corridor outside the dining room. "I've been waitn' here at the castle for hours."

Roarke noticed his worried eyes. "Aye. Go on, man. What is it?"

Duncan lowered his head and cleared his throat, then glanced up. "There's been a man in the village the last few days inquirin' about ye and the young lady. He's been snoopin' about the shops askin' all kinds of questions. The tobacconist told me yesterday."

Roarke frowned. Perhaps Cardinal Henry of York had been indiscreet, he thought with a ripple of alarm. "Who is he? What does he look like?"

"I ain't seen him, but everyone tells me the same thing. He's tall and thin. He talks real proper like. He's an English gentleman to be sure."

"Anything else?"

"Aye. The blackguard has a black patch on his eye."

The words stabbed into Roarke's heart. *Blackhurst?* But what was he doing in Scotland, and how in the devil had he found them?

"Are ye goin' to tell Miss Sassy?" Duncan asked.

"Nay, I am not, and you must vow to keep silent also. She had nightmares about Blackhurst for months after we left Boston." He clasped his friend's arm. "It's late. Stay here tonight and spend Christmas morn with us. Tomorrow afternoon go back to Killieburn and see if the villagers have seen more of this English gentleman."

As Duncan's footsteps faded away, Roarke renewed his decision not to tell Sassy—not yet. She had been terrified of Blackhurst, and there was a chance this stranger was someone else.

One of the ladies at the window laughed loudly, and Roarke's thoughts returned to the present. His heart heavy, he let his eyes trace Sassy's graceful form, and considered their predicament. Since the original incident, no one had seen the Englishman about the village. No, there was no reason to frighten the lass yet. He would simply protect her and keep her close. Better to let her think him an ogre than allow her to be terrified again.

Chapter 21

The year had barely begun when Sassy woke up at dawn to the sound of someone entering her bedroom. Half-dazed, she sat up in bed. Roarke stood there dressed in trews, boots, a lacy shirt, and a heavy, fur-lined jacket, for it was very cold.

"Roarke," she muttered sleepily. "What are you doin' here?"

He chuckled and laid a finger over her lips. "Shh. Don't say another word," he commanded. "I'm going to take you to my special room to see the sunrise." He clasped her hand and urged her from the warm bed.

Blinking, she stood on the icy floor and shivered. "Special room? Sunrise? What are you talkin' about? I ain't goin' anyplace."

"If you won't walk, I'll carry you." He pulled some covers from the bed, wrapped them around her, then gently scooped her into his arms. Like a father bundling up a child for an outing, he tucked the blankets under her chin.

"Put me down! I . . . I don't understand." She struggled in his arms. How dare he burst into her bedroom and whisk her off. Besides, she was still angry with him for restricting her activities . . . "Put me down!" she repeated.

"Quiet, lass. You'll wake the castle," he said,

drawing the drooping blankets tighter about her. Once out of the bedroom, he carried her up two flights of stairs and down a long corridor, then pulled back a large tapestry to reveal a narrow door. He ascended another steep, winding staircase carved out of stone. He carried her with little effort, but occasionally shifted her weight so he wouldn't brush her legs against the rough walls. At last they emerged into a small cubicle lined with windows, located at the top of Donkinny Castle. The turret room was hardly larger than a closet, but was furnished with a desk and a few chairs. Cobwebs covered everything, and the room smelled as if it hadn't been aired in years.

As the sun slipped over the horizon, blushing the clouds with pink and silver, Roarke sat down in an old armchair, holding Sassy on his lap. "I wanted to show you this place," he said as he cuddled her against him. "I woke up thinking of it this morning."

Her anger at him left her as she realized the room had a special significance for him. Curious, she looked about the small chamber. "It's so little. What was it used for?" she asked.

"It's a scribe's room. In medieval days when few of the lairds could write, my ancestors kept a scribe to copy manuscripts and write letters for them." He gazed out at the rugged HIghlands, which were just coming to life with rosy color. "The light is wonderful here. You can see for miles and miles. It's one of the oldest parts of the castle and was added after my forefathers started building out from the original tower."

Sassy's interest increased; in the security of the small room, Roarke had relaxed and was talking freely. The gift of the laurel leaf had touched her heart like nothing he had ever done, and she yearned to understand the man who was capable of giving such a gift.

"When I was a wee lad I used to come here often to watch the sunrise," he went on. "One of the cooks had a boy just my age. We would chase each other about the castle playing knights. When I wanted to get away from him, I'd pull back the tapestry, scramble up that winding staircase, and come here. Later when the British agent lived in Donkinny, this was my refuge from the world. I haven't been here for years. I'd almost forgotten it existed until this morning." He chuckled and tucked the blanket around her, holding her closer. "What wishing I used to do up here."

"And what did you wish for?" Sassy asked, favoring him with a smile.

"I wished for all sorts of things," he said with a sigh. "For important things like having my father alive. I wished my mother could have seen Kevin take his first steps." His eyes darkened with emotion. "And I wished for foolish, childish things. I wished I was a mighty Scottish king of old, for then I could march my forces to the South and drive the British from the Highlands. I wished I was a falcon so I could sweep down upon the haughty British officers and snatch off their stiffly curled wigs with my claws." He brushed back Sassy's hair. "I even wished I was a fly so I could sit on the walls of the British agent's office and listen to him tell his friends how he skimmed money from MacLaren lands."

During the early hour the castle was silent and the world seemed to belong to Sassy and Roarke alone. She guessed he was telling her things he had never disclosed to another person, and she sat very still. "And I thought Kevin was the dreamer," she said softly.

He smiled and traced her face with his fingertips. "The sense of being part of a conquered nation sometimes overwhelmed me. I felt helpless and defeated. I don't know what was more humiliating, seeing the British agent lord his authority over Robert, who was the rightful MacLaren chieftain, or seeing our clansmen afraid to wear their own tartan for fear of retaliation." He sighed heavily and gazed again at the snowy mountain peaks bathed in pink. "At last the roads and forts were built and the British moved southward again, feeling they had subjugated us to their rule. But they hadn't. By that time I was already at sea, working toward my dream of staging a new uprising."

Nothing else he had done or said had given her a better picture of the wealthy but orphaned child who longed for his parents and strove to see their deaths avenged. She relaxed under his approving gaze, feeling a new intimacy between them.

"Roarke?"

"Yes?" He gently kissed her hand.

"I understand how you hated the British, how you still hate them, and I understand why you went into privateerin', but . . . " She bit her lips, unable to finish.

"Go on," he commanded. "Don't be afraid to speak your mind, lass."

"Well, I'm . . . I'm just wonderin' about the reasons behind your rebellion. I can see the anger and hurt you carried as a boy. But are you fightin' for Scotland or to avenge your family?" Immediately she regretted her words, for his expression told her he was shutting himself off from her again.

"Does it make any difference?" he finally asked.

"Yes. I think it does. It makes a lot of difference. It's easy to plant your dreams in the past. But it's harder to see ahead . . . to figure out where you're goin'."

"I know where I'm going, and I'm making progress."

"Seems progress has more to do with direction than how fast you're movin'. Sometimes I think what you want for Scotland isn't . . . isn't—"

"Realistic?"

"Yes, I suppose that's the word."

He regarded her quietly, then rearranged the blanket and caressed her hair. His face was thoughtful.

Sassy knew they would talk no more of his rebellion that day, and she was content to sit in his arms and watch the glowing mountains. She felt honored that he would share this part of himself with her, and felt closer to him than she ever had before. He had wooed her and given her many gifts, but she realized that he was finally giving her something even more precious—part of himself.

Perhaps his insistence that she not leave the castle without him was for her own good. Perhaps he was genuinely concerned for her welfare and not simply restricting her activities to antagonize her. And yes, he had hurt her, hurt her deeply, but could she allow herself to nurse her anger forever? She thought again about Shakespeare's line that true love didn't try to alter the object of its affections. And life was too short to be lived in half measures, worrying about commitments.

In those quiet moments she realized how deeply she wanted to be completely his again. Pride had turned out to be a cold bedmate, and more important, an even colder friend. But she had rejected him for so long, she suspected he had almost given up on her. He might not believe her if she suddenly announced she was ready to accept his advances.

With some surprise, she realized she would actually enjoy flirting with him to let him know she had changed her mind about making love with him. Determined to go after him, she snuggled a little closer, imagining how surprised he would be when he discovered that *she* was now actively pursuing *him!*

* * *

A few days after her visit to Roarke's secret wishing room, Sassy sat at the dinner table, nervously awaiting his appearance. As she glanced down at her peacock blue silk dress, a blush warmed her cheeks. Although Roarke had given her the gown for Christmas, she hadn't worn it. The neckline was too low. But now that she had decided to flirt with him, it was just right.

She considered the last two days—busy days that hadn't gone as well as she had hoped. Wasn't it just her luck that Roarke would receive a stack of bothersome letters from the lairds just when she had decided to show him she was ready for love? Since then, he had been shut up in his study working each day from breakfast until dinner; the few precious minutes she had been alone with him, a preoccupied look had glazed his eyes. He had been so immersed in plans for his rebellion, he had hardly noticed her flirtatious gestures.

Flirting. How did one go about it? Obviously she had done something wrong; then with a flash of remembrance she thought of Eunice Snodhocker back in Potter's Lick. The silly chit had always made a fool of herself flirting with the men every Saturday when she came into town. How Sassy had laughed at her! Now she tried to remember exactly what the girl had done.

Dressed in trews and a silky shirt, Roarke entered the dining room with a stack of scribbled papers in his hand and sat down at the head of the table. Sassy felt a sting of hurt when he scarcely glanced at her.

He looked up at her as a servant placed dishes on the table and removed the silver covers. At the sight of her exceedingly low décolletage, his gaze lingered on her bosom. Her heart raced, but after giving her a puzzled look, he went back to his reading.

When the servant left, she asked sweetly, "Did you get a lot of work done today?"

He continued to study the papers without looking up. "Aye, but I have more to do tonight. I'm going to an important meeting at Dunsworth's castle tomorrow and need to get my thoughts in order."

She flicked the lace dripping from her long sleeves and raised her brows, thinking that men could be the dumbest creatures on earth sometimes. Male dumbness was what it was. They were all filled with it, filled right up to the top of their heads. And sometimes you had to hit them smack between the eyes to shake them out of it. She would just have to wage an all-out campaign against him. Kevin would be staying in the village tonight, and Mr. MacDonald was working late, so they wouldn't be interrupted.

There would be no more demure smiles or lowered lashes. Tonight she would make it as plain as frost on a window that she was ready for his lovin'. Tonight she would be Eunice Snodhocker!

Clearing her throat, she forked a pheasant breast from the serving platter and tossed it onto Roarke's plate. As the meat thudded against the china, he put down his papers and looked at her in surprise.

"I'm jest givin' you a nice piece of meat," she explained, moving the papers to where he couldn't reach them. "There ain't no gristle there, I'll wager."

As they helped themselves to the rest of the food and ate their meal in silence, she happily noticed his gaze drifting to her low-cut neckline once more.

"You ought to eat more meat," she suggested between bites. "It gives a man a lot of strength below the belt."

Roarke cocked a brow at her. "Strength below the belt?"

She put down her fork with a loud clink. "You

know, *lastin' power*. Course, fried squirrel is the best for that, but if you ain't got it, chicken or pheasant will do."

He threw her an odd look. "Sassy, what's come over—"

She put her fingers over his lips, then scooted her chair close to his. "Did I ever tell you about Eunice Snodhocker back in Potter's Lick?"

He took her hand away from his mouth. "Eunice who?"

"Eunice Snodhocker. She was the biggest flirt I ever saw. Every Saturday she came to town and flirted with the men hard as she could." She leaned forward, giving him a good view of her bosom, and batted her eyes. "Look at me. See how I'm battin' my eyes? Well, she used to bat hers so hard, I was afraid her eyelashes were goin' to fall right off."

Roarke smiled and continued to eat.

"And the dresses she wore!" Sassy went on. She tugged her dress even lower and was rewarded with a glint in Roarke's eyes. "Sometimes I was afraid she was goin' to fall right out of those dresses and embarrass everyone to death. Course, the men followed her around like hounds trailin' a meat wagon—till she got arrested."

"Arrested?"

"Yes," Sassy casually answered as she paced in front of the crackling fire. "One night she had a gentleman friend stayin' over at her house, and they got to arguing durin' the night." She widened her eyes. "Well, that man got out of the bed and started to leave, but ol' Eunice wasn't ready to let him go. She was naked as a jaybird, but she grabbed up her clothes and ran from the cabin after him, thinkin' she'd have time to put on her clothes later."

Roarke stopped eating, giving her his full attention.

"Eunice jumped on the back of that man's wagon, tryin' to put on her clothes, but he wadded them up and throwed them in the bushes. So there she was sittin' beside him naked as the day she was born. They drove through Potter's Lick like a streak of greased lightnin', but the constable saw 'em and arrested Eunice. The next day she had to sit in the stocks by Will Taner's general store with people laughin' at her till they was fit to bust. Course, she had clothes on by then."

"I hardly see what this outlandish story—"

"You would have thought that would have slowed her down some," Sassy continued, cutting him off. "But it didn't." She sidled up to Roarke and traced her finger along his jaw. "The very next Saturday she was in town runnin' her fingers over the men's faces." She swept her fingers through his hair. "Or playin' with their hair." She massaged his back. "Or kneadin' their tight back muscles." She brushed her bosom against his shoulder. "Or even rubbin' up against 'em like this. Can you imagine that!"

Roarke reached out to grab her, but she moved nimbly away from him, and sashayed over to the dining room door. "I decided I ain't hungry no more." She batted her eyelashes again and yawned. "I guess I'll jest *go to bed* now," she finished suggestively.

From the gleam in Roarke's eyes, she knew she had finally broken through his male dumbness. But she wanted to let him stew for a while and build up some steam. Before they made love, she wanted him hot as a string of red peppers. Tomorrow night after his meeting with the lairds, he should be *just right*.

As she ran up the stairs, she laughed to herself, proud of her accomplishment. Eunice Snodhocker couldn't have done better herself.

* * *

The next night, shortly before eleven o'clock, Roarke returned from yet another meeting with the fractious lairds, this one intended to decide how much money each laird would provide from his own pocket to finance the rebellion. Saddle-sore and half-frozen, he entered the castle from the courtyard and stripped off his wet coat. What a day! Since the latest war council had been held at Dunsworth's castle, the obstinate old laird had decided to dominate the morning session, and accused the other lairds of being misers; Leckie and Campbell had been at each other's throats all afternoon, arguing about "withheld funds"; and as if this weren't enough, Ramsay and MacNish had had a hellish row about money during the after-dinner session.

Thoroughly disgusted and numb with cold, all Roarke wanted was whiskey, a warm bed, and a woman in his arms—his woman, Sassy Adair. He tore off his damp hood and muffler and strode into the chieftain's room. At the grog tray, he poured himself a drink. Aye, he thought, after taking several large sips of whiskey, it was a bitter night, a night made for warmth . . . for love.

Thoughtfully, he put down the glass and considered Sassy. He had wanted her since he had first spied her under the oak tree in Virginia, slashing at the ruffians like a wild savage. The fire in her eyes and in her spirit had caught him by the heart and hadn't let go. He had wanted her in Williamsburg, and tried to sail away and forget her but angrily found he could not. He had wanted her in Boston, and resorted to a schoolboy trick to keep her with him. And Lord, how he had wanted her on the sea voyage!

Refilling his glass, he considered their time in Scotland, a miserable time for him, because she had been so temptingly close, but just out of reach, making him want her all the more. He had tried to court her . . . to humor her . . . to win her with romantic gestures, to speak to her in reasonable terms—but all to no avail.

Until recently. Until he had taken her to his secret wishing room and opened his heart to her.

From that day on, he had seen a great softening in her manner and a light in her eyes that had tempted him to distraction and set his loins on fire. It seemed they had traded places in he game of love. Although he had been preoccupied with work, he knew she had been flirting with him. Lately she had favored him with smiles and glances that made his blood tingle. Did the chit have any idea what her lowered lashes and soulful glances were doing to him?

She often trailed her hand over his when they met in the hall, and she took every opportunity to brush against him. And last night at the dinner table she had behaved outrageously as she told him a story about some silly woman named Eunice Snodhocker!

This morning when she had seen him off, she had told him she would be waiting up for him in the library when he returned that night. Waiting up for him in the library . . . Just thinking of it made his heart beat a little faster. Now it seemed she was trying to seduce him!

With new purpose, he tossed back the whiskey, feeling better than he had in months. Perhaps this would be the night, he thought as he left the chieftain's room. Perhaps this would be the night they made love.

Striding down the drafty corridor, he met Mr. MacDonald and whirled him about by the shoulder. "I'm relieving you of your duties tonight," Roarke said, pulling several coins from his vest and placing them in the servant's palm. "I want you to leave the castle and spend the night in the village inn."

Mr. MacDonald's eyebrows swept upward. "In this weather, sir? At this hour!"

"Aye, in this weather, at this hour!" Roarke slapped more coins into the man's limp hand, wondering how much it would take to buy him off. "And take Kevin with you."

"He's retired for the evening, sir."

"Well, get him up, dammit! And get up the maids and dishwashers and floor scrubbers and anyone else sleeping under this roof. Take them all with you."

Frail Mr. MacDonald stood his ground. "All of them? But that will be quite costly—"

"There's enough money here to outfit a regiment," Roarke said, taking a bulging pouch from his vest. "It should see you through the night." He dropped the heavy pouch into the servant's hands and stalked away, then glared back over his shoulder. "Don't come back until nine tomorrow morning . . . No, on second thought, make that noon."

Mr. MacDonald paled noticeably. "But what about Miss Adair? What am I to do with Miss Adair?"

Roarke chuckled and rubbed his chin. "I won't overburden you. I will take care of Miss Adair myself."

"But, sir—"

Roarke jabbed a finger into the air. "Do you understand your orders!"

The perplexed servant sighed and replied, "Aye, sir, I . . . I think so."

"Well, carry them out, man. Carry them out!" Wondering how an intelligent man could be so thickheaded, Roarke started to move on, then paused again. "I am not to be interrupted tonight for any reason!"

The discussion over, he whirled and left, eager to see Sassy's lovely face. He thought of the sparkle in her eyes and the softness of her hair. By the time he reached the open library door, he could scarcely wait to touch her silky skin. Just as he thought, she was sitting at a table poring over an open book, a flickering candle stand at her side. She wore a low-cut dress made in the MacLaren tartan, laced up the back and trimmed with fur at the cuffs. From behind her, light from the crackling fire washed over her loose chestnut hair and fine features.

She looked up with a start as Roarke entered the room. Then, seeing who it was, she raised her brows and smiled, her lips soft and inviting. "Did you have a good trip?" she asked sweetly.

He braced his hands on the library table and leaned toward her. "No. I had a horrible trip," he said with a chuckle. "Dunsworth, Ramsay, Campbell, MacNish . . . all of them fought like rabid dogs all day, and I nearly froze to death riding home." He raked a gaze over her luscious form and cocked a brow. "I need to talk to you about something, lass. About your flirtatious manner."

She looked at him innocently, but a smile lurked on her lips. "Flirtatious manner?"

"Aye. Perhaps this is all just a game with you, but I thought I might give you fair warning that your actions are having the desired effect. If you don't stop, I may soon lose control."

A blush stained her cheeks as she closed the book and stood up. "Those pants look so tight, it looks like it's going to take you two hours to wiggle out of them," she said, edging away from the table.

Roarke straightened and eyed her playful green eyes. "Burn me, if that isn't an invitation, my ears are deceiving me." He reached out to grab her, but she grinned and danced out of his way.

Laughing softly, she moved toward the open library doors, flashing her eyes at him. "If you see somethin' you like, you're goin' to have to come and get it," she called in a teasing voice. "I ain't had a good game of chase in a coon's age."

Just then there was a rustle of feet in the corridor as Mr. MacDonald herded some of his charges toward their icy destination. Sassy's gaze went to the door, then back to Roarke.

"Aye, it's true, lass. They're leaving—all of them. A Highland chieftain has the ancient power of pit and gallows over his clan, and I've just used that authority to send everyone away. Soon we will be completely alone." He drew nearer. "Think of it. Just the two of us—all alone in this huge castle."

A coy smile flickered over her lips. "Sounds interestin', don't it?"

When he came after her again, she ran from the library and took off down the long corridor, glancing back with laughing eyes. Roarke ran after her, watching her bright skirt disappear into the shadows as she skidded around the corner. His heart pounding, he followed her to the third story and trapped her in a sitting room; a low fire crackled in the hearth, barely illuminating the dim chamber.

First he spotted her moving in front of the flames, but like a kelpie, she disappeared—vanished from sight. Pausing, he listened to the wind and the sputtering logs, then heard a creaking footstep coming from the right side of the room. When he moved that way, she popped up from behind a chair and hurled an ugly pea green dish at him; missing him by several feet, it sailed past him and crashed into the door casement, breaking into many pieces. He glared at the broken dish, then at her. "What do you think you're doing!"

"I'm makin' the game more interestin'."

"Interesting, hell! You almost decapitated me."

"Oh, I was jest funnin'. If I'd meant to hit you, I'd a hit you. I was the best rock chucker in Potter's Lick."

After that, she was about the room like a fury,

crawling on her hands and knees, hiding behind chairs and settees. With careful footwork he managed to get near her, and once even got close enough to catch the hem of her flying skirt. But she let out a shriek of laughter and was off again, leaving a piece of the garment in his tight grip. Merriment sang through Roarke's body. He was thoroughly enjoying the chase, which made the idea of finally catching her all the more tempting.

She led him downstairs, then through Mr. MacDonald's office, swiping a ream of papers from the desk as she scurried past. Scrambling after her, Roarke slid on the slippery papers and fell on his backside. With a giggle, she peeked over her shoulder and slipped from the room.

"You little minx!" he shouted, getting up and racing after her.

As she ran down a long marble staircase, she accidentally brushed against several suits of armor lining the stairs. Metal helmets and breastplates clanged over the steps, sending up a terrible din and blocking Roarke's path. After negotiating the rolling obstacle course, he reached the bottom just in time to see her heading down a narrow staircase to the castle kitchen. Ah, she would be trapped at last! he thought, picking up his pace.

In the kitchen she surprised him by hurling a bowl of flour, which hit his chest and exploded upward in a great white cloud. "Are you goin' to let a little flour slow you down?" she taunted. A satisfied smile wreathed her face, and her flushed cheeks and glittering eyes made her more attractive. While he wiped flour from his eyes, she turned and scampered away.

"That little trick is going to cost you fifteen long kisses, lass," he shouted. Swiftly he followed her to the main part of the castle. She was weakening. She had to be. No mortal woman could keep up this pace forever. Excitement pumped through him as he realized she was leading him on a roundabout journey to her bedroom.

As expected, she flew inside the room just in time to slam the door in his face. With a smile, he turned the knob and found the door unlocked. He entered. She vanished behind a velvet wall hanging, which he in turn tore down with a mighty rip. With a giggle, she fell to her knees. The material tumbled over her in a cloud of dust. All flying arms and legs, she sprawled on the floor, floundering in yards of heavy velvet.

By the time she regained her feet, he had cast off his shirt. Inch by inch he followed her every move until he had her backed into a corner. He grabbed her wrists and held her arms against the wall. Tangled hair hung over her eyes, and sweat sheened her heaving bosom as she laughed up at him.

"I vow," Roarke murmured, gasping for breath, "if I had a regiment of men like you, I could take Edinburgh, and London, too. I see you play this game by your own rules." With a crooked grin, he met her teasing grin. "Let's hope you make love with as much spirit as you play cat and mouse . . . Eunice Snodhocker."

They both laughed as Sassy picked up Roarke's discarded shirt and wiped every trace of flour from his face and hair. Then, before she could make another move, he pulled the lacings at the back of her gown, finally tearing them from the placket. With a mighty tug, he jerked the garment over her smooth shoulders and tugged it down past her waist; it floated to the floor with a soft *whoosh*. In her chemise and ribboned pantalets, she was slender and graceful—but what interested him lay under the lacy underthings. Already his loins were aching.

He watched her startled eyes . . . and saw her nipples harden under the gauzy chemise. With a thudding heart, he ripped the filmy garment from her body. "Now we're going to play a game we'll both enjoy,'' he said with a chuckle. When he slid the pantalets over her smooth buttocks, she cried out and covered herself, but he brushed away her hands, exposing the silky triangle between her legs. ''No, lass, you're beautiful. Why are you trying to hide yourself?''

She held her tongue and stared back at him, her eyes shining; she was naked except for dark stockings, which set off her milky thighs and pink nipples and fiery hair. She looked so vulnerable standing there in the soft lamplight with her pantalets and gown pooled about her feet. But was that a spark of lust he saw in those lovely green eyes? Aye, it was. She wanted him as badly as he wanted her.

Despite her boisterous ways, her face was tender and sweet, her lips full, and her eyes glistened with suppressed sensuality. Holding her gaze, he impulsively brushed her lips with a tender kiss, as soft as swan's down. His heart leaped when she seemed to crumble under his scrutiny—a sigh caught in her throat and her bosom trembled against him. It was so quiet, he could almost hear her beating heart . . . and a sensual magic hung about them like a sweet fragrance.

His breath coming harsh and fast, he eased back a bit and slid a gaze down her body. Firelight shimmered over her soft breasts, flat stomach, curving hips. It glistened in the tangle of damp curls between her pearly thighs. Feeling his manhood stir, he looked at her rosy nipples, all hard and erect, ready for him to kiss . . . to suckle. Hungrily pressing her to him, he fluttered kisses over her creamy neck and cupped her breast, rubbing a thumb across her nipple. She gasped and sucked in her breath, and her long, silky hair fell over his arm. They were chest to bosom now, and he could feel her trembling, feel her heart pounding. With a contented sigh, she closed her eyes and put an arm around his neck in a gesture of surrender.

The long game of chase was finally over.

Roarke's head spun with delight. How he loved this hardheaded hellion, and how he wanted to take her to the heights of sexual pleasure! "My little love. My sweet lass," he whispered roughly.

He traced both hands over her cool back, then her hips, pulling her closer. Even damp and sweaty, she smelled wonderfully sweet and womanly to him. He could feel her swollen nipples rubbing against his chest, driving him to a frenzy of passion. A tremulous urgency ran through her as he lowered his head and caught one of the pebbly nipples in his mouth. She cried out softly and pressed her hand against his throbbing flesh; the warmth of her fingers penetrated his breeches as she instinctively stroked back and forth.

He moaned and kneaded her buttocks; his breath came hard and quick and painful in his chest. Then their mouths met and they were kissing, madly, furiously, ravenously, as if they couldn't get enough of each other. Both of her arms flew around his neck, pulling him closer. Their tongues intertwined in a deep kiss, and a hot shudder took his body, making him grind his abdomen against her.

She was moaning and trembling in his arms, and her hand clutched his hardness to stroke him once again. Groaning at the delightful pressure, he slipped a hand between her silky thighs, finding her already moist and pulsing. Gently he scooped her into his arms, and kicking away her discarded clothes, laid her on the bed and removed her slippers. He was vaguely aware of the richness on the canopied bed, heaped with lacy pillows at the head, and the sound of the crackling flames in the hearth, but he saw and heard everything through a thick mist of passion. In a matter of seconds he had divested himself of his boots and trousers, and lay down beside her.

Her eyes were dilated, her lips parted, her nostrils flared; her breath came in short gasps. He smoothed his palms down her warm, slender arms and moved to her legs, enjoying the silkiness of her skin, then he peeled off her stockings with a soft crackling sound and tossed them aside. She was the loveliest creature he had ever seen. Taking her mouth, he nibbled and sucked; at last he thrust his tongue between her lips and drove in and out, making her moan.

His hand strayed to the damp triangle between her thighs and he toyed with her there, teasing, arousing. Finally he broke the dominating kiss to lean over and draw on her nipple, feeling it grow hard as he swirled his tongue about it in swift circles. When the moist tip of his shaft touched her inner thigh, she writhed under him and groaned in delight.

He wanted to bring her to climax with his hand first, to prolong her pleasure as long as possible. He claimed her with his fingers while he continued nuzzling her nipple, toying with her swollen bud long and leisurely, flicking at it, stroking it, exploring the whole area behind it. With a sigh of delight, she relaxed and opened wider to him, enticing him to rub his wet tip into her moist valley in another teasing gesture. The scent of her womanhood was in his nostrils, sharp and sweet. Then he was again caressing the center of her desire with his fingers in long, firm strokes. He felt her quivering, warm and moist against his palm, and at last she clamped her thighs about his hand and shook convulsively.

Her face was soft and luminous, tender . . . almost glowing. "That was wonderful, so wonderful," she murmured thickly.

His heart lurched as he realized how much he loved her and how close she had come to leaving the castle. Now that she was his, he would never let her go. "That was only a taste, lass," he said, pulling her close; he kissed and caressed her hair and called her name tenderly. He brushed away her tears of pleasure and gave her a moment to recover, then began another round of lovemaking. Soon his hand was again between her thighs, stroking her, teasing her, bringing her to a fever pitch once more.

Sassy was light-headed and dizzy with pleasure. All her doubts about him had melted away like snow under the hot sun; she now realized that she loved him totally. The passion she felt for him was a thing beyond her control. Gasping for breath, she watched him position himself over her. His face was intense, all hard planes, and his maleness was thick and hard, its dark tip glistening in the light.

"Put your leg over me, lass," he ordered, lowering himself toward her.

Obedient, she slipped her leg over him. His mouth near her ear, he told her what he intended to do next. As she listened to his deep voice, chills raced over her arms and a throbbing pulsed deep inside her, deep in her womanhood and between her buttocks. He whispered more deliciously exciting things and rubbed his shaft against her, teasing her with entry, slipping the tip of his tongue between her lips.

Hungrily she pulled it into her mouth; she moaned and locked her other leg about him, spreading herself wide for him. Again he toyed with the sensitive area, caressing it with featherlight touches, grazing over the seat of her desire with his thumb and entering her deeply with two fingers. She whimpered and caressed his silky hair, then traced down his neck and corded back, and clenched his buttocks. She felt his maleness hard and wet and hot against her thigh.

He worked his thumb over her bud again and

again, bringing her to a fever pitch. For long seconds he stroked and flicked and pulled; at the same time his other hand found her nipple and he gently rolled it between his fingers. She was throbbing and bursting for release, but he eased off . . . then began again.

She moaned as if she could bear no more and pressed her hands against his tight buttocks, begging for entry. He fluttered kisses over her face and quivering eyelids, and with a masterful stroke, slid into her at last—huge, strong, and powerful. At first she stiffened and gasped at the burning sensation; then, as he began to move slowly and rhythmically, she surrendered her trust, wanting him to thrust deeper. What fire and ecstasy swirled through her body at that moment. Groaning, she dug her nails into his back and arched her hips toward him. Pulling back a bit to protect her from his weight, he started a tantalizing rhythm, plunging deeper and stronger as she rocked up to meet him.

Each masterful stroke heightened her arousal and she gasped and drew him closer yet. Her hips twisted beneath him as she struggled to meet his faster pace; a deep, glorious sense of excitement rolled over her, and she felt warm and glowing, as if she might burst with pleasure at any moment. Even in her sexual excitement she yearned for more than a physical coupling, wanting to be one with him in every respect. As he relentlessly continued, fire streaked from her womanhood to her belly, and pleasure rocketed through her.

She tightened her inner muscles about his long hardness. She was whimpering for surcease, but he kept steely control and pounded into her again and again, until with one mighty thrust, he jetted into her. Like a mighty river, the flood of ecstasy carried her away with a reckless force. Shuddering with rapture, she cried out his name, and he held her in his arms until their bright flame of passion was slowly spent.

Afterward they dozed peacefully. Sassy enjoyed a warmth and contentment deeper than anything she had ever known. Even as she slept, the glow of their love engulfed her body and spirit, leaving her deliciously satisfied. When she woke, her body still humming with joy, she stole from the bed and found her treasure sack. As she slipped back into the warmth of Roarke's arms, he stirred and opened his eyes. Gently she placed the laurel leaf into his open hand, tender emotion swelling inside her. "I think it's about time I passed this on to . . . to someone I love—before the luck wears out," she said softly.

Chapter 22

Clothed in a warm coral dress trimmed in fur, Sassy stood near her bedroom window watching snowflakes swirl from the sky. Bathed in the warm contentment of true love, she scanned the silvery landscape, aglow with sunset colors. At her urging, Roarke had put out trays of grain for the hungry deer that ventured from the wilderness. She laughed as a doe and fawn nimbly leaped a castle hedge and approached the grain.

As she watched the red deer, so beautiful against the snow and evergreens, she thought of her new life with Roarke. Although they had been sleeping together for over a month and a half now, it still seemed impossible.

She smiled to herself as she remembered the look on Mr. MacDonald's face when he had returned to the castle the day after she and Roarke had first made love. How shocked he had been to find papers littering his office floor—but like the well-trained servant he was, and although his expression reflected a keen curiosity, he asked no questions. Some of the maids had blushed and giggled and ducked their heads as they passed Sassy in the corridors. Otherwise, no one had commented on the night they had all been sent to Killieburn. Who would dare reproach the great MacLaren?

Now Sassy's heart thrilled with excitement as she heard beloved footsteps coming toward her; she whirled to find Roarke crossing the room.

Chuckling warmly, he came to her side and drew her close. Dressed in heavy winter clothes, he smelled of the cold outdoors. She snuggled against his chest, then glanced at his amused face; happiness flooded her.

"Last week it was the birds. Now it's the deer," he said, in mock despair. "Next you'll have me feeding the hares and badgers." With a groan, he kissed her forehead. "What a predicament for a thrifty Scotsman to be in love with a lass like you. You'll be the ruination of me yet!"

She stood on slippered toes to kiss his lips, but he swatted her behind. "Nay, you lusty wench. We'll not be dallying in bed when we have a social obligation to fulfill!"

Widening her eyes playfully, she caressed his jaw. "A social obligation?"

He sighed dramatically, then lifted her hand and kissed her fingers. "What a bother ye furrin women are!" he went on in a broad Scots brogue. "Ye waste a man's hard-earned money feedin' everything that crawls, walks, or flies, an' ye know none of th' local holidays!"

She giggled happily. "And what holiday might this be?"

" 'Tis Fastern's E'en, woman, and we've been invited to a celebration at a crofter's farm. Every year a tenant invites me to share his meal. 'Twould be the height of rudeness to refuse his hospitality."

She glanced at the flying snow, then back at Roarke's twinkling eyes. "But how can we go? The roads are filled with snow."

"We'll go in that," he said, pointing out the window.

Hearing bells, she looked out at the snow-packed

drive circling the great lawn. Their necks held high, a team of fine white horses pulled an antique sled on ornate runners. A servant held the reins and leaned back against the blue leather upholstery, his legs covered with a fur throw. With an exclamation of surprise, Sassy studied the fantastically decorated sled, thinking it looked like something from a fairy tale. A high peak topped with cupids holding lanterns crowned its prow, and golden scrolls decorated its sides. At last the servant pulled the team to a halt directly under the window, then got out and stood next to the horses.

Roarke stepped up behind her, feathering kisses over her hair. "My grandfather had flashy taste for a Scot, don't you think?" His hand cupped her breast as he talked, making her glow with warmth. "He *liberated* the sled on a raid over the English border one winter. He said he had always had a secret wish to glide over the snow in a fabulous sled with a beautiful woman at his side. Since I was a boy, I've shared that same romantic notion. Unfortunately my grandfather didn't live to fulfill his dream . . . but I feel I might get lucky today. What do you think?"

"I think you're right. That sled is the purtiest thing I ever seen!"

He kissed her tenderly and fondled her breast, making her nipple harden under the wool dress . . . then he held her at arm's length. His eyes were deep and warm with love. "Bundle up . . . and hurry, lass. I'll be waiting outside."

Fifteen minutes later they were on the road. Warmed by his presence, Sassy sat next to Roarke, the fur throw over her legs. Smiling down at her, he pulled her closer yet, then snapped the reins and called to the team. Sassy took in everything—the labored breath of the horses, the jingle of harness bells, the muffled thud of flying hoofs, the whisk of runners over packed snow.

The sled followed a twisting path that entered a small forest glittering with icy branches. Powdered with snow, larches and evergreens flew past on either side. The woods were silent except for the rush of an icy brook and the piercing cry of a bird. Soon they were out of the trees and on open moorland once again. The landscape's stark beauty tore at Sassy's heart. Snow mantled the distant mountains, and up ahead, thatched crofters' cottages huddled together like shaggy sheep.

Sassy realized she would soon arrive at one of these cottages and partake in a strange celebration she knew nothing about. She touched Roarke's arm. "What *is* Fastern's E'en, anyway?" she asked.

He shot her a crooked grin. "It's the night of the next Tuesday after the first new moon after Candlemas."

"It's *what!*"

He laughed and squeezed her to him. "It's the evening before Lent," he explained with a chuckle. "It's an echo of the revels from the South. After a big meal, the women make up scones and invite friends for dinner and a party—especially young unmarried people. The housewife puts favors in the scones. There is a favor for each profession. If you find a button, you'll marry a tailor. If you bite into a penny, you'll marry a rich man, and so on."

Sassy laughed. "That sounds like fun."

He cocked a brow. "If you find a ring, you'll be the first to marry," he went on. "There will be laughing and drinking and the scrape of the fiddle far into the night. And after all the fun is over, each lad chooses a lassie and squires her home." He flashed her another wicked grin. "No one talks about what happens then. That's the part of the game *I* like best."

As Roarke had promised, they enjoyed a wonderful evening at the crofter's farm. The low-ceilinged cottage was brightened with hanging copper pots and scraps of lace at the windows, and the burning peat smelled mellow and cozy. There were spirits to drink, lively music to dance to, and friends with whom to share the good cheer. Roarke's eyes twinkled with pleasure when Sassy broke her scone apart and pulled out a cheap brass ring. A blush stung her cheeks as she met his eyes, and the crofter's family laughed and congratulated her. A little embarrassed by all the attention, she silently slipped the ring into her pocket.

After leaving the crofter's farm, they flew through the darkness in the golden sled with the glowing lanterns. Stars lit the inky sky, and in the crisp night air, the landscape was a breathtaking silver-blue.

Sassy cuddled next to Roarke, thinking of all the wonderful lovemaking they had shared since their great chase through the castle. One night as she had lain nude on pillows before the crackling fire, he had caressed her body with fragrant warmed oil. He had begun with her shoulders and back and ended in the most intimate places, finally carrying her to bed to satisfy her mounting passion. And in one of Donkinny's storerooms he had found a huge metal bathtub so ornate, it might have belonged to King James himself. The room aglow with soft candlelight, they had bathed together in warm, sudsy water, laughing and drinking champagne.

When the sled gently glided to a halt before Donkinny, Roarke carried Sassy into the castle so she wouldn't dampen her feet in the snow; he kept his arm about her as they walked up the sweeping staircase. Once they were in her room and had taken off their damp outer garments, he stirred the fire.

"I had a wonderful night," Sassy said with a sigh.

He grazed his hand over her cheek. "Perhaps it isn't over—just yet," he replied, deftly unlacing her gown, which fell to her feet with a rustle. Scooping her up, he deposited her on the pillow-mounded bed. She remained perfectly still as he sat beside her and brushed her lips with a fiery kiss; as he removed her shift, she felt the warmth of his hands through the thin fabric, and her breasts took on a pleasurable glow, as if they knew what to expect. Hungry to touch him, she ran her hands over his fine shirt, feeling hard muscles beneath the silk. Soon the ribboned shift lay in a silken pool beside the high bed. The huge bedroom was slightly chilly, but his body warmed her, and the crackling flames in the fireplace cast a cozy glow on the fringed canopy above her head.

Roarke kissed her, then cupped her bare breast, flicked his thumb over her nipple until she trembled. He laid her back against the mound of pillows, and she raised her hips as he slid away her pantalets and slipped off her stockings. He lay down beside her and thrust his hard tongue into her mouth. Eliciting moans of delight, he parted her moist curls and slipped a searching finger into her womanhood. She was flooded with a feeling so deep and full and lulling, she thought her heart would burst with love.

Then he surprised her by clasping her in his arms and rolling her on top of him. She could feel his velvety breeches against her legs and his silky shirt against her bare breasts as his warm hands caressed her buttocks. Somehow the idea of being nude while he was clothed gave an extra measure of excitement to their lovemaking and made her feel like a wanton harem slave. He eased her up until her full breasts hung before his face, and her pulse fluttered with excitement. For a while he kissed her mouth and gently fondled her soft mounds, then he drew on a nipple while slipping a hand between her spread buttocks to toy with her womanhood until she ached for entry.

Just when she could bear no more, he turned her on her back and settled her against the soft pillows; she felt lace and the cool satin counterpane against her bare buttocks as he spread her legs. Then, beginning at her feet, softly, leisurely, as if he had all the time in the world, he planted tiny kisses from her arches up her calves to her knees and beyond to her trembling thighs. He stroked his tongue back and forth over her skin, and spurred on by her groans of ecstasy, bathed her with damp kisses.

Sassy gasped as she felt a moist warmth against her flesh . . . then a teasing flicking of his tongue. Shocked, surprised, delighted, she held her breath, wanting and not wanting him to continue. When he leaned forward, the savage tenderness of his tongue flooded ecstasy throughout her body and made it glow and pulse with deep satisfaction. Hot passion swirled wildly within her. He continued lavishing her with attention until she gasped his name and clenched his silky hair. Still he persisted in kissing her where she had thought she would never be kissed, until, her heart racing, she exploded in a shattering climax and sank damp and limp against the mattress.

Afterward he held her tenderly and fluttered kisses over her face and breasts. Then he pulled back the counterpane, and lifting her like a child, deposited her under the covers. As she watched him undress, the sheets were cool and silky against her body, which still glowed with sensual pleasure. With a soft whoosh, he blew out the lamp, leaving the chamber dark except for the rosy glow from the hearth. When he joined her in bed, they made love again, then he pulled her against his body and they settled down for sleep.

His breathing was quiet and regular as she lay in the darkness thinking, her nostrils still filled with the warm scent of their lovemaking. Already her body was a slave to his touch, and she couldn't imagine living without him. She knew deep inside that she was plunging headlong into reckless folly, and she knew she should be thinking about going back to America. But how could she when her heart cried out for his touch, for the sound of his voice, for the sight of his face? Even now as his warm hand caressed her breast in sleep, she felt a new and vibrant need for him. Pushing away unpleasant thoughts of leaving, she sighed and nestled against him, refusing to consider her precarious future.

Sassy and Roarke made love as often as they could and whenever the spirit moved them: in *her* bedroom and *his* bedroom; late one night in the chieftain's room; and in the locked dining room in front of the hearth. If it hadn't been so snowy, they would have made love on the castle grounds, on the moors, and beside Loch Tay.

To Sassy, life now glowed with joy.

One morning when spring's first warmth had reached the Highlands, she woke late. Outside, melting icicles dripped from the eves and fell to the cobbled courtyard below. With a yawn she opened her eyes: Sunlight crept between the half-closed drapes and wavered across the walls.

Since she had been sleeping with Roarke, she had grown used to the warmth of his body beside her, his manly scent, the sound of his deep voice as he woke her with a kiss every morning. She loved the way they fell asleep, with him cupping her breast, the way he snuggled her against his chest and pressed her bare hips against his stirring manhood. Even now her tender nipples and the tingling warmth between her legs reminded her of their lovemaking.

An empty feeling pulled at her heart as she rolled over, eased up, and looked about her. Roarke's clothes were nowhere to be seen. He had even taken his cheroots from the dresser. Of course, it was late morning now, she thought with amusement, remembering how they had made love until the wee hours. How nice of him to let her sleep late.

Presently a fresh-faced maid, all shiny curls and rosy cheeks, poked her head into the bedroom. "Miss, the laird sent me to wake you," she announced. "He'll be leavin' soon."

Sassy yawned and rubbed her bleary eyes. "Yes, all right. I'll be up in a minute."

Now she remembered, today was the day Roarke was to make another trip to Laird Dunsworth's castle, this time for a series of long meetings to discuss setting a firm date for the beginning of their campaign. More traveling, more discussions, more politics! Roarke had been gone a lot lately, and it hurt more each time he left; this time he would be away for more than a few days, and she would miss him terribly. With a rush of urgency, she slid from the silken sheets and snatched up her underthings tossed at the foot of the bed. After quickly slipping them on, she rushed to the tall wardrobe and pulled out a lovely green silk dress with a full skirt and flounces.

When she was dressed, she tugged a brush through her thick hair and glanced at herself in the dresser mirror. Did she look different now that she was a wanton woman? Maybe she hadn't changed outwardly, but she had changed inwardly. Roarke's lovemaking had weakened her self-discipline and diluted her purpose. Truth be told, she thought sadly, it had stolen her resolve.

Each morning, each afternoon, each evening, she had promised herself she would talk to him about returning home. But he was stubborn and clever, too. Every day he skillfully avoided the matter, taking her on visits to the village or providing some other diversion. How happy he made her.

Soon spring would be here, and she would be free to travel. Lord, what was she going to do? she wondered as she left the room and started down the corridor. She had waited to make her decision, but she could wait no longer. Either she was Roarke's kept woman—his doxy—or her own woman with her own mind and her own goals.

"Miss Sassy! Miss Sassy, I need to talk to ye!" came a voice behind her.

She turned to see Old Angus standing with his cap in his hands; mud stained his knees, and he looked anxious. Mixed feelings consumed her, for she distrusted the old man, yet still felt an affection for him because of their days together aboard the *Sea Witch*.

"I . . . I need to show ye somethin' ye'll want to see," he offered nervously. He glanced at some chairs grouped near a window embrasure. "Could we set down fer a minute?"

Her first impulse was to tell him no, but he had aroused her curiosity. "All right . . . but I don't have much time," she replied, taking a seat. "You'll have to hurry."

A proud grin brightened his face. "This came from London." She tugged a creased newspaper page from his vest. "I thought ye'd want to see it."

She unfolded the sheet and saw it was the front page of a London newspaper, only a week old. In summarizing recent world events, the newspaper stated the London merchants had petitioned the king to come to terms with his American subjects, and Lord North had asked Parliament to forgo taxation to the colonies. But it was another headline that caught her eye.

Her heart lurched as she read that last September a Continental Congress had met in Philadelphia. Quickly scanning the article, she learned they had boycotted British goods, agreed to back up

Massachusetts's defiance of the Crown, and drawn up a Declaration of Rights listing American grievances. Why, the colonies were practically at war.

"Angus, how did you get this?" she asked, glancing up sharply.

The old man raised his white brows. "I was drinkin' in the tavern last night, and a traveler came in from Glasgow. He was showin' the paper to everyone, sayin' how the British was losin' the American colonies. He said London is full o' the news."

Sassy's heart beat with renewed hope and enthusiasm—yet she sensed something was wrong. "Why would a man from Glasgow come to an out-of-the-way place like this, especially with a London newspaper?" she asked, studying the old man's veiled expression. "Don't you think that's about as odd as a three-legged duck?"

He tugged his whiskery ear and chuckled. "Aye. 'Tis a bit odd—but not impossible. Sometimes rich men come to the Highlands to hunt." He touched her arm respectfully. "When I saw the paper, I nabbed on to it. I told the man I used to live in America myself."

Standing, she folded the newspaper page. "I want to keep this."

"Aye. I knew ye'd want it."

Her mind racing, she strolled toward the library, wondering what to believe. The story of the traveler from Glasgow sounded farfetched, but as Old Angus said, not impossible. With narrowed eyes, she glanced over her shoulder, watching the old man loiter about the chairs. Perhaps he *had* talked the traveler out of the newspaper, for she knew he could be persuasive. Hadn't he wheedled his way into her confidence on the *Sea Witch?* Whatever his motives, the printed news could not be denied: The

Americans had convened a Continental Congress and were on the brink of war.

Entering the book-lined room, she sank into a soft chair and studied the paper again, absorbing all the fantastic news. America had taken the first major step in breaking with England, and she hadn't been there for any of the glorious events—and at that moment she wanted to be there more than anything in the world. The decision she had struggled with since she and Roarke had once again become lovers now seemed very easy.

When purposeful footsteps resounded in the corridor, she stood up, girding her courage.

"Good morning, lass!" Roarke said as he entered the library. "I'm glad to see you're up. I'd hate to leave without a kiss."

He was dressed grandly: His shirt was of silk trimmed with lace; his neatly cut black jacket was decorated with silver buttons; his trews were of the finest wool. She studied him closely—the gleam in his eyes, the humor in his mocking smile, the grace in his muscled body. And there was the smell of him—the scent of leather and tobacco, and that faint sandalwood aroma. All the images swirled and pooled together, making her joints weak.

"What's the matter, love? You look like you've had a shock." His voice was warm and deep with concern.

She snapped out the newspaper sheet and pointed at the headline about the Continental Congress. "I have, but it was a good shock. Look at this."

A smile brightened his bronzed face as he read the article. "Good for them," he stated, tossing the paper on a table. "Good for the American rebels. Let them tweak the Lion's nose in the colonies while we twist his tail in Scotland!"

Disappointment pierced her hopes. "Is that all you're goin' to say?"

He shrugged his wide shoulders. "What would you have me say, lass? You know I've always been sympathetic to the American cause, but there is little I can do about it. I'm beset with problems here. Perhaps we can talk about this later." He neared her for a kiss, but she moved away.

She wished there were another way she could *say* this—wished there were another way she could *do* this. But by now the ache in her heart could no longer hold her back. "No. I want to talk about it *now.* I want to talk about goin' back to America."

His expression turned stony.

"Don't you understand?" she asked. "The news in this newspaper changes everythin'. In America they're not jest talkin' amongst each other like you and the lairds . . . they're fixin' to fight!" Her words hung heavily in the quiet library.

A frown creased Roarke's brow. "I told you I can't talk about it now," he replied, glancing at a grandfather clock that chimed the hour. "The other lairds and I are going to set an important date today."

She walked away from him, stung by his reply. This very day last week she had tried to talk to him seriously, and he had brushed her aside. Again she had met a will stronger than her own. Again her emotions struggled with her intellect. Again things looked hopeless. "I thought it meant somethin' when we made love," she finally said. "I thought you had some feelin' for me."

He strode across the room and embraced her. "I do, lass. I do."

She gazed at his handsome face through a mist of tears. "Then what would you have me do?"

He tightened his arms about her and caressed her back. "I'd have you stand by my side all my life. I'd have you bear my babes. I'd have you stay in Donkinny safe and protected from anything that would harm you."

He proposed a safe life, a life filled with love and abundance, but he had neglected to make any real commitment to her—to ask her to marry him. A sudden thought chilled her. Perhaps he hadn't asked her to marry him because their social stations were too different. Surely he would need to marry the daughter of a great Scottish noble; such a marriage would greatly help his cause. It seemed as a mistress she was fine, but as a wife, she failed to meet his standards.

"It sounds to me you'd have me do whatever you say," she finally said. "It sounds like you want to do all the thinkin' for both of us." Something deep inside her cried out against her words, but a powerful resentment reared up to silence it.

His face troubled, he moved away. "No. You're a strong-minded woman, and I'd have you no other way," he stated, regarding her keenly. "But it's late and I must go now. Can't you see that?"

"I see everythin' real clear now," she snapped, her voice breaking. "I see that your rebellion is so important to you, you can't spare a minute to talk about what's important to me."

A surprised hurt flooded his eyes.

Hands on hips, she marched over to him, looking at his clenched hand . . . his stormy countenance. "You think you're more important to Scotland than I am to America, don't you?" At first he didn't answer, and she jabbed her finger at him, demanding an answer. "Well, don't you!"

"Aye!" he finally blurted out. His eyes were bright and angry. "Aye, I do. And if you haven't noticed, it seems the Americans have done fine without you!"

His words cut deeper than anything he had ever said. Her heart turned into a great stone and she backed away again.

Swiftly he clasped her wrists in an iron grip, and pulled her against him. His fingers bit into her arms, and his eyes flashed fire. "I'm sick to death of our fighting, lass. For the last time, I must go. We can talk later!" He released her and strode to the door without looking back.

Sassy sank into a chair, her eyes streaming. It had finally come out, the question they had so long avoided. She had tried to fool herself, to deceive her common sense, to make herself believe she could have Roarke *and* be faithful to her rebel cause—but she couldn't. How could she enjoy life as an aristocrat's mistress when her fellow rebels needed her in America? How could she dally about a castle making love while they risked their lives for freedom?

She rose on unsteady legs. She had been a fool to wait so long to leave. And she had been a fool to make love with Roarke again, risking pregnancy and heartbreak. When the first ice had cracked on the Firth of Lorne, she should have left Donkinny. With clearer insight, she admitted she had wanted their union as much as Roarke. He had melted her heart with his tender gestures and attempts to share himself with her, but she now had an indication of his true priorities. It was her fault she was trapped now, her fault she was addicted to his love—her fault her heart was broken.

She walked, then ran, down the castle corridors. Near her room she bumped into Old Angus, who was still lingering about the window embrasure.

"Miss! What's wrong? Why are ye cryin'?" he asked, steadying her with his work-worn hands.

Unable to speak, she pushed him aside and went into her room. He stood on the threshold with a downcast look. "Have you seen Kevin?" she choked out between sobs.

"Aye. He's in the garden. But what's wrong with ye?"

She threw open the mahogany wardrobe's carved doors. "I'm leavin'," she cried, tearing out an armful of gowns Roarke had bought her. "I'm leavin' Donkinny today. I'm goin' to borrow some money and take the post coach to Glasgow. From there I'm sailin' back to America!"

Haltingly the old man approached her. "But, miss, ye don't know Glasgow, do ye? It's a strange city to ye, ain't it?"

His words, soft and wheedling, scarcely touched her. "What does that matter?" she said, hurling the gowns on the bed. "I'll stay in an inn for a few days . . . then I'll be gone."

He spread his blunt hands in a beseeching gesture. "Not knowin' the city, ye might be cheated. If yer heart is set on goin', stay at the Wind and Foam. It's a clean, upstandin' place."

She sorted through the gowns, her mind in a whirl.

"Did ye hear what I said, miss?"

She stared at the bed, the bed she and Roarke had made love in just before dawn . . . and she wanted to weep. She swallowed hard, tears scalding her throat. "Yeah, I heard you," she answered at last, struggling to speak. "What difference does it make where I stay? If it'll please you, I'll stay at the Wind and Foam." She raised her head, her vision cleared a little, and with some surprise she saw Old Angus smile broadly. Lord, her world was sliding down about her like a crumbling mountain—and he was smiling.

What in God's name did the old man have to be happy about?

Chapter 23

The Glasgow coach was chilly and dank. With a shiver, Sassy tugged down the sleeves of her blue traveling suit and let her weary body melt into the seat. Leaving had been hard. So very hard. Thank goodness Mr. MacDonald was gone to visit his mother in Killieburn and she hadn't had to face his kind, flowery farewell. She remembered Kevin's stricken face as he handed her the money for her trip. Then, emotion tightening her throat, she had settled herself in the carriage and waved at her benefactor, knowing she would never see him again. He had looked so slender, so pale, so vulnerable, standing in front of the gray castle, his slim arm raised above his head.

In Killieburn her carriage had rattled past the *Sea Witch*, but she had turned her head aside rather than watch it. Duncan was on board. How could she ever say good-bye to Duncan?

Now the old coach hit a bump, making her open her eyes. Through the twilight gloom she glanced at the opposite seat, where a fleshy housewife sat surrounded with small baggage. Dressed in a cheap cotton dress and a tattered shawl, she cuddled a little girl who was also shabbily clothed.

The woman tugged down her ragged mobcap

and smiled, showing a broken tooth. "What's the matter, dearie? Are ye havin' troubles wi' yer man?"

Sassy felt compelled to lie. "No. I'm jest feelin' poorly. That's all."

Seeing the woman's doubtful gaze, she sat up and pushed back the swinging drapes. On the other side of the dirty window the desolate moorland slid past, silhouetted against a purplish sunset. Rain threatened and a stiff wind ripped through the low heather. Up the road, a deep valley opened and blue mountains soared upward, their peaks lost in drifting mists.

"Are ye leavin' him, then?" the woman prodded.

Sassy studied her face and found no guile in the coarse features. "Yeah, I am. That's jest what I'm doin'," she said, dropping her hand.

The housewife shook her head and laughed. "Well, ye're doin' the right thing. I left two men myself an' I'm better off fer it, I am. Aye, ye done the right thing!"

The right thing. Had she done the right thing? With a spurt of defiance, she told herself Roarke had left her no choice. His manner—thoughtless and overbearing—could not be tolerated. If she didn't follow her dream, she couldn't live with herself. But if she *was* doing the right thing, why did it hurt so much? Swallowing back her feelings, she peered out as they neared Glasgow.

The coach followed the sandy River Clyde, then rattled under a stone arch and entered the city proper. Hills and mountains, all glowing in the sunset, encircled the closely packed houses. It was almost dark and lights flickered from the dwellings lining the narrow street. To Sassy each light represented the warm domestic unity of a man and woman who loved each other—something she would never have.

The housewife shot her a motherly glance while she adjusted the little girl's bonnet. "Get yer things, dearie. We're almost there, ye know."

The slowing coach passed Saint Mungo's Cathedral, twinkling with soft light, then entered a section of town crowded with half-timbered inns displaying colorful signs.

Looking up the street, Sassy spotted the Wind and Foam. Two stories high and more prosperous-looking than the neighboring inns, it was made of brick and trimmed with wood. A sign depicting windblown ocean waves swung above the cobbled courtyard. Hope leaped in Sassy's heart as she gathered her possessions—this inn was the first step on her way home.

When the driver pulled the team to a stop, Sassy clasped the door lever.

"Good luck to ye!" the housewife called in a loud, friendly voice.

Sassy tossed the woman a smile and crossed the rough cobbles. With an expectant heart, she entered the old building. The crowded, cozy taproom smelled of ale and tobacco and roasting meat. A fire flickered in the hearth, its light touching the faces of the men clustered around scarred tables. Through a haze of smoke she finally spotted the landlord in a white apron standing behind a bar, polishing a copper pan. Laughter and rough banter bounced from the low-beamed ceiling as she made her way to the burly man and paid for a room.

With a key in hand, she walked up to the second floor, her heels clicking on the bare steps. Old Angus was right, she thought, looking at the risers worn smooth by thousands of feet; evidently the Wind and Foam was a popular inn. At last she reached the landing, and finding her door, unlocked it.

She noticed a musty odor, then immediately

became conscious of another presence. No . . . she was just imagining it, she told herself. The room had been locked. With a weary sigh, she shut the door behind her. Again the sense of another person in the room came to her, this time more powerfully. Her heart turned over as she sent her gaze over the chamber, seeing a moon-silvered window, shadowy drapes, and indistinguishable forms.

From outside the inn came the sound of creaking carriages and clopping horses; and from below there came a merry chatter—but inside the room, everything was so quiet, she could almost hear her heart beating. For a moment she stood frozen to the spot, trying to decide what was amiss . . . and then she heard a raspy breath behind her.

She whirled around . . .

Roarke dismounted and strode across Donkinny Castle's wet courtyard. The day was somber . . . just like his spirits. Handing his mount's reins to a servant, he glanced at the dark sky and felt cold rain sting his face. Only in Scotland could there be a thaw one day and a freezing rain the next, he thought sourly. The poor weather, his shaky plans for a rebellion, and his argument with Sassy—all weighed heavily on his mind. "Damn this foul weather," he cursed, stripping off his gloves and tucking them under his belt.

With a heavy sigh, he entered the castle, hoping to find the woman whose face had haunted him. All day he had thought of Sassy's flashing eyes and pouting mouth, her wild spirit and sharp tongue. He cursed their wretched argument of four days before. Why had he been so angry, so harsh?

No doubt she was still wound up, waiting for him in the library with more demands. He entered the room. She wasn't there. A terrible stillness settled in his soul, but he shrugged it off, telling himself she was somewhere else.

From the library he went to the chieftain's room. And the dining room. And Mr. MacDonald's office. All were empty. As he approached her bedroom, the servants turned their heads and vanished into doorways. Lord, let her be here, he thought as he entered the chilled room. Let her be here.

But she wasn't.

The room was in impeccable order . . . but she was gone. Its coldness and hollowness almost took his breath away. He wrenched open the wardrobe and found it empty; the sight hit him like a slap across the face. How had this happened? How in God's name had Mr. MacDonald let her go?

Suddenly his hurt receded, to be replaced by fear for her safety. He had protected her all winter, but she was away from his care now, possibly exposed to terrible danger. Although there had been no more reports from the village of a tall man with an eye patch and a military bearing, Roarke still suspected that Blackhurst was after them.

Three worrisome questions pounded at Roarke's brain as they had for days. Was Blackhurst trying to hunt down Sassy, as he had promised her in Boston? If so, how did he know of their whereabouts when everyone on the *Sea Witch*'s crew was sworn to silence? And how would Blackhurst know about Killieburn's secluded harbor? The sickening answer pointed to a traitor, yet Roarke trusted his men implicitly.

Trying to shake off such troubling thoughts, Roarke left the room in search of Mr. MacDonald. Halfway down the corridor he met Sassy's maid, but she rushed past him, avoiding his eyes.

"Where in the hell is Mr. MacDonald!" he shouted at the girl.

She paused and ducked her head. 'He's in th' village . . . His mother is very ill. He left th' castle only a few hours after ye did, sir."

"Where is Miss Adair?"

"I . . . I really don't know, sir."

Roarke waved the frightened girl on her way. Dammnit to hell! Why hadn't he checked with MacDonald before leaving? With a pang of guilt, he remembered Sassy had made him so mad, he had rushed off half-cocked. The memory of their argument filled his soul with a sharp ache. She had left him. She had really left him. He felt in a dark moment of acceptance, a leaden feeling that almost cut off his breath.

Back in the library he snatched off his soggy hood and tossed it on a chair; cold moisture trickled down his face. Angrily he raked back his wet hair, then went to the grog tray and poured himself a drink. "Why didn't I tell Kevin about Blackhurst?" he muttered to himself, moving to the hearth. Inside, he knew the answer. He had thought of Kevin as a child, lost in his own dreams—an ineffective child, not a responsible man in whom he could confide. With one hand resting on the mantel, he stared into the dancing flames, regretting his decision. Then, hearing a noise, he looked up, knowing whom to expect.

His face white, Kevin lingered at the open library doors, obviously gathering his courage. At last he drew in a long breath and stepped forward.

Roarke studied his pale face. "When did she leave?" he asked, forcing himself to speak quietly.

His brother sighed and glanced at the floor. "She left right after you rode off to visit old Dunsworth." He stood silently for a while, then looked up and added, "I'm sorry. I really am."

Roarke didn't move.

Kevin clasped his arm. "I gave her the money, of course. We made the arrangement months ago."

Roarke stared at his younger brother's youthful face, feeling mixed emotions. He couldn't blame him for letting Sassy go, because he hadn't explained the danger to him. At the same time he wanted to throttle him.

Kevin released his arm. "Damn it. Why don't you say something? You know I couldn't keep her here if she didn't want to stay. People are free individuals, you can't hold them against their will. Even you can't do that!"

"Don't you think I know that?" Roarke muttered softly. He swallowed the rest of the whiskey and hurled the glass into the fire, watching the glass smash into tiny pieces as it exploded against the hearth stones. He stared at the fire, seeing Sassy's face in the flames.

Then, feeling Kevin's eyes upon him, he looked up.

"You've got to make things right with her," his brother pleaded.

Roarke bowed his head and closed his eyes, filled with bitter despair. "I said things I shouldn't have said. It was a terrible argument. Sometimes there's too much pain between a man and a woman to heal the rift—no matter how much they love each other."

Kevin waited to speak, but at last ventured, "She's not vindictive . . . Maybe she can forgive you. Can . . . can you do the same?"

"I really don't know," Roarke replied.

"Are you ready to take her back to America? To go with her, if that's what it takes to hold her?"

"Again, I don't know! But I know I can't let her leave."

"*Then go.* Don't sacrifice her love. Go to her and together find a solution."

Was this his little brother speaking? Had the lad

grown wise while Roarke was away at sea? "If I only knew where she was," he murmured dully.

"*I* know where she is. At the Wind and Foam in Glasgow."

Roarke's body stirred with a hope. "How do you know that?"

Kevin tugged a creased paper from his jacket and held it out. "Old Angus gave me this for you before he left."

Roarke scanned the note; Sassy was indeed staying at the Wind and Foam in Glasgow on Old Angus's suggestion. Annoyance nettled his sensibilities; if the old man hadn't suggested the inn, she might still be here, hesitant to leave. Then he told himself she would have left sooner or later anyway. Old Angus was just a foolish old man. "Where did Angus go?" he asked, noticing a slight throbbing at the back of his head.

Kevin shrugged and sighed. "I have no idea. He just said he was leaving the Highlands, and walked away. No one could dissuade him."

This didn't make sense. Why would the old man walk away from the greatest security he had ever enjoyed in his life? Why would he leave his beloved Highlands? He wouldn't—unless he had been offered some great reward or was very frightened.

Then Roarke remembered he had hired Old Angus aboard his ship without really knowing much about him. The old man had seemed so innocuous, he had thought him harmless. Could Old Angus possibly be the traitor? Gentle, fumbling Old Angus whose protection Roarke had assumed out of pity?

He should have paid more attention to Sassy when she showed him her letters thumbprinted with grime. Had Blackhurst made a trip to Killieburn? Once he found out that Angus was handling Sassy's mail, he could have asked him to read it.

And Blackhurst could have provided Angus with the newssheet about America. Anxiety coiled in the pit of Roarke's stomach.

"I must find Sassy . . . She might be in great danger," he told Kevin. His voice, though controlled, was razor-sharp and fired with urgency.

"In danger? How?"

"I believe a British officer named Blackhurst might have followed her to Scotland from America. He's demented . . . only God knows what he has in mind. I didn't tell her, for I couldn't be certain—but now I suspect Blackhurst planted Old Angus on the *Sea Witch* while she was docked in Boston Harbor. I'm afraid Angus might have talked Sassy into going to the Wind and Foam because Blackhurst is waiting there for her."

Kevin's eyes widened and darkened. "I didn't know. I would never have let her leave the castle, I—"

"The fault isn't yours, it's mine." Roarke paced in front of the fireplace, trying to decide on a plan of action. The note might be an attempt to lure him into a trap, but perhaps there was a way he could avoid capture. With new resolve, he strode toward the library doors. "I'm going to Glasgow," he tossed over his shoulder.

"I'll go with you." Kevin hurried to catch up. "Here in the Highlands you're protected by Donkinny and the loyalty of your clan, even the old lairds. Anyone of us would die for you . . . but Glasgow is filled with English authorities." He looked at Roarke pleadingly. "I want to be with you . . . I *should* be with you. I'm your brother."

Roarke paused, studying Kevin's eager face, and made an important decision. "I may need a good man," he said. "How soon can you be ready?"

* * *

A brutal hand clamped over Sassy's mouth, then someone yanked her backward, pressing several hard objects into her back. Squirming, she tried to break free, but the attacker tightened his steely grip. His fingers covered her nose and mouth with suffocating force. Fear consumed her, but from a deep well of inner strength she found the courage to fight. She hadn't come this far to be stopped; she had to stay alive; she had to get back to America. She struggled to open her mouth, then bared her teeth and bit into the intruder's palm with all her might.

With a great howl, he heaved her aside.

She cried out as she landed hard on the carpet and rolled over. Terrified but still alert, she crawled across the room on her hands and knees, scrambling toward the moon-bright window, trying to escape. Her fingers like talons, she clawed at the window, mindlessly pushing upward; within seconds, the attacker was beside her, jerking at her long hair. Cursing, he pulled her up again and steered her across the room. Pain slashed at the back of her head as he threw her on the hard settee.

"Stay there!" he growled in a low voice. "Or I'll break your neck and throw you through the window!" Quickly the shadowy man took kindling from the fire and lit a lamp . . . revealing the contorted face of Colonel John Blackhurst!

The beast who had fueled her nightmares for months had materialized before her eyes like an evil apparition. A wild, almost unbearable panic sprang up in Sassy.

He was dressed in a red military jacket studded with brass buttons and medals—the same medals that had cut into her back. White breeches and highly polished boots completed the immaculate uniform. His face was filled with hatred. Highlighted by the shifting flames, the black eye patch looked like a gaping socket; the other eye glittered dangerously. Aided by the fire's glow, she saw he still wore the same ring that had scarred her arm in Boston.

Scarcely able to breathe, she looked at the door . . . Perhaps if she was quick enough . . .

Blackhurst tossed the kindling back into the flames, then locked the door and slipped the key into his pocket.

Now she was locked in with this madman who had tracked her halfway around the world. Nausea turned her stomach. Easing back on the settee, she commanded herself to stay calm, to retain a measure of control.

Blackhurst crouched beside her, trailing a cold finger over her cheek. He was so close, she could see the purposeful intensity in his eye and hear his boot creak as he leaned forward. Her first impulse was to look away, but like a vulture's gaze, his bright blue eye pinned her to the settee. Roughly he pushed up her sleeve and looked at the scar his ring had made. "I see you still bear my mark. Have you thought of me often?"

Her voice trembled and sounded faint. "How . . . how did you find me?"

With an abrupt motion, he tugged down her sleeve. "You are so childish . . . so trusting," he muttered. "How did I find you? I had eyes on the *Sea Witch* even before I visited you in Boston. Old Angus has always been in my employ."

Shock swept through her. Now she knew why the old man had opened her letters. The one she had taught to read had betrayed her.

"I met him in a dockside tavern near the *Sea Witch* after the ball . . . I was gathering information on Captain Rakehell. The old man was down on his luck and wanted to sell a worthless watch." He paused a moment. "I bought his soul instead."

Sassy felt dizzy.

"I sent him to MacLaren with a story about

wanting to return to Scotland before he died,'' Blackhurst continued. ''I was in no hurry to act. As long as Angus was living on the *Sea Witch*, keeping informed wasn't a problem. If Rakehell was arrested immediately, I would have lost my power to manipulate you and capture the rebel printing press as well. What I hadn't counted on was him sailing so quickly, sneaking out in the fog.''

''Didn't you think I'd try to warn Roarke?''

''Yes, despite my threats . . . I did,'' he replied with an ugly laugh. ''That's why I posted a man in front of your aunt's home. If you went out, he was to follow you and report to me.''

In her mind's eye, Sassy saw herself leaving Aunt Pert's back door that foggy night and sneaking behind the tall hedges until she was out of the neighborhood.

''Of course, the fool missed you,'' the colonel snapped. ''When you didn't show up at my quarters, I guessed what had happened. Needless to say, the man is no longer with me.'' His face hardened. ''When I arrived at the harbor, the *Sea Witch* was gone. Despite Rakehell's haste, Angus slipped away from the ship for a few minutes before it sailed. Thankfully the tavern where we met was close by. The old man had just enough time to leave a note saying the ship was sailing for the Highlands, but he would contact me here at the Wind and Foam if I would come to Glasgow.''

Sassy was stunned by the news. ''Angus could read . . . he could write?'' she finally whispered.

''Yes, I'm afraid he could. Sharp of him to think up an excuse to get near you, wasn't it?'' he asked. Then in an aristocratic drawl he remarked, ''Mere days after you both slipped away in the fog, I took a British packet for Glasgow. I've been here almost as long as you've been in the Highlands. In his own way Old Angus is extremely clever. Imagine hiring on as the castle gardener!" He chuckled and cracked his knuckles in satisfaction. "He came here to visit me once, you know. And I even made a trip to Killieburn to question the locals."

Blackhurst idly fingered her hair. "I had to wait awhile to snare you. In the castle you were both too well guarded. I told Angus to look for any excuse to get you away from the Highlands." A cold smile flickered over his thin lips. "Where you go, MacLaren follows, of course. It seems the newspaper stirred up just enough trouble. I thought it would work . . . and I was right."

"How did you know I was interested in the American cause? I never told you."

"*My dear,* you gave me so much free information the night of the ball, investigating you was child's play."

Sassy moistened her dry lips; her heart pumped a rough rhythm. Lord, how much *did* Blackhurst know about her and the Sons of Liberty? How much did he know about the secret printing press? "But how did you know I was comin' to this inn . . . this room?" she muttered dully.

"The old man rode like a banshee after you left Donkinny. Considering all the stops your post coach made along the way, it was easy for him to arrive before you. He came yesterday, proudly telling me he had arranged it so you would be knocking on my door.

"Don't you understand, my dear? This is my suite. The man at the desk is another British agent. He sent you directly to me."

She clenched her trembling hands, trying to control her anger. "Where is Angus now?"

"Somewhere in Glasgow drinking himself into oblivion, I suppose. His job is over. He's earned his thirty pieces of silver."

He raised his brows. "Of course, my superiors

were happy to reassign me when they learned I intended to snare Captain Rakehell *and* a member of the Sons of Liberty."

Sassy's heart lurched painfully. *He knew.* Law a mercy, he knew! Somehow he had found out what she had desperately tried to hide. Denying it now would do no good. With trembling legs, she rose and walked to the hearth. "How . . . how did you find out?"

Again he laughed deeply. His expression was brittle and blazing with contempt. "You *are* a vain little thing, aren't you? Surely you didn't think my interest in you was purely physical. When I saw you at the ball and remembered your father was a traitor, I suspected you were involved with them. The day after you and MacLaren left Boston, I visited your aunt's house once more."

Fury clutched at her heart. "You devil!" she cried, slapping out at him before she realized what she was doing.

He clamped his fingers about her wrist and pushed her arm down. "I didn't have to interrogate your silly aunt Pert, you know. I simply said I was investigating your disappearance and needed details about your daily life. Although she didn't directly mention the Sons of Liberty, I pieced things together. Those tidbits of information about meetings, visits to the Green Dragon . . ." He released her wrist and smiled icily. "Your aunt was very distraught . . . She gave me so many details, I was fairly quivering when I left."

"She didn't say anythin' about you in her letters."

"No. I told her not to. I told her MacLaren was vindictive and might injure you if he knew I was on his trail."

"How fine you are at twistin' people around your finger!"

"It's called manipulation, my dear. And yes, I'm

a master at it. You must understand people and what they hold most dear. Old Angus wants security in his last days and was willing to betray a friend to get it. Your kind aunt, on the other hand, has your welfare to mind. And you . . . well, I know what is most important to you."

"No, you don't!" She turned to walk away, but he twisted her around, hurting her arm. Fear choked her throat as she studied his mocking face.

"Take a look at this," he ordered, drawing her across the room. At the window he pointed to the street where several British soldiers lingered under a streetlamp. "In a few days Captain Rakehell will arrive, only to be captured by a unit under my command. And I know what you will sacrifice to me to save him."

She glanced up sharply, trying to free her arm.

"Why do you struggle so? It's useless. Don't you realize I also know about the secret printing press?"

Fear, cold and overpowering, knotted in her bosom as she stared at him, afraid to speak.

Blackhurst smiled. "You're clever enough to hold your tongue, but I see the surprise in your eyes. Let me explain," he added softly. "We managed to capture a member of the Sons of Liberty. Under torture, he told us there was a press—of course, we already knew that. But the wretch would never tell us where the press was located. He died keeping the secret."

Nausea rose up in her. The cold glint in his eye told her he would go to any lengths to achieve his goals.

Still clutching her arm, he glared down at her, a muscle twitching in his lean jaw. "There are reports you were seen passing out rebel propaganda. Surely someone in your position must know the location of the press."

"No, I—"

"*Yes,*" he added scathingly as he tightened his grip on her arm. "And I have a feeling you will tell me everything."

Chapter 24

On the fourth day after her capture, Sassy sat with Blackhurst at a specially reserved window table in the Wind and Foam's taproom. With trembling fingers she lifted a teacup and gazed through the window, trying to steady her nerves. Outside, the sky was low and gray, and water puddled the dirty cobbles. Carriages rattled up the narrow street, now busy with noontime traffic; the thoroughfare ran up a slight incline, and when a teamster's horses balked, he snapped his whip at them. Pedestrians in somber Lowland dress paused to look before strolling away.

With a weary sigh, Sassy returned her attention to the crowded taproom. How she wanted to proclaim to everyone here that she was being held prisoner—but she knew it would do no good. Just yesterday she had thrown herself on the mercy of a patron, only to have Blackhurst tell the man she was a criminal under his supervision awaiting deportation. Just to make sure she couldn't bribe anyone, the colonel had stripped her of Kevin's money, making her dependent on him for everything.

A London newspaper lay on the table in front of Blackhurst. He had underlined bits of political news about America and seemed to be mulling over them. Who knew what he was thinking? He kept his own council and he had dug in for a siege. Cold and ambitious as Lucifer, he would cheat the Lord's own angels.

Sometimes he grilled her about the Sons of Liberty, but most of the time he locked her in one of the bedrooms of his suite. At night she could hear his muffled voice in the sitting room as he conferred with a sergeant who would assist in the capture of Captain Rakehell. She was permitted out of the depressing chamber only for questioning and to take meals with Blackhurst in this taproom.

As they ate, red-coated soldiers brought messages to his table. He often gazed up and down the cobbled street. Clearly the idea of capturing Roarke consumed his thoughts.

When she glanced out the window again, her eyes locked on the face of one of Blackhurst's men posted at the corner of the inn. On his commander's orders, he had changed into civilian clothes, as had all his comrades. How young and pale the lad looked standing in the chilly outdoors. For an instant she felt sorry for him, and wondered if Blackhurst had offered him part of the reward for Roarke. No, she thought . . . the colonel wouldn't share a smile, much less a shilling, with anyone else.

Then someone stepped behind the lad, making Sassy's heart leap. Kevin. It was Kevin dressed in the English garb of a young merchant's apprentice! A moment later she spotted Roarke, who was outfitted as a prosperous merchant in a conservative coat with wide cuffs and brass buttons. Gone was the lace from his jabot; gone were the silver buckles on his shoes. But even in the dull Lowland clothes, he radiated a reckless, dashing air.

She felt all the color drain from her face. She had to warn him. Had to let him know he was walking into a trap!

Blackhurst looked up from his reading. As he studied her face, she glanced over his shoulder through the window. Roarke and Kevin had passed the young soldier, who apparently had no idea who they were; heedless of the danger that awaited them, they had started across the crowded street. In moments they would enter the tavern.

Sassy's eyes darted between Blackhurst and the window. He was studying her so intently, she could almost feel the weight of his gaze. Suddenly turning toward the window, he locked his eyes on Roarke.

For a split second, Roarke gazed back at him and Sassy with surprise, then he grasped his brother's arm and turned to escape; at the same time Blackhurst shot to his feet and ordered nearby soldiers into the street. Grabbing Sassy's wrist, he bellowed at his men: "Get him, you fools! Seize the tall merchant. He's Captain Rakehell!" He yanked Sassy to her feet and pulled her from the tavern.

Young soldiers streamed toward Roarke from doorways and street corners; one lad leaped from the roof of a low shed and raced down the street. Roarke fought them fiercely, but he was vastly outnumbered; more than fifteen men finally surrounded and arrested him.

At first Kevin struggled with some of the late-arriving soldiers, but one of the burly lads smashed a right hook to his jaw and sent him flying to the cobbles. Sassy's heart dipped when he rolled into a gutter, then righted himself and scrambled away. Poor hapless Kevin, she thought, as he melted into the crowd that had gathered to watch the excitement.

Her gaze swung back to Roarke. The soldiers now had him by the arms and were proudly displaying him for everyone to see. His lips were cut, and blood smeared his face.

"We got 'im, sir!" the sergeant cried. "We captured Cap'n Rakehell!'' The others roared their approval.

''Take him to the city gaol,'' Blackhurst ordered. ''I will question him later.''

For one sad moment Roarke's painful gaze met Sassy's, then the soldiers marched him up the street, cheering wildly.

Disappointment knotted within Sassy's breast as Blackhurst pulled her back across the puddled street. Shocked, defeated, hopeless, she bowed her head. As they neared the hated inn, a sense of utter desolation nearly overwhelmed her.

On the threshold, Blackhurst paused. His fingers biting into her chin, he lifted her face toward him. Despair sank over her like a great oppressive weight, but she choked back a desolate sob and gathered her courage.

''Don't cry for Rakehell, my dear,'' he said. ''The infamous captain won't be taken to an ordinary prison. After I question him here, he will be moved to the dungeons of Warwick Castle. If you aren't acquainted with the establishment, it's a medieval castle near Stratford—the most formidable in England.''

She shuddered and drew in her breath, then lifted her head in defiance. ''A trial,'' she said boldly. ''He deserves a fair trial.''

Blackhurst laughed as he pushed her into the inn. ''Oh, he will be tried, all right, but his crimes against the Crown are so numerous, the proceedings will be only a formality.'' A light blazed in his bright blue eye. ''And after he is tried, he will be taken to London—and hung till he's dead.''

''Ahh . . . I see you are up and about,'' Blackhurst said cheerfully as Sassy entered the sitting room. ''Good. We can resume our discussion.''

Two weeks had passed since Roarke's capture, and Sassy still felt as shattered as the day it had happened. Collecting her wits, she arranged the skirt of her plain blue gown and tried to remain calm. Her heart might be pounding, but she had to put on a brave show; she had to make Blackhurst think she wasn't afraid of him.

As always, his military uniform was impeccable; he carried not an extra ounce of fat. His silver hair was slicked back, and his medals and boots were highly polished. He had disciplined himself to utter control. But she knew a mighty river of rage coursed beneath that polished surface.

Under his arm he carried a stiff folder of heavy velum. When Sassy looked at it, he chuckled and held it in front of him. "I see you've spotted my little surprise already. Wonderful. Let's sit down and talk about it.

"Now, don't be shy, my dear," he ordered, pointing to the settee. "Come. Let's get this business over with. I'm sure you will feel so much better when we've finished."

The bruises from his fingers had faded on her cheek, but her bruised spirit still ached. Her legs as heavy as lead, she moved toward the settee, wondering what his sick mind had devised now. She sat down, and he eased beside her; he was so close, she could smell the spicy shaving soap he had used that morning. The scent made her nauseous. She clasped her hands to still their trembling.

With the enthusiasm of an eager schoolmaster, he flashed her a tight smile and opened the folder. "Do you know what this is?" he asked, laying the document in her lap.

She scanned the finely written black lines and the gold embellishments at the top and bottom of the page . . . the red wax seal. Blinking at the impressive document, she shook her head.

"No. I didn't think you did. Well, it *is* very rare."

He caught her eyes, then added, "It's a royal pardon—for Roarke MacLaren."

Hope washed through her, quickly followed by confusion. "I . . . I don't understand."

"I knew you wouldn't," he retorted with a superior air. "See . . . it's all written out." He ran his finger under several lines containing Roarke's name. "A courier arrived at the Glasgow gaol with the pardon just this morning, direct from the king's hands—just as I requested."

By this time Sassy realized he was taunting her, pulling her further into his trap, so she remained silent, denying him the satisfaction of a response.

Rising, he paced before the settee. "As you know, I questioned MacLaren here in Glasgow. He was further questioned at Warwick by His Majesty's representative, who made the trip from London to see our infamous prisoner. Of course, MacLaren was then tried and sentenced to be executed. But the king acted on my suggestion that MacLaren be pardoned."

Sassy stood abruptly, sending the pardon flying to the floor. "*You* suggested that Roarke be pardoned? Why would you do that?"

Blackhurst regarded her as if she were a foolish child. "Because I'm a reasonable man. I would much rather catch a nest of traitors than punish one man, no matter how much he deserves it.

"You see, my dear," he added, picking up the pardon and looking her straight in the eye, "this document is *conditional.*" He thumped his finger at a small paragraph at the bottom of the page, rattling the stiff paper. "Roarke MacLaren's life will be spared and he will be set free only if you reveal the location of the secret printing press."

The words cut into Sassy's heart like sharp thorns. She sank to the settee and stared blankly at the crackling fire. "You're the lowest man I ever met," she muttered at last.

Blackhurst raised her chin and glared at her. "Despite your views, the king thinks my idea very clever. I may even receive a promotion for my efforts." A smile flitted over his thin lips. "The rebels in Massachusetts have bedeviled the Crown for months. I've orders to return and crush the Sons of Liberty before they can stir up more discontent, and destroy the press that has spewed treason like a poisonous viper." He released her chin and knelt by her side on one knee. "We must act swiftly," he added in a rough voice. "You will tell me the location of that press or MacLaren will hang."

He twisted her face toward him. "Don't imagine you can lie. If you do, several members of the Sons of Liberty will be killed."

She stood and glared at him. "What are you talkin' about?"

He rose and sighed wearily. "Don't you see? After you tell the location, we'll be leaving for America. I've booked passage for both of us on *The Thistle.*"

She tried to understand the full implication of his words.

"By my diligent efforts, several of the rebels have been captured and are languishing in the Boston gaol," he went on. "They won't reveal the location of the press . . . but I'm sure *you'll* tell me. If you mislead me, the wretches will be killed." He smiled, triumphant.

She tore the pardon from his hands and threw it on the floor. "You're crazy if you think I believe that paper is real."

He looked at her contemptuously. "How lightly you throw away your lover's freedom. Can you be sure the pardon is not real?" He picked up the document and tapped at the scrawled signature of King George. "This is the king's own signature! Give me the location of the press and Roarke MacLaren will be released and all charges against the Crown stricken from his record." He smiled again, showing large teeth like wolf fangs. "It's your decision, my dear. What is more important to you? Your lover's life or your misguided rebellion?"

That same day Roarke restlessly paced about his cell in Warwick Castle. Clenching his jaw, he scanned the filthy cubicle: Cobwebs hung from the vaulted ceiling, and the walls were gouged with the last messages of condemned prisoners. In one corner, a musty straw mattress covered with greasy rags served as a bed; in the other corner a chamber pot reeked of urine. When he paused near the cell's small window, a rat scuttled over his boot and along the stone floor, then disappeared into a chink in the wall.

Drawing in a long breath, he gazed from the barred opening; the dungeons lay partially below ground, and his line of vision was almost even with the castle lawns. Torches blazed at a five-story gatehouse at the end of the drawbridge, their light reflecting in the water-filled moat. Guards in red uniforms talked as they strutted back and forth across the drawbridge. Although too far away to hear their conversation, Roarke caught their lazy tones. They laughed as a supply wagon from the village slowly approached, then rattled over the planks.

Drawing his team to a halt, the driver flashed a pass at the guards, then, after they called a command to raise the grilled portcullis, proceeded on. As Roarke watched the wagon, the scent of grass and trees wafted into the chilly cell. He thought of Sassy and all he had wanted to say to her; he thought of the terrified look on her face as she stood at the door of the Wind and Foam, trapped in Blackhurst's grip; and he thought of Kevin, who had begun the trip with high hopes, as if he were setting off on a stirring adventure, and instead had been hurled into a gutter when the colonel sprang his trap. Lord Almighty, where was the lad now?

A sharp cry reverberated down the stone corridor, and the odor of burning flesh assaulted Roarke's nostrils. Nausea swept over him. The king's men were busy extracting another confession. Since Roarke's arrival, no one had approached him with hot tongs. There had been no need for the rack or an iron maiden either. All his offenses were neatly written in a portfolio Blackhurst had sent with him from Glasgow. Roarke had already been tried in London and condemned to die.

Blackhurst. What a cold, miserable, twisted piece of humanity he was.

Roarke's thoughts flew back to the day he was captured. He had been beaten and forced down the cobbled street by the cheering soldiers. His mind had reeled with concern for Sassy and contempt for Old Angus, who he suspected had betrayed him. Fighting back had been useless; they had thrown him into the gaol, leaving him with two guards. The cubicle had been cold, and the jubilant soldiers had clamored nosily. "We done it, lads. We captured the bloody pirate!"

Later Blackhurst had appeared in his fashionably tailored uniform; his face glowed with triumph as he slammed the barred door behind him. "Well, Captain Rakehell," he stated, slowly pacing around Roarke, who sat on a rickety straight chair. "It seems I've finally won our little game of cat and mouse. You took the bait just as I expected you would."

Roarke glared at him, wiping blood from the corner of his mouth.

Blackhurst smiled smugly. "No response, hey? I know what you're thinking. You're thinking I corrupted a half-witted old man, aren't you? Well, Old

Angus is actually very cunning is his own way. I hardly corrupted him . . . I simply recognized his genius. Surely you understand that."

Here was confirmation from Blackhurst's own lips that Old Angus was indeed the traitor. Roarke's heart ached to think that the likable old man he had befriended was actually a spy and an informer.

"As for the girl," Blackhurst continued, "she's not all that innocent, either. The Sons of Liberty is a radical group, given to violence and treason."

"God Almighty, how far would you go to win?" Roarke shot out.

The colonel rubbed his temple and looked thoughtful. "Winning *is* all that's relevant, you know. How you win is not important."

"No. I suppose to you it isn't. I see that although your morals are completely lacking, your boundless ambition remains firmly intact."

"Very good," Blackhurst replied with a chuckle. "You were always quick. I like that in a man."

"I assume you'll collect blood money for my head."

"Of course. Before I leave England."

"What will you do with it?"

"Spend it foolishly, of course." He tapped his eye patch. "I earned it, didn't I? How convenient for the Crown to pay me for the eye you took." He scanned the bare cell. "I think you'll find your accommodations comfortable, but don't get too attached to them, for you'll be moved to Warwick soon."

Roarke clenched his jaw, refusing to respond.

The colonel rubbed his arms. "It's devilishly cold in here, isn't it? But I'll tell you something to put a little fire in your blood. A thought to mull over as you're whiling away your hours before execution. I'm going to present Miss Adair with a false pardon stating you'll be freed if she tells me the location of the rebels' printing press in Boston. Of course, you *will* be executed, but the pardon should put just enough doubt in her mind to make her reveal the secret."

Roarke shot up and rushed toward Blackhurst, but the guards grabbed his arms and pulled him back.

Blackhurst sauntered toward the cell door. "Oh," he added in afterthought, "I've also decided to make Sassy my mistress. I'll take her after all this political business has settled down. On the ship back to Boston, I think."

Roarke lunged forward again, trying to pull away from his guards. "You bastard!"

"Actually I am a bastard, but it doesn't bother me one whit. Freeing myself from conventional morality has been most liberating." He ran his gaze over Roarke one last time. "I'll miss our chase, Rakehell. You were a wonderful competitor. It was all very stimulating, don't you think?"

With that he had disappeared down the corridor.

Another sharp cry brought Roarke's mind back to the present. The king's men weren't finished with the poor devil in the next cell. Roarke clenched his fist tightly. Damn and damn again, he thought. His execution was scheduled for only a month away. He scanned the wall, noting its thickness, then looked up at the reinforced ceiling. No one had ever escaped from Warwick, but he had to be the first. What would happen to Sassy if he wasn't? He swept his gaze over the cell walls again. *But how . . . how?*

Shocked to be crossing the Atlantic once again, Sassy stared through a small porthole at the rolling breakers and listened to spray lash *The Thistle*'s hull. Events had transpired so quickly during the last week! she thought as she gazed at the white-capped water. Was it really possible . . . had she already been at sea for three days? A few minutes later nausea swept over her, making her move to her berth and slip under the mildewed covers. Dressed in her shift and a long, ruffled petticoat, she burrowed into the thin mattress, feeling wretchedly seasick.

She glanced about the second-class cabin, comparing it to Roarke's lush quarters aboard the *Sea Witch*. The clothes she had brought from Scotland filled a cheap wardrobe. A table, washstand, straight chairs, and a marred sea chest were the only other furniture in the shabby cubicle.

One lantern hung from the ceiling, and casting a ghastly light, creaked with the roll of the ship. Her eyes closed, she listened to rats chatter on the other side of the bulkhead as they scuttled over the timbers; the old packet creaked and groaned under a hard rain. Somewhere between wakefulness and sleep she remembered the humiliation she had endured before she left Glasgow . . .

Blackhurst had ordered her to pack, telling her they were leaving the Wind and Foam, then he had thrust the pardon before her again and demanded the location of the secret printing press. At first she had refused, but he kept browbeating her.

"Roarke MacLaren's execution date lingers very near, my dear," he said, twisting her face toward him. "The location of one small press seems a small price to pay for his release."

"I don't believe you. You're lyin'!"

"Perhaps I am lying. But if I'm not, you'll have thrown away a man's life on a guess."

He went on for hours, putting just enough doubt in her mind that she thought the document might be genuine. Finally she came to believe it was. The Sons of Liberty had told her the Crown often bartered prisoners for information.

She sank to the settee, her eyes filled with tears as she realized she had to tell him. The loss of the press and the men found with it would be a great blow to the rebel cause—but when all was said and done, her concern for Roarke outweighed everything else. She just couldn't take the chance that the pardon was not genuine. She consoled herself with the slim possibility that she might be able to escape and warn the patriots before they were discovered. "All right, all right . . . *stop.* I'll tell you!" she cried. "The press is in the storeroom of the Old North Church, behind . . . behind the altar."

Blackhurst glowed with satisfaction. "No wonder the authorities couldn't find them. I suspected something like this all along!" He snatched up a few papers. "I must inform my associates here in Glasgow before we leave."

Sassy sat without moving until he locked her in; then, lowering her head, she sobbed bitterly. She had betrayed her friends in Boston; she had let down the Sons of Liberty and all the other patriots who had trusted her. She might have saved one life, but she had doubtless endangered many others. How could she bear such a burden of guilt?

Now she would never see Roarke again; she would spend a lifetime regretting her bitter words at Donkinny—and she had betrayed her comrades. "Lord, what have I done?" she muttered. "What have I done?"

Sick and weary, she slept fitfully, dreaming of all the people she had met since she had left the Blue Ridge Mountains. Then, as rosy twilight streamed into the cabin, there was a noise in the passageway. Groggy, she rubbed her eyes and raised her head to see Blackhurst enter. With a hard stare, he slammed the door behind him. Instinctively she tugged the sheet about her shoulders and burrowed deeper into the mattress.

He smiled tightly and walked forward, staggering a bit. "I just wanted to check on you, my dear."

"You jest wanted to spy on me!"

He laughed, and putting out an arm to steady himself, moved toward her berth. At first she thought he was staggering because of the ship's roll—then she realized he was drunk. And he was coming right for her. Before he could trap her against the wall, she slid from the berth and edged around the table.

His face sick with lust and drink, he eyed her bosom and bare arms.

She scrambled across the cabin, but he grabbed her wrist and yanked her against him; the odor of rum flowed from his half-open mouth. He glared at her with his bulging eye and slowly lowered his wet lips to hers. Coming out of a trance of fear, she jerked back her hand and slapped his face: The *smack* resounded loudly. Amazed at her own courage, she watched a red stain flood his jaw.

His eye glittered with hot, murderous rage as he caught her other hand. "I ought to kill you just like I killed Angus," he mumbled in a voice thickened with drink.

"What did you say?"

He glanced away. "Nothing. I—"

"*No.* I heard you say you killed Old Angus. And I can see it in your face. That's why I never saw him in Glasgow!"

Blackhurst stared at her impassively for a moment, then smiled crookedly. "Yes, if you must know, I killed the old fool . . . the day before you arrived."

"Why, for God's sake? Hadn't he done all your dirty work?"

"He was useful for a time, but he became greedy. He came to Glasgow demanding more money." His face relaxed and he loosened his grip on her wrist. "He wanted half of the reward on MacLaren's head. He said we had been equal partners in the affair."

Seeing her chance, she yanked away from him. "You . . . you killed him at the Wind and Foam?"

He laughed with contempt. "I'm not a fool. I agreed to his demands, then suggested we have a drink to seal our partnership. When he was roaring drunk I put him in a carriage, drove to a country lane outside Glasgow, and shot him. I left his body sprawled in a ditch."

Chills traveled up Sassy's arms. "You shot him and threw him in a ditch . . . like a dog?" She realized Blackhurst would never have told her these things if he were sober.

He stumbled toward her. "Yes, why not? He was just an old man. No one will miss him."

She was almost at the door when he grabbed her shoulder. Crying out, she fought him off.

"Shut up, you little fool!" he ordered, trying to cover her mouth.

She jerked her head from his hand. "No! I *will* scream my head off!" With the strength of a cornered tigress, she squirmed and flailed about, overturning chairs, yelling, and making as much noise as possible.

At last someone pounded on the locked door. "Are ye all right, miss?" came the muffled question.

Sassy recognized the deep voice of *The Thistle*'s first mate. "No! Help me . . . please, help me!"

With a scowl, Blackhurst released her and spat out, "Keep quiet about what you've heard, and don't think I won't be back. The next time things will be different." He unlocked the door, then, in afterthought, curled his lip and announced, "When I return, I shall have some very interesting news for you." Haughtily he stalked past the burly first mate and disappeared into the dim passageway.

Weak and shaken, Sassy assessed the plain-faced man. "You have to change the lock on this cabin!

Can't you see what's goin' on? I must be able to protect myself from him."

The rawboned mate tugged down his hat and hung his head. "I'm sorry, miss. Colonel Blackhurst has papers showing yer a political prisoner . . . a traitor to the Crown. He . . . he can lock you in irons if he wants."

"The captain—"

The mate sighed heavily. "The captain and the colonel drink together. I don't think ye can look to the captain for help. And I can't always be about when ye need me. Ye'll just have to figure out some way to protect yerself."

She clutched the man's thick arms. "Please . . . give me a weapon."

"Nay, I cannot." Looking embarrassed, he pulled away from her and left.

Sassy clicked the door shut, then slumped against it, thinking she might faint. Blackhurst had killed Angus as casually as if he had been a worrisome mongrel; and now she was the man's prisoner to do with as he pleased. Lord in heaven, how could she protect herself all the way across the Atlantic . . . and what news did he have to tell her? Knowing Blackhurst, she was sure it couldn't be good.

The next evening Sassy had just finished eating when a key slid into the lock. Blackhurst closed the door behind him and moved forward, looking as if he had just stepped from a reviewing box. As always, at the sight of him, a panicky feeling almost suffocated her.

A sly smile creasing his face, he neared her berth and paused thoughtfully, eyeing her with a hooded gaze. "The weather is miserable today, isn't it? I thought you might be bored . . . and ready for a good piece of gossip. It concerns Captain Rakehell."

Scarcely able to breathe, she steeled her nerves and regarded him evenly.

Chuckling, he strolled about the table, scanning the dirty dishes. "Ah yes, I thought that would get your attention." He shook his head and sighed, then held her eyes with his icy gaze. "I was just wondering," he began, carefully pronouncing each word, "what you might say if you knew the villain was hung. All London is buzzing with the news. He is dead. The royal pardon was, of course, false."

For a moment shock held Sassy immobile, then rage exploded through her. A cry bursting from her throat, she lunged toward him and beat her fists against his chest. "You devil . . . you bastard!" she shouted.

Darting backward, he caught her arm and slapped her cheek; pain sent her to her knees, and soon he was above her. "You little jade! How dare you attack me. Do that again and I will kill you!"

Her eyes narrowed as she glared up at his twisted face. "No, I'll kill *you.*" She tossed back her hair defiantly. "Just give me a chance and I will. I promise before the good Lord, I will!" She rose, and impulsively snatching an empty bottle from the meal tray, smashed it against the table. The glass shattered with a loud tinkling noise and left her holding a jagged bottle neck.

Surprised, Blackhurst backed toward the door. Obviously he thought the news would crush her spirit and leave her open to his attack, but his plan had failed. Fueled with a white-hot rage, she brandished the broken bottle, her body quivering.

The colonel paused at the half-open door. "You're overwrought," he commented in a tense voice. "When you've calmed down, we'll talk again." Then he was out the door, rattling a key into the lock and shooting home the bolt.

Sassy listened to his quick footsteps retreat down

the passageway. Her bosom heaving, she dropped the bottle neck and fell upon her berth. All her fierce emotion left her like sand pouring through an hourglass, and a deep ache, more painful than anything she had ever known, welled up to replace it. Her hands trembling, she pulled the dingy sheet over herself and closed her eyes. Black despair rolled over her in great waves, and it seemed that someone had reached into her body and pulled out her very heart. With Roarke dead, what did she have to live for? Nothing, absolutely nothing.

Tears streamed down her face as she thought of Roarke's twinkling eyes, his warm voice, his hearty laugh. She remembered the tenderness of his hands as they made love during the long, snowy nights in Scotland. She remembered the pleasure, the excitement, the wonder, of resting drowsy and warm in his arms. She remembered how her heart leaped for joy when he entered the bedroom all wet from snow and smelling of spruce. She remembered everything about him and asked herself how she could live the rest of her life knowing he was gone.

Until now she had been able to hold on to some kind of hope by believing he was alive and well in Scotland. She could believe her sacrifice meant something. Now that flame of hope was gone, replaced by a burning hatred of the man who had used and manipulated her.

Then she imagined she could hear Roarke's voice saying: *"Don't let go, never let go of hope."* Yes, she thought. If he were here, that's what he would say.

Suddenly, in her grief, she understood what life was all about—loving someone and believing in something and fighting for it. How glad she was she had faced up to Blackhurst. She was relatively certain he wouldn't be back again. Like all cowards, he had collapsed at her show of anger. She glanced at the jagged bottle neck. If he did return, she would have a weapon. She had weathered this crisis and, with any luck at all, would eventually reach the safety of Aunt Pert's arms.

She held on to the thought like a lifeline.

Chapter 25

Roarke paced past his small cell window for the fiftieth time that night, despair spreading through his veins like a slow poison. Raking back his hair, he scanned the shadowy cubicle once again, looking for a way to escape. A torch located down the corridor cast dim light over the bars of his cell, and moonlight painted a bright patch on the wall. He had often thought of trying to overpower the guard who brought his food, but the door was never opened, the food slipped through a slot near the floor. His heart as heavy as a stone, he studied the window, also tightly barred. He grabbed the bars and jerked at them, knowing they wouldn't budge; then, with a growled curse, he rested his forehead against the cool stones at the base of the window. Lord, how much energy, how much hope, he had expended searching for a way out of Warwick.

Like the hand of a comforting angel, the scent of early spring drifted over Roarke's bowed head, and he heard the cry of a nightingale and the lap of water in the moat. His spirits lifting a bit, he tried to identify the harbingers of spring: trimmed grass and tender leaves and the odor of the wild primroses that grew about the castle walls. Near the moon-silvered moat, crickets chirped and frogs croaked, and in the distance he heard the creak of wheels. With fresh interest, he raised his head.

The forested land on the other side of the moat lay in darkness, but torches flamed beside the portcullis, illuminating the drawbridge. Slowly a huge supply wagon, pulled by a team of matched Clydesdales, rolled from the darkened trees and clattered over the drawbridge; several guards warily approached the wagon. Roarke himself wondered why the wagon was bringing supplies at this late hour.

The driver, an older man judging from his stooped posture, wore a tricorn pulled low over his eyes. A younger, bareheaded man sat beside him. As pieces of conversation drifted to the window, Roarke clenched the bars and listened attentively. Although Roarke couldn't make out all the words, the driver had a distinctive Scottish accent.

With a thudding heart, Roarke strained to get a better look. At first the guards blocked his view, but at last they moved, and torchlight flamed over the face of the hatless man beside the driver. Kevin! *It was Kevin.* And on closer inspection, Roarke knew that the driver was Duncan.

But how could two men in a supply wagon violate the security of Warwick Castle? Even if they managed to get past the gatehouse and under the portcullis, they had to pass the barbican. Roarke knew there was always a small group of soldiers atop this high tower, even in the wee hours. Although the other guards were asleep, a musket shot would rouse them and bring them scurrying to this part of the castle.

Eagerly Roarke peered at the drawbridge, waiting to see what would happen next. Duncan flashed papers at the guards, then an argument broke out; after a while, one of the guards threw up his hands and angrily motioned the wagon forward. Another guard gave a signal, and with a great screech, the portcullis was lifted. When the wagon was almost dead center under the grilled gate, Duncan yanked the team to a halt; getting out, he made a great show of examining one of the wheels with a long stick.

Laughter rushed up from Roarke's chest. It was the first time he had laughed in weeks, and it felt wonderful. He knew exactly what would happen next. He should. He and Kevin had both heard the story countless times when they were children.

In the Middle Ages the clever Scots had stalled a wagon under the portcullis of Edinburgh Castle so the device couldn't be lowered. Hundreds of fellow Scots had rushed into the castle and liberated it from the English. Evidently the English guards assigned to this drawbridge hadn't heard the story.

Roarke's gaze swung over the shadowy land on the other side of the moat. Just as he expected, dozens of men began running from the protection of sheltering trees and dashed over the bridge.

Back at the wagon, Duncan turned to the guard at his side and brought his stick down on the man's head. Kevin leaped to the ground, snatched back the canvas cover, and lifted a long bow from the wagon bed. Taking careful aim, he sent an arrow soaring toward the barbican, which flanked the gatehouse. Instantly a soldier plummeted from the high tower and splashed into the moat. After hitting two more soldiers, who quickly tumbled after their comrades, Kevin darted under the half-open portcullis. Roarke's heart leaped. Another watch wouldn't be posted for hours; at this moment the rest of the castle guards were snoring, ignorant that Warwick's security was being breached. Thanks to Kevin's silent arrows, it appeared a successful surprise attack was under way.

By now the other Scots had reached the gateway; soon a volley of arrows flew upward, and the unwitting soldiers atop the barbican plunged into the moat like falling pebbles. For once, Roarke was glad Kevin had spent so much time at his archery lessons.

While half of the Scots whizzed arrows at the barbican guards, another group followed Kevin under the portcullis. Within minutes, Roarke heard footsteps ringing down the dungeon corridors. His spirits high, he strode to the barred door and waited—seconds later, Kevin reached his cell. Dressed as a working-class Englishman, he proudly displayed a ring of keys and unlocked the door.

"Well done, lad!" Roarke said as he embraced his brother.

Kevin grinned. "Twenty of the clan's best men came with me. No one wanted to see an English rope tightened around your neck."

Roarke rubbed the back of his neck and cocked a brow. "A sentiment I share, I assure you." He clasped his brother's arm. "How did you know I would be at Warwick?"

"I went back to the Wind and Foam after the excitement had died down. Everyone at the inn was talking about how you had been taken." Kevin beamed like a schoolboy. "I thought of the plan, and Duncan and Mr. Cameron backed me up. We raided the countryside for bows and arrows, and held several practice sessions."

As they left the cell and hurried down the torch-lit corridor, they passed several burly Scots who had been standing guard. Immediately the men fell in behind them. Pacing ahead, Roarke looked at his brother. "How did you get here so quickly from Scotland?"

Another smile streaked Kevin's face. "Mr. Cameron sailed the *Sea Witch* into Bristol Channel. We made the last thirty miles overland in wagons. They're hidden in the woods, and the ship is berthed near Newport waiting to transport you to safety." Footsteps echoed down the corridor as they turned a corner and yet more clansmen joined the procession from the castle.

Roarke slowed his pace as he neared the armory. In front of the heavy, nail-studded door he paused and grabbed his brother's arm; the group of men behind them also came to a halt. "Sassy? What do you know of her?" he asked.

"I'm afraid she's gone," Kevin answered. Sadness shadowed his eyes as he chose his words carefully. "Reports from Glasgow say Blackhurst has already taken her and sailed for America."

The words twisted Roarke's heart with pain. He had lived each dreary day in Warwick yearning to escape and rescue her. Now a sense of longing and great loss swelled within his chest. Anguish tore through him. Lord, if Kevin had only freed him a bit sooner, perhaps he could have changed the outcome of events. Burning with regret, he clenched his fist and steeled his emotions. No matter how his heart ached, he had to push his personal feelings aside and go about the task at hand, for at this moment a chance of a lifetime lay within his grasp. "I think we have a bit of unfinished business here at the castle," he said, taking the ring of jangling keys from his brother.

Kevin's face glowed. "The Sword of Wallace?" he asked.

Roarke flashed a grin. "Aye, *The Sword*. What's the use of breaking into the enemy's castle if a man doesn't do a bit of plundering?"

A murmur of excitement ran through the clansmen, who glanced nervously down the shadowy corridor, watching for English soldiers. Roarke tried several keys before the door creaked open, and he and Kevin entered the large room. Suits of armor, claymores, battle-axes, and tall racks of swords filled the musty-smelling armory.

From a row of tall arched windows, moonlight shone over the armor and ancient weapons. Roarke swiftly searched the chamber until he found the Sword of Wallace, displayed alone in a case on a velvet cloth. He noticed his brother's pale face and rapt gaze. "It's been four hundred seventy-six years since a Scottish hand has touched that sword," Kevin muttered in an awed tone.

"Well, one is going to touch it now. And I'll vow several more before the night is over." Reverently Roarke retrieved the heavy sword from the open case and hoisted it in his hand. "Aye, this is a bonny night for Scotland. Once the sword has been returned to its rightful place, luck will be with us."

Kevin sighed, his joyous expression fading a bit. "I *hope* luck will be with us."

"What do you mean?" Roarke asked sharply.

"We've received another letter from the prince—it's at Donkinny. It's addressed to you, so it hasn't been opened."

"Why didn't you bring it with you?"

"I feared I might be captured by the British. Mr. MacDonald is holding it for safekeeping, guarding it with his life." Kevin glanced at the stone floor, then looked up. "A servant boasted of it in the village, and now everything is in an uproar. All the lairds are clamoring for you to return and open the letter."

Mixed emotions stirred Roarke's heart as he quickly wrapped the sword in the velvet cloth. Whatever news the letter held, he knew it would vitally affect him and his brother. Making a quick decision, he handed the sword to Kevin.

His brother blinked as he accepted the heavy weight in his arms. "Wh-what are you doing?" he stammered.

"I want you to carry the sword from Warwick. It's your responsibility until we have it safely inside Donkinny."

"But why me? I—"

Roarke eyed him sternly. "No arguments. Save your words, lad. We must hurry. Hurry back to Scotland!"

Four days later, Roarke and Kevin placed the Sword of Wallace on a table in the chieftain's room at Donkinny Castle. Carefully unwrapping it, they watched late afternoon sunlight play over its heavily scrolled hand grip. Hearing footsteps behind them, they covered the sword, then turned to see Mr. MacDonald enter the room. Deep lines of weariness etched the steward's face. "I didn't expect you so soon, my laird," he said to Roarke. His countenance serious, he pulled the red-sealed letter from his vest and handed it to Roarke. "You'd better read it quickly, sir. Laird Dunsworth is in the library, waiting to speak with you. I was just talking to him when you entered the castle."

"In the library?" Roarke shot out.

"Aye, sir. Once he learned you had received the letter from the prince, he came to Killieburn to wait for your return. Today when he saw the *Sea Witch* put into port, he rushed to the castle hoping to speak with you." Bowing his silver head, the old servant turned and left the room.

Kevin shook his head and laughed bitterly. "Isn't that just like the old fox," he stated coolly. "At least he could have given us time to take off our coats and get a night's peace before he appeared."

Roarke cocked his brow. "No doubt he wants to boast to the other lairds that he was the first to know the letter's contents." With a sigh, he tore open the letter and hastily scanned it. His spirits sank lower with every line he read, then he slipped it back into its envelope and put it into his vest pocket. For a moment even the bright battle pennants hanging from the walls seemed to lose their color. Feeling as if he had just received a blow to his stomach, he looked at his brother.

Sympathy showed in Kevin's eyes. "The look on your face tells me the news is bad."

"Aye. Very bad."

There was a firm knock on the door.

"Damnation! It must be old Dunsworth," Roarke said, glaring. He paced across the room's Oriental carpet and rubbed the back of his neck. "We need time to talk and plan. We'll offer to meet with him tomorrow evening. Perhaps we can distract him with the sword for now. Try to get him out of the castle and send him on his way to Killieburn."

Kevin nodded, then admitted Dunsworth into the room.

Dressed in a fine jacket, kilt, and badger-head sporran, the stocky old man marched into the chamber with a curious look on his face. "Glad to see you free from that damned English prison, MacLaren," he gruffly announced as he shook hands with Roarke.

He glanced at Kevin, then scanned Roarke again. "Look here," he announced, his bushy brows lowering in a frown, "I'll be blunt. There's word out that you've received another letter from Prince Charlie. If this is true, I'd like to know what's afoot. I have a lot invested in this rebellion, you know."

Roarke nodded thoughtfully and crossed his arms. "Aye. I have received a letter, but as you know, I've just returned. I need time to study it and gather my thoughts. Can you come here for dinner tomorrow? I'll present the letter then. The other lairds will also be invited."

A disgruntled look crossed Dunsworth's fleshy face. "I don't know. I—"

Kevin stepped forward and cleared his throat. "Would you like to see the Sword of Wallace?" he asked casually.

Dunsworth whirled and looked at him as if he had just lost his mind. "*The Sword of Wallace?* You have it in your possession?"

"Aye," Roarke spoke up, glancing at the table where the sword lay. "Kevin took it from Warwick when he and the other lads broke into the castle and rescued me."

Dunsworth gazed at Kevin for a long moment, then he stared at Roarke with incredulous eyes. "Kevin rescued you? And he brought back the Sword of Wallace?"

Roarke chuckled. "Aye, he carried it from the English castle in his own hands."

Dunsworth looked at Kevin with a beaming face and extended his hand in a gesture of fellowship. "May I be the first of many to congratulate you. 'Tis a great thing to bring the Sword of Wallace home. A great thing! What will you do with it?"

Kevin seemed taken aback by the attention, but he threw Roarke a conspiratorial glance and clasped Dunsworth's arm, ushering him toward the sword. "I'll wrap it in a MacLaren tartan and take it to the ancient Kirk of Dalmally and lay it on the altar. It should be safe there with the clerics. And there it can belong to all of Scotland."

Dunsworth's eyes grew larger as Kevin uncovered the sword; the old man reverently traced his blunt fingers over the dark blade.

Kevin picked up the weapon. "Come, let's take the sword outside the castle and study it in the afternoon light. Perhaps you would like to hold it yourself."

The stooped laird raised his head and studied Kevin anew, as if he were viewing him for the first time.

"I've also been thinking about something I'd like to discuss with you and the other lairds," Kevin said. "It's a plan to unite all our clans in wool production."

As they walked together from the library, the laird clapped Kevin on the back. "Aye. I would be eager to hear of it."

Roarke sank into a chair, relieved to be alone. Taking out the prince's letter, he read it again, a host of questions and ideas besieging him.

That evening, as twilight closed in about the castle, Roarke sat by the library fire smoking a rum-scented cheroot; a glass of whiskey rested on a table at his side. He looked up as Kevin entered the room, noticing he was now garbed in a fine kilt and jacket instead of the old garments he usually wore at the castle. Sitting forward in his chair, he drew on his cheroot and gestured to the seat across from him.

Kevin took his place, sighing heavily. "Well, I finally sent old Dunsworth on his way. I'll bet he took a hundred swipes at the air with that sword. At last I suggested the other lairds might be interested to know he had held the Sword of Wallace." Kevin chuckled. "His face lit up and he couldn't get away fast enough to brag about his luck."

Roarke blew out a stream of smoke and gave a wry smile. "Fine . . . Now that he's gone, we need to talk." He pulled the prince's letter from his vest pocket and handed it to Kevin to read. When his brother looked up, Roarke said, "I suppose you know that this letter signifies the end of all hope for a new rebellion in Scotland."

Kevin shifted in his chair. "Aye, I do."

"Without the return of Bonnie Prince Charlie, there is nothing to bind the lairds together," Roarke continued.

"Why do you think he changed his mind?" Kevin asked softly.

Roarke angrily stubbed out his cheroot in a brass tray. "His courage simply failed him. I suppose we all live from dream to dream. In youth we strike out boldly like Prince Charlie did. When we meet defeat, most of us recover and try again . . . But the prince is old and bitter now." Roarke gazed at Kevin. "The British so destroyed his dream, he never regained his fighting spirit. He wanted to begin afresh, but in the end he was simply too afraid."

"How sad."

"Aye, I'm afraid Scotland's rebellion against the English is finally over."

"Scotland's rebellion was over after Culloden. It's *your* rebellion that's finally come to an end, Roarke."

The words startled Roarke, especially coming from his soft-spoken brother.

Kevin's face was sympathetic as he continued. "After Father and Mother died, and later after Robert died, you took it upon yourself to continue Scotland's fight against the English. But it was really your fight."

Roarke picked up his glass of whiskey. "I was not alone," he said a little defensively. "The other lairds were with me."

"Yes, they were with you," Kevin said gently. "But it was the dream of old men who had been defeated again and again by the British." He smiled sadly. "Only after you pleaded and coaxed and cajoled—only by the sheer force of your will—could you keep the bickering pack at the same table."

Roarke sipped the whiskey, feeling the liquor burn his throat as his brother's words stung his heart. "Aye, there you speak the truth," he replied with a bitter laugh.

Kevin gazed at the crackling fire as if he were calling back old memories, then he smiled at Roarke. "Do you remember when you put the thistles under the British agent's saddle?" he asked with a laugh. "I'll never forget that day. After looking over our land's ledger books, the haughty Sassenach went out to his mount. I saw the gleam in your eye about the same time the horse started to rear."

Roarke laughed. "Aye—the beast threw him a

fair distance. The sight was well worth the trouble it brought me."

"After that, during all your privateering years, even as I admired you for your bravery against the English, I realized you were motivated by revenge, not by a true hope for Scotland."

Kevin's wisdom touched Roarke's emotions, and he remembered when Sassy had questioned him about his motives in the turret room. Then, with a shaft of sudden and painful clarity, Roarke knew they were both right. Every time he had struck at the heart of the English, he had remembered his father, his mother, Robert. Each encounter had left him wanting to give the British more pain for the pain they had caused him. All his grief had been channeled into his quest for vengeance. "I've failed," he said dully.

Kevin sat forward. "No, you *haven't.* You organized the Scottish lairds and have them cooperating more than ever before. They are in a position to work together for a change. And now you have a self-knowledge to match the valor and leadership you always had."

For a while Roarke sat quietly listening to the flames snap in the hearth; then, almost as if he were talking to himself, he commented, "What do I know besides being a rebel?"

Kevin fired his voice with enthusiasm. "The world needs a few rebels . . . and it will always need rebels to keep authority in check." He sank back into his chair and studied Roarke. "Tell me," he asked in an earnest voice, "do you still have that old medal of Saint Jude you used to carry?"

Roarke smiled and nodded.

"You used to believe in it, and I think you still do. You've always fought for just causes—and you've got to do that now."

Roarke focused on Kevin's face, wondering how often he had failed to give his brother credit. Rising, he placed a hand on Kevin's shoulder. "It seems I've underestimated you." He smiled warmly. "I won't again."

Kevin grinned broadly.

Roarke now knew what he must do, where he must go. Quickly forming his plans, he filled another glass with whiskey. "Will you join me in a toast?" he asked as he handed Kevin the glass.

"A toast? To what?" Kevin looked puzzled.

"To the new chieftain of Clan MacLaren. To Kevin MacLaren." Roarke raised his glass, smiling.

Kevin's mouth fell open. "To the new chieftain? To *me?*" he asked in amazement.

Roarke laughed, and the regret that had hung over him like a gray cloud was gone. "Aye, you. You've proven yourself capable. You rescued me. And you seem to have had an understanding of my situation long before I did."

"But I—I could never command the respect you do!" Kevin stammered.

"You will now. Not only will you be the chieftain, you're also the man who brought the Sword of Wallace home—you'll be a bloody hero! Until you die, you will be respected and revered, and they will write songs about you." He studied Kevin's thoughtful face and went on. "You saw how Dunsworth treated you today. He'll soon be bringing his homely daughters to *congratulate* you, I'll wager."

Kevin seemed lost in thought for a few moments. Then he slowly said, "I suppose I could be chieftain. I've determined already to come out of my dreams—to look to the future. Your capture forced me into action, and I found I rather enjoyed it."

Roarke chuckled. "I don't know of anyone better than you to carry the clan proudly forward. You always amaze me with your ideas. I already heard you discussing plans for wool production with Dunsworth."

"But what about you?" Kevin asked. "Even if you're planning another sea voyage, you'll soon be returning."

"No. No, I won't be returning," Roarke stated resolutely. "I'm going to find Sassy. I realize now that I was chasing a dream, and for all the wrong reasons. But my love for her is real. And that's what I'm going to pursue."

"How will you find her?" Kevin asked excitedly.

"I have some contacts at the Green Dragon Inn in Boston. If she manages to escape from Blackhurst, they will know where she is."

"And Blackhurst?"

Roarke hardened his jaw and stared at the orange flames as he thought of the man who, at that very moment, might be molesting Sassy and endangering her life. "I've already promised myself I will find him and settle our old score. Then I'm taking some brotherly advice and becoming a rebel again. Now that I understand myself better, I can put away my anger at our family's deaths and the failure of the Jacobite cause. I want to start a new life with a new purpose—in America."

Before Kevin could reply, Roarke added, "I'm leaving day after tomorrow."

"That soon?"

"Aye, tomorrow we will go over accounts with Mr. MacDonald, and at the meeting tomorrow night I'll present you as the new MacLaren chieftain."

"What of Duncan? I have a feeling he will want to accompany you to America."

"Aye. He has always been with me. And I'll ask my sailors which of them would like to begin a new life with me in America."

Kevin was silent for a moment, then he said quietly, "You knew, didn't you? You knew the rebellion was falling apart when you had me carry the sword back from Scotland. You were trying to prepare me for my responsibilities.''

''I felt it might turn out this way.''

''How could you have forfeited such an honor?'' Kevin asked with full eyes.

Roarke smiled. ''If I can find Sassy, I'll have everything I want.''

''But still—''

Roarke placed his hands on Kevin's shoulders, feeling closer to him than he ever had in his life. ''Say no more, lad. Consider it a gift of respect . . . from one friend to another.''

Chapter 26

From the open porthole Sassy heard laboring sailors singing sea chanteys; bright and strong, their voices expressed enthusiasm and thanksgiving for another successful Atlantic crossing. Seconds later a chain screeched and *The Thistle*'s anchor splashed into Boston Bay. A roar of cheers burst from the crew's throat.

Boston. At last Sassy had crossed the great Atlantic; at last she was in America—home. How often she had wondered about Aunt Pert and her friends in the Sons of Liberty. But now that she *was* here, a sharp sadness tugged at her heart.

Finding the sailors' excitement depressing, she closed the porthole and glanced at herself in the cracked mirror. After weeks of seasickness and despair, her green silk gown hung loosely on her slender body. Her hair hung limply, and her skin was pale.

Blackhurst had sent a note commanding her to be ready to leave the ship. Soon he would arrive to escort her away.

Even as she thought of his intimidating presence, the door creaked open and he entered the cabin. This was the first time she had seen him in weeks, and her stomach lurched as she scanned his scarlet tunic and flashing medals. Then she spotted something new under his arm—a long, metal-tipped walking stick.

"I see you are ready," he stated. "Leave the cabin and proceed to the deck. I have a carriage waiting on the dock." Utter contempt iced his voice.

The sight of the pointed stick fired her anger. Obviously he intended to prod her along like a milk cow if she didn't move fast enough.

"Once you are down the gangplank, get into my hired carriage," he ordered. "I will be directly behind you."

"Where are you takin' me?"

"You're too valuable to relinquish to the common gaol. I'll lock you in my house." A cold smile crossed his lips. "Then I'm going to Old North Church."

Despair made her weak-kneed; she was helpless to warn the rebels. Her heart raced with excitement as she looked past the colonel to the open door . . . Perhaps she could run into the crowded Boston streets once they were on the dock. She pretended to stagger a bit, testing to see how close an eye Blackhurst would keep on her. "I haven't got my land legs . . . I need help," she muttered.

"Don't expect me to assist you. You must get to the carriage on your own."

Good, she thought. With a sigh, she looked about the room at her packed clothes. "What about my things?"

"Someone will bring them later. Go on, now. *Move.*"

As she left the cabin, Sassy felt her treasure sack swaying on the cord around her neck. Thank goodness she at least had her precious mementos to reassure and comfort her.

Blackhurst jabbed the stick into her shoulder. "Move ahead!"

As a sharp ache spread over her back, she resisted an almost unbearable urge to whirl and wrench the stick from his hands. But she controlled herself and kept alert for an opportunity to escape.

Once she was on deck, a tangy breeze revived her. Long Wharf swarmed with red-coated soldiers who were unloading gun crates from British merchantmen or stiffly parading back and forth with bayoneted muskets. Like annoying mosquitoes, small boys hurled stones at the soldiers, then darted behind packing crates. Everywhere there was hurried activity and an air of urgency.

She noted a forest of Union Jacks snapping in the salty breeze, and farther out in the bay, several men-of-war bobbed on the glinting water.

Back on the wharf, sour-faced colonists watched the laboring soldiers and the British officers commanding them with obvious distaste. It was apparent that Boston had never been closer to open rebellion.

Blackhurst stabbed at her back again. "What are you staring at? Move along, wench."

All thoughts of running away evaporated when she saw a crowd of red-coated soldiers milling about the wharf—one word from the colonel and they would have her. Be calm, she advised herself. Bide your time. After he thinks he has you safely in his home, he will relax, then perhaps you can escape.

Just as Sassy's feet touched American soil, a group of British officers filed past the end of the gangplank. Pausing, a fresh-faced lieutenant spied Blackhurst and threw him a snappy salute. "Colonel Blackhurst," he piped up in a clipped accent. "I haven't seen you in months!"

"No, Wilson. I've been in Scotland . . . apprehending a prisoner."

The young man eyed Sassy uneasily. "Well,

you've arrived just in time, sir. We in intelligence feel the rebels are grouping for an attack."

"Oh, really?"

"Yes, sir, but we're ready for the beggars. General Gage has put a reward on the head of John Hancock and Samuel Adams, dead or alive. It's those blasted Sons of Liberty who keep everything stirred up."

Sassy felt a surge of pride at his words, but resisted commenting, hoping to hear more.

"I don't think the scoundrels will escape," the lieutenant continued. "The single road across the Neck is Boston's only means of communication with the outside world—and we have it well guarded. And we've stopped all shipping. Even the ferries to Charlestown and Cambridge are out of business. We expect hostilities to break out soon."

Sassy glanced at the harbor again. Many American sloops and schooners lay useless at the wharfs. And on the narrow, winding streets feeding into the docks, hundreds of idle seamen wandered dispiritedly. Yes, she thought, the British had done a fine job of choking the life from the port.

"I wish I could meet the rebels in battle myself," Blackhurst proclaimed.

"Perhaps you can, sir," the young man went on. "General Gage is looking for a senior officer to accompany our troops as an observer and historian if the rebels are foolish enough to fight. I'm on my way to headquarters now. Can I tell him you would consider the assignment?"

"Yes, indeed you may. And tell him I will be at his office before the sun sets with that bit of news he wanted so badly."

The lieutenant saluted again, saying, "Yes, sir. Glad to have you back, sir!" Then he hurried to catch up with his comrades.

Afterward, Sassy noticed Blackhurst staring at an older, heavyset man mounted on horseback.

Dressed in the fine clothes of a prosperous businessman, the man turned in his saddle to address a British officer. His gaze met Blackhurst's, and surprise registered on his face. For a moment he seemed about to speak, then he nodded discreetly. Obviously the two men knew each other.

Blackhurst pointed to a hired carriage with an open top. "Stop staring and move on, woman." With heavy footsteps she did as he ordered. Thirty minutes later, Sassy entered Blackhurst's large two-story house, located in a quiet section of Boston. On her way up the stairs, she passed a sitting room furnished with a camelback sofa and wingback chairs clustered about a large, marble-manteled fireplace. A huge grandfather clock stood in one corner.

Blackhurst jabbed his cane at her again. "What are you gawking at? Get up the stairs."

She gasped and stumbled forward.

"Hurry. Up, up, up," he commanded. "Why are you so slow? I have a carriage waiting."

She whirled and snatched the end of his metal-tipped cane. "I could go a lot faster iffen you'd quit jabbin' me with that thing!"

Blackhurst twisted the cane away from her. "I'm happy to see you've retained your spirit. I like that in a woman. After I return from my duties, I may bed you after all." Hate and lust stamped his thin features.

Sick desperation surged through Sassy as she reached the top of the stairs, where another prison awaited her just a few feet away—a room where she would be questioned and grilled and possibly assaulted.

Blackhurst opened the door. "Move," he ordered. "The room is yours while you're here."

Sassy stepped onto a red Oriental carpet and scanned a large, multipaned window draped in filmy fabric. A four-poster bed and a tall highboy dominated the chamber, which was also furnished with overstuffed chairs and gold-framed portraits. The room smelled stuffy and unused.

Blackhurst prodded her forward, forcing her toward the bed. When she stumbled on a fold in the carpet and fell to her knees, he whacked the cane across her back. Unsteadily she tried to rise, but he hit her again, infuriated by her awkwardness; pain streaked over her shoulders as he continued to beat her.

How dare he touch her! How dare he beat her like an animal! Empowered by her white-hot rage, she snatched the end of the cane. Tears streamed from her eyes as she proudly lifted her chin. "Don't think you can beat the spirit outta me, 'cause you can't! If you touch me with that damned cane again, I'll beat *you* with it!"

The colonel jerked back the cane and moved toward the door; he took a key from his pocket and gave her a cold smile. "I must see General Gage for a moment, then I will destroy that foul press. Crying out will do you no good, for there are no servants here to help you." He threw her a last, menacing glare. "I'll deal with you later."

He left the room and locked the door. Sassy listened to him hurry down the steps and lock the front door. With a sob, she crawled to the bed and lay down upon it. She shuddered and clutched at her treasure sack as deep despair swept over her.

Then, as she thought of the rebels, she realized she couldn't afford the luxury of such self-pity. Her friends at the Old North Church were in terrible danger. No matter how tired she was, or how impossible the task seemed, she had to escape and warn her friends.

Weak and dazed, she stood and went to the window. Outside stood a great oak tree with fine thick branches. She had shinnied up and down lots of trees just like this one in the Blue Ridge Mountains.

On the street she saw Blackhurst's hired carriage move away from the mansion; then, when it was no more than half a block away, a rider signaled the driver to stop. Sassy's interest picked up when she realized the rider was the same older man who had nodded to the colonel at the harbor. The rider dismounted and spoke with Blackhurst. After they had talked for a moment, the driver turned the carriage about and proceeded back to the mansion; the rider remounted and trailed behind. Sassy realized Blackhurst was returning home to speak with the man. Who was this mysterious guest who was so important that Blackhurst would postpone his visit to General Gage?

A few moments later, the front door opened and footsteps rang on the marbled foyer. Sassy pressed her ear against the door. Maybe she would hear something important. Muffled voices came to her; the men had remained in the foyer. Trying to better understand their concerned words, she knelt and pressed her ear against the keyhole.

Now Blackhurst's cold, aristocratic voice was discernible. "So you think the rebels have stored most of their supplies at Concord?"

"Yes, indeed," came the other voice. "You will find arms and foodstuffs there in abundance. Thank God I saw you at the harbor. I dared not speak there, but I knew you would want the information."

"Yes, Dr. Church. You did the right thing. Now that I am back in Boston, I will be your contact as I was before I left. See no one but me. Wait a moment while I unlock a strongbox and get your money."

Sassy's heart lurched in her bosom. Dr. Benjamin Church, the colleague Dr. Warren had spoken of before she had left America, was a traitor!

A dry, cottony feeling filled her mouth as she strained to hear more.

"Here's your money, all good silver coins," Blackhurst said as he returned to the foyer. From below came the sound of clinking coins. "For your own safety," Blackhurst continued, "you should leave the Boston area."

Dr. Church sighed heavily. "I'm sorry I wasn't able to obtain information about the rebels' printing press."

"Never mind, sir," Blackhurst replied with a laugh. "I found out everything I wanted to know from a different source. In fact, I'm going to see General Gage about it right now. I will relay your information as well." The men exchanged a few more words, then footsteps rang out again and the front door was closed and locked.

Feeling weak and stunned, Sassy went back into the window and watched Blackhurst and Dr. Church leave in the gathering dusk. Sassy's head spun with the importance of what she had heard. She had to tell the rebels that Blackhurst was on his way to destroy the press. More important, they needed to know Dr. Church was a traitor.

Once again she studied the big oak tree outside her window. All she had to do was open the window and climb down to freedom. But her spirits plummeted when she discovered the window was nailed shut! With a frustrated moan, she scanned the chamber. She ran to the hearth and grabbed the poker.

Back at the window, she studied the situation. At first she considered breaking the window, but it would be difficult to smash through the strips of wood grilling the tiny panes. Instead, she placed the tip of the poker under the window and leaned down against it. Moisture rolled down her face as she repeatedly prized at the frame with the poker, working around each nail. Finally the wood splintered, the nails gave way, and the window budged open an inch or two.

With a gasp of relief, she tossed away the fire tool and pushed upward with all her might. Again the window moved—enough for her to squeeze through. She knew Blackhurst had a head start, but he had mentioned seeing General Gage before going to Old North Church. She had a chance to warn her friends. "I must speak with Dr. Warren," she murmured.

Gathering up her long skirt, she leaned out the window and reached for a sturdy tree limb. The air cooled her flushed face as she swung her legs over the sill and planted both feet on the thick branch, then began shimmying down the trunk. A few feet from the ground she jumped, hitting with a jolt and rolling to her feet.

With a thumping heart, she raised her torn skirt and raced down the street, toward the Green Dragon Inn.

Chapter 27

A half hour later, Sassy reached the Green Dragon, gasping for breath. Her pulse raced when she saw a gangly boy dressed in a homespun shirt and tattered knee britches. Jack O'Reilly was sweeping the cobbles in front of the inn. With some amusement, Sassy noticed that although he had shot up at least an inch in height since she had last seen him, his red cowlick sprouted up as stubbornly as ever. "Jack!" she called, raising her hand.

The boy whirled at the sound of her voice and threw down his broom. "Sassy! Where did ye come from? I thought I'd never see ye again."

She caught her breath as he pressed her against his slim body. "Oh, Jack, I have such a story to tell. You won't believe it. And I have to see Dr. Warren right away. It's important rebel business."

"Well, come on!" he urged, tugging her to the inn's front door. "The taproom is filled with customers as always, but we can talk in our storeroom—Ma's there now. And Pa can fetch Dr. Warren for ye. He lives nearby."

The inn's familiar scents and sounds wrapped themselves around Sassy like a mother's comforting arms—the scrape of benches, the tang of tobacco, raucous laughter, and a blur of merry faces as Jack hurried her through the noisy public room.

Seconds later, she was wrapped in Mary O'Reilly's ample arms. Smelling of freshly baked bread, the innkeeper's wife wore a much-washed gown and a ragged mobcap. "Saints preserve me, are ye all right, girl?" she asked in a worried voice.

Between long breaths, Sassy blurted out her story, ending with an urgent request to see Dr. Warren. Easing her down in a rickety chair, the older woman brushed back Sassy's disheveled hair, then looked at her son. "Jack, tell you father to bring Dr. Warren right quick. And fetch the girl a tankard of ale. She's white as milk."

As soon as the boy had left, Mary demanded, "Now, what's all this blabberin' about Blackhurst discoverin' the rebels' secret printing press, dear heart?"

Sassy placed a hand over her pounding heart. "Blackhurst tricked me into tellin' him where the press is. And he's goin' to Old North Church to destroy it!"

A twinkle enlivened Mary's blue eyes. "Love, the press used to be there, but it ain't anymore. The Sons of Liberty decided to keep movin' it to avoid detection."

Relief left Sassy weak, but seconds later she remembered Blackhurst's vindictive nature.

"What's wrong, child? You still look so frightened."

Sassy heaved a troubled sigh. "Blackhurst will think I lied to him. He's crazy, you know. He'll kill the rebel captives being held in the Boston gaol jest for spite."

Mary patted her hand and laughed. "You need have no fear of that either, dear heart. The patriots freed the captives in a recent raid. I'm happy to say there are now no rebels in the British gaol."

His eyes large, Jack entered the storeroom with a pewter tankard and handed it to Sassy.

"Come with me to my room, dear," Mary said

as she clasped Sassy's arm. "You should rest a bit before Sean returns with Dr. Warren."

Sassy followed Mary and Jack up the back stairs to a cozy chamber. Mary opened a dormer window, and a gush of cool air washed over Sassy's warm face. Taking a seat in a wingback chair, she sipped the ale, which cooled her parched throat. She had just finished the drink when heavy treads on the stairs announced the arrival of Sean and Dr. Warren. Sassy embraced Sean, who, as always, was wearing a long white apron, then she turned to Dr. Warren.

"There, there, what is it, girl?" he said. "You look like you've seen a ghost." Dr. Warren was as handsome and well dressed as ever, but it seemed there was more gray in his hair and new lines in his strong face.

As Sassy's incredible story poured from her lips, the O'Reillys and Dr. Warren looked at her with astonished eyes.

The doctor sighed and rubbed his jaw. "So Church is a traitor?"

"I'm afraid so," Sassy replied. "I've been out of the country for so long, I hardly know what's goin' on in Boston."

Dr. Warren stood and cleared his throat. "Well, let me bring you up-to-date, then. We know General Gage is intent on capturing our stores of powder and food. Thanks to Church's treason, he now knows where they are hidden. I'll wager the British will soon attack Concord to destroy those supplies."

"Have we a way of knowing when they might be comin'?" Sean asked.

Dr. Warren chuckled dryly. "The militia has already been alerted to march as soon as they hear church bells ringing. And we have a rider, a local silversmith, who will warn the outlying towns."

Sean lifted himself from his chair. "With the

danger of attack, seems to me we should be gettin' more muskets to Concord."

"Yes, I think you're right," Dr. Warren replied. "I'm thinking Sassy and Jack could take a wagon-load there tomorrow morning."

"Where are we goin' to get the weapons?" Sean asked.

Dr. Warren laughed again. "Don't worry. The Sons of Liberty will liberate them from a British man-of-war late tonight. I'll have the men bring them directly here."

"How are we goin' to get the guns past all those British blockades?" Jack piped up, scratching his head. "They're thick as fleas on a dog's back between here and Concord."

Dr. Warren smiled slyly. "You and Sassy will be carrying two coffins in the back of your wagon. Of course, the coffins will be filled with muskets. If the guard wants to see inside, offer to open the coffins and show him the bodies—but tell him your departed cousins died of smallpox. That should put them off."

Jack laughed and slapped his leg. "I like that idea!"

"But Colonel Blackhurst will be lookin' for the girl," Mary offered in a concerned voice. "Surely *she* can't go to Concord."

Jack ran a speculative gaze over Sassy. "She's about my size, Ma. We can dress her as a boy and put that flaming red hair up under one of my slouch hats."

Finally all the plans were completed and the older men left the room.

Mary caressed Sassy's arm. "When bedtime comes, you can use the little room across the hall. For now, come down and eat, then return here and relax before the fire." She tugged down her mob-cap. "I best go help Sean." With a warm smile, she also left the room.

As Jack knelt to attend to the dying fire, a sharp sense of homesickness overcame Sassy. She thought of Aunt Pert. How she wanted to see her and tell her about her love for Roarke. There, on her aunt's rose-scented bosom, she could pour out her long story and find release; there she would find help to heal her broken heart. She smiled as she imagined her aunt dozing over tea or working in her garden. She could almost hear the old lady's soft southern drawl.

Jack put the fire tools aside. "Why are ye so sad, girl? We'll get those muskets to Concord."

She smiled into his freckled face. "It's not that. I was jest thinkin' of Aunt Pert, and how I'm longin' to see her."

"Ye can't go there! I'll bet Blackhurst has a guard on the house jest waitin' to catch you." He looked thoughtful for a moment, then snapped his fingers. "But ye *can* write her a letter, and I'll take it to her." He removed some writing utensils from a drawer in his mother's desk. "Here," he said, spreading the paper on a small table. "Jest write what ye want and I'll carry the letter to her."

"That's wonderful. Come back in thirty minutes and I'll have the letter ready." Sassy dipped a quill into a pot of ink and gathered her thoughts. Then she began to write.

At eight o'clock Sassy paced over the braided rag rug, wondering if Jack would ever return. In her letter to Aunt Pert she had poured out her heart about her life in Scotland and mentioned her love for Roarke. If bad luck befell her at Concord—if she never saw her aunt again—she wanted her to know what had happened since they had last written. In the letter she mentioned she and Roarke had never resolved their differences. They were just too different—like the roses Aunt Pert had tried to cross-pollinate.

There was a soft rap on the door and Jack entered, startling Sassy. His hair was damp with perspiration, and his shallow chest rose and fell rapidly. Her hopes fell. "Where's Aunt Pert's letter?" Sassy asked.

Jack drew in a long breath and shook his head. "She didn't have time to write," he said. "While she was readin' your letter, I looked from her sittin' room windows, and the sight I saw nearly scared the freckles clean off my face." He widened his eyes. "British soldiers were walkin' your aunt's street. She said I should slip out the back door jest like I came in—and real quick, too, before one of those soldiers decided to search her house. I ran all the way home."

Sassy noticed he was holding his left hand behind his back. "What have you got there?" she asked.

"She didn't write, but she sent this for ye." He held out a rose.

A great lump wedged in her throat as she took the rose, a lush pink one veined in red. The color was gorgeous, like nothing she had ever seen. "How did she get a rose so early in the year?" Sassy asked with a cry of delight.

Jack shuffled his feet, looking a trifle embarrassed to be delivering the sentimental token. "She said she grew it in her little greenhouse 'cause it was some kind of special rose she had been workin' on. She said it was her *perfect rose.* She told me ye would know what that meant."

Aunt Pert had finally created a perfect rose, a rose that reminded Sassy of her love for Roarke.

"How come that flower makes ye look so sad?" Jack asked at length.

Sassy reined in her rising emotions. "It reminds me of a man I love . . . I mean that I loved. And the rose will soon be gone."

The somber comment dampened Jack's buoyant

nature for only a moment before he grinned. "Well, why don't ye press it in a book, silly? That way ye'll have it forever. Ma does it all the time. Now, cheer up and save your long face for those British blockades tomorrow." At the door, he looked back over his thin shoulder. "I've got to go. Pa's got some work for me downstairs before we close."

His footsteps fading away, Sassy sat alone on the bed and studied the flower. She knew exactly what her aunt was trying to tell her. Sometimes it *was* possible to combine two different strains. The child of two very different parents, this new rose would be stronger and more vital than either of its ancestors. Like this new rose, she and Roarke could have become one spirit and forged a love that brought out the best of both of them. She swallowed back her tears. If they had only realized it before it was too late, she thought sadly.

Two days later, Sassy and Jack raced away from Concord on foot, down the dusty Lexington Road; in the east, the rising sun spread its rays like a glowing fire. They scrambled up a grassy knoll to a hedgerow, then knelt on a patch of soft earth behind the shrubs to catch their breath. Their high position offered a fine view of the road cutting across the wide valley.

Shivering a little as the morning chill seeped through her boy's clothes, Sassy peeped down the road. She groaned and flopped back down. "The road's empty. Mebbe the British ain't comin'!"

Jack leaned back on his elbows and crossed his skinny kegs. "Oh, they're *comin'*, all right. Didn't you hear what the rider from Lexington said? All we got to do is wait. Bein' here outside of town, we'll be the first to see 'em, too."

The air was sweet and cool and filled with birdsong. Having spent the night at Concord after having delivered the muskets, the pair had been awakened before dawn by the sound of clanging church bells. Then a rider had thundered into town from Lexington and reported the British were slowly but surely marching to Concord.

Jack playfully tugged at Sassy's floppy hat. "This Yankee hat may cover your long hair, but I still don't know how we got through those British blockades yesterday."

Sassy stretched out beside Jack on the sweet-smelling earth. "We got through, though. That's all that matters."

Jack laughed and shook his head. "Did you see that grenadier's face when I offered to open the coffins and let him see our cousins' bodies?"

"I sure did," Sassy replied with a chuckle. "It's a good thing I had that handkerchief up to my face, actin' like I was brokenhearted with grief. I could hardly keep from grinnin'."

Jack laughed some more, then yawned and closed his eyes. In a matter of seconds he was lightly dozing. Sassy smiled, amazed that he could sleep at a time like this. She recalled the excitement that had stirred Concord when they had delivered the muskets. The coffins had been hastily opened and the weapons passed to eager, but ill-trained, militiamen. Today, despite their inexperience, those men would use the weapons against the British army.

A host of tender emotions stirred Sassy as she sat up and carefully took Aunt Pert's rose from her deep jacket pocket. She had wrapped its stem in a damp cloth, and it was still relatively fresh; as she studied its vibrant color, she sorted out her feelings.

All that she had worked for, and her father had died for, was about to reach its culmination. Her great moment had arrived. In a matter of minutes American citizens would be at war with the British, fighting for the right to build a new country. She should have been joyous—but she felt subdued. If Roarke had been here to share this moment with her, everything would have been wonderful. Without him, the victory seemed empty. Without him her success was meaningless.

Gradually the sound of tramping feet and jingling bridles broke into her thoughts. She slipped the rose back into her pocket, then cautiously peeked over the tall hedge. A chill ran up her arms at the sight of long columns of British foot soldiers led by officers on horseback. Marking time on their snare drums, a company of musicians followed; several supply wagons with creaking wheels trailed after them.

Morning light glinted on the soldiers' bright red uniforms and shiny bayonets. With narrowed eyes she studied the mounted officers . . . Her heart jumped when she recognized Blackhurst on a spanking white mount leading a column. Stunned, she ducked down and roused her friend. "Wake up!" she whispered roughly. "Take a look at this. They're here, and they've got ol' Blackhurst with 'em!"

Sucking in his breath, Jack clambered up. "That's him, all right. With that eye patch and scowl, he looks like Lucifer himself. I'll bet he's enjoyin' every minute of this."

Sassy shivered when Blackhurst paraded past, leaning back importantly in the saddle. Evidently General Gage had been pleased with the information Dr. Church had given Blackhurst, and as a reward, had selected him to accompany the fighting force.

Jack narrowed his eyes. "That was fat ol' Colonel Smith on that fine white stallion, and Major Pitcarin on the black mare," he said, studying the passing officers. "I've seen 'em in the Green Dragon. And it looks like they've got the whole British army with 'em."

The army's bright drum and fife music now swelled loud and clear. Sharp orders flew like arrows and the soldiers tramped ahead, their boots making rhythmic sounds on the hard earth.

"Law a mercy, there must be eight hundred soldiers!" Sassy whispered. "Thank goodness we delivered them new muskets. Mebbe they'll even up the odds a little."

Jack whistled low under his breath. "They're a pretty lot, all right. And they play a lively tune."

"Yes, but can they fight? Look at their faces. They're scared to death."

A gentle breeze whipped out bright pennants and fluttered the soldiers' turned-back coattails. Finally the last columns and supply wagons passed in a cloud of dust.

The excitement of the moment sheened Jack's freckled face with moisture; pulling out a tattered handkerchief, he wiped his brow and threw Sassy a dark look. "Come on, we better get back to Concord."

Sassy scanned the road. "How are we goin' to get around *them?*"

Jack jerked his thumb at the grassy farmland. "We'll cut through the countryside. It'll take longer, but we ain't got any choice."

As they scrambled down the knoll and raced over the fields toward Concord, the wind carried the *rat-ta-tat-tat* of British drums.

Chapter 28

Sitting near the crest of a hill, Roarke leaned against a cool boulder and listened to the muffled sounds of hundreds of British soldiers marching toward North Bridge. According to a citizen who had just escaped from the town center, the British had ransacked the town and were spreading out to search for rebels in the hills.

Yesterday evening after the O'Reillys had told him their son and Sassy had brought muskets to Concord, Roarke had dressed in simple country attire and left Duncan and his sailors aboard the *Sea Witch*, berthed in a hidden cove outside of Charlestown. Roarke had hoped to find Sassy here in Concord this morning, and several people had reported that she and the boy had delivered the muskets the previous afternoon. But no one seemed to know where they were now. Before Roarke had known what was happening, someone had slapped a musket in his hand and asked him to join a group of militiamen near the bridge.

He chuckled at his luck. Because he had followed Sassy to Concord, he had become an American rebel even sooner than expected.

The scent of daisies made him think of Sassy. He remembered how she had twirled a daisy in her fingers the first time he had kissed her . . . then their conversation almost a year ago on a Virginia road:

"I still think you ought to join up with us."

"It's not my war, Sassy. I'm a Scotsman. My allegiance is solely to Scotland . . . I have responsibilities there. And I would never want to live anyplace else."

"You keep sayin' that, but it sounds to me like you sail out of Williamsburg all the time."

"For the last two years I have."

"I'll bet you have rooms there."

"Aye, I do."

"Well, there you go—you're an American!"

He smiled at the memory. Here he was doing just what she had begged him to do when they had first met—helping the rebels.

Deep in his heart he knew that today of all days he truly *was* an American. But she wasn't here to share the moment with him, and a great, aching loneliness filled his soul. His anxiety increased when he considered the danger she was in. Was she still near Concord or had she returned to Boston? Had she been captured or met with some other violence?

When the wind carried a scrap of drum and fife music up the slope, he forced himself to turn his attention to the British. Standing, he searched for the first arrivals at the bridge: He spotted four companies of marching redcoats, their brass glinting in the morning sunlight.

Roarke saw some of the eager rebels stray from their hiding places, but he turned and waved them back. "Not yet, men! Let's see what they do!"

Some of the British soldiers loitered on the town side of the bridge while others started tearing up planks; the remaining redcoats moved up the slopes, their white crossbelts contrasting sharply with the green grass. "Fire now!" Roarke shouted.

With a Scottish war cry, he raised his musket

and ran down the hill. Scores of rebels darted from the safety of sheltering trees and joined him in his rush to the bridge, all yelling and brandishing their weapons.

Startled, the British clattered back over the bridge; a sergeant shouted an order, and the grenadiers knelt and fired. Black smoke darkened the air as the redcoats squeezed off round after round.

As the British continued the earsplitting blanket firing, Roarke fell to his knees to shoot and reload before moving on again. As if by instinct, the rebels fanned out and moved forward in a thin line, firing steadily, pausing only to kneel and reload. The surprised grenadiers started tumbling from the bridge, splashing into the water.

As the battle continued, the crackle of musket fire rent the air, and lead zinged past Roarke on all sides. Like a choking fog, black smoke drifted over the bridge and up the slopes. Shouts and oaths echoed, and smoke burned Roarke's lungs as he rushed ahead.

Several downed redcoats lay sprawled over the bridge while their comrades, panicked and confused, began to scramble back to Concord. Victorious rebel yells reverberated through the air as they chased the British troops.

Roarke knelt to reload. Biting off the end of a bullet, he shook powder in the priming pan and dumped the rest down his long musket barrel. Before he could jam wadding on top of the powder, he heard someone ride across the bridge. The man ordered the British soldiers to stand and fight. Roarke looked up, but battle smoke veiled the man's face. Then, as the smoke cleared, his gaze locked on Colonel Johnathan Blackhurst.

When Sassy and Jack finally arrived back in Concord, the British had already set some buildings on fire and were ransacking the town. Separated from Jack in the smoke and confusion, Sassy snatched a musket and powder horn from a downed rebel and raced toward North Bridge, the new center of conflict.

She was breathless from running and dizzy with fear and exhaustion as she approached the bridge. Yet, despite the terrifying melee going on around her, in the instant that a patch of smoke cleared, her gaze went straight to a figure on the other side of the bridge. A familiar figure. Her heart fluttered wildly in her breast. No, it couldn't be. The man dressed like a Yankee farmer just looked like Roarke. He was on his knees swiftly reloading his musket. She knew her eyes were deceiving her; then, with knee-trembling certainty, she realized it *was* Roarke!

She ran blindly toward him. Through the dark smoke she spied a mounted officer chastising the fleeing British troops. Blackhurst's eye patch was visible, as well as his raised pistol, which was pointing directly at Roarke! Her blood ran cold. Raising her own musket, she raced forward. "Blackhurst!"

Her hat flew off, exposing her flaming hair, which billowed out in the spring breeze. Blackhurst jerked his head about to stare at her. He pointed his pistol at her. From the corner of her eyes she saw Roarke finish reloading and stand; he took aim and a shot rang out. Almost simultaneously, Blackhurst tumbled from his saddle and rolled lifelessly to the bridge. Seeing that he was dead, most of the British soldiers panicked and ran wildly toward Concord and the Boston Road.

Sassy's heart thumped madly as Roarke raced toward her. His face aglow with joy, he scooped her into his arms and, running from the bridge, carried her behind a stone wall sheltered by a huge tree.

The lovers sat beneath the huge tree, much like the sycamore in Virginia a year ago; about them the ground was dotted with white daisies and pink buttercups. How shocked Sassy was to see Roarke's face! Stunned speechless, she wept tears of happiness as he rained kisses on her face.

"You shouldn't have attracted Blackhurst's attention," Roarke admonished as he pressed her against him. "You could have been killed!"

"Don't be silly. It gave you 'nuf time to reload."

"Burn me! You're a fearful hardheaded woman, Sassy Adair!"

Safe in his arms, she noticed some British stragglers disappear into the hills and green meadows, whooping rebels at their heels. The sight of Jack made her heart leap for joy. He was still alive.

Around the village, the hills still smelled of bitter smoke . . . yet everything was silent and still, now that the battle had passed. From the Boston Road, faint musket fire could be heard—but for Sassy and Roarke, the day's fighting was over.

Questions poured from Sassy in a tangled torrent. "Blackhurst told me you were dead," she said, clutching the lapels of Roarke's coat. "How did you get here?" It was still hard to accept the miracle of his presence.

Roarke put a finger to her lips. "Quiet, you little magpie. I'll tell you later," he said, caressing her hair. "For now, let me prove to you 'tis no ghost who holds you in his arms." His eyes warm with happiness, he kissed her thoroughly.

Starting deep inside her, pleasure spread through her body and blossomed into a flame of desire. As his lips roved over hers in sweet exploration, she ached to abandon herself, to revel in their passion—but steeling her will, she eased away and shook a finger at him playfully. "Don't think you can get out of answerin' all my questions by hushin' me up with kisses, Roarke MacLaren! What about your rebellion and all those *responsibilities* you talked about?"

Roarke's intent gaze held hers. "The day you left Donkinny, I knew you mattered more to me than anything else in the world." Gently he moved his warm hand over her arm, spreading heat throughout her body. "I've cut my ties with Scotland. Kevin is now chieftain of our clan."

Surprise widened her eyes. "But *you're* the MacLaren chieftain."

He shook his head. "Not anymore. Now both the *Sea Witch* and I will sail under an American flag."

For a moment she couldn't speak, then at last she managed to sputter, "You're . . . you're sure? You'd give up your castle . . . your riches?"

He searched her face, then kissed her gently. "You're my greatest treasure, Sassy Adair."

She snuggled against his hard chest, relishing his words and their deep significance; then, raising her head, she reached into her jacket pocket and retrieved the rose.

Some of the petals had curled and dropped away, but the remaining flower retained its wonderful color. Reverently she held it before him. "This is Aunt Pert's perfect rose. Sometimes when I watched her work, I thought she wouldn't be able to create a new color. I used to think the roses were too different—jest like us."

He smiled and touched her face.

"Some things can't be brought together, you know—they can't be mixed," she went on. "When I saw she *had* crossed the roses, I realized *we* could grow a true love, usin' the best parts of both of us." Tears misted her eyes.

Roarke laid the rose aside and brushed away her tears with his thumb. "Now, now, lass. Let's have no more tears on this fine day. I finally realized that I was holding on to an old dream—an impossible dream—so hard that I couldn't open my hand to grasp a new dream." He fluttered kisses all over her face and throat, then, in a deep voice, added, "My original dream may have failed, but I stumbled upon something finer—I found love and wholeness and a shining new future . . . I found you under a sycamore tree in Virginia. And you've taught me to lay aside old hurts and look toward the future. I was born a Scot, but I can be reborn an American, just as this new country is being born."

He lifted her chin and grazed her lips with a kiss.

Wild happiness swept through her; she felt dizzy with joy.

He raised his head. "After the war . . . after these colonies are free, I intend to buy a fine tract of tobacco land in Virginia. Will you be my bride and help start a new MacLaren clan?"

Sassy laughed and cried at the same time. He had sacrificed everything for her and he loved her . . . and they would always be together.

A shaft of golden light gilded Roarke's strong features, and his eyes glinted with intense passion. Tracing her cheek with his hand, he took her lips once more, kissing her with hunger. As the full power of his lips engulfed her, warmth swept over her, making her head light and her joints weak.

Slowly she eased away from him. "Yes, I'll be your bride," she answered quietly. "And even though Kevin may be the new chieftain, to me you'll always be *the MacLaren.*"

Laugh lines crinkled his temples as he smiled at her.

She playfully clasped his shoulders. "I guess it's a good thing I took all those dancin' lessons when I first got to Boston. Now that I'm goin' to be a fine southern lady, I'll be needin' 'em.'' She was having trouble picturing herself among the southern gentility. ''It jest seems such a shame.''

''What's a shame, lass?''

''Well, you know, it's a real comedown for me—the best rock chucker in Potter's Lick bein' reduced to traipsin' around a dance floor.''

Roarke laughed heartily. ''Don't worry, lass. We'll both don ragged work clothes regularly and play in the woods. If I know you, you'll be out early picking herbs for your mountain cures. And that's just what I want you to do. I don't want to lose the country girl I fell in love with.''

A last doubt flitted through her mind. ''You . . . you really don't mind that I'm not a fine lady?''

Roarke kissed her hand. ''My bonny lassie, don't you realize you're the greatest lady I've ever known? Your heart is full of love and you care about people. That's what being a lady is all about—not stiff, formal rules of etiquette.''

She frowned and opened her mouth to speak, but he lifted his brows. ''I'll not hear another word of protest. We'll live happily and do as we please. We'll get up at dawn and catch a fine string of fish, or stay in bed and make love all day long.''

''All day? Careful now, don't pick up more than you can tote!''

Roarke flashed a cocky grin. ''I'll admit making love all day will be a heavy responsibility, but it's one I'll happily fulfill.'' Mocking her mountain speech, he added, '' 'Sides that, ma'am, my shootin' iron ain't brand-new, but it never missed a target yet.''

Sassy burst out laughing. ''I can see you're feelin' good!''

''I *am*,'' he replied. He looked at her tenderly, his eyes full of deep meaning. ''I want many babes to dangle on my knee. And I intend to be there by your side when they come into this world.''

Sassy understood the significance of his words. At that moment the last lingering pain of her miscarriage melted away.

Roarke added, "I'm sure our children will be the first MacLaren clan in history to be raised on corn pone instead of scones. But perhaps we can take them on a visit to Scotland so they can taste a wee bit of haggis."

"They'll have the best of America *and* Scotland," she exclaimed. "Oh, love, we've got the world by the tail on a downhill pull!"

Roarke cupped her face in his large hands. "I'm finally home," he whispered, reclaiming her lips. With a teasing movement, his tongue entered her mouth, beginning a savage exploration. Trembling, she clung to his hard arms as he inflamed her senses and stirred her spirit.

His mouth triggered a raw hunger she thought she would never satisfy. Finally able to release her imprisoned need, she responded to him totally and shamelessly. A great shiver ran over her when he slid his hand into her shirt and touched her breast with his warm fingers. Gently he caressed the pliant flesh, flicking his thumb over the nipple until it hardened with an aching sweetness. Already her limbs glowed and her womanhood throbbed . . . and the long spring day, heady with the scents of fresh earth and wildflowers, still lay ahead of them.

Roughly she pushed him away and, glancing at him mischievously, studied his dancing eyes. "Law a mercy . . . you don't need much kindlin' to start a fire, do you?"

"Nay, I don't," he replied, humor lurking in his exaggerated brogue. "Bein' a proper Scot, I practice thrift in all things, lass."

Giggling, she shoved against him with all her might. When he sprawled backward, laughing in surprise, she straddled his chest and locked a hand in his hair. Narrowing her eyes, she looked at his merry face and cried, "Hush up and kiss me again . . . you vile pirate!"

Author's Note

The Sword of Wallace is my invention, but the idea was inspired by a group of young Scottish patriots who, over thirty years ago, stole the Coronation Stone from Westminster Abbey and returned it to its rightful home in Scotland after an absence of six centuries. The "criminals" were later apprehended and the Coronation Stone brought back to England, but the audacious deed fired the imagination of a nation.

The Green Dragon Inn, a favorite haunt of Samuel Adams and John Hancock, was actually located in colonial Boston. Dr. Joseph Warren, one of the most courageous revolutionary figures, organized the rebel spy system; he met his death at Breed's Hill in 1775. The war had hardly begun when it was discovered that Dr. Benjamin Church had sent coded documents to the British. After he was tried and found guilty of treason, George Washington recommended that he be hung; instead, he was deported to the West Indies, where he died a lonely and broken man.

Concord was truly the birthplace of the American Revolution. Armed with old bird guns and pitchforks, angry farmers poured in from the countryside to help the local militia fight the British. Surprised and confused, the redcoats scrambled back to Boston with colonial marksmen at their heels. By the time the British reached the city, they had lost 274 soldiers, and the most exciting chapter in American history had begun.